SAWDUST EMPIRE

A Novel

J.D. HOWARD

Editing: Allison Hitz & Skyler Cuthill

Cover design: Susan Harrell

Front cover photography courtesy of the Everett Public Library

Rear cover photograph courtesy of the Stanwood Area Historical Society

Chapter art-work: Miles Auckland

sawdustempire@gmail.com

Son Earth Publishing

SAWDUST EMPIRE

Diane

And all of the fallen who made the ultimate sacrifice in labor strife

HISTORICAL NOTE

It was the Free Soil Party in the mid-1850s who demanded that the lands opening up in the new west be made available to independent farmers, instead of wealthy plantation owners they claimed would develop it with slaves. Southern Democrats had continually defeated previous homestead proposals. They feared the free land would attract immigrants from across the Atlantic and that entire populations of the southern states would depart in droves, drawn by the opportunity and promise of the west.

Eventually the Homestead Act of 1862 was passed by congress and signed by President Lincoln during the Civil War, when there were no southern votes in the senate or congress to oppose.

By the late 1880s, fertile soil and virgin timberland was still ripe for the picking in the outlying areas of western Washington Territory. If you were a US citizen, the head of a household and married, a husband and wife could make a Homestead Act claim for 320 acres, or if single, 160 acres. Either claim could be made for the application fee of eighteen dollars. As long as a cabin was built, the land improved, and the homesteader(s) lived there for five contiguous years, deed and title would be earned.

President Benjamin Harrison, during a 10 day period in November of 1889, brought Washington Territory into statehood along with the Dakotas and Montana. Two years later Harrison signed the Land Revision Act, which took back surplus lands that had been granted from the public domain to the railroad syndicates. The act quickly accrued 22 million acres of Forest Reserve (outside of the Pacific NW) to be set aside, instead of being made available for short term timber company profits. With the power of his pen, Harrison's signature set in motion the industrial race for virgin timberland via any means possible before lands in the west were added to the newly created reserve.

During that same period a successful 48 year old lumberman by the name of Henry Hewitt left Wisconsin and headed west to seek a greater fortune. When Hewitt stepped off a Northern Pacific Railroad car at Tacoma in 1888 he quickly sought out investments in land and timber and soon became a partner in the St. Paul and Tacoma Lumber Company.

The next year he happened upon a newspaper article about a place called Port Gardner Bay near the village of Snohomish City, rented a boat, and headed north. Once at his destination he followed the Snohomish River upstream and was impressed with what he estimated as an eight-thousand acre timbered bluff that the river circumnavigated.

When he was one and a half miles directly to the east from where he'd started, Hewitt came-about and sailed back around on the current and an outbound tide. Close to the shore he measured the water's depth and found that it was suitable for a potential deep saltwater port. Henry Hewitt instantly knew he'd found the perfect location for the city he envisioned and the profits it would bring. He returned to Tacoma invigorated by what he'd found.

Wyatt and Bethel Rucker had arrived at Port Gardner Bay that same year of 1889. The two brothers from Ohio purchased fifty acres of bayside land to plat, along with other parcels, (properties that Hewitt wanted) and planned to name their town site Port Gardner. Shortly thereafter Henry Hewitt began acquiring land on and around the peninsula from the homesteaders that had arrived on the peninsula previously, in a few months he held title to 5,000 acres. He sought out the Rucker brothers, took them into his confidence, and divulged the plans for his, "City of Smokestacks." Hewitt then began conversations with them about selling some of their holdings. They reached an agreement after the Rucker brothers insisted on a contract that required of Hewitt's soon to be formed company to build certain industrial developments; paper and lumber mills, salt water docks, a nail works, and ship yard.

Hewitt returned to Tacoma and met Charles Colby, an investor and former business acquaintance from Wisconsin who had recently replanted from New York City to Tacoma. Colby was extremely wealthy, Ivy League educated, and looking for new business investments. In the summer of 1890 Hewitt and Colby boarded the Queen of the Pacific for a round-trip Alaska steamship cruise to outline plans for a city of industry. When Hewitt unrolled a bird's-eye-view map of the peninsula platted in streets showing the main north-south thoroughfare as Colby Avenue, Charles Colby was probably flattered. Going over the map, Hewitt deftly hinted that this new city should be called Everett, after Colby's fifteen-year old rambunctious son. The city's name was thereby solidified at a dinner party in Colby's home during October of 1890. The settlement on Port Gardner Bay had its name, the Everett Land Company was founded with Henry Hewitt as its president, and the east-west street that started from the proposed pier on the saltwater bay and crossed Colby through town to the banks of the Snohomish River became Hewitt Avenue.

Colby returned to New York and convinced businessmen Charles Wetmore and Colgate Hoyt to invest in Port Gardner and build the industrial requirements that the Rucker contract had spelled-out. Colby then received news from Hewitt that he'd hired a prospector to do a mineral survey of the towering Cascade Range to the east at Monte Cristo, where other miners claimed to have discovered huge deposits of iron, silver, and gold ore. After Hewitt sent word of the ore deposits a shock wave of enthusiasm surged through Colby's New York group. This became the news Colby needed to land the richest investor of them all, John D. Rockefeller. After numerous meetings the group convinced him to spend millions on a railroad from a proposed smelter at Everett to Monte Cristo, and municipal improvements for their new city.

News of the multi-million dollar investment by Rockefeller fanned the flames of a major speculative real estate and development wildfire, causing the Hewitt group to file for a 484-acre plat that would become part of the town.

During that same year, Rockefeller's money built the Monte Cristo railroad, mines at the site, and a smelter. At the same time, the Hewitt consortium used a majority of Rockefeller's cash to begin building city services after rumors that the Empire Builder, James J. Hill, was planning to bring his Great Northern Railway over the four-thousand- foot summit of Stevens Pass, sixty-five miles to the east. Hill's plan was to join it with his recently acquired Seattle and Montana Railway that had been extended north from Seattle to Port Gardner Bay in the fall of 1891. Two years later the Great Northern was connected to the Seattle and Montana at Everett and the Bay View Hotel was built on Bond Street, it became the first train depot and one of only two Everett locales where Henry Hewitt would reside, the other being the Monte Cristo Hotel.

Soon the Great Northern station was filled daily with hundreds of excited newcomers who were looking for a fresh start and get in on the elevator at the bottom floor with jobs, homes, and the promise to be part of building something great, while others came on the run from past troubles. The city transformed from a muddy backwater outpost of trappers and speculators into a commercial hub that was brimming with immigrants full of joyous hope.

With Rockefeller's dollars the Everett Land Company built a water system, city pier, coal-fired electric plant, and primitive gravel, plank, and brick roads with trolley cars, and a jail. Newcomers who came to Everett unemployed or without family support were put to work building the city for the lowest of possible wages. If a man refused to work on the new city he was threatened with jail and if he continued to resist work he'd find himself behind bars.

Hundreds of men were hired by the Everett Land Company to clear the land for the city, stonemasons and carpenters were hired to erect brick buildings. There was also great chance for fast profit: bars, bawdy and box houses, gambling dens, burlesque halls, and saloons soon filled those buildings turning Hewitt Avenue into a path to impurity where respectable people would never be found. By March of 1892 so many ill begotten and down trodden came to Everett that community leaders created a stop gap form of government they titled "The Committee of 21," to help control the boozing, brawling and general mayhem that seemed to be overtaking the town. Eventually, when the settlement of Everett became an incorporated city in the spring of 1893 a mayor was elected, and an ordinance was passed that allowed saloons only on the north side of Hewitt Avenue, thereby segregating not only businesses but the inebriated from the sober.

Then the New York Stock Exchange crashed in June of 1893, causing an economic panic across the nation. Three of the five Everett banks collapsed; banks that held city, county, and eastern investment funds. The Everett Land Company found itself in a fiscally desperate situation and could no longer pay the interest on its bonds which were held by Rockefeller. Rockefeller became incensed with what he felt was Hewitt's financial irresponsibility's and forced Hewitt to resign as the president of the Everett Land Company in 1894. In doing so Rockefeller confiscated Hewitt's stock and most of his personal interests in the development company.

The economy took another blow in 1897 when a major flood washed out the Monte Cristo railroad for the second time in two years, most of the bridges, tracks, trestles and road beds were slept away in Robe Canyon, east of Granite Falls. Rockefeller announced that the railroad would not be rebuilt at that time through his local representative, who stated that there was very little iron, silver, or gold ore in the Monte Cristo mines and that, "the investment never paid dividends." The east coast press soon claimed that Rockefeller had been duped into a number of unfortunate investments in Washington State by Henry Hewitt.

Rockefeller eventually sold his holdings in the Everett Land Company in January of 1900 to James J. Hill, who believed in the town not only because of his railroad but because of the abundant timber resources that surrounded it. Hill then hired John McChesney to run the former Rockefeller Corporation and renamed it the Everett Improvement Company.

That same year James J. Hill sold nine hundred thousand acres of timberland in Snohomish County, from his acquisition of the Northern Pacific, to Frederick Weyerhaeuser, his neighbor in St. Paul, Minnesota, for six dollars an acre. Weyerhaeuser then purchased the Bell-Nelson Mill on the Everett waterfront. Once Weyerhaeuser made a commitment to Everett, James Hill was able to lure other timber barons from his logged off state of Minnesota and the rest of the northern Midwest to Everett by telling of available land for mills along his railway line on the shores of Port Gardner Bay and the wall of timber that surrounded it.

Two years later, nine lumber mills were producing over a combined million board feet of lumber daily and thirteen shingle mills cut a million and a half shingles a day. In Lowell, the Puget Sound Pulp and Paper Company was producing eighteen tons of finished paper daily and provided over 250 non-union jobs. James J. Hill funded the construction of the 1,200-seat Everett Theater, which in the years to come hosted performances of Al Jolson, Lillian Russell, and Fatty Arbuckle. Hill also oversaw the organizing of the Everett Flour Company, which produced barrels of Best "Ever"-ett flour.

In 1906, the San Francisco earthquake and fire created a nearly insurmountable need for lumber and cedar shakes, and the mills of Everett boomed. More mills were built on the waterfront, along with foundries, machine shops, piers, and another ship yard. At one time Everett had ninety-five wood-based and manufacturing plants from the bay up the Snohomish River and around the peninsula to Lowell.

James J. Hill began building a permanent seawall from Everett to Seattle in 1907 to prohibit the washout of his double-track line along the shores of the Puget Sound. Steam derricks were used to place two-hundred thousand cubic yards of granite from Index. Quarried and cut into pieces six feet long and four feet wide, the nearly thirty-mile bulkhead took four years to construct.

The positive economic conditions created by the lumber and shake industry spread county wide. By 1908 the greater Everett area held roughly forty-two lumber mills, ninety-six shingle mills, and thirteen logging railroads with over six-hundred miles of track. But the commerce of Snohomish County and Everett's golden age could not overcome the basic laws of supply and demand.

The boom and bust cycle of Everett's sawdust economy turned the town into a place of incredible extremes. When timber prices rose, the mills would hire, over-produce, and flood the market. But as soon as the price of lumber and cedar shingles dropped, the mills would shut down. Street brawls were a common occurrence, sin and vice ran rampant in the streets during downturns, and prominent citizens turned to the clergy for answers.

With the community unruly, a number of Protestant ministers that had cobbled together enough tithes to build churches eventually brought the evangelist Billy Sunday to Everett in the summer of 1910 to shore-up the river of wickedness that flowed freely on the streets. Across five weeks the evangelist conducted three thousand prayer meetings throughout the city and held seventy-six revival meetings in a wooden hall that was 140 feet wide and 200 feet long. The timber tabernacle was built by volunteers ahead of his arrival on a vacant lot between Lombard and Oakes, directly south of Everett Avenue, it seated 6,500. A total of 220,700 people attended over those five weeks, 18,000 on the final night. From those attendees, roughly 2,400 were converted to church membership even though Billy Sunday left disappointed in Everett's overall lack of Christian spirit. The wooden tabernacle was promptly torn down.

Also arriving in 1910 was the Interurban Railway that connected Everett with Seattle. Made up of electric trolleys, the ride between the two cities took one hour and thirty-five minutes, stopping along the way to pick up passengers at designated stations.

The Anti-Saloon League, through the power of Voter Initiative, put the statewide ban of alcohol on the ballot in 1914. The measure prohibited the manufacture and sale of intoxicating liquor, but not its possession. However, drugstores were authorized to sell liquor if prescribed by a doctor or requested by a clergyman, while residents were allowed to import liquor for personal use. The Prohibition ballot was carried by the rural areas and won, the new law was finally put into effect on January 1, 1916.

At that time Everett was fourteen square miles in size and had a population of over thirty-four thousand people, an estimated six-hundred cars in the city limits traveled on twenty-four miles of surfaced roads. The daily capacity of the shingle mills was 4.5 million cedar shingles while the lumber mills produced a combined total of two million board feet of lumber per day. Everett was the lumber and shingle center of the Pacific Northwest, if not the world, and the mills of the great timber town of Everett and the loggings camps of western Washington was where a person could land a job and earn a payday.

PART ONE

Chapter 1

THE MILL

After an extended winter the climate was once again fervent and promis-ing. The color of life painted the landscape, brilliant greens of multiple shades brought vitality and balance to every eye and warmth and well-being to every heart. Sepia fields were plowed and furrowed until the earth was black and rich, ready and willing to accept new seed. Warm prevailing winds car-ried cherry blossoms through the air; the sight of their floating white petals brought rejuvenation and hope. Vermilion Rhododendrons and Mary Christian Camellias flowered and spread their fragrance at the same time that silt choked streams and high water rivers rippled and tore at their banks. Nature's balance was resurrected. The sap was up, and spring was in hand.

On one such glorious morning in western Washington, when the air was fresh and the world felt new, a chauffeured burgundy Pierce-Arrow pulled out of the portico of a white mansion on Laurel Drive and headed for the Northern Imperial Mill. Rolling past other finely appointed homes overlooking the indus-trial bay, the limousine's paint sparkled with a hand buffed shine, its white wall tires spotless, and its lone back seat rider, Luther MacCullock, always looking straight ahead. Taking the same route through town every day, his short grey beard perfectly trimmed, a freshly pressed suit top pocket holding pince-nez glasses and a packed but unlit pipe held with one hand, he was a man that thought only of his lumber and cedar-shingle company and the profits it created him.

The sedan turned west and headed down brick paved Hewitt Avenue towards the waterline. A block from the turn for the Northern Imperial head office the driver swerved to miss a square pothole.

"Get back next to the trolley tracks where the grade is smoother," MacCullock ordered, "And take me to the mill today, my camp foreman came in on the train last night so he should be there."

At the bottom of bayside Hewitt, just before the railroad tracks, the chauffeur slowed the car to a crawl, careful not to jostle the cargo. The driver angled along the elevated trestle plank road beside the railroad spur that fronted so many other mills and then slowly came to a stop as workingmen darted in front of the vehicle making their way to the Smith-Edgerton and Seacrest Mills farther upriver.

At the Northern Imperial gate the overweight, unshaven guard stepped out of his tiny station house and tipped his hat as the car rolled past. The sedan pulled into the mill owner's parking place to deliver its passenger, turned around and headed back to Laurel Drive. The guard, seated again in the gate house, opened the breech of his shotgun to check his shells, and then leaned back in his chair. He closed his eyes but kept his ears opened as the workers walked by, listening for any line of talk against management.

The mill owner strode past the company bunkhouse and placed his pipe in a coat pocket just as the logging foreman poked his head out of the bunkhouse door, "Mornin', Captain. I'll be right up," he said and hitched his suspenders.

"Good," Luther MacCullock replied.

MacCullock briskly strode into his mill with a straight back and firmly set jaw. As he walked by the line of workers punching timecards, their clothes smelling of wood pitch, grease, and sawdust, he kept his eyes fixed forward, his briefcase hanging straight down at his side. With each step the stiff soles of his leather shoes slapped a clip-clap sound against the scarred four by twelve clear-fir decking. Once past he climbed the stairs to his mill office and stopped at the landing where he unlocked the door.

Inside, he took off his coat and placed his briefcase on the dusty, oversized oak desk his father and him had built in Minnesota over fifty years before when he was just a lad. Its massive hardwood desk top finish was now faded and worn, the lathe turned legs dented but still sturdy, the carved ornate handle on the single top drawer black from use. He took his Churchwarden pipe from a coat pocket and set it in the ashtray next to the upright telephone and sat down.

***

County Sheriff Donald McRae drove through the gate of the Northern Imperial as the guard nodded, not bothering to tip his hat. The sheriff, his setter dog Champion Tom, and a deputy parked next to the main building's entrance. He got out of his roadster, closed the door, and then spread both arms in the cool salt air to stretch as he yawned.

Donald McRae was sturdily built, tall and wide shouldered. He was round faced and blushed at the cheeks but the skin on his face was tight. A pair of brown trousers were held up by a leather belt that a blackjack and single-action Colt revolver hung from. His rolled-brim black Stetson was tilted forward, and a red pamphlet stuck out of his wool coat. He bent over and looked through the windowless door of the Chevrolet 490, saying to his deputy, "Jefferson, wait here with Champ. I've got to go check in with the Captain."

Walking up the stairs to the office McRae hesitated at the door, knocked, and then stepped inside.

"Mornin' Cap'n," Sheriff McRae said brightly, "I stopped by yer main office first, but the lights weren't on."

"Yes, good morning, Donald," Northern Imperial owner Luther MacCullock replied, looking up from his desk. "I've got rare business here this morning."

Luther MacCullock was a firm believer in the ten hour work day with only Sundays, the Fourth of July, Christmas, and Easter off, yet he constantly schemed of how he could deny his workers any time off at all, pay them less and work them more. He loved the daily sound of machinery running and the odorous smell of freshly cut cedar, the organic scent of rough-cut fir, and the smoke of burning scrap wood fueling the hot steam; each one filled Luther MacCullock's senses with the tingling aura of money.

Luther MacCullock had built his mill from scratch. Twenty years after the fact MacCullock was a man standing tall, proud of what he'd accomplished. To him his mill was a church and if its smokestacks were steeples, then his original office, was the inner sanctum.

Picking up his pipe, MacCullock continued to address the sheriff. "What's the latest on the strike, are they still walking off the job today?" the mill owner asked, seated behind his desk.

"As far as I know they are but I haven't heard anything else since the last ultimatum," McRae said as he pulled the red pamphlet from his coat pocket and placed it in front of MacCullock. "I took that off a hobo my men brought in last night."

MacCullock lit his pipe and carefully placed his pince-nez on the bridge of his nose. He picked up the thin, creased pamphlet and took a pull from his pipe. Reading a few sentences, MacCullock let the smoke slowly escape from his mouth and rise around his head. The aroma of his lifelong habit filled the room, but then he quickly exhaled.

"Sabotage?" MacCullock coughed, his voice rising. "Now somebody is advocating sabotage?" He continued reading, his eyes darting through the leaflet, one hand holding the lanyard on his glasses: "'Workers should only work eight hours in a ten-hour shift by slowing down on the job.'"

"What in blue blazes is wrong with these agitators printing such rubbish? Can't these rabble-rousers mind their own business instead of putting lazy thoughts in my men's heads? I pay a perfectly fine wage, and I will not allow any of my men to be sitting down on the job!" MacCullock tossed the pamphlet into the garbage can. He turned back to the sheriff with narrowed eyes. He was about to say something but his concentration was interrupted by the shrill cry of the shift whistle inaugurating another work day.

MacCullock turned his head to listen for the familiar sound of saws slicing timber and shingles being cut, a sound he never bothered to conceal his pleasure of. But his mill was silent. He took off his glasses, got to his feet, and strode over to his office window that looked out over the inside of the mill. Every worker in the plant stood still at their stations.

He focused his eyes through the dusty windows and watched as one worker stepped back from his upright shingle machine and walked towards his office. It was the union shop steward.

"Not him again," MacCullock muttered.

The steward climbed the stairs to the mill owner's inner sanctum and knocked. The sheriff looked at the captain. Luther walked over and sat back down at his desk, and then motioned for the sheriff to open the door. The union steward came in and glanced at the sheriff and nodded a hello, he stepped in front of MacCullock.

"Well," MacCullock grumbled and started to clench his fists under the desk, "what are you going to annoy me with now?"

The steward pulled a small slip of paper out of his pocket and began to read the scribbled words with slightly shaking hands. "The shop stewards," the man said, rolling his r's, "at all the mills are requestin' that each mill owner return our vages to vhere they vere two year ago —" MacCullock cut him off.

"That's enough. I've heard it all before and don't need to hear any more."

But the union man continued.

"Ve vere promised res-tor-a-tion of our vages an' now the market for clear shingles is a dollar an' ninty-one cents a square an' it vas less back then an' ve vere paid more. Right now you are paying fifty cents an hour. Ve vant a raise to sixty cents, and an eight-hour vork day, or ve vill go on strike," the Finnish shop steward said calmly.

MacCullock glared at the man with seriousness. He stood up to his full height, inhaled, and bellowed, "Are you done? Because I've heard enough. Now you listen. There will be no raise and I don't care if the whole lot a' ya go on strike. I've heard all the talk about higher wages and a closed union shop, and I don't give a lick. If you want to walk off the job, then go ahead!" he roared and motioned for the steward to leave as he sat down. "I've shut down this mill before, and I've got no problem doing it again! Donald! Get him out of here!" The sheriff tromped over, grabbed the steward by the arm, and yanked him towards the door.

"Ve vere promised," the union man said loudly over his shoulder. Taking little stutter steps with the sheriff pulling him along he declared, "Ve vant res-tor-a-tion!"

McRae pushed him out of the office and onto the landing, slamming the door behind him. The black-haired Finn pulled a small brass whistle from his pocket at the top of the stairs, and as he went down he blew louder and louder with every step. Quietly every worker picked up his lunch pail and walked out, not bothering to punch the time clock.

Luther MacCullock's mind buzzed like a trim saw snipping a shingle for square. "That little foreigner comes in *my* office and tells me *they* want a raise!" the mill owner shouted as he slammed a fist on his desk. "They can all go straight to hell!"

The sheriff watched as the gruff old mill owner got up and began to pace from one end of his office to the other. MacCullock's pipe billowed behind him as he walked to and fro. Back and forth he went in front of the office window, his steps slow and precise, while the sheriff stood quietly with his hat in his hand. McRae waited for the sound of a voice with the lung power that could cut a man in two, the kind of vocal venom and regimentation that only Luther MacCullock could inflict.

But MacCullock kept quiet. He stepped over to the other window in his office that looked outside to the mill pond below and contemplated his next move with his hands clasped behind his back, his long-stemmed pipe clamped in his teeth. A fresh raft of logs was tied to pier booms next to the curved elevated ramp that pulled them up from the salt chuck. The shipping pier jutted out at a right angle for one hundred feet from the main mill pier. An elevated gangway connected to the shipping pier to the mainland for crew access. As expected, the stream of Northern Imperial workers was joined by streams of workers from the Smith-Edgerton and Seacrest mills, trooping out in silence. MacCullock walked back to his desk and stood behind it. His words were loud and sharp.

"I'm going to need *you* to keep things under control," MacCullock said. McRae looked at him.

"I'll keep the peace," the sheriff replied.

"But you used to be an officer in their union," MacCullock asserted, "you worked with those men and represented them, and *that*, could be a problem."

"Nope. It won't be a problem, Captain," the sheriff said nodding his head. "It's only a strike, it'll pass like all of the others. Besides, most of those men are good decent folks."

"Well! They're certainly not decent if they walked off the job," MacCullock replied with a glare as he sat down behind his desk. "And what about that shop steward? You know him, right?"

"The shop steward?" the sheriff asked.

"Yes," MacCullock replied, "that stupid little Finn who was just in here."

The sheriff coughed as he glanced up to the ceiling, "I think he was hired on right before I ran for office. Yep, now that I think about it, he worked the green chain."

"So you know him?"

"No, I don't know him. Just know who he is," the sheriff answered.

"But what about the rest of these workers? You know them, don't you?"

"Some of them, I suppose," McRae answered in an uninterested tone.

"Damn it! This is serious business!" the mill owner snapped.

"I'm not gonna argue with you," the sheriff shot back. "Most of the men I worked with are gone. There's only a few left."

"Okay, but still, things could get rough. I can't have you being sympathetic towards a union that you used to be a member of."

"I can understand that."

"So you'll be able to stand up to these strikers if things go bad?" MacCullock asked, watching for any sign of weakness on the sheriff's face.

"My duty is to uphold the law and keep the peace," McRae replied.

"No matter what?"

"No matter what," the sheriff answered. "But the less news of my boys bashing heads gets in the headlines, then the better for my reelection."

MacCullock rocked back in his squeaky wooden chair. He crossed his arms for a moment and then said, "You see! Now there you go! You're already worrying about getting votes."

"Do you want me to be sheriff again or not?"

"Dammit Donald! Of course I do. I think you've done a fine job cleaning up the jail with your progressive ideas and all. Hell, you're the best sheriff this county has ever had, but I'm the one that financed your campaign. I'm the one that put you in office, remember? And now I have a strike on my hands and that means *we* have a strike on our hands," MacCullock said and then paused. "But as far as you being reelected or not, I'll keep you in work. Give you a position with good pay and easy hours."

The sheriff scratched the side of his head. "Work? Hell! If I don't run for sheriff then I'm runnin' fer mayor!"

"Mayor? You've got a long way to go before you'll ever be mayor," MacCullock chided.

"I'd make a perfectly fine mayor," the sheriff responded.

"Yes. Well. If this strike causes some trouble and you put it down, then you probably could be elected mayor," MacCullock acknowledged.

"That sounds good." McRae grinned. "But I'd have to move to town, I guess."

"All that's in the future, right now we need to be more concerned about this strike, but tell me. If things turn bad are you going to be able to go toe to toe with men that you used to be one of?"

The sheriff rubbed his unshaven chin with a thumb and forefinger, "I'm not gonna take any guff from anyone, anywhere, no way no how, no matter if I was a union man before or not."

"You're sure about that?"

"You have my word, Captain," the Sheriff Donald McRae promised, "as long as I have your word about keepin' me in work. That is, if I don't end up being re-elected or get to be mayor."

MacCullock eyed the sheriff briefly, stroked his well-trimmed grey beard, and then said, "You can probably have any job you want in Everett if you keep this town, *and* this strike, under control, but we won't have to worry about that. Everything will be fine, and you'll stay sheriff."

"Okay, but I'll probably need more deputies."

"If you need more deputies then hire some! By God and country, McRae, I will break this strike! If I could beat the Sioux, then I can beat this strike!" the old Indian killer exclaimed and rocked back in his squeaky chair. He stared at the ceiling and then re-lit his pipe.

"Now," MacCullock began as he puffed, "I know you're out of jurisdiction across the tracks over in town, but this strike happened on county land, so, I say you have legal cause to act. When those workers picket, they'll be down here at the mills, in the county, so that would put you in charge." MacCullock sucked on his pipe and then blew a cloud of smoke into the room. "I know the police chief pretty darn good from the Commercial Club, so I'll get a handle on him and make sure he stays out of our way, and the mayor for that matter. And I want you or one of your men at that soapbox corner every night keeping an eye on things," the mill owner ordered. The sheriff nodded his head as MacCullock continued.

"I think we should let the Everett workers have their say, so let them be for now, we don't want to start throwing our weight around too soon. However, if any agitators from out of town show up talking about a closed union shop and what have you, then you'll need to act and enforce that street ordinance if there's trouble," MacCullock maintained.

The sheriff put his hat back on and set it straight. "I'm gonna do whatever I got ta' do ta' keep things in line. And if I need to get some more deputies then I will," the sheriff said as he eyed MacCullock coldly, the already tight skin on his raw boned face stretched thin.

"Very good then," MacCullock acknowledged.

"So, where do we start?" the sheriff asked.

"Every worker in town is headed to that damn meeting corner right now, so I think it would be best if you got up there and checked on things," MacCullock ordered.

"I've got a deputy already in the car. We'll go back to the jail and get some more men."

"Good, and tonight stop by the club," MacCullock said and then turned his attention to the top of his desk and searched for a pen.

"I will." Sheriff McRae stepped out of the office and closed the door behind him. Coming up the stairs were Charlie Purvis and Butch Barnell, the logging camp foreman and mill manager.

McRae grabbed the brim of his Stetson and tipped his hat.

"Mornin'," the sheriff grunted to both men, then glanced at the logging camp foreman and cracked a smile. "Charlie, haven't seen ya in a while. How the hell are ya?"

"I'm surviving," Purvis said. A slight grin formed on his face and he asked, "You?"

"Surviving, too, I guess. Fine day for a strike, wouldn't you say?"

"Those lazy-assed sumbitches don't know how good they got it here," Purvis uttered as they passed each other on the stairs.

Barnell spoke up. "I bet them bastards 'er headed up to that corner right now!"

"I'm headed that direction too," the sheriff said as he turned out of sight at the bottom of the staircase.

***

Purvis and Barnell continued up to the office and then knocked.

"Come in," MacCullock said from behind his desk.

"Looks like we've got another strike to deal with," Barnell observed, stepping inside.

"Yes, yes we do," MacCullock replied, not looking up.

"Those shingle-weavin' bums ain't worth spit," Purvis cracked. He walked over and stood in front of MacCullock's desk, then clasped both hands behind his back.

"Gentlemen, we are going to break this strike come hell or high water," MacCullock grumbled, "and the only way we are going to break this strike is to keep this mill pumping out lumber and shingles! And that means Timber Creek *must* keep this mill supplied with timber. So under no circumstances will I allow word of this strike to get up to my logging camp. Do you understand me, Purvis?" MacCullock said, now staring at his foreman.

"Yes, sir," Charlie answered rocking up on his toes.

"And Barnell," MacCullock boomed, "I want you to hire as many men as you can find, anywhere you can find them, at, let's say, forty cents an hour.

I want flyers at the train station, the interurban station, the city pier, everywhere. I want this mill back up and running at peak performance immediately. Put a 'Now Hiring' sign out front, and take the company truck around town with a hiring sign on it, too." MacCullock shooed him away with a flip of his hand and snapped, "So get to it!"

"Right away," Barnell replied, nodding as he headed out the door.

"Good," MacCullock acknowledged to his mill manager's back. He turned to his logging camp foreman.

"And Purvis. You have got to keep the logs coming no matter what!"

"I've got another raft just about filled. It'll be ready to come down-river in a few more days," Purvis said with confidence.

"OK. Now, your crew needs to be kept in the dark about this, understand? If they find out and join the strike then we're doomed. Those logs must keep coming!"

"Yes, sir," Purvis responded, nodding his head, "But the camp is only forty, fifty miles away. Word gets around."

MacCullock glared at his camp push with a morose, hard stare. "Mr. Purvis," MacCullock groaned, "it is *your job* to make sure that word doesn't get around to *my* logging camp!"

"Oh, uh, yes sir," Purvis said as he straightened his back to attention with his hands at his side.

"Good. The paymaster won't be up till the end of the month," MacCullock stated and then paused to relight his pipe. Waving out the flame he started again, "But there will be the supply deliveries. Other than those two, there really isn't much contact with the outside world up there. I'll make sure the paymaster and supply men keep their mouths shut. As long as you do your job like everything's normal we should be fine."

"Consider it done," Purvis said. MacCullock set his pipe in the ashtray, spun in his chair, and began to dial the combination on the old payroll safe behind the desk. He pulled a strongbox from inside, opened it, pulled out an envelope, and placed it on the desk. Then he stood up and stepped over to his tall oak cabinet of flat file drawers. MacCullock opened one, pulled out a color coded map, and set on it top. The blacked out sections of the map signified already clear-cut parcels, while the white plots were not yet logged and available. Those marked with red ink were his competitors holdings, yellow were potential homestead buy-outs, brown, mineral claims with timber rights, and the many marked in green, important Northern Imperial un-cut parcels. The map was a checker-board of uneven colors that symbolized money made, money to be made, and the vile insult of money made by his competition. The highly profitable virgin timber world of trees still standing was shrinking. Luther found another map and placed it on his desk.

"There's a carbon copy of the timber deed and road building agreement in this envelope, plus an extra map. Everything in it," MacCullock said, nodding at the envelope, "shows that we have the right to cut, fill and dig grade for the Shay, *and*, cut and yard every single bit of harvestable timber in the section. The owner said he was up at the end of March. You see him?" MacCullock asked as he handed over the items.

"You mean Grover Cromwell?" Purvis replied, grasping the package.

"Yes, Cromwell."

"Yeah, saw him and his two sons. Talked to him," Purvis said.

"Good. The Cromwell family has had two claims northwest of Mineral Ridge for over twenty years. I'm not sure how they fooled the auditor in getting that claim way up there but they must have built a cabin years ago, and now that I think about it, they must have got up there from the Pilchuck drainage back then. Well, that doesn't matter anymore because they've decided to sell every tree, it borders the north line of the last Timber Creek parcel. The snow should be gone up there soon, if not already. He said he'd been up on snowshoes and marked each corner, flagged the lines," MacCullock stated.

"Yep. Said the same thing to me," Purvis replied.

"You and your timber cruiser have been at this long enough to figure everything out, so I have full confidence in both of your abilities."

Purvis nodded and then boasted, "I'm the best damn camp push there is. I'll handle it."

MacCullock put his hand on the base of the upright phone, motioned with his right hand towards the door for Purvis to exit and then finished, "Don't let me down. And keep those logs coming." Purvis nodded again and walked out.

Behind his closed office door, Luther MacCullock picked the receiver up off its hook and dialed city hall.

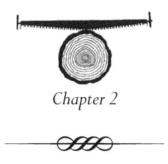

Chapter 2

FREE SPEECH CORNER

M en walked out of the Northern Imperial in a silent parade past the mill guards led by their leader, shop steward Renny Niskanen. His handmade slipshod work shirt did not set him apart from his fellow workers. Swinging his dented black metal dome lunch pail from its twine handle, he marched past the lumber trust watchmen with a reinforced heart and mind after delivering the final ultimatum to Luther MacCullock.

"Where the hell are you bunch a sliver pickers goin'?" mill guard Buck Mullaney shouted from his little gate shack. He stood up and stroked his thick brown mustache that connected to thicker mutton chops.

"Ve are on strike!" the little Finn cried.

"Why you lumber bum sons a' bitches! What's wrong with you?" the over-weight mill guard yelled as he followed the procession toward the railroad tracks, a thin smile formed on Mullaney's face as his finger found the safety on his shotgun.

But the shop steward and every man kept walking past the guard as the baritone voice of Jesuit Nathan Bywater rang out from his ad-hoc pulpit on the cut-bank, just across and above the railroad tracks.

"Take Jesus into your hearts today, men! Let me pray to the good Lord for you, to guide you and keep you safe in your endeavors and —"

"Shut your face ya damned Bible-thumper. Go on back to your church where you belong!" he hollered, the butt of his shotgun against the hip of his dirt-covered grease pants. Mullaney spit on the ground and then glared at the preacher.

But the sermonizer held no fear of the long-time lumber trust brute. Holding the Bible against his chest and pointing a finger at the mill guard, he declared, "The Lord is your Savior, too, and the church has the right to free speech on the streets of Everett. I would hope you of all people, sir, would know the laws of this city, and this country!"

Buck spit another greasy brown wad of goop on the ground and stared at the priest with scorn and then at the mill workers walking off the job. He swaggered over in the clergyman's direction holding his shotgun with his right hand, but he stopped at the end of the mill property.

"Go on ya worthless quitters!" Mullaney yelled at the men. He turned around and walked back to the gate house.

As the last of the striking workers crossed the tracks and headed uptown, Father Bywater abandoned his pulpit and followed them. The closed sign was still in Mulligan's window so a few of the men ducked into the Big 5 Café to see if there was a quick, affordable backroom morning snort available when an electric trolley car rolled past going up Hewitt Avenue towards the city center.

"What's going on?" the motorman yelled.

"We're on strike," one of the men replied, "and headed up to Wetmore." The smiling motorman cranked the hand-wheel brake, stopped the trolley, and said, "I'm going that way. Hop on, this ride's for free!" as a horde of strikers climbed aboard, quickly overfilling the car.

Shopkeepers came out on the sidewalk to watch and listen as the massive procession headed up the Hewitt hill, some onlookers shouting encouragement, others watched with concern. Women darted out of nearby houses carrying babies to watch for husbands, the look on their faces indicating how proud they were of their spouses for standing up to the powerful timber companies.

At Wetmore Avenue, Renny Niskanen picked up one of the ever-present wooden crates from in front of Spanjer's Dry Goods and Grocery and walked out to the center of Hewitt. He turned around, paced fifty feet back on the sidewalk past the front door of Bachelder and Corneil's men's clothing store and set the crate down short of Weiser's Café and the Gospel Mission. He stepped onto it and addressed the crowd.

"Good-a morning!" he shouted to his fellow strikers. A nervous cheer went up in the air. "Today, on this May 1st, the International Vorkers' Day, ve strike for better pay, and better vorking conditions." Shouts of approval rang out over a small chorus of boos as a growing crowd of raised fists, some with missing fingers, began to form around him. Stopping what little traffic there was, the crowd groaned with apprehension as Sheriff McRae pulled up across the way with another patrol car loaded with deputies. A moment later, Everett Police Chief Tom Kelly pulled up in his Oldsmobile behind them. McRae got out and walked back to the chief. They had a few quick words, and the sheriff returned to his roadster while Kelly pulled out and drove away. From his soapbox perch, Niskanen saw the encounter, paused, and then resumed with vigor while off to the side a newspaper reporter from the *Daily Tribune* scribbled on a notepad.

"Thank you, my fellow vorkers for joining us in our strike this morning! Ve vill stay on strike until every thieving mill owner caves in to our demands! They vill pay us more by the time this is all over," the little shop steward yelled above the gathering.

"The mill owners promised that they would restore our vages! And they have not! They make a promise!" Niskanen hollered to cheers.

'That's right!" Imperial striker Hank Hillstrom shouted.

"Yeah!" another striker spoke up. "A promise is a promise!"

"The lumber trust agreed that they vould pay us! It is time for them to keep their promise! Ve vill vin this strike and ve vill vin it right away!" Renny yelled.

"You're a liar!" shouted a man in a dirty, plaid pork-pie hat. "How am I supposed to feed my family if we're on strike?" Niskanen looked right at him.

"Nobody vill starve. Everyone who has been paying their dues to the Shingle Veavers' Union is going to get two dollar a veek to valk the pickets, and the union is going to organize a food bank. Ve had all the meetings. The majority voted to strike against the mill owners who favor profits over their vorkers. How many of you have lost a finger, or a hand, or an arm for MacCullock and the others?"

"I did," answered one worker, and then another yelled, "I lost a finger and a thumb at the Seacrest."

"How much do you think your fingers, your thumbs, made MacCullock and the rest of that gang of thieves? How much is a finger or a thumb worth? It is a lot cheaper for MacCullock and the rest of his lumber robbers to injure us than to replace all of the vorn out junk they run in their mills."

"To hell with you!" the man in the pork-pie hat spat out. A few loyal strikers standing behind Renny moved to surround the heckler as the shop steward continued.

"Low vages and poor vorking conditions must end, and the only vay ve vill ever gain any progress against these mill owners is to strike and stay on strike until they bleed like ve have bled for them," he proclaimed as the expanding multitude of two opposing sides responded with tense huzzahs.

"Ve vill valk the picket lines as long as it takes to earn a better living! Ve must have solidarity!" he yelled out into the street while women, some of them with toddlers, sat at opened upstairs apartment windows to listen.

Waves of echoing cheers poured over him, Renny Niskanen felt more alive than he had in a long time. He felt a growing purpose to lead his fellow workers to victory. Swelling with confidence, he shouted above the mob, "Do ve vant progress?"

"Yes," the massive swarm replied in an uneasy unison as they pumped their fists in the air.

"If its progress ve vant, then progress is made only if ve STRIKE and ve BOYCOTT and ve REVOLT!" he screamed as the sheriff and deputies leaped from their patrol cars and ran toward Niskanen.

Blackjacks in hand, McRae and his men forced their way through the crowd in a rush of power. "Surround him, men!" the sheriff yelled as they started to form a shoulder-to-shoulder circle around the soapbox.

"That's it . . . Renny . . . I'm takin' you in," an out-of-breath McRae hollered as his deputies began to pull men out of their circle.

"I haven't broken any law! You cannot arrest me!" Niskanen shouted from the soapbox.

"Like hell I can't!" the sheriff snapped.

"I thought you vere a union man?" Niskanen cried, but the sheriff ignored him.

One deputy got inside the circle and began pushing out one striker at a time until they had closed ranks and put a struggling Niskanen in handcuffs. The sheriff turned back to the crowd, not bothering to mount the soapbox, and said, "If you men are to strike, then walk your pickets down at the mills! I will *not* tolerate any talk of revolt!"

The crowd of strikers jeered while Niskanen was led away to the sheriff's patrol car and then driven to the county jail.

As soon as they drove away Father Bywater took to the soapbox, the crowd buzzed with anger. "Brothers and sisters please join me in prayer." But the crowd booed at the preacher. "Please, please let me talk to God for you and ask for help," the long faced preacher pleaded as he began to recite the Lord's Prayer. "Our Father who art in heaven —"

"Shut-up! We don't need some priest to talk to God for us!" one riled-up striker yelled as the remaining crowd motioned and hollered at the priest to go away. The people slowly dispersed, most of them heading for home or the speakeasies on Hewitt.

***

At the county jail, Sheriff McRae and Deputy Jefferson Beard took Niskanen to a dusty storage room that was half-filled with barrels and boxes stacked next to the steel-bolted back door.

"I did not break any law, and I have the right to free speech."

"Dammit, Renny. Settle down," the sheriff said as he took the handcuffs off Niskanen, his deputy standing behind him.

"Free speech is the law of America. I have my rights," Renny said, rubbing his wrists.

"Would ya' shut up," McRae snapped, "You've had your say for the day but I can't let you stand on that soapbox and say a word like revolt. That's a riotous word, and I'm not gonna have it. You understand?" the sheriff said, glaring at Niskanen. "Now listen. I'm gonna let the workers who live here walk the picket lines all they want and talk at that soapbox. I know my job and —"

"Your job. What job? You mean your job to stop us speaking?" the Finn said with contempt.

"Stop it, Renny," the sheriff growled. "Don't be givin' me guff in my jail."

Deputy Beard stepped next to the sheriff and placed a hand on his blackjack.

"Who do you work for, Sheriff? Who?" Niskanen boldly asked.

"I work for the people of this county, and they want law and order."

"I saw you in MacCullock's office this —" but Niskanen was hit by Deputy Beard's blackjack. Beard aimed for his shoulder but missed and hit Niskanen on the side of his head instead, splitting open the top of Niskanen's ear.

"Don't be givin' the sheriff here any a' yer bellyachin'," Beard snapped.

"Knock it off, Jeff!" the sheriff hollered as he grabbed hold of his deputy's arm, and then glared at Beard. "Let me handle this."

Niskanen staggered backwards onto a barrel and sat in silence while McRae stood over his former working acquaintance. The sheriff put his hands on his hips.

"Okay, you're right, I was a union man. But now I wear a badge, and that means I'm the sheriff of this county and responsible for the safety of its citizens. So you listen up. I ain't gonna arrest you today. I'm gonna let you out that back-door instead," he said, nodding at the dead-bolted steel door, "but only after that crowd has gone home. And you are not going back to that soapbox," McRae ordered, pointing at the wall in its direction, "so don't give me any more lip or you won't be home for supper. Just sit there and be quiet and, Jeff, let him out the backdoor later this afternoon. I'm going over to city hall . . . 'n don't you dare lay another hand on him!"

But first the sheriff went upstairs to his office, closed the door, and sat down at his desk. Champion Tom was lying on his dirty blanket in the corner but got to his feet when his owner came in. The sheriff looked at his dog and grinned.

"Come 'ere, Champ," he said. Tom loped over and sat up at McRae's feet. The sheriff scratched him behind his floppy ears. Champion Tom looked at his master with sad eyes, groaned, and laid down, he put his head down on extended paws and exhaled, jowls flapping.

Opening the bottom drawer of the file cabinet, the sheriff pulled out an old bottle of Canadian whiskey and set it on his desk. He stared blankly at the unopened bottle for a few seconds and then shifted his gaze to his hunting rifle and fishing pole in the corner, his mind wandering. He closed his eyes and let his head fall back for a brief moment, then stared at the bottle some more. He glanced at his dog and back to the bottle. McRae grabbed the dusty whiskey jug, held it, then put it back in the cabinet and kicked the door closed.

***

Later that afternoon the blood on Renny's ear had dried leaving a long streak of reddish-black going down his neck. When the heavy jail door slammed shut behind him the sound aggravated his throbbing injury. He headed down the trash strewn alley behind the jailhouse and back to Wetmore. Up ahead he saw Noah Spanjer outside of his market stocking the fruit racks. As he walked, Renny looked for his lunch pail along the sidewalk but he didn't see it. Spanjer had just pulled the last bunch of bananas out of a crate when he saw the shop steward approaching him.

"Renny!" Noah cried, "What happened to you?"

"Oh, a deputy rough me up. I be okay."

"Here, come inside, sit down. Let me get something for that," the plump and balding store owner offered as he led Renny through his market to the storeroom. The bell above the store door rang. "Hold on a minute," Noah said. "I've got customers." Spanjer walked back out into the market, a group of lumberjacks were coming in with cork boots on.

"Nope, nope, nope," Spanjer said, waving a finger. "No corks allowed boys. Didn't you see the sign in the window?"

"Aw, mister," one logger in a plaid work shirt complained, "we just blew in and we're starvin'."

"That's fine there, fellas. Just take off them boots, those spikes have ruined more shop floors in Everett than fire and bankruptcy put together. Yer money's still good. Be right with ya."

Noah scurried back to the storeroom and grabbed some medication along the way. He found Renny sitting with his head in his hands. Noah opened the cotton and iodine and dabbed at his laceration.

"I was around troubles like this in Spokane before I came over here," Noah offered. Renny flinched at first and then welcomed the healing medicine.

"Which deputy hit you?" Noah asked.

"I think his name vas Jeff."

"Jeff, oh, Jefferson Beard was it. Hmm. He's tough, but he's always been fair and even handed as far as I know. What'd he hit you with?" Noah asked.

"One a' those black sticks they carry."

"Ah, well, considering what else could have happened, I guess you got off easy," Noah said.

"Yah, I guess so," Renny replied.

"It might get worse, you know. Bloodier," Noah said.

"No, it von't. MacCullock vill see reason. He has to."

"But the mill owners have money. They can hold out a lot better than you" Noah countered as he looked him in the eye then added, "and if the sheriff and his deputies take their side, they could get away with . . . well, they could get away with almost anything."

Renny looked at the store owner and said, "Nobody is going to get away vith anything."

"Well," Noah said calmly, "I'm behind you and your union all the way. And I'll give you all the support I can, but you still need to be careful," Noah cautioned as he finished up and handed Renny the small bottle.

"Here, take this. Have your wife put some more on tonight and again in the morning. You feel all right? Can you walk home?" Noah asked.

"Yah, I be fine," Renny said.

"Oh, I almost forgot," Noah said, handing his friend his lunchbox. "I found it out on the sidewalk."

"Thank you, Noah. That vas good of you," Renny said, grabbing the black domed pail by its twine handle.

Noah turned and went to take care of his bootless customers. Renny left and headed north on Wetmore past IXL Hardware and the Holten Hotel. People were walking all over downtown — strikers headed home and mothers shopping with toddlers. At Everett Avenue he turned and headed east towards the Riverside District. Renny waited for two cars and a horse and buggy to go by on Broadway before he crossed. Up ahead was the usual afternoon crowd of men in line and lingering in front of Dupree's Employment Agency. It was a place where an out-of-work man could buy a job lead for three dollars. The head job shark was writing down openings on a chalkboard outside.

Milling around were footloose floaters, fresh-in-town lumberjacks wearing cork boots, hoboes, truckers, itinerant farm hands, along with a group of mill workers who had voted against the strike. Renny recognized a few and could feel their eyes glaring at him, so he stepped off the sidewalk and walked out onto the plank-covered road to avoid any potential altercation. Their scowls changed to smiles once they saw the cut on the side of his head, black from iodine and blood.

At Virginia Street a Baker Electric car with a lady behind the wheel wearing a feathered hat turned west toward uptown, the only sound the car made was from the wheels clacking against the road planking. In front of Saint Dominic's Academy crews of city workers stood with teams of Dray horses hitched to wagons loaded with pieces of ripped out road wood. They were pulling up the planking and tarred in place wooden blocks, getting the road prepared for cement paving.

A few blocks later Renny trundled past Rudebeck's feed store where clerks were loading a flatbed truck with sacks of grain, when the smell of fresh bread and pastries wafted out of the Scandia Bakery over on Chestnut Street, Renny stopped to smell the wonderful, sweet aroma, and then continued down the avenue. Up ahead at Sovde's Grocery there were horse drawn carts lined up in front ready to go out on delivery runs as people came and went carrying sacks of groceries.

Once he got to Market Street, Renny could see a few kids hanging around outside of a bawdy house, peering through the gaps and knotholes in the tall fence, waiting for something to happen. Then he heard a clatter and the sound of breaking glass. It was coming from Lafayette House, the big new brothel on the corner. Renny stopped in front of the green, three-story Victorian and gazed at its steep roof lines, the gingerbread railings along the covered porch, the architectural adornments, and the corner turret with teardrop shake siding. A few chickens were scratching in the yard.

Suddenly, the front door of the house swung open and a screaming man in a suit flew out like he'd been shot from a cannon. The man landed in a dusty heap at the bottom of the stairs as the kids all laughed. A second later the house body guard appeared holding another well-dressed man by the throat with his right hand in between taking bites from a turkey leg in his left. The hulking ruffian was nearly as tall and wide as the entrance. He slammed the man's head repeatedly against the door jamb. Teeth and blood spurted from his mouth. The ruffian heaved the john off the porch with a huge smile on his face.

"Nobody slaps my gals around! Now git yer lily-livered, panty-waisted asses out of here. I don't want to see either of you two here again!" he hollered and then laughed like it was the most fun he'd had all day.

All the kids were snickering when a prostitute in a frilly pink and black corset with a bloody lip materialized in the doorway holding a vase of colorful flowers. "You sick bastards!" she yelled and threw it at the men, the vase shattered to pieces when it landed on the walkway. Harvey, the body guard, wheeled around, grabbed the fancy lady by the arm, and pulled her inside, saying, "Aw, Cora, why'd ya have ta' go an' break one of Goldie's favorites?" He slammed the door behind them.

Renny looked at the parlor house as he scratched his head and watched the men pick each other up off the ground. After living in the neighborhood for four years Renny had heard all about the recently built Lafayette House and its body guard, Harvey Keel. The bordello's customers were always in the neighborhood, coming and going through the gate in the tall fence that surrounded it and all the other brightly painted brothels on Market Street.

The local line of talk had Harvey Keel as a man of unexplained origin who was so darn right mean and ugly that nobody dared to ask him who he was or where he came from. He had a bent nose, a scar on the left side of his neck that looked like an ending parenthesis, arms the size of a tree stump, and girth as big as a fifty pound sack of hog feed seemingly held up by a white sleeveless t-shirt.

The two thrown-out bordello customers made their way to the gate as they dusted themselves off. One had a series of lacerated welts and lines of blood on the side of his face — he was so disoriented that he walked right into the fence as he felt around in his mouth for missing teeth. The other man had the look of revenge in his eyes. Renny thought their faces looked familiar, but he couldn't remember where he'd seen them before.

"OK, kids, you should not be hanging 'round here," Renny said as he tried to shoo them back to their neighborhoods.

"Did you see him beat up that guy?" one of the boys asked, his eyes as wide as saucers.

"Yah, and if you keep hanging 'round here he might just beat you up too," Renny lectured.

"So? It was still fun to watch, especially when that whore threw the bottle of flowers at 'em," another boy said.

"You kids need to go on home. I don't vant to catch you here again," Renny said.

"Yeah, OK, Mister," one boy said as they all ran off snickering.

Renny walked away. He turned left on Summit Street and followed the trolley tracks up the slight grade. The street was lined with shacks, shanties, clap-board hovels, and a few cottages, none of which had seen paint in years. Some neighborhood children were playing in the middle of the road, skipping rope and playing ball.

"Hi Mr. Niskanen!" one of the happy kids said.

"Hi Holly," Renny replied as nicely as he could, his ear still pounding.

"We haven't heard any mill whistles today. How come?"

"That's because the mills are on strike."

"Again?" Holly frowned. Another girl spoke up, "But guessing whistles is our favorite game." Renny stopped and looked at the kids.

"Don't vorry, the strike vill not last long." He continued walking.

At home Renny slowly climbed up to the porch on creaky, worn-out wooden stairs. He took off his muddy boots, opened the door of the weather-beaten cottage and stepped inside the sparsely furnished two-story house.

"Yah, Renny, you are home?" Petra asked from the kitchen. "How it go?"

"Oh, it vent pretty good 'til the sheriff and his deputies got a hold of me," he said. Renny slowly went back to the rear of the home, set his lunch pail on the counter, sat down, and laid his head on the table he'd built. Petra looked at her husband.

"Vhat is this! Your ear?!"

"A deputy hit me," he said as he rolled his head to the side and pulled the bottle of iodine out of his shirt pocket. "Here, this is for the cut. Noah gave it to me."

"Vhat? Vhy did they hit you?"

"After ve valk off the job, everyone vent to the corner and I make a speech. McRae did not like vhat I said, so he took me to jail," Renny explained as Petra got him a glass of water.

"He took you to jail for vhat you said? Vhat did you say?"

"It is all right. He did not arrest me."

"A deputy hit you?"

"Yah."

"Vhy?"

"I vas talking back, and he just hit me."

"Oh, Renny. Vhy this? I knew it vould be trouble. This is not right to do?"

Lifting his head from the table, Renny looked at his blonde, small boned twenty-three-year-old wife and said loudly, "Yah, it is the right thing to do! MacCullock not pay us enough to live on! An' he ride around in a fancy car! Ve have to fight! Ve already talk about this." Renny drank some water.

"I know. But ve are already starving and now you are striking!" Petra said, raising her voice.

"The strike von't last that long, not to vorry. The union is paying two dollar a veek to every man that valk the picket line, and I already pay forty dollar for the next two month rent. Our garden is growing, so ve vill be fine. Ve have no place else to go. Ve came to America because ve had to, remember?"

"Yah, I remember," Petra said not wanting to ever see her alcoholic mother again, or see the father that abandoned her and her sister when they were just toddlers.

"I still glad ve come here," Renny added and grinned.

"I guess I like America, too," she said quietly.

"Ve vill be all right, I feeling better already. Vhat's to eat?" Renny inquired as he sat up and took another drink.

"I make some rye bread. Ve still have a piece of pork from yesterday and some eggs. Can you get a few turnips from the garden?" Petra asked as she ruffled her husband's black birds-nest hair.

Renny gazed into his wife's blue eyes and reminded himself again how much he loved her. He loved everything about her. The way she spoke, the way she moved, her smile, her shape, her soft skin, just being around her Renny was forever reduced to a puddle of melting admiration. The love he held for her could never be erased.

"*Mina rakastan sinua*," Renny said with a warm smile. Standing up he gave Petra a kiss on her forehead and started towards the back door then turned around and said, "But I think only the radishes are ready."

Chapter 3

TIMBER CREEK

Twenty years before all this, in 1896, the wilderness was everywhere. Back then, once you were headed east across the Snohomish River, walls of timber pushed up from the rich ground to tower over two hundred feet in the air. The trees were so tall they seemed to be holding up the clouds and so wide as to block out the sun on the Fourth of July. It was a seven hundred year old timberland garden of pure, pristine Douglas-fir, western red cedar, hemlock, and spruce in forests so vast and green and lush it all seemed endless. Vine maple, buck brush, decomposed trees, duff, and ferns covered the forest floor. Moss was everywhere, it covered the soil like skin and grew on every tree.

Western Washington was a temperate rain-forest that grew in a mild climate of wet winters and rainy springs. It was a place where dreams could come true for lumberjacks and industrialists, a land that was tamed by western expansion, the need for natural resources, and the opportunity to profit from opening up and logging the last continental frontier at the edge of the Pacific Ocean.

By 1916 the bottom land across the Snohomish River was mostly clear cuts, stump farms, and homestead corn fields. Only here and there remained untouched portions of virgin land, the owners waiting for the price of lumber to go up or holding out for the time when money was tight and they had to sell their timber. There the trees waited patiently for cross-cut saws and the violent sound of crashing timber.

Lost in the clickity-clack of the rails and turmoil of the day, the logging camp foreman gazed from his window seat on the Great Northern Railway Cascadian car on his way up-valley to the logging camp.

From his window Charlie Purvis didn't see a single tree he didn't want to cut down or a stump he didn't already know. To pass the time he evaluated the standing trees he saw, silently adding up the profits each one would bring and the time it would take to fell, buck, skid, and either raft or flatcar haul to the Northern Imperial Mill. He saw beauty in the devastation, good work already done and wages already paid.

The Cascadian whisked past clear-cuts and stumps until it broke into a field of corn next to a small log home where a woman with a baby in her laundry basket was hanging out clothes, a zigzag split-rail fence encircled the house. Then it was back to the cornfield until that too ended and another homestead came into view. A small house sided with hand-split cedar with one window sat next to a lodge pole paddock that held a drove of hogs beside a log barn surrounded by more stumps. Then virgin forest began again. Charlie admired an old-growth cedar, with long curving limbs, but all he wanted to do was cut it down and haul it away.

Another farm of rough-cut buildings sat beside the tracks, a man with a team of horses was pulling stumps. The dirt-covered farmer had a cable wrapped around a stump, the taut cable went through a pulley block anchored to a lone still-standing tree and back to the farmer's straining beasts of burden. The farmer stopped, took off his hat, wiped the sweat from his brow, and waved at the train. The guy looked like a fellow Charlie had knocked out in a barroom brawl back in the fall, but there'd been too many broken faces and bloody lips for Charlie to try and remember.

From a railway river bridge near the town of Snohomish he saw two men in a long boat towing an entire cedar tree, headed for a mill to sell for cash. It reminded Charlie of his youth, doing the same thing years before. But these days very few trees were left along the river bank to fell, limb, and row to town.

At Sultan the Cascadian stopped for water, so Charlie headed over to the Northern Imperial rail and log yard next to the elevated flume that dumped logs into the splash pond at the river inlet. As he got closer he could hear the ringing of the bell that hung over the flume to signal that a log was coming, he knew Timber Creek was in full operation.

In the flume house sat a squat figure of a man with a grizzled face who'd done just about every logging job he could. His body was shot by now but he could still count and add figures in his head, making him useful. Charlie climbed the rickety stairs to the little clapboard station and called out, "Lum, you old sumbitch, how goes the world today?"

"Aw, Charlie, is that you?" Lum drawled lazily. "You know how it goes for me. It's screw or be screwed, and everybody's stupid," Lum mused while keeping an eye on the logs crashing into the pond below, each one hitting the pond with a boom, shooting a twenty-foot fountain of water into the air. River pigs in cork boots scurried from one floating log to another with pike poles pushing the bouncing pieces of timber towards the raft boom. Suddenly, one of them tripped and fell into the cold spring water.

"That's right, ya dumb log hopper! Cain't nobody walk on water 'cept maybe Luther MacCullock!" old-timer Amos Wade shouted in delight at seeing his much younger colleague splashing and gasping for breath. "Son," the old river pig said, jumping over to a closer log, "tell me now? Does it feel like the good Lord's intention for your life and soul is bein' reveled to ya at this very moment?"

Charlie saw the commotion, stepped out of the flume house, and walked out to the end of the gangway.

"Get that man outta the water! Amos! You hear me, Amos Wade?! You're gonna be the one fishin' his body out of the river if'n ya don't!" Charlie yelled with his hands cupped to his mouth.

"He's gonna need to learn how ta' swim sometime!" Amos replied, slapping his thigh.

"Amos Wade! I'm gonna be pickin' out yer headstone real soon if'n . . ."

"Yeah, yeah!" Amos hollered back, then turned and sniffed over his shoulder, "Oh, but I already know you can walk on water ya . . ." his voice fading, drowned out from the splash pond noise.

"What's that?" Charlie screamed after seeing Amos' lips move as he stuck his pike pole out for the half-submerged man. Charlie walked back to the flume station shaking his head.

"Someday I'm gonna fix that sumbitch," Charlie remarked and then said, "Looks like things are running smooth."

"Yep, smooth enough until you kill some poor bastard up at the camp again," the squat, unshaven flume man piped.

"Shut up, I don't need yer damn sass. Besides, I'd damn well kill every stupid Scandi in these woods if it kept the logs a-comin'," Charlie said as Lum's right hand quickly scribed a mark in the ledger.

"Stove off Charlie, I'm trying to count," the old timber bum growled as the train whistle blew.

"You're a credit to yer race there Lum, and I'll have you know I ain't got anybody kilt up at the camp since last fall," Purvis said as he turned and walked back to the switching yard, then boarded the train.

When the Cascadian stopped at Startup Charlie jumped off and headed over to the small Northern Imperial steam-powered speeder car, the utility miniature locomotive used for hauling tools and men. It sat idle on the company spur right where he'd left it the day before. The company log train was still up at Timber Creek being loaded, so he knew the track up to the camp was clear. He checked to make sure he had plenty of water in the boiler tank, got a roaring fire built, and opened up the piston valve and away he went.

The Northern Imperial Timber Company was a tree-eating machine that bored its way through the western Washington forests with overwhelming force, no tree of any value was left unharvested. The first plot of land that Luther MacCullock purchased in the district was the 320 acre Robinson Homestead in 1896, for five dollars an acre. Arlee Robinson had built the skid road northerly for a mile from the river and the Great Northern railroad tracks starting between Startup and Gold Bar. Once the homestead was MacCullock's and then clear-cut, Northern Imperial extended the skid road farther north to other purchased claims and timber sales, going farther and farther into the wilderness. Back then it was only a half mile up to Camp 1 from the Great Northern line. A year later the road was extended a mile deeper in the forest to Camp 2. As the trees were cut and the forest denuded, the whole operation moved further and further into the woods until Camp 9 was established, which they now called Timber Creek.

In 1898 when thirteen-year-old Charlie was a swamper, he used whatever the camp cook would slop in his bucket — bacon fat, used vegetable oil, spoiled butter — to grease the wooden skids on the ground that the logs were pulled over. Yoked oxen traveled the path as bull whackers prodded their teams pulling logs down from the hills to the river, until the log train grade took the skid road's place. Beginning in 1906 at Camp 5, the elevated water flume was built for small-diameter logs, while the big timber was loaded on locomotive flat cars. Charlie by then was a side-rod and hook tender; he liked being the boss of the rigging crew, giving orders to the men. Over the years, the flume and the company rail line were extended for miles up to a now completely isolated Timber Creek, except for the hardiest of souls that walked the ten plus miles up the spur from the river and the Great Northern line. Charlie rode through mile after mile of clear-cut devastation, over trestles above creeks, past lakes and cut-banks on Northern Imperial land.

When he sped past Shep Clausen's small log cabin, at the old Camp 8 site, he saw two side-hill salmon and wished that he had his rifle, imagining the taste of fresh venison for dinner. He tried to remember the last time he went hunting and then wondered if he even had any ammunition up at the camp.

Timber Creek had grown from what started years before as a cluster of tents and shacks into a permanent settlement over the years. More than a dozen frame and log buildings, built on skids and hauled from one camp to the next, surrounded the flume pond that was fed by the year-round creek that the camp was named after. The timber cruiser and foreman house was the first building at camp, its white-washed siding stood out from the rest of the dilapidated structures. Next was the string of long, low bunkhouses, all of them looking worse for wear than the previous, with an outhouse behind each one. A wide trail snaked out through the stumps and brush past the privies to a single small building standing alone in the clear cut. Next to the last bunkhouse was the mess hall, then the wood shed, the tool and file shop, the chicken coop, and milk cow and hog shack.

At the edge of the pond was the main spar tree with a two-drum steam donkey that towed the logs into camp. At its base was the last turn of logs at the landing ready to be sorted and either hand-leveraged with peavey poles and dumped in the water or heel-boom-loaded onto flatcars. Across the pond was the flume dam and sluice gate, a gangway ran the length of the dam for the flume herders to work the logs. A massive clear-cut encircled it all, with Cascade mountain peaks to the south and east.

Charlie rolled into Timber Creek. He pulled the brake lever in front of the gear-driven Shay logging locomotive, then jumped out, threw a track switch, and parked the speeder next to the steam shovel on one of the three side spurs that paralleled the main line. The side spurs reconnected with the main line at the opposite end of the camp, stacks of hand-hewn railroad ties and track rails were stored all around.

He walked over to the mess hall and opened the door. It smelled of pork and beans, pickled beef, sour milk, fresh biscuits, wet, rotten wood, and the sound of slobbering lumberjacks. Only the long-time bull-cook, Tubs Donovan, acknowledged Charlie, saying, "I've got another pot a' beans comin' fer yer table."

"Good," Charlie grunted and then sat down next to his second-in-charge and timber cruiser, Shep Clausen.

"How was the log count today?" Charlie asked his right hand man.

"Down a little," Shep replied, "but not bad."

"How 'bout Mineral Springs? You get up there?" Charlie asked. Shep took another bite before he said anything.

"Nope."

"Then we're both going up there with an ax crew first thing in the morning," Charlie said as Tubs set the fresh pot of beans on the table.

"We had a short stake wander in today," the cook said, "He's the one by himself over in the corner."

Purvis slopped a full ladle of beans on his nailed-down plate, looked over at the new stiff, and swatted a bug on his neck. He shooed the flies away from the biscuits, took one, and got up. Charlie Purvis was short in stature but long on nerve. Wearing his ever present brown leather jacket, grey trousers, a collared black work shirt and tan suspenders, he walked over to the short stake with his eyes fixed on the stiff, sizing him up.

The logger had a hook nose, a square jaw, and a dark knit hat on a head of sand colored hair. He wore a pair of pitch-stained tin pants, a flannel coat, and a damn- near-shot pair of cork boots with busted laces. A gunny-sack, bindle, and double-bit ax were leaning against the bench next to him. He had the look of an experienced timber bum, but Charlie was skeptical of any new-comer who wandered into his camp.

"What's your name, short stake?" Charlie asked with a mouth full of biscuit.

"Harry Dolson," the bum replied, looking up.

"And who are ya, Harry Dolson?"

"Just a fella lookin' fer work."

"Where'd ya last work?"

"Down in Oregon fer Western Pacific."

"Did ya now?"

"Yep. I set choke, topped a few spar. I was a faller most the time."

"Okay, well, we'll see about that. who is yer closest relative?"

"Ain't got none."

"You expect me to think you were hatched 'er something?"

"Nope, orphaned."

"Where?"

"Our Mother of the Sacred Cross, in Portland."

"How old are ya?"

"Nineteen. Twenty next month."

"Are ya right- or left-handed?"

"Left."

"Good. I could use a left-handed ax man right now."

"I can chop an undercut just as fast as anyone."

"Can ya now?"

"Yep."

"You know how to stay out of the bight?" Charlie asked.

"I know where to be in the woods and how to stay out of trouble."

"Okay, all right then. So ya got a full belly there, Dolson?"

"Yes, sir."

"Well, I'm the head push here, and my name's Charlie Purvis. An' you don't be doin' nothin' you ain't told to do, ya got that?"

"Yes, sir, Mr. Purvis."

"Settin' choke at this show pays three dollars a day, swingin' ax is four, and rigging pays four-fifty. I'll put ya on the cuttin' crew, but there's no cards, no liquor, no women, no talking during meals, no pistols, and if'n ya got a rifle ya have to lock it away in the file shop. Ya get Sundays off to do laundry 'er go huntin', 'er whatever, but if ya ride the flume to the rough house in Sultan on a Saturday night and you're not back by Monday morning, then just don't even bother comin' back at all. Now take your bindle over to bunkhouse four. You'll need to sign a contract first thing in the morning. We'll start ya out on the cuttin' crew with Bill and see how ya do."

"Thank you, Mr. Purvis," Harry Dolson said with an appreciative smile. Purvis started to walk away but then stopped and turned around, remembering he had one final question. With a cold, hard glare that nearly lopped off the top three inches of Harry's head, he asked, "You carryin' a red card?"

Harry's eyes seemed unfocused and his face became calm, as though he had prepared for the question. He looked away and scratched the side of his head and said, "No." After a short pause he turned back to Charlie and added, "Sir."

Purvis stared at Harry for a moment and then nodded his head. Charlie seemed satisfied and went back to his meal, signaling the short stake to move along. Harry picked up his bindle, ax and gunny-sack and followed a few men out the door.

"Which one is bunkhouse four?" Harry asked the group.

"Just start countin' as ya move on down the line, ya stupid green horn," one logger replied.

Counting through them, he made his way over to the bunkhouse and stepped inside. The stench of bean gas and wet, moldy clothes hit him square in the face. The wood floors were shredded from cork boots and the room was loud with talk, most of it coming from two pairs of men in the back corner. One pair was bantering away in Norwegian as they puffed on their pipes and whittled wood, the other pair was locked in an intense arm wrestling contest with a gaggle of men surrounding them. Harry went over and looked over the shoulders of everyone. But instead of watching the contest he scanned the faces of the men and took a mental survey of who his future work and living mates would be.

"You can do it, Silas. Take him!" one onlooker yelled. "I've got a day's pay bet on ya! Come on, put yer back into it! Don't let him beat ya!"

The two arm wrestlers groaned and strained as they pushed and pulled against each other, the massive muscles on their forearms bulging and gleaming with sweat. One lumberjack stood next to them with his hands on the table, watching for a pin.

"Take him, Joe. Take him! Silas ain't no good. Beat that son of a bitch!" a logger cheered as the wrestler named Joe just about had his man's arm pinned, and, Boom! Down went Silas' wrist on the table.

"Joe Frytag wins!" the one lumberjack hollered, and half the men cheered. A young logger bolted for the door, but an older-looking barefooted man wearing a filthy, smelly shirt grabbed him from behind.

"Hold on there! You owe me three bucks!" the lumberjack hollered, spinning the other one around.

"We never shook hands," the younger one said as he broke free and ran out the door. The other one caught up and tackled him outside. The bunkhouse emptied, except for the Norwegian whittlers and a few others, and the men circled round the two loggers outside as they wrestled on the ground. Once the older logger got on top of the other he started pummeling him. Left, right, left, right.

"Uncle!" the younger one yelled. The winner pulled the loser's billfold out of his front pocket, took three dollars from it and shoved the money in his own pants pocket.

"That'll teach ya to welch on a bet, ya damn bush-wah," the older logger said as he stood up and strutted back in the bunkhouse and then vaulted up onto his bunk. He put his hands behind his head, crossed his dirty bare feet, and grinned.

Harry followed the men back inside and found one last open top bunk at the end of the run. A pile of sawdust, bits of cloth, and shredded paper were in one corner of the bunk. When he threw his bindle and gunny-sack on the berth, a mouse scurried from the little pile, ran up the wall and disappeared in the shadows. He paid it no mind. Harry gave the whittlers a nod.

"Ya got any tobacco for me pipe in yer yunny sack new feller?" one Scandi asked. Harry was surprised to hear him speak English.

"Nope, just some snoose," Harry answered.

"Yah vell, dats okay. I don't wanna be smokin' no snoose," the Scandi said with a grin. "I is Jorgen Jorgensen and dis is me brudder, Jaako. Vat's yer name?"

"Harry Dolson."

"Ve is pleased to meet ya, Harry," Jorgen said. Jaako asked, "Who did Charlie put ya vorking vith?"

"He said I'd be with Bill," Harry replied. The two brothers nodded and one pointed at a man sitting on the bench reading, they went back to their whittling.

The dank smell of pitch, sawdust, wood smoke, and unwashed socks permeated the air, but Harry was comforted by the sound of a lone logger playing a quiet harmonica in his bunk. Filthy long underwear, pairs of stiff, paraffin soaked, canvas pants that the lumberjacks never washed called tin pants hung from wall pegs. Wet, rumpled cork boots with their laces tied together were slung over the roof beams for drying. The boots showing sharp, steel spikes jutting out from their soles.

A row of double bunks ran along the side walls, both had a bench seat running the length in front. There was a potbellied wood stove in the middle of the room, where an old grey haired dog was sitting up on the floor scratching itself. Dog hair seemed to cover everything. The logger the Scandi pointed at looked up from his Bible and eyed the new hire.

"What'd you say your name was?" the man asked.

"Harry Dolson."

"Well, Harry, I'm William Redbrick. That there is Frank Cargill," Redbrick said as he set down his worn-out holy book, pointed at Frank laying in his bunk, and cracked a grin, "But everybody 'round here knows us as Reader Bill and Dirty Shirt."

Harry nodded and thought, *Oh, I saw that shirt and how he can use his fists,* then he said, "Pleased to meet you both. Charlie said I was gonna be with Bill tomorrow, is that you?"

"I believe that would be me, son," Bill said as he picked his Bible back up but didn't open it, "and tomorrow I believe we are gonna begin cutting up in Mineral Springs."

"That's right, by gobs," Dirty Shirt said from his bunk as he shoved a hand deep in a pants pocket, felt around, and pulled out a stubby pencil. He licked the end of it and began to jot pay time in a little worn-out notepad. Dirty Shirt smiled, nodded to himself, looked up and said, "We's just 'bout done in the Timber Creek Basin, after how long? A year?"

Reader Bill gave him a long suffering look. "It's been over two years now that we've been pulling logs outta this camp. Is your head in the clouds or something?"

"What? How d'ya figure that?" Dirty Shirt answered and glanced at his scribbled pay money figures. "'Cause I only got fifty-two, no," he held up a hand and counted off three fingers, "*fifty-five* bucks saved up."

Reader Bill stared at Dirty Shirt with a sour look and said, "That's because you keep riding the flume to Sultan every other payday since you been here. Isn't it about time you start saving your money and maybe go to church for a change? Are you ever gonna gather up all your sins?"

The corners of Dirty Shirt's mouth turned upwards, he chuckled and replied, "Now why would I want to go and gather up all my sins? There's too many of 'em. And besides, why would I want sit in church all day Sunday when I could be out shootin' side-hill salmon?"

"For the love of Pete, Dirty Shirt. If you go to church you can gather up all your sins under one roof. That way you can deal with all of them at the same time," Reader Bill said as he opened his Bible.

"Why'd I ever want to deal with my sins? Sinnin's all I got," Dirty Shirt said and then turned to young Harry and changed the subject.

"If'n you need to fix up yer bunk sack, there's some straw out in the cow shack. Go ahead and get some," Dirty Shirt offered.

"Thanks. I will," Harry replied.

The same lumberjack that called Harry a greenhorn came in wearing a crusty, stiff pair of tin pants covered in black pitch and sawdust.

"Evenin', Axel," Reader Bill said, but the lumberjack didn't acknowledge him or look his way. Instead, Axel Chambers looked at Harry and grunted, "what the hell are you, some kind a' pilgrim?"

"Nope. Just a fella lookin' fer some steady work," Harry answered.

"Yeah, well, we'll see if ya can work once we're yardin' timber up Mineral Springs," Axel said as he climbed into his bunk. "An' don't be buggin' me or provin' to me how stupid ya are, pilgrim. Ya got that?"

"YA GOT WHAT?!" Charlie Purvis bellowed from the doorway. "Axel, you need to shut that punk-assed blow hole of yours, ya hear me? And why was the log count down again today?" Charlie shouted as he glared at him.

"Why you always doggin' me, I ain't in charge of the log count," Axel shot back.

"Bull-shit you ain't! The faster you choke 'em the faster we count 'em! And if you ain't chokin' 'em then we ain't countin' 'em! That's why ya worthless scamp!" Charlie barked.

"Aw, I was digging out gopher holes on every turn today. Those fallers need to be dumpin' them trees so they land on slash and such so I can choke 'em off easier," Axel replied.

"Don't start moanin' about yer station or blamin' yer slow-assed work on the cuttin' crews! Now I want YOU," Charlie yelled, pointing at Axel, "and all the rest a' ya to be high-ballin' it tomorrow, or I'm gonna start dockin' pay again. We've got another raft to fill down at the river by the end of the week, so all a' you ladies need to shut yer traps 'cause I don't wanna hear any more belly aching!" Charlie tromped out the door.

Harry glanced over at Reader Bill and asked quietly, "He always like that?"

"Oh yeah. Mr. Charlie's head push here, and you don't ever want to get in his way," Bill replied warily.

"Or yet on his bad side," Jaako said from the back.

Harry nodded and headed out the door. Outside he took a deep breath of cool, fresh air and looked up into the night sky. The stars were out and the sound of croaking frogs and singing crickets surrounded him. As he started walking he could hear men talking and laughing in the file shop. Harry walked over and looked in through the window, two men were sharpening crosscut saws in the glow of a dozen kerosene lamps hanging from the ceiling and resting on benches. They had saws clamped to long, narrow wooden vises on work tables, the teeth of the blades pointing upward. Each vise had a single shelf that ran the length underneath it holding files and tools. One filer stopped sharpening a bit and picked up a raker gauge from his shelf. He set it on the run of teeth he was working on and checked the height of the bits, then felt the sharpness with a thumb and finger. Once he was satisfied he set the gauge down on the workbench shelf, pulled a small round can of snoose out of his back pocket, and tapped the lid as he noticed Harry staring at him from outside.

"Something you need there, fella?" the filer asked.

"Nope. Just headed fer some straw."

"This ain't no cow shack, sonny. The cows and hogs is that a'way," the filer said as he pointed the direction for him to go. Harry moved on down the line of buildings.

The faint sound of a guitar and fiddle filtered out of an open bunkhouse door, and the dark silhouette of a lone night watchman walked the gangway on the splash pond dam. A few men were sitting in front of a bunkhouse smoking pipes, and Harry could hear the sound of pots and pans clattering in the mess hall. In the cow shack, Harry bent over to grab an armload of bedding straw and two of the biggest rats he'd ever seen ran from deep inside the pile and out through a hole in the wall. Harry dropped the straw and jumped back right when the cook house flunky walked in with a bucket of slop for the hogs. He was a young kid, much younger than Harry, barefooted and lean.

"Watch out! Hog slop comin' through," the boy said as he carried a heavy bucket with two hands walking bowlegged.

"Need some help?" Harry asked.

"Nah, I's fine brother," the barefooted worker said as he dumped the load of kitchen scraps in the feeding trough. "Who 'er you?" the boy asked.

"Just got hired. Name's Harry Dolson," Harry answered. "You?"

"I'm Little Stovie. I help in the mess hall at night an' feed the donkey boilers in the day."

"Pleased to meet ya," Harry offered.

"What crew ya on?" Little Stovie asked.

"The cuttin' crew. Your pa work here?"

"Nope. Don't got no pa."

"What about yer ma?"

"No ma, either."

"Well, where ya from?

"Sultan," Stovie said, pushing the slop around in the trough with a stick.

"Who raised ya then?"

"Oh, I had a bunch a' ladies raise me at the bawdy house. But when's I turned seven, Miss Cora said I had to go to school but didn't wanna, kept runnin' away. She said if I weren't gonna go ta' school that I had ta' work an' that was fine by me. So Charlie brought me up on the log train an' I been up here ever since."

"That right, huh? How old are ya?"

"'Ten in July, I'll be! An' Charlie's gonna have me chasin' up at the next show!" the young boy said proudly.

"That's a good job, startin' out an' all. But do ya think you'll ever go back, to school that is?"

"Nah, but once in a while on Sundays Reader Bill has me work on my ABC's.

Stovie started to push the slop around in the trough again as the hogs gorged themselves. Harry glanced out the opening in the back of the shack.

"What's that building out behind the outhouses?" Harry asked and motioned in its direction.

"Oh, you mean the powder house?"

"Yeah, I guess so," Harry replied and looked away.

"That's where Charlie and Shep store all the dynamite," Stovie said. Then a voice called out.

"Stovie, how long's it gonna take ya to slop them hogs?" the bull cook yelled. "And ya forgot yer milk pail! Daisy's gonna be mighty darn mad if'n ya don't get ta milkin' her."

"I gotta get goin'. See ya in the morning, brother," Little Stovie said over his shoulder as he ran off to the mess hall. Harry scooped up an armload of straw and headed back to his new home.

***

It was still dark when Harry woke to the sound of the bunkhouse door being kicked open. "Come on! Let's go! Get up, ya bunch a' lazy brush apes!" Charlie Purvis yelled into the stinking room of snoring lumberjacks, "Get ta movin'! Now! We got logs ta' yard and a raft ta' fill!"

Harry snapped upright in his bunk and immediately started scratching the flea bites on his arms and legs. He rubbed his eyes, jumped into his tin pants, lashed on his cork boots, and headed for the mess hall. There was a line going out the door as loggers slowly trudged in and sat down to tables filled with plates of pancakes, butter, syrup, biscuits and gravy and coffee. Harry sat down at the end of a table and started filling his plate.

Shep Clausen walked up with a cup of coffee in his hand.

"Okay son, Charlie says yer comin' with us today," Shep said.

"What about Bill and the contract?" Harry asked as he grabbed two biscuits and put them on his plate, then reached for the gravy.

"We'll find Bill in a minute. I got yer papers right here," Shep said as he put a Northern Imperial contract in front of him.

"What's it say?" Harry asked taking a bite.

"Can't ya read kid?"

"A little, not much really."

"Well, OK," Shep replied. "It says that Northern Imperial owns your ass, son, now make yer mark on both of those lines at the bottom, then grab one of the cook's nosebags from the table so ya got a lunch and meet us out front." Harry nodded and began to wolf down the rest of his breakfast.

Outside, Timber Creek buzzed with activity as men headed out of camp and into the woods. Logging sections of forestland was an endeavor that took great planning and skill, first the timber cruisers and foreman determined the area to be cut and laid out the rigging path for the high-lead operation, each area was called a side. Next, the fallers fell every tree in the side and limbed and topped the designated spar and tail trees, then moved on to the next side of trees to cut. Buckers would follow and cut the logs in lengths of forty-feet. The riggers came in after that to climb the spar and tail trees, hang the pulley blocks and set guy wires. They'd do it for a series of high lead operations in each logged off side. Once the trees were down and the rigging was hung the donkey puncher yarded his steam donkey over the landscape and positioned it at the base of a spar tree. The riggers would finish by running the cables from the steam donkey drums and hanging the choker rigging for the donkey. The whole system was constantly being built, ran, then torn down and moved in a steam and steel mechanized ballet of power and force.

Smoke poured from the main steam donkey near the flume pond where Little Stovie was chucking wood into the boiler firebox. The head donkey puncher checked his pressure gauges and opened a condenser valve spewing off excess steam. Blasts of hot air hissed from the donkey engine like a locomotive. The operator opened a piston valve, released a hand lever, and the two haul drums began to turn. They were wound with steel cable that moved upward through pulley blocks hung high from the spar tree, which was called the haul-back. Separate choker cables hung from butt rigging on the haul-back cable, they clanged together as the choker rigging made the first run of the day up Timber Creek Basin. Men grabbed freshly sharpened cross-cut saws and double-bit axes from the file house when Harry saw Shep, Bill, Frank, and the two Norwegian brothers nearby waiting for orders.

"Ah! Another balmy spring morning in the beautiful Washington woods," Dirty Shirt said, and then added, "How cold do you think it is today, fellas? Thirty, thirty-five degrees?"

"Thirty degree is a varm summer morning in Norway," Jorgen said as everyone laughed. Then Charlie showed up.

"I think it's warm enough for the bunch a you bastards to do some honest work for once in your lives. Now get to it," Purvis said.

"Grab yourself a Swede fiddle and meet us over at the speeder," Reader Bill said to Harry as he headed over near the Shay.

In front of the file house was a rack of crosscut saws, all of them with bright, freshly sharpened teeth. Harry grabbed a ten-foot double-handled crosscut saw and walked over to the speeder car, where he found the men hooking a tote wagon to the back of it.

"Hop on, kid," Charlie said and nodded at the tote as he got inside the speeder cab.

Harry dropped the saw and his ax next to an assortment of tools, sledge hammers, spring boards, a leather sack of wedges, some kerosene bottles, and a few nosebags.

He jumped on the wagon and asked Bill, "So, we get to ride to work?"

"Only a couple of miles or so. We hoof it the rest of the way to the new section."

Harry sat down and the speeder started to roll. He could see Charlie and Shep in conversation through the rear-window in the cab, and, when he glanced over to Reader Bill, his eyes were closed but his lips were moving. It looked like he was praying.

Even if the view was only stumps and slash piles, busted tree tops and worthless shook timber all around them, Harry still loved it. The fresh air, solitude, wildlife, and the views of distant snowcapped Mount Baring and Mount Persis to the east were invigorating. It helped him forget about the rest of the world.

At the base of Mineral Ridge they were at the end of the tracks. Charlie hit the brakes, closed the piston valve, and hopped out.

"All right, Dolson, show us what you got, and lead us up that creek bed," Charlie said as he pointed the way to go, the mossy stones in the creek pointing out a natural uphill path towards their destination.

Harry looked up the side of the hill, he knew he was being tested, so he latched onto his gear, glanced at Bill, and then headed up the grade.

Two hundred yards up the sloping, wet rock bed, Harry stopped. Centuries of spilling water had opened up a wide rock face and exposed square blocks of granite that looked like milled four-by-four pieces of short lumber posts. The top six inches of each piece created a staggered hillside staircase of rock drenched in rich mineral water, it looked ancient with its mossy treads. Small stalks of cedar sprouts forced their way up through the hard, tight cracks between each step of stone. Everyone stopped to look at the beauty of the granite stairway.

"What is this place?" Harry asked as Charlie pushed him out of the way.

"It's called the Devil's Staircase — I'll take it from here," Purvis said as he started climbing.

"I've heard about this place before," Reader Bill said out of the side of his mouth. "For such a beautiful place it's too bad it's named after Satan."

"Get your timber bum asses a' goin'," Charlie yelled as the rest of them followed, "This ain't no picnic!"

Once they got to the top of the western shoulder of Mineral Ridge, an enormous basin stretched before them. A virgin forest of huge timber, vast and unbelievably magnificent, spread out on a gentle downward slope as far as the eye could see.

"Bill, you and Harry take yer misery whips and start in on that grove," Charlie ordered and motioned at a grouping of trees, "and dump everything back uphill. Shep and I are gonna scout out a haul-back path and figure out how much timber is in this first side. I'm thinkin' we'll use that big Doug-fir over there for the spar. This first side we'll be yardin' everything up ta' here," Charlie said as he pointed at the extra tall tree.

Harry set the sledge-hammer, ax, and his lunch-bag down by some snow-flattened ferns while Reader Bill looked up the trunk of their first victim and counted the limbs on the uphill side. "Yep, she's limb heavy on the good side. If we can get this one down without hanging up then it'll open it up for all these others. She'll be on the ground in no time there, Harry, my-boy," he said with a grin.

Harry and Reader Bill grabbed their double-bit axes and cut some spring board notches on either side of the nine-foot diameter tree. Harry got his notch done first. He slammed the metal hook end of his board into the notch, and then hopped onto the narrow springboard and waited on the left-hand side of the tree. When Bill was done he swung the other end of the saw over to Harry, and they began the bottom cut. The freshly sharpened crosscut saw sliced through six inches of bark and bored into the heartwood of the old-growth fir. At the first sign of pitch flow they pulled the saw out and doused kerosene on the blade until the saw moved freely through the wood again. Once the cut was a good third of the way into the tree, they pulled their axes and started the undercut.

With every ax swing they bit deep into the yellow-white wood. Large chips of fir fell to the forest floor as the cool morning air filled their lungs. After four hours the undercut was done, and a breeze picked up. The crowns of the trees rustled and swayed.

"You know, they say a good ax man can fell timber all day long in the wind," Reader Bill said as he swung the Swede fiddle handle over to Harry from his springboard.

"Yep, I've heard that saying, too," Harry answered as they doused the blade with kerosene and started in on the back cut. The tree's pitch began to ooze out.

"We had a fellow come down here from B.C. last fall, and he didn't have enough wedges set in his back-cut to keep the tree standing on a windy day, and sure enough that big old fir kicked back on him and squashed him dead," Reader Bill said as he quickly wiped the sweat from his brow with a free hand when Harry pulled and then continued talking and sawing.

"If need be, we might do a second undercut on this one to make sure the tree bucks away from the stump and pushes forward more, that way it won't break up when it hits the ground. Northern Imperial doesn't want any split an' shook timber for the mill. But we'll need to use a wedge with a tree plate so this big old thing doesn't set back on us or pinch our saw," Reader Bill instructed.

From the pouch strapped around his waist Harry grabbed a wedge, and a flat square piece of steel that had one side hammered and curled over, and placed them one on top of the other in the center of the back-cut. He struck the wedge and tree plate a few times with the ten-pound hammer and then went back to cutting. A dozen saw pulls later, the tree made a cracking sound.

"Keep sawing, Harry. She's about to go," Bill ordered. Five strokes later, the tree began to move and it cracked as loud as the day is long. Then a deep-rooted pop sounded. The old growth moved some more and began to pitch as Bill yelled, "Timber!" Both he and Harry let go of the saw, jumped from their springboards and ran away from the tree as it slowly tipped. The uncut wood between the back and undercuts ripped and peeled loose, its fibers tearing, breaking free, snapping, splitting, and then exploding. With a rush of air the tree came violently cashing down. The forest floor shook like an earthquake as the massive Douglas-fir crushed the mossy ground and sunk into the spring soil. Small green sprigs floated down. All was quiet in the woods once again, only the slight breeze moved the branches.

With a huge smile on his face, Bill put his hands on his hips and said, "Grab the saw and I'll get the axes. We'll buck the top off first and then get to snipping the limbs."

An hour later they had most of the tree stripped of limbs when Charlie and Shep showed up.

"That opened it up," Charlie remarked. "These others will come down clean now. If you can get two of those done every day for the rest of the week we'll be in good shape. Grab yer nosebags, ladies. It's lunch time."

"What'd ya get?" Reader Bill asked as he took a bite out of a pickle. Harry opened the brown paper sack, buried his face in it, and smelled what was inside. He pulled the biggest sandwich he'd ever seen from his bag and smiled, then opened the waxed paper around it. Harry picked up the sandwich but the bread was hard as wood on the outside, then it started to drip slop and fell apart in his hand.

"What the —," Harry groaned as his sandwich drooled all over the forest floor. "It looks like a ladle of beans an' molasses." Charlie started to chuckle.

"Yeah," Shep said with a grin, "I've seen those before. When Tubs gets behind he throws those things together. He calls 'em sloppy shingles." Reader Bill ripped his ham sandwich in half and handed it to Harry. "

"Here ya go," Bill said, "it's always a good idea to take a look inside of Tubs' nosebags before ya head out in the morning."

Five minutes later Charlie was done and got to his feet, saying, "OK, you two get one more on the ground while Shep and I figure out and stake where we're gonna run the grade ta' get the Shay up here, an' that'll do it for the day."

***

Over the rest of the week Reader Bill and Harry fell a dozen more old-growth fir and opened up a good-sized area around the one still-standing tree that was going to be the spar. On Saturday morning the climbing gear was on the tote wagon, and Charlie had a smirk on his face.

"OK, Dolson. Ya said you've topped spar before," Charlie said.

"Yep," Harry answered, thinking he knew what was next.

"All right. Yer toppin' it then," Charlie stated.

"I'll top that big ol' Doug-fir you picked," Harry replied with confidence.

"Well, since there's no wind today, we'll just see about that," Charlie grunted, the corners of his mouth turning downward.

As soon as Charlie opened the steam piston valve and the wheels of the speeder were turning, Reader Bill looked over to Harry and asked, "You've topped spar before?"

"More than I can count," Harry answered.

"OK, good. I wouldn't want to see another young buck find the end of his days from the orders of Charlie Purvis," Reader Bill said warily.

"I'll be fine," Harry sniffed.

At the end of the tracks, Harry hopped off the tote and grabbed the climbing spurs, a waist belt with rope, a short-handled liming ax, and led the way up the creek. At the Devil's Staircase, he didn't hesitate to gawk at the beauty of it and kept climbing until he was at the base of the designated tree, where Charlie felt inclined to talk.

"When was it we quit using dynamite to blow the tops of these things off, Bill?" Charlie asked with the same smirk plastered on his face.

"You darn well know when it was," Bill replied with a touch of bitterness in his voice.

"Oh yeah, I remember now," Charlie said. "It was back when old Anders Nielsen done blew himself up three years ago when he lit that fast fuse and it jumped up to the charge just a little bit too soon. Two halves of old Anders hit the ground before that top landed on him. Hell, he got himself kilt twice!"

By the time Charlie was done with his story Harry had the spurs and belt strapped on and was tying a hand saw and the liming ax to the climbing belt with two pieces of three-foot hemp line. Reader Bill walked the end of the belt rope around the tree and then handed it to Harry.

"Aw, don't be payin' Charlie no mind," Reader Bill said, "he just likes scarin' people."

"Good luck, son," Shep offered, "and don't be chopping your rope. Every logger only gets one mistake out here, so do yerself a favor and don't be using it today. Up you go."

Harry dug his spurs into the bark and started to scale the tree. After every three short steps he stopped to flip the rope up higher on the other side of the tree as the hand saw and ax rocked back and forth under him, clanging together with each movement. Charlie and Bill stood off to the side and watched him, both with their right hands on their foreheads to shield their eyes from the sun. The first fifty feet of the tree were without limbs, and they could hear Harry breathing hard as he climbed.

"You OK?" Bill yelled. Harry signaled back that he was fine with an arm wave.

At the first limb Harry stopped, pulled up the ax, and then lopped it off with a swing. The limb turned in the air as it dropped down to the forest floor. He took two more steps and his left spur came loose. He dropped, but with lightning-fast reflexes Harry jerked on his rope with both hands and stopped his fall. Reader Bill held his breath.

Harry dug his spurs back into the thick bark and tightened his rope, and then started climbing again. At the next limb he missed his mark, and the ax bounced off the tree first before cutting the limb clean off. It flew out away from the tree like a spear through the air.

"Look out!" Harry shouted as the limb took flight. It landed closer to Charlie than to Bill and Shep, its sharp end going deep into the soil, standing straight up like a javelin.

"What the hell are you trying to do, Dolson, kill me?!" Purvis screamed at the top of his lungs. "You ignorant bastard! I may not be married, but I don't need to be done in by you with a widow-maker!"

Harry yelled down, "I said look out!"

"That's OK," Shep shouted back. "We know it was an accident." Shep turned to Charlie. "He didn't mean it. Let's go sit down and take a break."

Away from the tree and after a moment, Charlie calmed down, saying, "Yeah, well, we'll see if this Dolson kid can snip off the top forty feet. If he pulls it off it'll make a fine spar for hauling out of this drainage."

"I guess you'll be working with the riggin' crew ,and hangin' gear next week?" Reader Bill asked.

"Yep, I suppose," Charlie said and then scratched the side of his head and wondered out loud, "So, whatcha think of this Dolson fella?"

"Seems like a good worker to me," Reader Bill said.

"I figured you'd say somethin' like that about some young kid who just tried to kill me. I ain't sold on him yet."

"Charlie, he didn't try to kill you," Bill said firmly. "He's a good kid, and I like him. Besides," Bill frowned, "are you ever sold on anyone?"

"Hell no," Charlie snapped. "This punk-assed kid doesn't know how stupid he is yet. He's still a bit wet behind the ears if ya ask me. There's something about this kid that don't cut right to me."

"Why's that?"

"I don't know yet. I guess he seems a bit too friendly an' eager to please 'er somethin'."

"Charlie, the kid's far better an' any of those other short stakes wanderin' in and out a here, or even the ones you fired lately," Reader Bill reminded his boss and then looked up in the tree.

Harry had most of the limbs off and stopped to take a break where the tree was less than two feet wide. From his vantage point he could see the towns of Sultan and Gold Bar in the distance, and the rail yard, all of it in miniature. The peaks to the east were still white with snow, and the wide Skykomish River below was a thin ribbon of blue. It snaked and curled its way down-valley to merge with the Snoqualmie at Monroe, forming the Snohomish, then towards Puget Sound and the mill smoke of Everett. Harry felt like he was on the summit of a mountain at the top of the world. After he caught his breath, he looked up into the tree to see which side was limb heavy.

Charlie stood up and cupped his hands to his mouth, he yelled, "That's good enough. Now decapitate that sumbitch!" Harry signaled back with his arm to show that he'd heard him and pulled up the saw.

After working his way around to the limb-heavy side, Harry began to make the undercut. Since the tree was narrower than his saw was long he finished the top-angled cut with it instead of chopping out the undercut and then watched the wedge of wood fall away. He worked his way back around to the other side for the back-cut, made sure his rope was tight and below the undercut, and then dug his spurs deeply into the bark before he started.

With each draw of the saw, Harry took a deep breath. He knew that if he pinched the saw he'd have to chop it out, and that was the last thing he wanted to do one hundred and twenty feet in the air. But the saw kept cutting smoothly and he prayed that a gust of wind wouldn't come out of nowhere.

Then he heard a crack. He sawed faster, and it cracked again. He thought he heard Bill yelling when the top of the tree started to move away from him. Harry let go of the saw, held the rope tight, and screamed, "Timber!" as the limbless tree swayed back and forth under him. Three seconds later he heard his echo bounce back at him just before the top of the tree came crashing down to the forest floor below.

Reader Bill cracked a satisfied smile, nodded his head, and thought, *I knew he could do it.*

***

After dinner, when all the dishes were done and his kitchen was closed for the night, Tubs Donovan handed Charlie a steaming cup of coffee.

"Goin' down ta' Sultan tonight?" the bull cook asked.

"Naw, not tonight. Cora moved on down ta' Everett an' workin' at some brand new fancy crib," Charlie confided. "Guess she was tired of the same old timber bums up here." He lifted the cup to his lips.

"Ya might have to look her up the next time yer down in mill town," Tubs offered with a sly grin.

"No doubt about that," Charlie said with a rare smile. Tubs grinned back.

"You think you'll ever tell the men about Cora and —" Charlie raised his hand and cut him off.

"You damn well know I'll never say anything, so quit askin'," Charlie snapped.

"But some of the men in camp know, I think," Tubs said.

"And they all damn well know to keep their traps shut, too," Charlie cracked, glaring at his only friend.

The long-time cook changed the subject.

"Yeah. OK. So, how'd it go up there today?" Tubs asked

"Well, that new sumbitch Dolson landed a widow-maker near me today."

"Did he now?"

"Yep."

"He call out?"

"Bill said he did, but I didn't hear him," Charlie said as he took another drink.

"If he called out, then it was just an accident."

"Yeah, maybe. But there's somethin' about him that rubs me the wrong way."

"What's that now?"

"Well, the day he showed up I asked him if he was carrying a red card."

"You mean IWW?"

"Yeah, a Wobbly card. We don't need any a' them up here."

"What'd he say when you asked him?"

"He said no. But it didn't sound right, and then he looked away."

"Oh," Tubs scoffed, "that don't mean anything. Besides, yer short of men right now."

"Yeah, I know. I could use as many ax men as I can find and they sure ain't walkin' into camp like they used to. You know," Charlie said rubbing his unshaven chin, "Since we're movin' the show up to Mineral Springs, and, now that I think about it. I might just know what ta' do with this new short stake who came a wanderin' on into my camp, especially this week an' all."

Tubs raised an eyebrow and asked, "Whatcha mean, this week and all?"

Charlie looked away and took a sip of coffee. He turned his head back around and faced the cook.

"This week?" Purvis said with a grin. "Because, here we're' startin' a whole new show an' this new kid come wanderin' in as if he knew there was gonna be work up here, that's all . . . We'll see how he does."

***

That night as some of the crew were huddled around the glow of an outdoor fire, Harry reached for the jug of moonshine as Shep Clausen congratulated him. "You done good today, son. Here's to Mineral Springs' new tree top-per, Harry Dolson!" Everyone let out a cheer, especially Dirty Shirt and the Jorgensen brothers.

"Now that we've got Harry, I guess my spar toppin' days is over," Dirty Shirt said with a smile.

"Yah, sure, ve all done toppin' I guess," Jorgen Jorgensen said. "But can ya rig a spar, too?"

"I sure can, and I sure will," Harry answered. He took a drink from Shep's moonshine jug and wiped his mouth with his sleeve. "Where'd you get this stuff?"

"Make it myself back in the lean-to," Shep said as he pointed around the back of his log cabin. "I grow my own potatoes and twice a year on my trip to Sultan I get my yeast and sugar. Last winter I tried cookin' the mash in the cabin but damn near burned the place down, so I got myself all set up outside this spring, and this here's my first batch. Not bad if I say so myself."

"Yah, vell, in Norway ve make aquavit with potatoes and sugar, too, but ve add caraway seeds and den ve let it sit in da oak barrel for about as long as ve can vait. Den ve drink it all!" Jaako chuckled.

"Yah, maybe you drink it all," Jorgen added to laughter.

Harry took another swig and offered, "Did you fellas ever hear the one about the timber baron and the stump farmer?"

Everyone looked at each other, and then Dirty Shirt piped, "Let's hear it."

"OK. Well," Harry began, "one day a well-dressed timber baron was out hunting grouse. He had on his fancy boots and a brand new mackinaw. He'd been walking around through some stump farm for a while when all of a sudden this grouse took to flight. The timber baron drew a bead on it and shot it clean, but the grouse landed on the other side of a fence in another field. So the timber baron looks all around but doesn't see anybody, so he jumps the fence and walks over to his grouse. Just then this filthy old farmer jumps out from behind a stump. He was missing a few front teeth, but he could still shout pretty fine, and he yells, 'Whatcha think yer doin' thar, mister?' And the timber baron, he says, 'Getting my grouse that I just shot.' So the farmer says, 'Well, you cain't jess jump a fence and take a grouse from another man's field.' The wealthy timber baron, he says,

'But I shot it. Therefore by rights it's my grouse.' And the farmer goes, 'Not so fast there fella. Round these parts we tend to settle our differences the old country way. You see, I'll flip a coin, and whoever wins gets to beat on the other one for three minutes, and then the other one gets to beat on the first one for three minutes. We go back and forth like that until one of us stays on the ground.' And the timber baron, he says, 'Why that is ridiculous. I'm not going to diminish myself with a fist fight like that.' So the farmer says, 'Well, you ain't a-gettin' that thar grouse then.' The timber baron, he thinks about the farmer's proposal and starts to size up the farmer, thinking he's old, missing his teeth, smaller than him, and worn out. Then the baron thinks about how he's young, tall, and strong, and decides that he could whoop the farmer's ass pretty good, and he says, 'OK, I'll fight you for that grouse.' Since they'd come to an agreement, the stump farmer pulls out a coin and flips it in the air. The timber baron calls heads, but the coin lands on the ground tails. So for the next three minutes the stump farmer beats the heavenly daylights out of the timber baron until he's on his knees and about an inch away from his life. The timber baron slowly gets back on his feet, barely able to stand, and he says with his hands on his knees and breathing hard, 'OK you worthless stump farmer, it's my turn now.' But the farmer looked at him and says, 'Oh, you can have the grouse — it's not even my field.'"

The whole crew burst into laughter as the young Harry Dolson beamed with delight.

Chapter 4

PICKET LINE

"A fair day's vage for a fair day's vork!"
"Say it again!"
"A fair day's wage for a fair day's work."
"Vhat do ve vant?"
"A fair day's wage for a fair day's work!"
"A longer picket line, get-a shorter strike!"
"A longer picket line, gets a shorter strike!"
"Say it again!"
"A longer picket line, gets a shorter strike!"

Buck Mullaney took a big bite from his sandwich and watched the picketers march and chant from behind the newly erected fence and just inside the large mill opening with the rest of his guards. Most of the strikers who had been walking the picket line for the last three-months at the Northern Imperial had saved up a little money to tide them over, prepaid their rent, and stocked up on food supplies for the duration.

"My wife woke up sick last night," Fred McCorkel mentioned to a striker in front of him after the chant died out, "so now my kids will get it, too."

"Yeah, well, my wife and kids have been sick all week," the striker replied.

"Fever?" Fred asked.

"Yep."

"With a cough?"

"Yep."

"I ain't got any money to go to the clinic," Fred said.

"Me neither, and my kids need to see a doctor, too," the striker said.

"Maybe the union should pay," McCorkel offered.

"MacCullock should pay!" the striker yelled at the guards.

"MacCullock ain't never gonna pay for squat, but the union should. Hey, Renny," Fred yelled, "how 'bout we see if Jake Michel can get us some free doctor or clinic visits? My kids 'er sick." The little shop steward nodded his head and quickly agreed.

"Yah. I talk to Jake. And vhere is Hank Hillstrom today?" Renny asked.

McCorkel glanced towards Hewitt, he turned back to Renny and answered, "Don't know. Haven't seen him all day."

"Yah, vell. He should be here," Renny said and then pointed at a rusty flatbed and called out, "Here they come again!" Another truckload of scabs came bouncing up the frontage road. He recognized Northern Imperial foreman Butch Barnell behind the wheel.

Buck Mullaney saw the rolling, rumbling hulk of metal and opened the mill gate. The well-armed group of mill guards fanned out to make sure the jeering picketers stayed back.

"Keep yer sorry asses where they are, ya bunch a' bums! I've got a new load of real men who want ta' work an' feed their family an' kids coming in!" Mullaney yelled as he opened the breech and checked the shells in his gun.

"Go to hell, you scab bastards!"

"All we want is a decent wage!"

"Why doesn't MacCullock come down from his fancy office and face us?" The gang of strikers yelled at the truck as it drove through the fence gate while the guards walked backward, behind the vehicle, the gate quickly closed.

Once inside the fence the workers filed past the bunkhouse and mess hall and into the mill. The exterior of the mill was a mix of constantly mended weather beaten board and batten siding, grey-black and dilapidated from disrepair and neglect, its sheet metal roof was a patchwork of rusty colors. The mill's condition was proof of the owner's concern for gain over upkeep.

Barnell sat behind a desk at the entrance where he took their names and set them to work.

"You ever do any mill work?" Barnell asked the first bum in tattered clothes.

"Yep, lots," the bum answered.

"Where?"

"Spent a good while in Darrington at the U.S. Mill and then that darn cousin a' mine got me down to Granite to work fer the King Bolt shingle outfit. But it was tough gettin' paid. Seemed like we was always gettin' shorted and such. So I left," the man explained. "Came down here."

"Yeah, well, we're payin' shingle weavers and sawyers forty cents an hour with room and board. You can take it 'er take a hike," Barnell grumbled. "Makes no difference ta' me."

"I'll cut shingles, I suppose," the bum said. "Ya runnin' Caldwell's?"

"I've got two-dozen Sumners upstairs," Barnell replied, "but three ain't workin'."

"Uprights, or them new gold high-standards I heard about?"

"You want a job 'er not, fella?" Barnell countered, glaring at the hobo.

"Yeah, yeah," the man answered. "I said I'd take a sawyer job."

"OK. Good. Ya' got a name?"

"Tompall."

"That yer first and last name, Tom Paul?"

"T-o-m-p-a-l-l is my first. Tharp's the last," the man said.

"OK, here's yer time card," Barnell said, handing him a time sheet. "Punch in and then go past the time keeper's office and up the stairs to the shingle area. You'll see it. Next."

"What about lunch?" the new hire asked.

"You'll get fed when I say so," Barnell growled, "now git to work."

Tompall made his way inside the mill. Soot covered windows allowed only enough filtered sunlight to show the floating sawdust particles hanging mid-air, the building shook and hummed with the sound of working equipment. Ten-ton logs were pulled up the ramp from the salt chuck and rolled onto the carriage to be milled. The carriage and floor shook from the log's weight as workers clamped the log in place. The head saw buzzed through fir logs, spitting sawdust into the air. Freshly cut slabs slammed onto rollers and moved on to gang saws where the four-inch thick pieces of fir were cut into lumber. Next the lumber slid to the graders for inspection, and moved on down to the green chain, where men sorted the different-sized pieces and lengths and loaded the lumber onto carts then taken to be stacked for kiln drying. Steam blasted out of overflow valves, men yelled orders, and the whole mill seemed to shake like a faint earthquake.

Tompall found the time clock, punched in, and went around the corner and up the stairs to where a long row of sawyers tried to keep up with their shingle machines. He pulled a sponge mask from a trouser pocket to cover his mouth and tied it around his head as he walked down the sawdust-covered aisle. The saw stations were to his right, and the conveyor bolt roller was on the left. Cedar blocks slid down the bolt roller to shingle cutters who grabbed a new one every minute or two.

There were four empty shingle saw stations down at the end. Three of the machines were torn apart, used for parts to rebuild the machine he was to operate. It looked like it was ready to go. Tompall pulled the lever to engage the pulley on the overhead axle crank and stepped on the clutch floor pedal. The shingle machine roared to life, its sharp steel teeth spinning as its bolt carriage slid back and forth. Satisfied that the machine was running right, he stepped off the clutch and waited for the two saws to quit spinning. Then he yanked on the carriage set works lever and locked it open. Tompall picked up a cedar block from the rollers and mounted it in the set works, released the spring tension, clamping the cedar block in place, and stepped on the clutch pedal again. The machine sliced off two shingles. Tompall let them fall to the floor and took his foot off the clutch when a shingle weaver called up the chute from below, "You about ready up there? Let's go!" Tompall pulled the sponge mask down on his chin.

"Yeah, yeah!" he yelled back, "Just makin' sure this thing runs!"

Tompall adjusted his sponge mask and kicked away inches of sawdust from under his feet for better footing and stepped on the clutch pedal again. The machine sliced off a shingle, he caught it with his left hand. He quickly transferred it to his right, set it on the hinged table on the trimmer saw in front of him, and pushed down, cutting off a knot hole. Then he flipped it over with his right hand, and trimmed the other side square. At the same time he caught a new shingle with his left hand. Tompall tossed the finished shingle down the chute and began the process over. He did another, and another, and another.

Outside the mill, three rowboats of men floated up to where a worker was feeding wood into a steam boiler.

"Not you bastards again!" the worker yelled.

"I've been telling you all week that you're doin' my job ya worthless scab! What's it like takin' food out of a family's mouth, you pig of a hangman!" Hank Hillstrom yelled from one of the boats.

"You're the ones who walked off the job! If you want your job back then come up here and get it!" the worker yelled and threw a round of wood into the firebox.

"Damn you, ya chicken-hearted, mud-suckin' mule!" a man in another boat screamed.

"Why, you pig-snouted slaughter-house cur! You strikers are nothing but a bunch a' swine herders!" the scab barked back and then threw a piece of scrap wood at the boat, hitting it square on the gunwale. One man in each boat stood up and began throwing the rocks that they'd brought with them at the scab while the rest of the men started shouting.

"You low life!"

"You're the pig of a hangman, not us!"

"And the son of the devil!" Hillstrom shouted.

"You're the grandson of the serpent and nothing but an idiot before God!" one oar-man hollered as they began to row their boats away while the others pelted the scab and the mill with rocks.

Inside, the mill hummed with the sound of MacCulloch's profits. The six teen-foot steam driven head wheel groaned as it turned the axle crank that ran along the top of the support beam through the entire length of the mill. At each work station separate drive belts came down from the axle to turn the worn-out machinery when a rock broke through one of the dusty mill windows. It landed right in a drive pulley wheel causing the belt to spin off making a screeching racket. Barnell jumped from his station desk and ran outside where he saw men in three rowboats paddling out of the salt chuck headed upriver.

***

Near the northwest corner of Hewitt and Wetmore the Salvation Army band played *Nearer, My God, to Thee* in front of the Gospel Mission as a crowd of concerned citizens and off-picket strikers gathered. The secretary of the Everett Building Trades, Jake Michel, walked out to the center of Hewitt, paced off fifty feet back along the west side of Wetmore, set down a wooden crate, and stepped onto it.

"Good afternoon, Everett!" he hollered out over the building crowd. "It's good to see all of your tried and true faces today! I say that because we are fighting the good fight, and when we win this strike it will give equal rights to all members, an eight-hour workday, and decent working conditions."

"Right now every shake mill in the state is up and running, and all of them have returned wages to where they were two years ago. But the Everett lumber trust will not restore our former wage scale. They refuse! The mill owners cannot stand against this evidence!" Michel yelled.

"There is nothing to hold back the rising price of shingles right now. The price of clear shingles will probably be higher than it's ever been, over two dollars a square, and soon! Every scrap of steel is going to the European war effort, the war has taken away the market for metal roofing. More cedar shingles will be needed, and that means more profit for the lumber trust. They can more than afford to pay us the 1914 scale right now! And with those enormous profits they'll pay a decent wage to the brave union men out there on the pickets!"

"Our plan is to bring into the Shingle Weavers Union all the mill workers: the timber sawyers, the shingle cutters, the packers, the filers, the engineers, and the firemen. When we win we will welcome all these skilled positions into a new industrial union!" Michel roared. The crowd boomed back with cheers and raised fists. Michel smiled back and raised an arm.

"All right! Very Good! Thank you! Stay strong Everett!" Jake hollered. "That's all I've got for now, there's other people here that want to talk today," he said stepping down and walking away.

Another speaker stood behind the soapbox and waited. He was tall, broad shouldered, and light haired. He wore grey wrinkled trousers and a white uncollared shirt buttoned at the neck under a brown suit coat that was frayed at the sleeves. The man put a hand to his mouth and coughed a few times, then stepped onto the wooden crate and scanned the onlookers with sharp blue eyes. His mouth was covered by a light brown handle-bar mustache. The crowd quieted. He nodded once and then spoke with a clear, earnest voice as he reached out to the crowd with an open right hand.

"Greetings fellow workers, and citizens of Everett! It is good to see you today. My name is James P. Thompson and I am from the IWW," he began. "And as a proud member of the Industrial Workers of the World I am here to tell you that we are all here for something better than being wage slaves! I have heard a great deal about what is happening in Everett, I and every single decent person in Seattle and up and down the coast are rooting for your cause. I tell you now that we shall begin the march towards victory!" Thompson yelled out to a few scattered cheers.

"We should never allow ourselves to be exploited or degraded by the lumber trust, we must fight them now. If we don't fight them now who will fight them tomorrow? If we don't fight they'll hold down our wages today and then reduce our wages tomorrow! These barons are only concerned with their massive profits. Do not allow these industrial aristocrats to look down on us with disdain while they luxuriate in their mansions. I say this because the IWW will allow every man who joins our one big union to be able to lay his head down at night and sleep with an unfettered conscience," Thompson explained to louder cheers and fewer boos.

"Now, the AFL has the Shingle Weavers Union affiliated with them as a craft union. In the AFL every job is a separate craft, and every craft is a separate union, so when one craft goes on strike the others are forced to remain on the job. If other crafts remain on the job, then they scab against each other. But with the IWW all crafts are one, if we go on strike, then we all go on strike. The IWW will always win with the power of being together as one!" Hundreds of anxious faces in the crowd stared at him while a reporter from the *Daily Tribune* stood across the street and took notes.

A man in a brown derby hat with a bowtie and cane stood next to a woman with four barefooted children in hand-me-down clothes as two malingering teenagers worked their way through the crowd, not caring what the speaker had to say. Noah Spanjer shooed the last of his customers out, closed his market and leaned against the door to listen. He nodded in agreement in a blood-stained butcher's apron next to a banker in a neatly pressed wool suit. Helen Pomeroy, the widowed wife of a former timber worker stood with her two children on the sidewalk next to Father Nathan Bywater, all of them paying close attention. Every out-of-a-job man and every woman and child strained to listen as litera-ture, pamphlets, black cat stickers and copies of the *Industrial Worker* newspaper were handed out and stuffed into faded overall pockets and cloth purses. A few boos rang out when the sheriff pulled up and parked his dark green Chevrolet across Hewitt, the paddy wagon full of deputies pulling in behind him.

Thompson saw the sheriff and looked back into the crowd, his eyes seemed to catch fire, and his voice got louder.

"I say this theft of labor must stop! Why is it that this land is so rich when we are so poor?" he asked with outstretched arms. "Why is the divide between hard-working families and their employers so wide? I'll tell you why. It's because these industrialists see us as their slaves, with no rights and no brains, that's why. And if we are to narrow the gap between us and them, we must strike and stay on strike until they find themselves as poor as we are!" The crowd's enthu-siasm began to swell and the speaker started to move his arms, a workingman's conductor using graceful movements with open palms as he spoke.

"Labor is entitled to all it creates. We are the ones working all day long making the capitalists richer by the minute. We are the ones who are making the profits for all the timber barons in this town!" the Wobbly speaker yelled. Then the afternoon vaudeville show at the Rose Theater let out. Three hundred citizens flooded onto the Wetmore sidewalks and spilled out into the street, blocking traffic. Mothers pulled their daughters close and fathers turned their heads to listen as their eyes darted around the street scene. Thompson contin-ued speaking.

"If these wealthy mill owners are going to use scab labor and pay them less than they were paying you, then the scabs will soon be on strike, too! Soon enough the scabs will be joining you on the picket lines and be at the street meetings because they will not be able to afford to feed their families on slave wages." The crowd roared as Thompson paused for a drink of water. Then he noticed the sheriff and his deputies walking towards him through the crowd. He raised his right fist and pointed a stiff index finger straight up to the sky.

"Hear me now! We must not mourn the death of our former IWW member Joe Hill. We must organize. Joe Hill was executed in Utah for a crime he didn't commit. He was executed, no, he was murdered, by the wealthy elite afraid of his power to organize us, we the people. On May First when this strike started, hundreds of IWW members scattered the ashes of Joe Hill in every state in the union, even here in Washington. So I say, long may labor live! Long may Joe Hill live! And long may the IWW live!" James Thompson hollered out over the crowd.

"Liar! None of that stuff is gonna happen. Go on back to Seattle, you Wobbly scum!" yelled the man in a dirty, plaid pork-pie hat.

"What did you just say?" a man in the crowd barked.

"I said he's a liar!" the pork-pie hat cracked again.

Instantly the men handing out IWW literature pounced on him, pushed him to the ground, and hit him repeatedly, one of them snarling, "Big Jim Thompson's no liar!"

The deputies rushed into the crowd with blackjacks raised. They forced their way to the speaker, not caring about the man on the ground or the commotion taking place around him, while Sheriff McRae stayed back and watched. Deputy Beard jerked the speaker from the crate and cuffed the speaker, Thompson yelled out, "A victory for one is a victory for all! If we work together, we'll all benefit! If we all fight together, we'll win this battle against the lumber trust!" Beard's blackjack came down on Thompson's lower neck and shoulder, silencing him.

The timber widow, Helen Pomeroy, quickly mounted the stand and began to recite as loud as she could, "We hold these truths to be self-evident, that all men are created equal, that they are endowed by their Creator with certain unalienable Rights that among these are Life, Liberty, and the pursuit of Happiness." She was pulled from the crate by a deputy but continued even louder, "And we have the right to free speech!" The same deputy started to push her away.

"How dare you —" Pomeroy shouted and swung her purse at the deputy. "Is there a decent man in the crowd who will take the stand?" she hollered over her shoulder as she trundled towards the Gospel Mission with her children.

Thompson was led away by three deputies and thrown in the sheriff's backseat. The crowd jeered while shaking their fists. Then Father Nathan Bywater took the soapbox.

"Let us be calm, citizens of Everett! Please, please, we must control ourselves in the eyes of God in Heaven. We are all children of God and the path to Heaven —"

A voice in the crowd cried out, "How 'er we supposed to get to heaven when we're stuck here in this living hell?"

***

For the last three months Luther MacCullock sat upstairs in his walnut-lined room at the Northern Imperial head office and watched strikers in picket lines march with their signs across the tracks over at his mill. He looked down upon the horde of hungry and tattered striking workers with his hands clasped behind his back, his pipe clamped tight in his teeth. The telephone rang, he walked behind his desk and picked up the receiver.

"Yes?" he said into the phone.

"Captain, it's the sheriff."

"What is it?"

"We just had a blow up at the corner. A Seattle IWW speaker was here today, got folks pretty riled up. He's a trouble maker for sure. Hell, the whole thing ended in a street fight. But I've got him in the holding tank now."

"For Christ's sake, McRae! Now the IWW has sent an agitator here?" the crusty old mill owner yelled into the receiver. "There've been picketers in rowboats outside of my plant harassing my workers and throwing rocks through windows all week, this kind of thing has got to stop!"

"I told you months ago that I was going to need more deputies. I've hired everyone I can, and there's no more money in the budget," the sheriff shot back.

"Okay Donald, all right. Meet me at the Commercial Club at six after the picketers have left. I've got a new idea I want to talk to you about," MacCullock said curtly. He hung up, and then picked up his pipe.

He struck a match and sucked on his pipe so hard the flame went out. "Damn match," he complained, dropping it in the ashtray. Once the pipe was re-lit, he rocked back in his creaky chair. "The hell with this strike," he cursed to himself. Pipe smoke billowed behind him as he got up and opened a window. Fresh salt air filled his office, but right behind it came the sounds of picket line chants.

Slamming the window shut, MacCullock went back to his desk but just stood there thinking for a moment. He opened the top drawer of the file cabinet and found the folder that contained the information he needed to make his next move. Placing it on his desk, he sat down, opened the folder, and picked up the phone.

"Get me St. Paul, Minnesota."

***

James Thompson held onto the iron bars of the cement walled holding cell of the county jail.

"Why have I been brought here?" he yelled. "Under what charge?"

Two minutes later, Sheriff McRae and Deputies Jefferson Beard and Walt Irvan came around the corner. One of the deputies opened the cell door.

"You are a vagrant and not welcome in *my* county!" the sheriff bellowed as he walked into the cell with the deputies next to him.

"I haven't broken any law, unless Everett has a law against free speech!"

"You ain't gonna speak at that corner."

"Do you have an ordinance against it?" Thompson asked.

"Yep, back in '13 the city passed ordinance 1501, meant for fella's just like you," the sheriff proclaimed.

"But I hear you're letting others speak on that corner. Sounds like you're discriminating against me," Thompson boldly stated, standing toe to toe with McRae.

Instantly Deputy Irvan stepped between them and slapped Thompson across the face, opening a cut at the corner of his mouth, a small trickle of blood running out. Thompson stood his ground. "Knock it off, Walt," the sheriff ordered and glared at Irvan. The sheriff turned his attention back to Thompson.

"Listen, fella, we have strikes and labor troubles here."

"Do you believe in free speech?" Thompson snorted, eye to eye with the sheriff.

"That's not the point!" McRae snapped.

"Then you *do* believe in free speech?"

"Dammit!" the sheriff hollered, his face reddening. "The people of this town want law and order and I aim to keep it that way!"

"You're the sheriff of the county, and I was speaking in the city limits. Where's the police chief?" Thompson said, staring down the sheriff.

"Now you listen up!" McRae yelled, the veins in his neck bulging. "This strike happened on county land, so that give *me* authority."

"You're the authority? You're no lawman! You're nothing but an errand boy and a fool that believes in —"

"Don't you be calling me a fool?" McRae hollered.

"Well, you're no lawman."

"I'm the iron hand of the law!" the sheriff screamed, cutting him off.

"What law? This is a farce. You're a farce you damn —" The sheriff silenced him with a quick right-hand blow to his midsection. Thompson's knees buckled and he bent over.

"Nobody calls me that in my jail!" McRae hollered over Thompson. "You listen up fella, I believe that only the citizens of Everett have the right to free speech. You are not from here, and you do not live here, but since this is the first time I've had the pleasure of doing business with you I'm gonna let you go."

"If you let me go, I will come back to speak again," Thompson said, gasping for air as he stood back up.

"No, you won't, not after you see what's on the other side of that door," McRae snarled. "If I ever catch you in *my* county or *my* town again, let alone speaking on *that* corner, then I will send you to the devil!" McRae barked and then unbolted the back door. He opened it to three deputies with clubs, and ax handles at the ready. One of them stood holding a shotgun off to the side.

"If you come back here, yer just gonna be borrowin' trouble. You got that? Don't let me find you here again. Now git!" the sheriff yelled as he pushed the Wobbly speaker into the deputies. Irvan followed him out the door. A storm of blows came down on Thompson's body. He tried to run at first but then stumbled to his knees and crawled. Thompson got up, and a black boot kicked him in the trousers, a fist hit him in the stomach, and an ax handle swing from Walt Irvan landed squarely on his back. Thompson moaned in agony, he fell to his knees and crawled to the alley where he got to his feet. A shotgun was fired in the air as a battered and blood-stained Thompson stumbled off into the city.

***

The Commercial Club was located in one of the original brick buildings in Everett. Its four-foot wide oak door opened to waxed maple floors that stretched into the main room, ornate brass lights hung from coved ceilings. There was a bar and restaurant with walnut wrapped picture windows of Port Gardner Bay, Whidbey Island and the Olympic Mountains to the west.

Club members sat at tables in leather wingback chairs or in booths playing cribbage or chess. Waiters scurried about, making sure all needs were attended to. The kitchen was hidden beyond the bar, and a wide hallway led to the many back rooms used mostly for state prohibition-banned whiskey, brandy, and wine storage, while other rooms held tables and chairs for poker and private conferences. The hallway ended at the rear entry that accessed a small delivery area off the alley.

The creation of the club in 1912 was born out of boom-time profits. Luther MacCullock had spurred its founding after talking other mill owners and businessmen into contributing the assorted materials and the time to build it. Once completed, it became a private entity that sold shares of stock to an exclusive group of area businessmen and companies that controlled the town behind its closed doors. Every wealthy timber baron bought shares, the *Daily Tribune*, bankers, lawyers, executives, businessmen, and developers bought memberships and made decisions over imported prohibition whiskey and fine food brought in on the Great Northern Railway. Backdoor affiliations were granted to every mayor, police chief, and sheriff. By 1916, the club had well over three hundred members.

Most evenings the air was filled with the aristocratic sounds of staunch conservative values that spoke to power and wealth, future destiny, and the current price of timber products while it smelled of grilled beef and onions, cigars, and liquor.

As Luther MacCullock strode into the club that evening he was greeted by the usual faces.

"Good evening, Captain," Ralph Edgerton said from his booth, looking tired and wan, wearing a pressed white shirt and bowtie.

"Hello, Ralph. How are things running at your plant?" MacCullock asked.

"Oh, fair to middlin', I'd say. How long do you think we can hold out?"

MacCullock looked down his nose at his competitor and said, "As long as we have to," before continuing to his designated room down the hall. There a disheveled sheriff sat eating a steak, his face pale and hollow, his black Stetson sitting on the table. Champion Tom was lying on the floor next to him.

"Criminy, Donald, you don't look so good," MacCullock observed.

"Yeah, well, I don't feel too good, either," the sheriff groaned, the corners of his mouth turned downward, "and now I hear they've been slayin' rainbow trout up on the Skykomish while here I am fightin' yer war for ya."

MacCullock shot the sheriff a disconcerting scowl.

"Listen here, this town needs you. A lot of good people are depending on you to put this trouble down," MacCullock chided as his voice grew louder. "Don't you understand that the fate of this town rests on your shoulders? It's time to raise some sand and get your sap up!" MacCullock snapped. "And now we've had an IWW speaker here! Good God, man. If the Wobblies are sending organizers here, then that means they'll probably try to open a union hall. And we cannot, we can never, ever tolerate the IWW having a meeting place here!" MacCullock boomed with a cold expression.

The sheriff just sat there and stared back at the mill owner. He took another bite of his rib-eye steak and chewed it slowly.

"Luther, I had a long day," the sheriff replied. "I'll fight yer war for ya. But I'm not gonna let you forget about keeping me in work, or me being mayor."

"For criminy sakes, we have more pressing matters than some job or political pipe dream down the road!" MacCullock cracked. "I'm telling you right now that the IWW is never going to get so much as a toehold in this town! That can never happen!"

McRae didn't answer and took another bite. After a moment the mill owner relaxed, and said, "You'll get your job, Donald. You could be my timekeeper."

"Timekeeper huh? Good," the sheriff belched, "OK then, I'll take care of the IWW. So what's this about a new idea?"

"In a minute. First I want to hear about that speaker you locked up today."

"Well, the guy's a Seattle Wobbly, name of James Thompson. Lost my nerve with him a little. I told him he shouldn't be comin' round where he don't belong and sent him on his way."

"You let him go?"

"Had to, didn't break any law."

"Then we need to pass another stronger ordinance that stops all these street meetings for good."

"How're we gonna to do that?"

"There you go again with that no-can-do attitude," MacCullock said.

"It's your strike, not mine."

"Dammit, man!" Luther MacCullock yelled, slamming his fist down on the table. "We need to get something perfectly clear. This is not my strike, this is the workers' strike. They're the ones who walked off the job. Do I need to remind you again that the safety and stability of this town and this county is on your shoulders?"

McRae leaned back in his chair, crossed his arms, and glared at MacCullock, then shifted his eyes to the dinner in front of him. He looked back to MacCullock and said, "I'll keep the peace, and I'll do whatever I have to do. But right now I need more men, and my budget is spent."

"All right," MacCullock grunted. "I'm gonna get you some more men right away. But I want these strikers to get the message that we mean business, and soon. You need to do something and take control of this situation."

"OK, Captain. I already said I'd take care of it," the sheriff said. "So, what's this *new* idea about?"

MacCullock lit his pipe and then said, "It's really very simple, you have the power to deputize, right?"

"Yeah, so," McRae replied.

"Well, the only way we are going to get any decent deputies that understand our difficulties and not cost the county any money is to deputize every member of the Commercial Club."

"What? You want me to deputize all the men out there?" the sheriff said motioning with his thumb towards the main room out front.

"Yes, just think. You'll have an entire army of men at no cost," MacCullock replied.

The sheriff took another bite and chewed on the idea as a slight grin formed on his round face.

"That's good," McRae grunted.

MacCullock got up and motioned with the stem of his pipe for the sheriff to follow him. Once he was out of the room McRae glanced behind himself then leaned back in his chair, opened a liquor box behind him, and pulled out a bottle of Canadian whiskey. He cracked the seal, closed his eyes, poured the brown liquid into his mouth and let his head rock slightly back. But he didn't swallow, he just let the liquor rest for a moment on his tongue and savored it. Then he lowered his head, sloshed the whiskey around in his mouth and pushed it back and forth through his teeth. McRae held it up against his inner upper lip and let it soak. He swallowed but then took another drink. McRae spun the cap back on and got up, he set the jug back in the box and left, bumping into the door jamb as he put his Stetson on.

Luther MacCullock strode into the main room, which was filled with talk and the smell of smoke.

"Gentlemen," he said. "Gentlemen, can I have your attention? Listen up." MacCullock raised his hands above his shoulders, clapped, and waited for the men to quiet down. "Now, I know we're all very upset about the situation that's going on in our town and quite frankly, we need to do something and do it right away. The way I see it, to end this strike for good we must supply Sheriff McRae with more men. And the best place to find more men who understand our labor difficulties is right here in the Commercial Club. Right here is where we are going to make a stand," the Captain said, pointing his pipe stem at the floor. "I say that because today there was an IWW speaker at the corner of Hewitt and Wetmore. And it ended in a street brawl! So, gentlemen, we are the ones who are going to do something about this situation because the sheriff is shorthanded and the county is broke. He needs help, and he needs more men. We are going to arm and defend this town ourselves."

"What?! Are you talking about martial law?" banker David McGivney said.

"We can't do that!" Lester Blankenship jeered.

"Luther's talking about protecting our town from the IWW," Mayor Dennis Merrill proclaimed, rising to his feet.

"But we've got the sheriff and his deputies to handle this," pharmacist Virgil Postlewait contended, "and let's not forget about the police department."

"That's right!" Blankenship argued. "Trained men need to do this kind of thing, not us."

"Gentlemen!" MacCullock said loudly. "Our police and sheriff's departments are too small to handle this situation. We have no choice. Sheriff McRae is here and he is going to deputize every able-bodied man who is a member of the Commercial Club, and he is going to start with *me* and then you, McGivney," he said as he pointed at the banker. "And then you Blankenship."

"Those who are not in attendance will sign up, too," MacCullock said confidently as he looked around the room. Everyone eyed each other and then slowly nodded their heads and agreed to volunteer. McRae stood slouched with his arms crossed against the hallway entry, his Stetson tilted forward and to the side, with a sad-looking Champion Tom standing next to him.

"And the man who is going to save Everett is right here," MacCullock said making a sweeping movement of his arm towards McRae. "So we will begin to swear in everybody right now. Sheriff, the floor is yours."

McRae snapped his fingers at his dog and pointed to the floor. Champion sat down. The sheriff stepped into the main room and slightly lost his balance. While the attention shifted to the sheriff, tailor Lester Blankenship walked out.

"Captain, would you like to go first?" the sheriff said as he stepped over next to MacCullock.

"I would be honored to be the first member here tonight to step forward and be sworn in," MacCullock stated.

"Raise your right hand. Do you solemnly swear that you will support and defend the Constitution of the United States and the laws of Snohomish County against all enemies, foreign and domestic, and . . . that you will bare true faith and allegiance to the same? So help you God?"

"I do," Luther MacCullock vowed, and then added, "OK McGivney, you're next."

When McRae finished his third deputization, he turned to the group and said, "OK, you all know the drill. Everyone just raise yer hands and say the pledge at the same time."

Once McRae was done, he tromped down the hall and out the back door of the club with his dog just as the little man in the dirty plaid pork-pie hat came in the front door. MacCullock spotted him and stepped into the hallway out of view as a waiter came by. He grabbed the waiter by the elbow, pulled him aside and whispered, "Do you see that dirty little fellow at the door?"

"Yes, I do, Mr. MacCullock," the waiter answered.

"Go over there and kick him out and then lead him around and bring him through the back door to my room," MacCullock quietly ordered and then ducked down the hallway. Moments later the waiter brought the foul-smelling fellow to the mill owner and closed the door.

MacCullock glared at him and snapped, "I told you to never come here."

"I did what you said, and I want more money. I got the tar beat out of me today so if I'm gonna take your beatings for you then I want more dough," the man said.

"You'll get paid what we agreed on and nothing more," MacCullock sneered as one black eye squinted back at him.

"If you're not going to pay me more then I'm going to the police," the little agitator sputtered.

"Go ahead and go to the police. They won't do a thing, and neither will the sheriff! Don't you know I own this town?" MacCullock growled.

"Well, then, I'll go to the Seattle police and have them get in touch with the Governor," he shot back. The smirk on MacCullock's face instantly dissolved.

"Listen, you little son of a bitch," MacCullock said as he jabbed his finger into the man's chest, "I hired you to plant yourself in the crowd of those street meetings and agitate the strikers and any union people that show up. Plus I've got more help on the way," MacCullock snapped as he pulled out is wallet. "Here's another five dollar bill, and don't ever try to contact me or find me again. If I get reports that you're doing more of what you're supposed to do, then I'll get you more money through my mill guards. This meeting is over."

MacCullock glared at his little instigator and pointed to the back door exit, the man in the pork pie hat left. MacCullock walked back out to the main room.

"Here we've got a southern Democrat in the White House who wants to get us involved in a European war that we've got nothing to do with," mill owner Fred Baker complained as he dipped the half-chewed end of his cigar in his brandy snifter and then pointed out, "We should let the Europeans destroy each other. Besides they're just going to buy more lumber when it's all over."

The whole room laughed as a businessman chimed in, "Washington was right in his farewell letter when he said that we need to avoid attachments with European countries."

"But we can't sit on our hands and let the Krauts run all over the place and destroy Europe! Not to mention the Lusitania last year," David McGivney replied. MacCullock quickly commandeered the floor.

"That's enough talk about Wilson and the war. We've got our own war to fight right here! Gentlemen, I think it would be best to break our citizen deputies and the city itself into sections. Neighborhood boundaries should be determined, and those volunteers living in those neighborhoods should patrol their area and set up schedules," Luther instructed. "And, we must keep a constant eye on the city pier, the train depot, and the Interurban Station. Any threat of IWW intruders must be eliminated before it begins. All traitors and vagrants must be kept out of Everett!"

Chapter 5

SUMMIT STREET

R enny Niskanen had been walking the picket line and leading his fellow strikers for months, they had gotten nowhere. Tensions had been mounting at the mills and on the streets of Everett. By the middle of August, the Northern Imperial mill looked like a battened-down fortress. Barbed wire was now strung on the top of the fencing that encircled the entire mill and pier, and two new bunkhouses had been erected to accommodate the workers that didn't live in Everett. Search-lights hung from the sides of the building, and a dozen lumber trust guards stood watch as a dwindling number of strikers walked the picket line.

Buck Mullaney spat a greasy wad of brown goop on the pier planking and squinted at a rumbling wreck of a flatbed truck rolling and bouncing across the tracks. When he recognized the red badge on the truck door he muttered to himself, "Now what in the hell are those damn Sallies doin' comin' down here?"

Renny was watching, too, as the Salvation Army truck stopped near his gang of strikers. A man sat behind the wheel, and two women were squished next to him in the cab. Two other men sat on the flatbed next to boxes and crates. The men wore dark blue uniforms and white military-style hats with red bands, the women wore blue dresses and red bonnets. When the truck parked, the Sally behind the wheel hopped out and started to walk over to Renny. The women climbed up on the flatbed and started to sing. One was young with long, auburn hair, the other, heavy and older.

> "Abide with me, fast falls the eventide
> The darkness deepens, Lord, with me abide
> When other helpers fail and comforts flee
> Help of the helpless, O abide with me."

Their voices rang out through the harbor. All of the picketers stopped to listen, a few followed Renny over to them.

"Greetings brother," the driver said to Renny.

"Hello there, fella," Renny replied.

"We've got some sandwiches and coffee for you," the Sally said.

"Yah, ya do?" Renny said brightly. He turned around and yelled with a wave, "They got food!" to his fellow strikers. The men dropped their signs and ran over.

The strikers surrounded the Salvation Army truck in no time, all with outstretched arms and their hands grasping for the free food.

"My kids are starving! Give me two sandwiches!" Hank Hillstrom yelled.

"Yeah! Me, too!" Fred McCorkel hollered.

"My daughter's sick! And starving!" a man in a tattered work shirt yelled.

"Sure, sure. Here ya go. But we have more stops," one of the men in uniform said, handing a striker a brown paper sack.

"My kids get all the food, the hell with yer other stops!" Hillstrom said. More men in frayed work clothes snapped at the brown lunch sacks and started to climb up on the truck.

"Stay down, please," the driver said. The two Sally women continued singing, but their once joyous uplifting voices began to crack and started to lose tempo. Two strikers circled around to the other side of the truck and took one of the sandwich crates.

"Hey! Hold on there!" the Sally yelled, and jumped down to get the crate back. More crates of sandwiches were taken. Some of the strikers from the Seacrest Mill showed up, one ripping a crate from another striker's hands.

"What the hell do ya think yer doin'?" the stolen from striker yelled, hitting the man in the face and then lunging at the crate. Two other Seacrest men threw themselves into the fight, while still more Seacrest men showed up. They pushed their way into the crowd and ripped open crates. The two Sally ladies started screaming. Fists flew and crates were ripped apart. Brown paper sacks dropped. Strikers snatched them and shoved them in coat pockets. Some ran off with armloads of lunch sacks while still more strikers ran over from the Smith-Edgerton.

"Start the truck! Start the truck!" one Sally yelled.

BOOM! Buck Mullaney's shotgun sounded in the air. The two ladies gasped as they ducked and covered their heads. The lumber trust brutes had formed a semicircle around the melee with shotguns raised.

"Goddammit! All of ya, get back. Now!" Mullaney yelled. "You heard me! I said to get back. Go on back to yer pickets. Now! And what the hell are you damn Sallies doin' down here? We told you to stay uptown and not come down here with free food for these bums."

"What do you mean not to come down here?" Renny shouted at Mullaney.

"None a' yer damn business is what it means." Mullaney barked.

"These men are starving, and they are helping us!" the shop steward yelled.

BOOM! Mullaney fired off another round and then opened the breech and shoved in more shells.

"Get the hell outta here. NOW!" Mullaney screamed, his face beet red, the veins in his neck swelling. He eyed his men on both sides of him. They stood their ground with shotgun butts on their hips.

"My superiors are gonna hear about this!" The Sally driver hollered at Mullaney.

"Shut yer trap and get back uptown. If I ever catch you 'er yer kind down here again, I'll tan yer hide!" Mullaney hollered at the truck as it pulled away.

Renny glared at Mullaney and raised his fist, "*Olette kaikki paskiaisia!*" he yelled in Finnish.

"Shut up, ya damn foreigner." Mullaney snapped and took two slow steps backward.

"Those people vere here to help these men," Renny said defiantly.

Mullaney fired one last round into the air as his lumber trust brutes started walking slowly backwards. The strikers from the other mills began to clear out.

Renny looked at his remaining strikers as a flock of cawing seagulls landed where the truck was parked and pecked at the pier planking.

"That's it for today," Renny said. "That's enough."

They started to walk away, eating what was left of their sandwiches. Once they were across the tracks Hank Hillstrom said, "What was it that Mullaney yelled at those Sallies?"

"Yeah," another striker started up. "You mean when Mullaney said that they knew they weren't supposed to be coming down to the picket lines with food. What was that about?"

"Right, Mullaney said something about how they told them that," Fred McCorkel added.

"MacCullock's been payin' 'em off I bet," Hillstrom said.

"I think maybe that's right. Maybe MacCullock been paying them off," Renny remarked.

"I bet that's right."

"I bet so."

"That bastard MacCullock."

Renny led his men up Hewitt, then past the Commercial Club, where the ever-present guard was posted at the door. Renny raised his fist and began a union chant aimed at the club while a half dozen citizen deputies came out of the building and followed them at a distance.

"Dump the bosses off your back!"

"Say it again!"

"Dump the bosses off your back!"

"Bread and roses is vhat ve vant!"

"Bread and roses is what we want!"

"Say it again!"

"Bread and roses is what we want!"

When the chant died out, one of the strikers stopped and complained, "I only got one of those sandwiches, and I'm still starving. Fer criminy sakes, it's been over three months, and we haven't gotten anywhere. Why can't we just go back to our old wages? I think we need to have Jake Michel help get this thing figured out." The rest of the men stopped.

"Yah, vell. Maybe ve should ask for less of a raise?" Renny reasoned.

"Well, maybe. But you're the shop steward. Do something," the striker replied.

"Yeah, Niskanen, do something, fer cryin' out loud," Hillstrom added.

"Yah, yah. OK, I go by the Labor Temple and talk to Jake," Renny said and walked across Hewitt.

At Spanjer's market Renny reached for a wooden crate under the sidewalk fruit racks, Noah Spanjer came out of his store.

"Renny, how are you doing?" Noah said.

"Oh, I is okay."

Then Spanjer lowered his voice. "A man from the Seattle IWW was here today. He was looking all over downtown for a union hall. He came in 'n' asked about my basement room off the alley. He said they would pay rent."

"Rent is good. Vill it be good for business?" Niskanen asked.

"I'm willing to find out. But the strikers and their families on our side *are* my business. The families associated with the lumber trust don't shop here. They boycott me," Spanjer said.

"Vell, if you are villing to let them have some space, then I guess that vould help our cause."

"With the Wobblies here, I think you'll have a better chance to beat this thing."

"Yah, maybe," Renny replied.

"Well, I watched them win in Spokane," Noah stated with his hands on his hips.

"That sounds good," Renny said.

"The IWW is a good union. They stand for the same things your union wants. Good wages and shorter work days."

"Yah. Maybe the Vobblies vill help," Niskanen said as he turned and carried the crate out to the center of Hewitt, spun around, walked off fifty feet, set it down and dropped the gunny-sack he'd started carrying, he stepped onto the crate.

"Good-a afternoon, people of Everett and all of you citizen deputy's vith the vhite handkerchiefs around your necks!" the little Finn yelled to the small crowd.

"Ve are still valking the picket lines, and MacCullock is still vorking scab labor. Ve must hold out as long as ve can until the scabs find out that they too cannot feed their families with the vage scale the lumber trust is paying them," he said as a few more men wearing white handkerchiefs showed up with ax handles.

"The only force that can break the mill owners' hold on low vages is the Shingle Weavers Union and all of its members!" Renny exclaimed. "Ve have to stay the course ve have been on if ve are going to end this strike! MacCullock and the rest of the lumber trust has to come to the bargaining table and start negotiating."

The Salvation Army band marched out of the Gospel Mission blowing their brass horns and beating their drums as loud as they could playing *Battle Hymn of the Republic*. Niskanen tried to speak over them.

"Yah. Yah. I think the Salvation Army has been getting their donation checks from the lumber trust again! Yah, MacCullock has turned them into his own private army. The Starvation Army!" Niskanen yelled. But the crowd was small, and he didn't think they were listening, so he quit and headed to the Labor Temple.

Renny walked east down the north side of Hewitt with the gunny-sack slung over his shoulder. Prostitutes in frilly corsets and feather boas watched him from open second-story windows as men in tattered clothes lay passed out along the sidewalk. He ambled up to the Hayes Theater where *The Floorwalker*, the latest Charlie Chaplin silent movie, was playing. Renny stopped briefly to look at the movie poster and wished he could take his wife to see it. He shoved a hand deep into an empty pocket and continued walking until he was at Lombard where he headed around the corner. Renny stepped into the wood frame Labor Temple building and walked down the corridor towards the main hall, he poked his head in the last door on the right. Jake Michel was in his office seated at his desk reading a copy of the *Daily Tribune*.

"Jake," Renny said, "Can I come in?"

"Renny! How are ya? How's your week been? Come in, come in," Michel responded, greeting his labor associate and motioning for him to sit down. Then pointed to the newspaper on his desk.

"I swear this paper. They ought to call it the *Northern Imperial Tribune* or the *MacCullock News* for criminy sake's!" Jake remarked. "Just look. The front page says that most of the mills are turning a profit with scab labor and that they will probably continue to run and beat the strike. That's hogwash. Why can't we get the straight skinny out of this paper?"

Then Michel looked at Renny. "How's the picketing going? What can I do for you?" Jake asked as he tossed the newspaper in the garbage.

"Vell, it does seem like the strike is not vorking," Renny said dejectedly, "but I vas told that the IWW is going to open a union hall here."

"What? The Wobblies!" Michel exclaimed.

"Yah," Renny answered.

"Aw, we don't need them here, they ain't welcome," Jake snapped, his black eyes narrowing. "Dammit. I should-a figured as much with Thompson speaking here the other day," Michel said. He paused for a moment and then added, "This is crap, they don't know anything about us 'er what's good for our mill workers."

"Yah, vell, they still could help us? They are union men. Right?" Renny asked.

"Yeah, sure, they're union. But not like us," Jake said. He leaned back in his chair and crossed his arms. "Ya see, the IWW wants all the skills in one union, they want to lump everybody together in one big happy family. It'll never work. Each craft needs to have its own people to stand up for them and know exactly the job they do and the issues that affect them."

"Yah, but, they are against MacCullock and the other mill owners just like ve are," Renny offered.

"Oh, I know. The IWW is just as sick of the lumber trust as us. No doubt about that! That's true. And, ya know," Michel said rubbing his chin, "I guess I must admit. I did hear that they helped a few years ago during a strike back east."

"Vell, ve could use all the help ve can get," Renny said.

"Aw, I don't know, maybe. But I do know they're for the 8-hour day and the 40-hour week. I do agree with that. Crap, well, I guess if they're coming then we're just gonna have to deal with 'em, and then see what happens," Jake replied.

"The Salvation Army brought some free sandwiches to the picket line today," Renny said, "but it did not turn out very vell. It vas a big fight. The men are starving."

"What's this now?" Jake asked.

"Yah, the Salvation Army came vith free food but Buck Mullaney fire his shotgun and told them that they knew they ver not to be coming down there. I think MacCullock is paying them off."

"What! Nah, if MacCullock is paying them off then they wouldn't have brought you free food."

"But Buck said they knew not to come down," Renny replied.

"Well, who knows, maybe they took his money and still brought the food?"

"Yah, maybe," Renny said scratching his head. "The men vanted me to see if ve could start negotiations with MacCullock and the other lumber men."

"Sure. But a federal mediator has already been here for a week of meetings, and he hasn't gotten anywhere," Michel said.

"Yah, but ve have to do something," Renny replied.

"Like what?"

"I think the men vould be happy with a smaller raise," Renny stated.

"OK."

"How about fifty-five cents an hour instead of sixty cents?" Renny offered.

"So a five cent raise?"

"Yah. Just five cents."

"OK, I'll call MacCullock."

"Very good. Thank you, Jake," Renny replied. "And some of the workers' family members are sick. Can the strike fund pay for doctor visits?"

"I'll check, but don't hold yer breath," Jake Michel replied with a somber look.

"But the union needs to do something," Renny pleaded.

"Yeah, OK. I'll see what I can do," Michel said. Renny headed for home. Winding his way through the Riverside District he noticed a few bits and pieces of wood on the ground in an alley next to a chopping block. He walked over to the tiny pile of wood scraps, opened the gunny-sack and stuffed them inside.

***

At Summit Street Renny kicked his boots off on the porch, opened the door, and stepped into his little home. He walked into the kitchen, set the gunny-sack of kindling down, and gave his wife a kiss. "Is there anything for dinner?" he asked.

"Yah. Dinner vill be ready in a minute. I trade laundry and ironing vork with the lady across the alley for a little bit of codfish, and ve have some eggs. How vas the picket line?" Petra asked as she bent over and fed the fire with the bits of wood from the gunny-sack. Renny gazed at her diminutive frame and shapely hips and cracked a smile.

"Oh, there vas a big fight today. The Salvation Army brought us some sandwiches, but the men from the Seacrest stole dem. It vas not good. It ended in a big fight."

"Did you get hit again?" Petra asked.

"No, no. I not in the fight. I just watch this time."

"That's a good."

"But there is better news, ve are going to start negotiating vith MacCullock. And a Seattle union is going to set up a hall here. They vill help, I think."

"Yah, good. Ve got a letter from your mother today," Petra said in a quiet voice as her husband grinned. She added, "It is on the table."

Renny sat down at the scrap-wood kitchen table he'd proudly built and thought about his parents' farm that he had to leave, since he was the youngest of six children. He opened the envelope and started reading.

"'Momma vants us to come back. She misses us,'" he reported with surprise. "'And she says that brother Dieter is getting marry to a girl he just met! Her name is Ronja.'"

Petra frowned, and then exclaimed, "Ve did not travel halfway around the vorld just to go back to Finland!"

"I know. America is our home now. Ve vill never go back there," Renny said with a firm tone that comforted his wife to hear.

"But if the strike do not end soon, maybe ve should think about going to Seattle to find vork?" she asked.

"No, our home is Everett. Ve need to keep fighting for better vages. It is the right thing to do, and I still vish ve could raise children here someday. Don't you?"

Petra hesitated, and then said quietly, "Yah, Renny I do, but ve been trying since ve got here and I not pregnant . . . And children take money, ve don't have any!"

"I know, someday ve vill have money again and maybe someday ve vill have a family. But the strike is needed to be done and ve vill vin. I know it. Ve are going to try for fifty-five tents an hour now," Renny said and turned his focus back to the letter.

Petra kept her back to Renny as he read the letter while she prepared dinner. She hated the thought of ever going back to Finland.

That night, as she tried to fall asleep, desperation covered Petra like winter snow. She tossed and turned and then lay on her back and stared at the ceiling in darkness. Her apprehension had been building for weeks, and tears pooled up in the sockets of her eyes. The joyous expectations she'd had when they first stepped from the train four years before had dissipated, they'd been replaced with the fear of an unknown future and the pangs of hunger. Finally in the middle of the night she fell to sleep.

In the dark of early morning, a starving Petra crawled out of bed, put on her clothes, sneaked downstairs, and put on an overcoat. She quietly slipped out the back door into the soft gray light of daybreak. The alley was quiet as she sneaked along next to fences and horse barns up to Twenty-Sixth Street, where she turned left and crossed Market, and turned left again at the next alley. At a tall fence she pried free a loose board and carefully placed it aside. Petra reached into the chicken house, felt around in the straw, and found two fresh eggs. With a rush of excitement she quietly placed the board back and glanced around before quickly walking back home to start a fire before Renny got up.

When she returned he was already in the kitchen. Petra hesitated and didn't know what to do at first, then she pulled the eggs from her coat pocket and smiled, hoping he'd be happy.

"Look Renny, I got breakfast," Petra said showing the eggs in her hand.

"Vhere did you get those?" Renny asked.

"Oh, someplace."

"Vhere, someplace?"

"Renny, ve are starving."

"Did you steal those eggs?"

"Somebody has to feed us!"

"But you can't take vhat's not yours."

"Oh, vhat's a couple of eggs? Is harmless."

"No, it is not harmless. It is stealing. You have been feed-ding us stolen eggs. Now vhere did you get them?"

"From behind a fence in an alley."

"Vhat house, vhat street?"

"I not sure."

"Vhich house?" Renny shouted.

"The big green one, on the corner."

"Petra!" Renny yelled, "That's Goldie Lafayette's roughhouse!"

"So?"

"Harvey Keel vorks for her. He is a mean man."

"And how do you know that?"

"I know because I have seen him beat people up. If he finds out, I don't vant to think about vhat he vould do to us."

"Nobody saw me. Is OK. I von't do it again."

"Promise?"

"Yah, I promise. Now sit and relax. Let me cook some breakfast," Petra said. She turned to the stove and frowned.

***

A half-hour later Renny stepped out of the house and headed for the picket line.

The fog had moved in overnight. It enveloped the city in a thick, damp cloud. He noticed that all was quiet at Lafayette House as he walked by on the north side of Everett Avenue. Then he made his way past Dupree's Employment Agency, across Broadway and uptown, then down to the mill.

Only ten picketers were at the Northern Imperial mill pier walking the line by the time he got there. A striker with two signs handed one to Renny that said, "Union Strong."

Buck Mullaney and his gang of lumber trust brutes were in their places, but the front barbed-wire fencing had been moved back overnight, it was closer to the mill, exposing and giving access to the shipping pier that jutted out at a right angle from the main mill pier. The land's end gate for the gangway that crossed over the water for lumber ship crew access was unlocked and open. Renny noticed the differences but paid the changes no mind, he called out a chant.

"A victory for one is a victory for all!"

"Say it again."

"A victory for one is a victory for all."

"Vhat do ve vant?"

"A victory for one is a victory for all."

"The boss need you. You do not need him."

"The boss needs you. You don't need him."

Sheriff McRae drove up in a patrol car full of deputies. The picketers stopped in their tracks and glared at him as he got out of the car.

"Traitor!" Hank Hillstrom shouted and pointed at the sheriff.

"Yeah. You used to be one of us!" another striker added.

"Turn-coat!" Fred McCorkel hollered.

"You're worse than those scabs!"

McRae snapped his head around and glared at the picketers. He walked over with Jeff Beard and two other deputies. They stood four abreast in front of them. The sheriff glowered at each one with his hands on his hips, his Stetson slightly cocked.

"Shut up, you bunch of damn quitters. I ain't about to take any crap from the likes of you," he snarled and then yelled over the group, "We got a report that some of you bums are carrying weapons, and we're' here to make sure that you're not."

"Ve do not have veapons!" Renny cried as he stepped out from the small cluster of strikers.

"Well, we got a report and now we're here ta' make sure that ya' don't, ya' little foreigner," McRae barked, "so we're gonna search the lot of ya.'"

"This is America, you can't just search us," Renny said. "Vhat is wrong vith you?"

"Shut yer face, or I'll knock yer head off!" the sheriff hollered just as two city police cars parked across the tracks. A few policemen got out and stood beside their cars. Some of them lit cigarettes as they talked, but they stayed on their side of the tracks, across the invisible line that divided the city from the county and watched.

Renny pointed at the police, "Are they here to keep an eye on you?"

"Dammit! I've heard just about enough a yer crap," McRae snapped and glowered at the shop steward.

"And vhat about your boss MacCullock? Vere is he today?" Niskanen nagged the sheriff, "Is he in his office writing checks to the Starvation Army?"

"I told you to shut your damn face, Niskanen. Now go over and stand against that fence and spread 'em. All of ya!" McRae yelled and pointed at the fence next to the shipping pier.

Nobody did a thing until Mullaney fired his shotgun in the air and yelled, "You heard the sheriff, ya bunch a bums! MOVE IT!"

Renny looked at his picketers, then turned and walked over to the fence. The others followed.

"That's right, there ya go," the sheriff said as the strikers shuffled over and lined up. "After each one a' ya is searched I want ya ta' go out and wait on that shipping pier until the whole bunch a' ya is done. And Niskanen, you're first."

"Me? Vhy me?" the shop steward protested.

"I just told you ta' shut yer damn head!" McRae roared. He spun Renny around and pushed him up against the fence. The sheriff patted him down, shoved him towards the pier, and said, "No weapons on this one."

Halfway through the shakedown, four cars and two trucks pulled up and parked at the shipping gangway gate. Two dozen strikebreakers carrying clubs and ax handles got out of the vehicles and moved towards the gate. As soon as they did, Buck Mullaney and his brutes moved out from behind the mill pier fence and surrounded the few strikers yet to be frisked. Mullaney reached under his coat and pulled a pistol from his belt. He walked over behind Hank Hillstrom, dropped it with a thud, and stepped back.

"This man has a weapon!" Mullaney hollered as he bent over to pick it up. The sheriff spun around on his boot heel, pulled the blackjack from his belt, and struck the closest picketer. At the same time, Mullaney and his gang formed a blockade behind the strikers, giving them nowhere to run but the shipping pier.

"Judas!" Hillstrom yelled, and then he pointed at the sheriff and screamed, "I didn't have no gun!" The butt of a shotgun slammed into the side of his head, knocking him unconscious.

"Get those sons a' bitches!" the sheriff yelled pointing his blackjack at the picketers. Clubs and fists came down on the unarmed group of strikers. With nowhere to turn they ran out on the side pier, where they were greeted by the strikebreakers coming up the gangway swinging ax handles. Some picketers fought back, others jumped into the water.

One strikebreaker beat his way through the melee. He lunged at one striker, took a swing, and dropped back. He lunged again, swinging and baring his teeth like fangs, and then dropped back until he saw Renny.

"This'll teach ya, ya little foreigner. Ain't nobody gonna call the sheriff Judas!" the strikebreaker barked as he came at Niskanen from the side.

"I not call him that —" Renny yelled just the man struck him in the head with his club. Niskanen hit the dock with a thump. A few strikebreakers saw Renny go down and began to stomp on him.

Once every picketer was down, the sheriff and his deputies walked out to the shipping pier to congratulate the strikebreakers while they stepped over the injured men. A few soaked-to-the-bone strikers who had chosen to jump pulled themselves up on the shore and ran off while the city police got back in their cars and drove away.

***

"The sheriff and some of his goons beat up the picketers down at the Imperial!" a man wearing overalls exclaimed as he ran into the Palace Pool Room on Hewitt, east of Rucker.

"What's that?" someone asked.

"When?" another man said dropping his cue on a pool table.

"Just now," the man in overalls said out of breath. "I'll go down to the Labor Temple and tell Jake. The rest of you spread the word. I think it's time we start getting even on this crummy deal," the same striker said, going out the door.

Word of the mornings beating moved through town like wildfire. By the end of the work shift that day every union man was ready to hand out a bit of their own justice. Agitated strikers, along with a few longshoremen and a dozen sympathetic citizens, stood on the sidewalk of lower bayside Hewitt with clubs and baseball bats hidden from view as the Imperial scabs crossed the tracks into town after their shift. Other strikers waited next to the railroad tracks and watched as they walked past them and up the Hewitt grade.

Once MacCullock's workers were close Jake Michel led his men out into the street and stood in front of the strikers with a downturned mouth and narrowed eyes. Behind him, men pounded the pavement with their clubs, ax handles and bats while others pumped fists into the air and yelled. The strikers from the tracks came up from behind and surrounded the Imperial workers.

"Bastards!"

"You're all scum!"

"What's it like being a scab?"

"You're all motherless slags!"

"Go back to hell!"

The Imperial workers stopped in their tracks and yelled back.

"You're the ones who walked off the job! Not us!"

"Quitters!"

"Go back to yer picket line!"

"Leave us alone. We're just trying to make a living!"

Michel glowered at the Imperial men, his quick black eyes darted from man to man. He turned around to his group and said, "OK, boys, are ya ready to throw into a fight?" Every man nodded back at the brave labor leader in agreement. Jake grinned at the loyal men behind him and then he snarled at the other men before them.

"Shut up all a' ya worthless scabs!" Michel yelled, "Let's see if you'll be able to walk to our jobs tomorrow morning. Get 'em, boys!"

The angry collection of strikers swept down on the scabs with clubs and fists swinging in a fury.

Imperial workers dropped to the ground as strikers kicked and struck them. A scab swung his lunch pail at one striker's head just as another picketer's ax handle knocked the Imperial to the ground. Soon enough most of the scabs were face down and bleeding on the bricks of Hewitt. One Imperial, a hulking galoot, fought off one striker after another until a wallop in the back of his head knocked him out.

Police sirens blared in the distance, the brawl had crossed the invisible line into the city limits. Three cop cars pulled up and officers leaped out, one fired two shots in the air, and the battle quickly ended. All the participants scattered. Once the crowd dispersed, the officers got back in their patrol cars and drove off, not bothering to pursue and leaving the fallen.

***

That night the Labor Temple hall was overfilled with concerned citizens, strikers with their families, and other union men. Everyone was seething with anger at the mill owners, the police, and especially Sheriff McRae.

"What are you gonna do Jake?"

"Yeah! What are you gonna do about that sheriff?"

"The sheriff has to go!"

"The sheriff is the devil!"

"We need a new sheriff!"

"We need our jobs back!"

"Who hired those strikebreakers today?"

Jake Michel got up to speak.

"People!" Michel hollered as he looked out over the packed room. "Workers of Everett! Can I have calm please? Please? People?"

"As you have probably heard, today we gave the mill owners and a few of their scabs a bit of their own medicine. If the mill owners are going to have picketers beat up by strikebreaker goons then we are going to retaliate. They need to know that we are more than willing to fight back," Michel proclaimed to cheers and boos. He raised his hands for calm. "I am going to have a conversation sometime soon with Luther MacCullock at the Northern Imperial about a wage of fifty-five cents an hour. So we are going to take a vote tonight about it."

The crowd flew into an uproar.

"MacCullock can go to hell!"

"We want a bigger raise!"

"There's no way! No way!"

"He can take his pennies and shove them up his ass!"

"Let MacCullock keep his damn scabs!"

"I vill vork for fifty-five cents an hour!" Renny shouted.

"I will, too!"

"Then you're just as bad as those scabs!"

"Yeah! You want to be a scab!"

"Hold on! Hold on here!" Michel pled. "I know we all have different opinions but, we still need to vote."

"To hell with MacCullock! He owns that worthless sheriff!"

"Yeah! The sheriff works for MacCullock!"

"People. Hold on just a minute here!" Michel hollered, trying to get control. "We are still going to have an up or down vote on bringing forward a new proposal. Now please listen up," Michel raised both hands in the air.

"But we want that worthless sheriff arrested!" someone yelled. "And what about those mill owners? They're the ones pulling the strings on all of this!"

"Ve need to vote," Renny Niskanen called out.

***

That same evening at dusk on the corner of Hewitt and Wetmore James Thompson stood against the display window of the men's clothing store. He watched as a few dozen citizens milled around and listened to speaker after speaker say their piece about the strike, the union, the sheriff, the war in Europe, the national debt, and which store to boycott or buy from. Thompson checked his watch and looked up the street. He recognized a Model-T coming down from Pacific, it drove through the intersection and parked across from him.

Two men hopped out of the cab and raised their arms at Thompson and then carried small boxes over to the crowd, they began to hand out IWW pamphlets and Black Cat stickers. Thompson nodded to them, stepped over behind the soapbox and waited for the speaker to finish. He closed his eyes, dropped his head, mouthed a few unheard words, and twisted his mustache. Then he raised his head and cleared his throat just as the other speaker finished and got down. Thompson stepped on top of the wooden crate and looked out to all the faces.

"Brave citizens of Everett and fellow workers! Greetings! My name is James P. Thompson, and I am here to help you and your cause!" Thompson began with an outreached and open hand. "I am here because I believe in your cause! And the Industrial Workers of the World believes in your cause!"

"I am an organizer for the IWW, and we must recognize that we are fighting a war between two classes. One class owns the means of production but doesn't operate it. Our class owns the means of labor but doesn't own the production. I say this must end. Industry must be owned by the people and operated by the people. Industry should not be owned by the few, and operated by the many for the few. It is vital that we organize our army of production against the lumber trust's army of destruction," the organizer said to a few nodding heads.

"The IWW believes that the worker is the backbone of America. The IWW also believes that these thieving industrialists cannot be allowed to steal any more from the workingman. We cannot allow that!" Thompson yelled as the crowd began to come to life with applause. More people walked up and stopped to listen.

"What we need to do is organize, not along craft lines, but along industrial lines much the same as these industrialists have conspired to fall in line against us. The time has come for us to realize that we should not be exploited any longer. We cannot!" Thompson's voice rang out with an honest conviction. Citizens clapped their hands and a few cheered.

"We must never compromise. It's with compromise that trouble begins. We must fight the good fight and stand together with solidarity. I for one do not care what others think or what others say or what others do. I do not care about those things because I am foursquare with the cause. I am right with myself and right with my union, and my union is right with me."

"Please hear me now, workers of Everett," the speaker said with one hand raised and a finger pointed upward. "When we rise together, it will be with the rank and file of our brothers, because when we rise, we rise together. We win together!"

Thompson's voice sounded like an alarm and his eyes seemed to burn. Everyone began to yell back with enthusiasm while Thompson stood with both arms extended down and out to the crowd, his palms open. He nodded his head to the crowd's cheers, raised one hand, and then dropped it to his side and began again.

"I was at Spokane and Fresno when we won the free speech fights in '09 and '11 and I was part of the Lawrence strike for better wages. I am here to tell you that the IWW will support you 100 percent in your fight against industrial tyranny," he said as the crowd yelled in approval.

Thompson raised his hands once more, "The news of your troubles has gone out on the jungle telegraph to every IWW member across the western states! Soon enough we will flood this town with thousands of loyal men until the mill owners, the police chief, and that rotten-to-the-core sheriff recognizes your right to free speech and decent wages!" Cheers filled the street as fists pumped in the air. A reporter from the *Daily Tribune* stood off to the side and took notes.

"A few years ago in Lawrence, Massachusetts, the textile mill workers were automatically shorted pay without being told. The mill owners just stole their money. It may have only been thirty-two cents a week, but to those shorted workers it meant three fewer loaves of bread a week. It meant starvation to those already underpaid striking mill workers. It was then that they realized that it was better to starve while fighting for better wages than to *starve while on the job*!" Thompson hollered. The crowd roared back.

"When that strike started, the IWW had only three hundred dues-paying members in Lawrence. But by the end we had organized twenty three thousand textile workers into a strong base. In two months the mill owners capitulated, the strikers there won, and so can you!" The union organizer screamed as the crowd thundered. "Always remember that the heart of a union man never beats a retreat and that we must always vote as we strike, and strike as we vote!"

"Please, people of Everett. Spread the word that I will be having a street meeting here," Thompson said and pointed at the sidewalk, "tomorrow, at this very same corner that I was removed from last month. I would like to see all of you and the rest of the citizens of this fine city then." Thompson stepped off of the soapbox as another speaker took the stand.

Noah Spanjer immediately approached the IWW man.

"Excellent speech, Mr. Thompson. Welcome to Everett," Noah offered, reaching forward to shake his hand. "I'm Noah Spanjer. I spoke with one of your representatives before."

"Good to meet you. You spoke with someone?" Thompson replied with a firm grip.

"Yes, I did. The man from your Seattle office, huh, Jim Rowan I think he said his name was, he asked about my basement room of the alley. I own the market up the street, just closed for the evening," Spanjer replied. "But I think it would work well if you'd like to rent it for a union hall."

"Yes, yes, by all means we'd love to have a union hall here to spread the word and sign up new members," Thompson said in earnest.

"Excellent, it's yours if you'd like," Spanjer said. "You know, I heard once that you chained yourself to a telephone pole with Elizabeth Flynn in Spokane," Spanjer said.

Thompson chuckled, stroked his mustache, and said, "Oh, that's a line of talk, set in motion by a political comic in some newspaper. But yes, Flynn was in Spokane in aught-nine, and she's a fine patriot, a grand lady. You see, after she wrote in the *Industrial Worker* that the Spokane jail was a brothel the powers that be had a cartoon published showing Elizabeth and I chained to a lamp post, not a telephone pole. They tried to ruin both our marriages, it didn't work. But it was only Elizabeth Gurley Flynn who chained herself to that lamp post."

Spanjer smiled back. "Well, I guess one can't believe everything one hears."

"My associates have more boxes of literature and pamphlets. We'd like to get a hall established here right away. Can we go there this evening?"

"By all means," Noah replied. "It's right around the corner."

"Would there be a place for my two comrades and me to bed down for the night?" Thompson asked.

"Absolutely," the portly market owner replied.

**

Jake Michel addressed the Labor Temple as Renny and a few strikers handed out ballots.

"Strikers. Strikers!" Michel said, "Can I have your attention. We are now handing out the wage proposal ballots. It is a simple yes or no vote. Yes to work for fifty-five cents an hour or no to stay on strike."

"But five cents isn't much of a raise!" one striker proclaimed.

"That's right. We need to stay united," another agreed.

"That's fine. If you still want a ten cent raise, then vote no," Michel countered, "but if any of you are willing to work at fifty-five cents an hour, then vote yes."

One striker stood up on his chair and protested, "What about that sheriff? What are we going to do about him and those strikebreaker goons beating up picketers?"

"Yeah, we want the sheriff arrested!" another striker hollered.

"Yes, I would like to see him arrested, too, but the police aren't going to do anything," Michel confessed. "I'm afraid there's not much we can do about the sheriff for the time being."

Strikers quickly marked their ballots and placed them in ballot boxes which were taken to the office and counted. Ten minutes later Jake Michel stepped back to the podium and raised his hands for calm. "Strikers, the votes have been counted and you have voted no on the five-cent wage increase. So, fellow members we have no new proposal to take to the lumber trust and we are still on strike."

**

By the next afternoon word had spread through town that a street meeting was to be held and James Thompson was to speak. Hundreds of curious townsfolk milled around downtown waiting. Twenty other IWWs soon arrived by car and truck and met up with Thompson and his two associates in the alley behind Spanjer's market. They hung a Local 248 union sign above the basement stairs, pinned posters on the walls inside, set up an American flag next to a yellow and black IWW flag, and put copies of the current *Industrial Worker* with other literature on tables they'd brought. A few hours later the IWW group came out on the sidewalk to mingle with the crowd as the Salvation Army Band played *Rock of Ages*.

Jake Michel picked up a crate from under the fruit racks, walked out to the center of Hewitt, turned around, and paced off fifty feet back along the Wetmore sidewalk as Mr. Bachelder stared at the union leader from his men's clothing storefront. Bachelder went back into his shop, shut the door, and put a closed sign in the window.

Standing on the soapbox, Michel proclaimed, "Good afternoon fellow citizens! Last night the Shingle Weavers Union voted on going back to work at fifty-five cents an hour. They voted on a raise proposal from us that would have paid them five cents more than they were getting before going on strike, and they voted a resounding NO!"

"What kind of strike is this?" someone hollered.

"You've already lost it!"

"Yer just spinnin' yer wheels!" another shouted.

"Let him speak," a striker in overalls and a newsboy hat called out.

"People, I am trying to schedule negotiation meetings, but nothing has been set, so for now we are staying the course," Michel said. He stepped down from the wooden crate, and saw James Thompson. He glared at Thompson with sharp black eyes. Jake took two steps to the side and watched the IWW move over to the crate.

"You don't know anything about Everett," Michel said calmly.

"Yes, I do," Thompson replied.

"Is that so? Well . . . I think yer a liar," Jake said, his voice rising.

"Nope," Thompson quickly spat out. He stared at Michel and said, "The only liar in Everett is the lumber trust and I know that both of us are against them." Then Thompson's eyes sparked and he declared, "I know our unions have differences but I'll go toe to toe with that Sheriff and fight tooth and nail with those mill owners. You'll see!"

Michel looked long and hard at Thompson, thinking things through. Slowly, a slight grin formed on his face and Michel nodded an OK. He turned his attention away from Thompson and headed to the back of the gathering.

Thompson watched Jake Michel walk off. Dressed in a brown suit coat and trousers, the IWW speaker stood behind the soapbox for a moment. He closed his eyes and touched his chin to his chest, mouthed a few words, and then opened his eyes and stepped up onto the crate. Thompson raised his right hand to the sky, and then lowered it and reached out to the crowd. His voice was clear and strong.

"Greetings fellow workers! And greetings Everett citizens!" he called out to the crowd. "My name is James Thompson and I am from the Industrial Workers of the World. At this very moment there is a federal mediator here from Chicago trying to negotiate a settlement between all parties. But the chances of the mill owners coming to a compromise with the Shingle Weavers Union are slim. They are still operating with scab labor and making profits while the strikers starve. As the wealth piles up in one hand, misery piles up in the other. And this must end. And it can end fellow workers if the Shingle Weavers join the IWW and end their affiliation with the AFL," Thompson said to a few scattered citizen's hand claps.

Three police patrol cars pulled up across the way but the sheriff was nowhere to be seen. Thompson continued his speech.

"Those who hold power in this town are kith and kin with the mill owners and not friends of labor. I say that because labor has nothing in common with industry and power. Those who think labor and industry go hand in hand are mistaken. The monarchs of industry only wish to pay the least and get the most while they luxuriate in their castles. But the wage slave is the one who grants these monarchs of industry their self-indulgent elegance. We are the ones who are providing them with their excesses!" Thompson exclaimed as the street began to fill with louder cheers. As he waited for calm, his piercing blue eyes caught fire, and he began to pound his right fist in an open left palm.

"I say enough is enough. They think that we should be privileged to lick their boots of polished leather. Imagine that. But I say enough! They gloat in telling us that we live in a free country and that the world is democratic. I say enough! They would have us believe that this democracy we live in is fair and just. Fair for who? I say enough! These industrial parasites have squeezed thousands of dollars from our backbreaking work. And I. Say. Enough!"

"He's right. Enough is enough!" one striker yelled, pumping his fist in the air.

"I've had enough too!" another shouted.

"People, people," Thompson cried out to the still-building crowd, "We must find the courage to stand and face these red-handed robbers. For we are the ones who speak the truth against their lies. The mill owners say they can't afford to pay you a decent wage. I say they can! I am ready to stand by your side and fight for what is right and just for the workers of the world. I tell you we must organize to control the use of their labor power. We should have eight hours for work, eight hours for rest, and eight hours for time to spend with our families. The workers of the world must unite. The workers of the world must awaken! If you join the IWW then you can win this strike," Thompson yelled out over the now enormous crowd when the dirty little man in the pork-pie hat showed up and pushed his way to the front of the gathering.

"Go back to Seattle, Thompson!" the agitator shrieked.

"I won't go anywhere until this strike is won!" the Wobbly roared back.

"Well, my wife and kids are starvin', and you ain't puttin' no food on my table!" the pork-pie hat yelled.

"The IWW will establish a food bank here, and if you join the IWW, then your family won't have to starve. We'll provide —"

"Aw, we don't want yer charity. Go back where ya came from ya filthy Wobbly!" the little agitator cried and shook his fist. Then a few IWW pounced on him and pushed him to the ground. At the same time, a dozen policemen ran from their patrol cars and began to push through the crowd. Thompson tried to get in a few last words.

"Keep fighting Everett!" Thompson screamed as Noah Spanjer tugged at his sleeve. "Never give up! The shining sun of our revolution is rising people . . ." Spanjer jerked Thompson from the soapbox and dragged him into his market as a couple of the IWWs followed. Spanjer locked the door behind them. He quickly put the closed sign in the window, turned off the lights, and then hustled them into his storage room.

"At least I got to talk for a few minutes," Thompson remarked.

"You know, that fellow in the pork-pie hat is always showing up at the meetings," Noah observed. "I don't think he's a shingle weaver or a mill worker."

"Yes, well, that may be true," Thompson replied.

"I'd say the little rat fink is getting his due," Spanjer said.

"Sure looked that way. It'd probably be a good idea to hole up in here for a while, at least until its dark, if that's OK?" Thompson asked.

"Well, we've got plenty to eat," the market keeper happily replied.

Chapter 6

LAUREL DRIVE

Luther MacCullock drummed his fingers on his desk in the Northern Imperial main office while going over the books with mill manager Butch Barnell. He stabbed a finger at the bottom line of the paperwork and held it there. Then he looked up and stared at Barnell.

"So our man-hours are up and production is down?" MacCullock grumbled, looking down his nose at the foreman, his left hand holding pince-nez.

"Yes, but we're still making a profit," Barnell answered.

"Well, not much of one," MacCullock countered. "Why's production's down?"

"Because we're down three shingle machines," Barnell stated, "and I'm constantly hiring and firing and training. But I've got all the stations filled, and there should be more replacements coming to town," Butch said.

"And what about the three machines that aren't in production?" MacCullock asked. "Can't you fix them? Get them producing again?"

"Four were down to be exact. Two of them need bearings, another needs new set works and still another needed a clutch. So I used the parts from the broke down machines to keep one going," Barnell answered, "and I ordered three new Sumner Gold Medals."

"You did what?" MacCullock boomed. He dropped his pipe and glared at his foreman. "You ordered three Sumners without talking to me?"

"I have before. Our accounts are backlogged and these new Gold Medals are safer, when a sawyer steps off the clutch it engages a brake to stop the blades," Barnell said confidently.

"And you're guessing that some decent laboring men are going to come to town to get me back to top production?!" MacCullock thundered. "Hell, man, I've got this whole town geared up for a blockade to keep out all comers! And you ordered more Sumners!"

"Well, yes, sir, I —," Barnell started to explain when the phone rang.

"MacCullock," the mill owner hastily said into the receiver.

"Mr. MacCullock, this is Jake Michel from the Building Trades."

"Oh, you. What is it?" MacCullock snorted.

"How are you today, sir?"

"I'm working, Mr. Michel. What do you want?"

"I read in the paper that all the mills are turning a profit. Did you see the article?"

"No, Mr. Michel, I did not see or read some article in that rag of a newspaper — However — I must say if the daily is printing that, then they are speaking the truth. Because I am running at peak production."

"The *Daily Tribune* also claims the mills are going to beat the strike."

"Well, I'd say that's very accurate reporting," MacCullock replied with confidence.

"I'd say that's false," Michel quickly contended. "Everyone in this town knows the mills are running slow."

"No! I'm sorry Mr. Michel, but you are completely off base! Is there anything else you wish to bore me with?"

"I understand there was a bit of a fracas in front of your mill the other day with the Salvation Army handing out free sandwiches."

"Yes, my guards told me all about it."

"Well, did your guards tell you that they slipped up and told the Sallies that they knew they weren't supposed to be going down there feeding the pickets?"

"What are you saying, Mr. Michel?"

"I'm just repeating what your guards said, Mr. MacCullock. That's all."

"Now you listen here. I am a fine, upstanding, respected businessman in this community and I've done more good in this town than anyone knows. I think you've said enough for today."

"Hold on, I'm scheduling a meeting at the Labor Temple with you and the mill owners."

"What kind of meeting would that be?" MacCullock asked.

"For negotiating," Michel said in a firm tone, there was a pause while MacCullock gathered his thoughts.

"So, Mr. Michel," MacCullock said, "you think I have time to leave work and come to some Labor Temple meeting? I've already been contacted by some government mediator who is here and wants me to listen to him and take up my time. I told him to go back to Chicago!"

"Ralph Edgerton has met with him. Why can't you?"

"Are you not listening to me?" MacCullock snapped. "You're wasting my time. I've got a mill to run!"

"I understand that Mr. MacCullock. But the union members *might* be willing to take less of a raise," Michel offered, knowing that they'd already voted against it and silently hoping that MacCullock hadn't heard.

"What does 'less of a raise' mean?" MacCullock replied.

"I might be able to persuade the men to take fifty-five cents an hour," Michel answered, relieved.

"Well," MacCullock said, "my mill is operating at full capacity, and maximum efficiency. Why would I want to rehire a bunch of strikers that walked away from their jobs?"

"The union would like to schedule a meeting with you and the other mill owners at the Labor Temple to talk about it."

"I wouldn't set foot in that building you call a temple!" MacCullock boomed. "But I'll tell you what —" MacCullock paused again to gather his thoughts, "I'd be willing to go back to the same wage of fifty cents an hour and not a penny more. You-have-forty-eight-hours," MacCullock quickly said as he pulled the receiver away from his mouth and abruptly hung up.

"What was that?" Michel said into a silent phone, but there was no reply. He hung up frustrated.

MacCullock rocked back in his squeaky chair, breathed deeply, looked at his mill manager, and dropped his glasses on the desk.

"OK, Butch," MacCullock said, "I'll deal with this order you made, but from now on you clear it with me."

"Luther, I'm sorry. I thought I was doing the right thing," Barnell apologized.

"Yes, I understand. Just don't do it again. Now get back down there before anything goes haywire," the mill owner replied, picking up his pipe as Barnell walked out.

Luther MacCullock lit his pipe, took a long pull, and blew smoke out from the side of his mouth. He got up from his chair and began to pace in front of the window with his hands clasped behind his back, the pipe clamped between his teeth. Smoke billowed behind him as he organized his thoughts. After five minutes he sat down in his chair and opened his personal phone register. Finding the number he needed, he picked up the phone in one hand and held the receiver against his ear while he dialed. He drummed his fingers on the desk until the other end picked up.

"Hello, Tom? Are you there?" MacCullock said into the receiver. "MacCullock here. Can you hear me?"

"Yes, Luther. I'm here," Tom Sumner answered. "How are you?"

"Very good. And yourself?" MacCullock asked, rocking back and holding the long shaft of the upright phone.

"Things are good. Never been better," Sumner replied. "The Canadian market is excellent right now. Things are humming along just fine. And with the war going on, lumber and shakes should start to really take off."

"Yes, well, that may be true," MacCullock cautioned, "but with this strike and the Wobbly blockade, not to mention the fact that I'm running my plant with, well, minimal workers and a . . . well, just between you and me, I'm keeping my head above water."

"I can understand that," Sumner said. "Guess I'm a lucky man, my moulders and machinists have new union contracts. I may be paying them more, but it's worth it. We're all working."

"So things are good?" MacCullock reiterated.

"Yes, more than acceptable, I'd say."

"Well, then, I hope this isn't too much trouble because I need to modify the order my manager placed for those three Gold Medals."

"What's this? But Butch said you needed them."

"Yes, I know that Tom and —"

"Luther, we've already started," Sumner said firmly.

"Tom, my mill manager made a mistake. We can't take on three new machines right now, so I'd like to make an adjustment."

"An adjustment?"

"Maybe slow it down or—"

"Luther, those molds have been rammed, cored, and set. I've got them scheduled for the first heat and pour tomorrow."

"Good, then you haven't started."

"No, Luther, the molds for the castings have been built. The sand has set."

"Now, Tom, I've been a good customer of yours for twenty years, and I need a favor," MacCullock said in earnest. "How about if you build me just one?"

"You're asking me to junk the molds for two machines that my men have worked dozens of hours on," Sumner replied.

"Now, Tom, do I need to remind you about the Commercial Club loan we did for you after your plant burnt down?"

"Yes, Luther, that was a wonderful gesture, but after all we are paying off that debt, and with interest I might add," Sumner remarked.

"Once I win this strike and all of the mills are up and running like gangbusters again, we'll be calling in more orders than you can keep up with."

"More orders than I can keep up with, huh?" Sumner said.

"Yes, Tom. The market will rebound bigger than ever before."

"OK, I'll tell you what. I'll build the one and junk the others, but you owe me dinner. Me and the wife, at the country club after a round of golf. *And* you can hire me a caddy!" Sumner countered.

"Very good, Tom, dinner and a caddy it is," Luther replied brightly.

"OK. How about after I get back from San Francisco? I've got a Metal Trades convention there next week. We'll get together when I return. I'll get back to you."

"That would be perfect. Call me then and, thank you, Tom," MacCullock said, hanging up the phone.

✳ ✳ ✳

Pounding rain bounced off the burgundy Pierce-Arrow parked in the alley between Norton and Grand just north of California Street. Small rivulets of muddy water trickled through miniature trenches in the gravel under the sedan as the rain sullied and washed away its hand-buffed shine. Luther opened his private entrance office door and stepped out onto the landing. He checked the lock twice then walked down the stairs holding his briefcase at his side and a black umbrella over his head. His chauffeur, George, stepped from the driver's seat and opened the back door.

"Good evening, sir," George offered, tipping his cap. A stream of water ran off the brim.

"Yes, good evening," MacCullock automatically replied, closing the bumbershoot and getting into the cab.

"Martha is preparing a fine Friday night meal," George related, getting behind the wheel. He accelerated the hand throttle and disengaged the clutch.

"That sounds good," Luther replied.

"How'd it go today?" George asked, turning up California.

"Well," Luther began, "we're running and filling orders, so that's good, but it's not very profitable right now. And Jake Michel and that damn union are a pain in my neck, I'll tell you that. But by God, I am still going to beat this strike. I didn't come all the way out here to lose money."

"I'm with you all the way, Mr. MacCullock," the devoted chauffeur replied, looking at his employer through the rear-view mirror, he turned south on Grand.

"Thank you. You've been a good friend and loyal worker," Luther smiled. "How long is it now that Martha and you have been with me?"

"Ten years, sir," he quickly answered.

"Has it really?"

"Yes sir, Mr. MacCullock," George said, nodding his head as he turned on Pacific. "You hired the wife and me back in the '06 boom. Remember?"

"Has it really been that long?"

"Yes, sir. I wouldn't have traded it for anything else."

Luther grinned in the back seat as George angled around the Kromer corner and towards the neighborhood.

Laurel Drive was where timber barons, capitalists, developers, bankers, and railroad executives lived, all of the upper crust. It was the first neighborhood with sidewalks and electricity.

Every home on the west side of the hill had a view of the bay and the Snohomish River. The river wrapped around the Everett peninsula in a deep, wide highway of water, its shore-line filled with floating logs waiting to be milled and smokestacks, incinerators, piers, and railroad tracks. It was a view of industry.

Luther MacCullock built his house on Laurel, a white Colonial three-level mansion that rested back from the street and stood proudly behind vermilion rhododendrons, fragrant camellias, holly, juniper, and lilac. Tall cherry trees flanked the property. Dark green shutters were mounted at the side of each multi-paned window, and ivy climbed drain spouts. Three brick chimneys jutted above a cedar shingle roof, each stack constantly belched smoke, fueled by scrap wood from the Northern Imperial. A circular driveway turned through the manicured lawn and into a portico supported by round columns with white lattice between.

Behind the home was a terraced yard that continued down to the alley, where a converted stable house served as a garage, work-shop, and tool shed. A moss-covered concrete walkway went from the basement door through Martha's well-tended flower and vegetable garden cultivated in black, rich soil. Stairs continued down two more levels of quay-like walls built of rock and brick. One held a thicket of blackberry vines, the last an overgrown strawberry patch.

It was after six p.m. when the Pierce-Arrow pulled up the driveway, slowly entered the portico and parked. George stepped from behind the wheel and opened the passenger door. Luther got out from the back seat with his briefcase and umbrella at the same time that Martha opened the forest green front door from inside.

"Thank you, Martha," MacCullock said, walking into the foyer.

"Good evening, Mr. MacCullock," Martha responded brightly, greeting her employer.

He set the briefcase down, Martha assisted him with his coat, and she hung it up in the entry closet. Varnished fir floors stretched from the foyer throughout the main level of the tidy, spotless home. A grand staircase carpeted in a patterned broadloom reached from the entry up to the second-story bedrooms. Next to the stairs rested the upright harmonium that Martha occasionally played.

In the living room, unused provincial furniture was arranged in groupings for conversation. There were chairs of soft leather, multiple sofas of corduroy and calfskin, and black walnut tables, flowered chintz draperies framed the windows. A painting of Luther's father and mother, both of them expressionless, hung above the living room fireplace, numerous photos of his first lumber mill in Minnesota covered nearly every wall.

Around the corner, the dining room was filled with picture windows that looked west through evergreens to the industrial waterfront and a portion of the bay. Directly above it and the kitchen, on the upper floor were MacCullock's master bedroom and sitting room, both with commanding vistas above the tree tops. On clear days Luther had a bird's eye view, south towards Mukilteo, north to Mount Baker, west to the Olympics, and all of Port Gardner Bay.

"Dinner will be ready soon," Martha said and headed down the hall to the kitchen.

"Very good, I'll be in the library," MacCullock replied.

"Would you like some tea?" Martha asked as Luther walked down the opposite hall.

"Not tonight," Luther answered and then mumbled, "Sure could use a scotch," under his breath.

Luther went directly to the wheeled serving table in the library, picked up the stippled crystal decanter, removed the stopper, and poured an inch of liquor into a double old fashioned. Then he sat down in his favorite chair, a leather recliner that rested in front of the small fireplace, and took a drink. Above the mantle hung a photo of himself when he was an army captain, standing in his dress uniform, saber at his side, Colt in his holster. Every wall held shelving for books. Behind him was a mahogany desk where the daily mail waited. On one table beside him was an ashtray and Tiffany lamp, on the other table, a copy of *The Dubliners* by James Joyce, a bookmark wedged between the pages of short story number four.

Beside the book was a framed photo of his deceased fiancée, Evelyn O'Dowd, killed in a Minneapolis flour mill explosion in May of 1878 at the age of 22, while he was away serving in the Indian wars. An ignition of grain dust had demolished the mill and instantly killed eighteen workers.

Luther sipped his drink, set it down, and picked up the photo. He stared at his one and only wife-to-be who never was, and then touched the fading black-and-white picture with his fingers, his eventual death the only thing between them now. He began to daydream of the life they had had when they were young and optimistic. His thoughts took him back to the day he'd asked her to be his wife on the banks of the Mississippi during a picnic. He tried to visualize her beautiful blue eyes and raven hair, her soft alabaster skin.

Luther kept his fingers on the picture and closed his eyes as his breathing slowed. Primordial feelings began to rush inside of him. All the bitterness that had hardened his heart softened, and the paragon of Evelyn flew through his soul, the ecstasy that marked their short life restored. A tidal wave of perfect joy washed over him, and his coarseness melted away, replaced with the warm, inner glow of her spirit returned. He bathed himself in her memory.

"Dinner's ready," Martha's loud rosy voice rang out from the kitchen and down the hall. Luther's body flinched, and he jerked his hand away from Evelyn's image. The solace he'd found in his momentary dream was over.

PART TWO

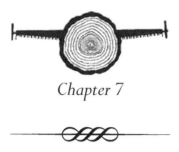

Chapter 7

SHADOWS & LIGHT

As the sun rose over the Cascades, it produced shafts of smoky light through early morning clouds. Beams of sunshine streamed through every tree, the branches making foggy shadows as vapor droplets shifted in midair, dissipating. A single strand of spider silk hung horizontally from a tree trunk, suspended in the ether, waving, reaching out, and searching for a new home. As the daystar climbed the sky, it slowly burned off the haze until it shone bright, permeating every neighborhood in Everett with optimism and warmth.

School kids were still on summer break. They filled the parks and playgrounds, rode bikes, or played hop-scotch on sidewalks with siblings and friends. Teenagers fished, swam, and skipped rocks in the Snohomish River or spent the afternoon at the city beach, if they had a nickel they went to see a movie matinee at the Princess or Everett Theaters. Mothers with extra spending money went clothes shopping, or hung laundry and weeded gardens in backyards. Trolley cars ran over the hill on Hewitt and through the town streets carrying citizens and businessmen on their way to work and important meetings.

In the countryside near Marysville the sheriff walked out of the backdoor of his two-story farmhouse on a Tuesday morning. Champion Tom sprang from his doghouse, shook his body, stretched with a yawn, and followed his master to his Chevrolet 490 parked in the garage.

"Come on boy," the sheriff said as he opened the rear car door. Champion jumped in and sat up at his usual spot in the middle of the rear seat. They headed down the driveway and into town, then stopped and parked on the corner of 4th and the Pacific Highway. He looked to his dog and said, "Sit, Champ."

Getting out of the car the sheriff stumbled, and his Stetson slipped off. The bright sunshine blinded his vision. "Damn sun," he grunted to himself as he bent over to pick up his hat and then walked into the small pharmacy.

"Where's the aspirin?" he grumbled at the aproned young attendant behind the counter.

"It's down the second aisle, sir."

The sheriff found what he needed and hastily opened the little box. He pulled out the glass bottle before he got to the counter.

"How much?" he asked, handing the box to the attendant to throw away.

"Ten cents," the young man replied as he adjusted his horn-rimmed glasses.

"For a bottle of fifty?"

"I'm sorry, sir. I can get the owner if you'd like to complain. He's in the backroom."

The sheriff shook his head no, fished a nickel and five pennies from his trousers, dropped the coins in the attendant's open hand, put the pills in his pocket and went back to the car.

McRae turned back east and drove through the Sunnyside area of Marysville, across Ebey Island and Deadwater Slough, then over the Snohomish River and into Everett. Once on Broadway he turned at Twelfth Street and parked behind Althea's Diner, his favorite greasy spoon. The frame building rested comfortably on the corner, a torn and faded open sign in the window, an arrow of peeling paint on the side of the building with the caption, "Good Grub, Eat Here." The sheriff parked in the alley, left Champion Tom in the car, and walked in through the back door.

"Mornin', Sheriff. Or should I say good afternoon?" Althea said from the kitchen as the sheriff sat down at his regular spot at the U-shaped bar. The place was empty. She set a cup of steaming coffee in front of him.

"What'll it be? The usual?" she asked.

"Can I still get breakfast?"

"Sure."

"Ham and eggs then, over easy," he ordered as the mailman walked in.

"I'm setting your mail down by the register, Althea," the olive-skinned man said.

"Hey, fella," the sheriff beckoned, "I've got some mail out in my car. Go get it and mail it for me."

The mailman looked at the sheriff with a sideways grin and tilted his head.

"Sorry, can't help ya. I can only take mail from a mailbox. They changed the rules," the carrier said as he slipped outside.

"Huh? What 'er ya talkin' about?" the sheriff grumbled at the closed screen door. He picked up a newspaper, skimmed through a few news stories, and then found a baseball article.

"Looks like the Red Sox are gonna take the pennant," the sheriff said to Althea.

"Yeah, I heard that," she answered from the kitchen.

"This new kid, George Ruth, he's a hell of a pitcher. Says here he's won twenty games and the season ain't even over yet." Three women came in for an early lunch and sat down at a window table. Althea set the sheriff's ham and eggs down in front of him and went over to her customers. McRae glanced at them. He recognized Helen Pomeroy but not the other two. He turned back to his meal and began to wolf it down.

"Good afternoon. What can I get ya?" Althea asked the group. Mrs. Pomeroy noticed the man at the bar and a scowl swept across her face.

"Is that Sheriff McRae?" she asked quietly.

"Why, yes it is."

"You are serving that man?" Helen asked a little louder.

"Well I should say so, he's been coming here for years," Althea answered when the sheriff turned his head and looked at the women.

"I thought this was a respectable diner," Pomeroy snapped. "We will not be having lunch then. Ladies, we need to take our business elsewhere." She and her friends got up from the table.

"You got a problem, lady?" the sheriff snarled at Pomeroy, a cold expression on his face.

"Mr. McRae, if I want to have lunch somewhere else then that's my business, not yours," Pomeroy said. "Why, I wouldn't get caught in the same room with a thug like you!"

"Aw, you and your group can home and make yer own lunch fer all I care," the sheriff scoffed.

"How dare you speak to me like that? Why, you're nothing but a childish bully. And how dare you talk poorly of us," Pomeroy snapped as the three women stormed out of the diner, the screen door slapping shut behind them.

"For criminy sake's, Don," Althea popped, "now you're scarin' off my business."

"Oh, their business ain't worth squat. How much they come here anyway?"

"That's not the point. You're costing me money!" Althea said, but her old friend ignored her.

Althea huffed and shuffled off to the kitchen with her hands on her hips. The sheriff went back to his meal. A fly landed on the newspaper page he was reading.

"Christ," he said and ruffled the newsprint. He took another bite, but the fly lit on his coffee cup. He shooed it away. It landed on his plate. He slammed his fist down, hitting the fork on the edge of the dish sending it and a knife flying through the air, the silverware landing on the floor as the plate wobbled on the counter.

"Damn it, Don, what's going on out there?" Althea asked from her grill.

"Aw, nothin', just dropped a fork," the sheriff answered and then asked, "So, how much I owe ya?"

"You mean for your meal and theirs, too?" Althea cracked.

"Damn it, Althea, don't be givin' me no grief! And don't get me started! Besides, how long I been comin' here?" the sheriff said.

"But ya still cost me three meals, and they'll never be back."

"Here's a dollar then," the sheriff said as he grabbed a piece of ham he'd been saving for his dog and went out the front entrance.

In the car he held the strip of ham out for Champion Tom. It disappeared with a sloppy chomp. The sheriff turned the ignition key, stepped on the floor starter, and backed out of his parking place. McRae started to pull onto Twelfth Street when a squeaky horn sounded. He slammed on the brakes as a woman in a Baker Electric car drove by glaring at him. She was sitting with a straight back behind the wheel in the tiny boxlike green and black wooden cab, her wide brimmed feathered hat nearly touching the side windows.

"I didn't hear ya, lady!" the sheriff yelled as he threw up his hands while she silently rode by. He mumbled, "Can't stand those stupid battery cars. Good thing they quit makin' 'em."

He turned right on Broadway, at East Grand he turned left and drove around the peninsula to Hewitt where he turned on Norton, and then onto the elevated wooden trestle that ran along the waterfront. He saw a few picketers at the Clark-Nickerson Mill but he recognized their faces. As he got closer to the 14th Street dock he saw a group of teenagers coming down the stairs on the bluff. They were carrying fishing poles, he slowed down and thought, *Dammit, that's what I should be doin'*! McRae watched the kids for a moment and wondered if, and when, he'd ever get back on a riverbank somewhere to cast a line. He tried to watch them as he turned around. The sheriff popped the clutch, stepped back on the gas and shifted gears, the tires started to clack faster as they rolled across the plank on pier trestle. He slowed down in front of the Clough-Hartley Mill, but every striker's face he saw he remembered, and continued on his way.

At Hewitt he turned east, drove through the Colby intersection and then parked a block down the street from Lowman's Grill, leaving Champion in the car. He could hear conversation as he approached the low-slung single-story brick building. Inside the restaurant, every booth along the exposed brick wall was packed with patrons having lunch while businessmen in suits and overcoats stood at the bar, each man nursing his soda, wishing it were beer.

Right as the sheriff stepped through the door an unseen patron hollered, "Look out it's McRae!"

"Who said that?" the sheriff spat.

"I did," a man in a booth said.

"Where are ya?" the sheriff said taking a few steps in the direction of the voice. He started to put his hand on the blackjack and then recognized his old fireman friend, Sean O'Riley, sitting in a booth with an empty plate in front of him.

"Aw, I was just messin' with ya," O'Riley said with a laugh.

McRae stopped, and then walked over. "Why — I shoulda figured."

"How's things?" O'Riley said with a smirk and put four-bits on the table for his meal.

The sheriff half-chuckled, "Oh, you damn well know how it is for me, ya bastard. I bet you been fishin' all week. Huh?"

"Nope, just changed out this mornin' but I'll be up on the Stilly this weekend," O'Riley said as he stood up and grabbed his coat.

"Ah, yer a lucky man, O'Riley," the sheriff replied with a rare smile.

"I heard ya had a little bit of trouble down at the Imperial the other day," O'Riley said.

"Did ya now? It wasn't much, just a little bit a' fun."

"Yeah, well. Maybe yer version of fun. But how 'bout them Red Sox?" O'Riley mentioned as he put on his coat.

"Oh, yeah. After they win the pennant they'll take the series, I bet. Hold on," McRae lowered his voice and asked, "You know if the houseman's here?" O'Riley smiled, titled his head at the bartender and said, "Yeah, I think so. Gotta get. See ya 'round."

McRae nodded to O'Riley and touched the brim of his Stetson as the fireman walked away. The sheriff went over to the end of the stool-free mahogany bar, glanced around the room, and then looked at the bartender.

"Someone in the backroom?" he asked and tilted his head at the curtain next to the bar.

"Yep, houseman's here, but —" the bartender replied quietly. He shook his head not looking at the sheriff and said, "Just a second." He glanced around the room as he dried a glass. He set it on a shelf, dried another then looked at McRae and tilted his head towards the curtained hallway just past the bar.

"Good," McRae grunted. He stepped over to the curtain, pulled it back and ducked into the hallway as the bartender closed it behind him. At the end of the hall McRae pulled out his blackjack and rapped it on the door. "You there?" the sheriff mumbled, and rapped again.

"Whose zat?" a muffled voice answered from the other side.

"Don," the sheriff said, sliding his blackjack back into its leather belt loop. The sound of deadbolts opening clanged, and the heavy door slowly opened just wide enough for him to slip through.

"Gemme a jug of Canadian," the sheriff said as he stepped inside. The long-time transgressor closed and bolted the door behind him. The walls were stacked with wooden boxes of liquor and quarts of beer. A table had a single lightbulb hanging over it.

Another man sat in the corner. McRae looked at him and sniffed, "How goes it?"

The man nodded slightly, saying, "Howdy," with a sober face as his eyes started darting around.

The sheriff turned back to the bootlegger. "So, Bud — what'd ya got?"

"I've got some B.C. bourbon for two dollars," the bootlegger said, pulling a bottle from a wooden box.

"Two dollars? For bootleg 'shine? Don't be tryin' ta' sell me rotgut liquor!" the sheriff bellowed.

"Well, I've got some real Canadian for ten dollars," he offered and pulled another jug from a different crate. McRae glared at him, his narrowed eyes boring into the man's skull. The scofflaw snapped his head back and quickly changed his tune, "But you can have it for five."

"Give it," McRae said and pulled a clip of money out of his trousers. He peeled off a five dollar bill and dropped it on the table as the fellow slipped the jug into a brown paper sack and twisted the top. The sheriff snatched the package out of his hand and stepped to the door.

"Good seeing ya, Don" the bootlegger offered as he unbolted and cracked open the door. McRae walked back down the hall and looked over the curtain. The bartender saw him and slid the curtain back halfway. The sheriff stepped over to the bar.

McRae stood at the bar and held the jug down under it. He looked around the room and recognized a couple of men he used to work with in the mills, they were whispering to each other. The sheriff turned his focus to the long mirror behind the bar and watched as the two men got up from their booth to leave. McRae turned to get a good look at them just as three drunks walked through the entrance. They had their arms wrapped around each other's shoulders as they stumbled in. One of them lifted a mangled hand with a thumb and four stubs cut off at the knuckles. He shouted, "How 'bout three beers!" The patrons snapped their heads around to gawk at the dirty drunkards and then exchanged glances at seeing such a sight.

"There's no beer here for you!" a man in a suit hollered.

"No beer?" the fingerless man said, and then belched, "then why the hell did we leave the Pastime."

"The Pastime Parlor is selling again?" another businessman remarked.

"Yep," one of the other drunks hiccuped and wiped his mouth with his sleeve, "they been spillin' beer all mornin' in their alley." A few men picked up their coats and walked towards the door while the three drunks made their way over to the only empty booth. The fingerless one yelling at the men leaving, "But we's already drunk 'em dry."

McRae shook his head and turned to leave. The drunks were laughing to themselves and opening menus while the third had already dropped his head on the table passed out.

"That's it! You're out! We're closed!" the bartender yelled as he headed towards them while men in suits watched on. The sheriff slipped out the door.

Leaving Lowman's, McRae walked down the sidewalk and could see his dog sitting up as usual in the back seat, the sheriff hopped in. He shoved the bottle under the seat, turned the key and stepped on the starter, then he saw something on the windshield. With the car idling he got out to see an IWW black cat sticker.

"What in the hell!" he hollered and glanced up and down Hewitt. "Whoever did this is gonna pay!" he yelled.

The sheriff tried to pull the sticker off, but his worn, crudely chopped fingernails were too short so he couldn't get an edge. He continued to pick at it as his blood pressure rose. The black cat with its arched spine just stared back, making him even more furious. Finally, he got it off and flicked the sticker remains into the gutter. He hopped back in the car, pulled out the bottle, took a drink, and then drove east on Hewitt.

At Rockefeller he turned right and drove through the intersection. A couple of teenagers walked right behind his bumper as he drove through the Hewitt crosswalk. The sheriff looked in his rearview mirror to see them and screamed, "God dammit!" at the sight of another sticker on the rear window. He slammed on the brakes and stopped in the middle of the street at the base of the hill.

A red-faced sheriff leaped from his car while the teenagers watched. Soon enough a crowd of people had gathered around watching him pick away as the teenagers snickered. A car pulled up behind him and honked. Champion Tom started baying like he was hot on the trail of some criminal.

"Don't you people have something better to do?" McRae barked as loud as Champion Tom and then glared at the onlookers. The teenagers looked at each other, shrugged their shoulders, and said, "Nope, not really."

"Well, scram, dammit! Get out of my sight!" the sheriff roared as he got back in the roadster and drove up the hill. The crowd watched and then slowly dissipated into the shadows of the downtown buildings.

***

The sheriff parked on Rockefeller, walked through the arched entrance of the two- story, white mission-style county jailhouse with his dog at his side, and climbed the stairs to his cluttered office. He sat down in the wooden swivel chair and put his feet up on the desk covered with paperwork while Champion spun around a few times on his dusty corner blanket and plopped down. McRae pulled the black Stetson down on his brow and tried to relax. Ten minutes later Deputy Beard came in the room holding a half-eaten sandwich.

"One of the men said there's a union sign hanging behind Spanjer's," he said as the sandwich disappeared under his bushy, black mustache.

"What's that?" the sheriff spat out and jumped to his feet, a hand reaching for his blackjack, his hat landing on the floor.

"Oh, sorry, boss. I didn't know you were takin' a break. There's a union sign hanging behind Spanjer's market," the deputy said, as he stroked and cleaned his whiskers.

"What union?"

"Local 248," Jefferson replied, licking his lips and smiling.

"That a new one?" McRae asked.

"Yep, none of the men have heard of it."

"That a plumber's union?"

"Nope, they already have an office down at the Labor Temple," Beard answered.

"Well, I bet it's the damn Wobblies. Let's go take a look," the sheriff replied, rubbing his eyes. He picked his hat up off the floor, looked at his dog and said, "Sit, Tom. Stay."

The sheriff got behind the wheel of the patrol car, felt for the jug under the seat but didn't take a drink, and dropped it in reverse as Deputy Beard hopped in.

"What's the plan?" Beard asked.

"Got no plan. Just goin' over there."

"Maybe we should have another man or two?"

"Nah, we're OK for now."

McRae turned into the narrow alley behind Spanjer's market. Overflowing garbage cans were beside every backdoor and an old woman wearing a flowered scarf was hanging laundry from an apartment on a second-story fire escape. A hand painted sign over the basement stairwell had black letters that read "Local 248." The sheriff stepped out of the car, went down the stairs, banged on the door, and yelled, "Who the hell's in there?" He waited a second, then banged on the door again. No one answered, so he tried the doorknob but it was locked. McRae went back up the stairs and got behind the wheel.

"What d'ya think?" Beard said.

"Well, I'm thinkin' you're gonna stake it out. Let's go back, and you can drop me off. Then I want you to watch the place 'til ya see something," the sheriff said.

"And if it's the IWW?" Beard asked with an eager voice.

"If it's the Wobblies, well then, they are gonna end up wishin' that they never set up shop here," the sheriff said as he drummed his fingers on the wheel, "but since that federal mediator is still in town, I guess we need to take it slow."

McRae circled around the block looking for anything out of place. Finding nothing, he drove back to the jailhouse and parked in the alley. Deputy Beard got out and jumped into the other patrol car while the sheriff took the whiskey from under the seat and locked it in the rear compartment.

The sheriff walked into his office and went straight to the file cabinet, opened the bottom drawer and pulled out the old, dusty bottle of whiskey. Without hesitation he cracked the seal and took a long drink, then looked at the phone. McRae took one more pull and called Luther MacCullock at his head office.

"Yes," MacCullock answered.

"It's Don."

"Yes, Sheriff."

"I found a new union hall in the alley behind Spanjer's market."

"Did you?" MacCullock asked.

"It's got a sign says Local 248."

"And what union would that be?" MacCullock asked.

"Well, since Spanjer's a Socialist I think it's probably the IWW."

"If it is, we cannot allow them to get established here, never."

"Yeah, I know. I've got it staked out."

"And then what?" MacCullock quickly asked.

"Once I know who it is, I'll deal with it, Luther," the sheriff answered.

"I'm counting on you, Sheriff. And so is this whole town."

"I'm well aware of that. I'll take care of it. Anything else?"

"Just keep doing your job, Donald. Sounds like you've got it handled, for now," MacCullock said as he hung up. He gathered his thoughts and began to formulate his next move. Luther called his foreman at the mill with a slight grin.

"Butch, I've been thinking we should do something for the men," MacCullock said.

"Like what?" Barnell asked with a sarcastic tone.

"I thought we'd take our crew to the playhouse."

"What? You mean the pictures?"

"No, I mean the playhouse. I heard there's a magician appearing, and that it's quite a show."

"And how are we supposed to do that? Take 'em up in truckloads?"

"No, no. Just walk on uptown."

"What? You mean like a parade?"

"Exactly."

"You want me to march our workers through the streets?"

"Are you not listening to me, Barnell? I'll get the whole thing arranged and paid for at the Everett Theatre. But, Butch, I think it would be best if the guards and you just carry clubs. You should have them leave the shotguns behind."

"Oh, uh, well if you say so. I'll take care of it."

At 6:30 p.m., after the mill shut down and the men had been fed, Butch Barnell stood up in the mess hall and announced, "All right, Northern Imperial is taking you to see the magic show at the playhouse, so I want everyone outside right now. We're all walking straight up Hewitt to the theater, and then after the show you can all do whatever ya want."

Tompall Tharp stood up and said, "All of us?"

"That's right!" Barnell replied. "All a' ya."

Tompall sat back down and looked up and down the table. He whispered to the man next to him, "Nah, this sounds like trouble to me."

Outside, Buck Mullaney and a dozen club-toting brutes lined up the thirty-five workers with Barnell in the lead, while the rest of the lumber trust guards walked beside and behind the ragtag group. Unwashed and unshaven with some in cork boots they were a bedraggled sight to behold as they headed out of the mill. A group of local strikers were huddled around a small campfire cooking a kettle of mulligan on the city side of the railroad tracks. One of the strikers saw the Imperial scabs walking up the frontage road and gobbled down the rest of his meal, set down his bowl, and ran uptown.

The theater-bound parade of men tromped across the tracks and headed up Hewitt. Soon a group of strikers and sympathetic citizens were following the parade and heckling the filthy display.

"Would ya look at all of these scabrous Northern Imperial prairie chickens!" one onlooker exclaimed. "Where you boys goin'?"

A few teenagers saw the marchers as they got close to Grand and ran off through town spreading the word. A block later, the ragtag group of men was past Rucker and stomping by the Palace Pool Room. Every patron inside flooded onto the sidewalk and followed them up Hewitt Avenue as the jeering intensified. The crowd recognized Barnell.

"Where the hell do you think you MacCullock rats are going?" a striker yelled.

"This looks like nothin' but hell on a holiday!" another one hollered.

"You finks goin' ta' church on a Tuesday night?"

"Sure don't look like no church meeting to me."

"There ain't nothing to worship north of Seattle, you fools."

"What are you trying to prove, Barnell?"

"Looks like you boys just got let outta prison!"

"Ya dumb bastids, we already had the Fourth a' July parade!"

"Shut up, you worthless quitters!" Buck Mullaney yelled at the jeering sidewalk crowd.

At Hoyt, more citizens began showing up in ones and twos. Men and women, kids on bikes, shop-keepers, and businessmen all watched or followed on the sidewalks until a hundred people were following the ragtag procession.

When the procession passed the Commercial Club, Luther MacCullock stood at the window and watched with Ralph Edgerton and a few other members.

"Are those your workers, Luther?" Edgerton asked.

"Sure are," MacCullock answered with a smirk.

"What's going on?" Edgerton said.

"I'm taking them to see Alexander the White Mahatma tonight," MacCullock said.

"The magician? What on earth? Well, this has got to be the first time you've ever spent a penny that you didn't need too?"

"It's good for morale."

"Morale! When have you ever cared about morale? What about the strikers?"

"The strikers should have stayed on the job," MacCullock said bluntly.

"For criminy sakes, Luther, when my workers find out about this they're gonna want the same thing. This is not a very well thought out idea," Edgerton groaned.

"I don't care if you like it or not, Ralph. If it keeps my men in good spirits and my mill running then that's all that matters," MacCullock flatly replied and went back to his booth. David McGivney and a few of the other club members went outside.

An electric trolley car came up and over the crest of the Hewitt hill. It rolled through Colby and then stopped for the men coming up the middle of the street. The confused passengers turned their heads as they looked at the forlorn group. The parade turned south at Colby, stopped at the theater, and lined up to go inside.

"You mean ta' tell me that the Northern Imperial is taking you scabs to the magic show? Hell, MacCullock never did anything like that when we worked for his three-penny outfit!" a striker yelled as the ticket-taker began to let them in.

Jake Michel walked around the corner from Hewitt, stopped in his tracks, and asked a man on the sidewalk, "What the devil is this?"

"Looks like MacCullock's taking his scabs to the show," the man replied. "They're all goin' inside."

"Why that son of a — what's he trying to prove?" Michel spat, and looked at the crowd.

"No strikebreaking scab is worth a show ticket!" someone yelled.

"You dumb union bastards can go to hell!" an Imperial worker shouted over his shoulder.

"That'll be the last night on the town you worthless swine will ever see!" a striker screamed as more union men chimed in.

"You'll all be working fer Lucifer come morning!"

"At least we'll all be working!" another man yelled back, waving his ticket in the air.

"What kind of devils asses are you?"

"You're all pigs of the hangman!"

"You're the ones who walked off the job!" one of MacCullock's last workers to enter the theater yelled.

Jake Michel quickly walked across Colby and joined Hank Hillstrom and a few strikers he knew. The sidewalk was shoulder to shoulder with curious onlookers. Minutes ticked by. Jake saw two strikers from the Seacrest Mill show up with a gunny-sack full bats and ax handles. They started to hand them out, one of them saying, "Go over in the alley beside the theater and wait for them to come out." Jake's heart jumped up in his throat. He glanced around at the crowd again. There were plenty of strikers but also a good number of citizens, husbands and wives with their families, and teenagers.

"Where the hell are the cops? You see any cops since you've been here?" Jake asked Hillstrom.

"Nope," he replied, not taking his eyes away from the scene.

"There's too many citizens. I think the cops need to be here," Jake said. Hank didn't reply. Michel grabbed him by the arm.

"How 'bout you run over to city hall?" Jake said to him. "The police need to show up."

"Nope, I ain't leavin'," Hillstrom said, he glanced at the union activist and back to the street. The striker jerked his arm away from Jake and grumbled, "I'm plannin' on kickin' a few scab asses real soon."

"Listen here! I'm ready to throw into a fight, too! Right now! But there's women and children here. Somebody's gonna get hurt," Michel said.

But Hillstrom ignored him. Jake calmly said in his ear, "Don't you have a wife and kids at home?"

"Yeah, so?" the striker replied, not taking his eyes away from the commotion.

"Yeah, well," Michel said, grabbing Hillstrom firmly by the back of his neck, "any man who's not home with his family right now should be. Now get yer ass over to city hall and tell the cops!"

"All right! All right!" Hank grumbled and pulled himself away from Michel's grip.

"But I'll be back!" He ran off up the street, past the Strand Hotel, crossed over, and headed toward the police station a block away.

Jake watched him run around the corner and turned back to a building mob. Once Hillstrom was out of sight Hank stopped, rolled a cigarette and waited just out of view.

Men began to beat ax handles and baseball bats against the sidewalk curb and on street lights and telephone poles in unison. The crowd kept growing and began spilling out into part of Colby. Horns honked and drivers yelled.

A few minutes later, the theater doors opened and the first few men emerged. Jake looked up and down the street, but the police still weren't there. A striker in the crowd threw a bottle. It landed with a crash in front of the theatre.

"Take that ya stinkin' scabs," the striker yelled.

More bottles were hurled. One hit a display window next to the theater entrance, shattering the glass. A few of the Imperial workers darted out, picked up rocks from the gutter, and began throwing them when Tompall Tharp walked out. He immediately reached in his tattered overalls pocket, pulled out a machine bolt, and pitched it across the street. It landed at Jake Michel's feet with a clang, then a rock hit Michel in the forehead, a gash opening above his eyebrow.

"Why, you —" Michel hollered and wiped blood from his eyes.

When Hank Hillstrom heard glass breaking, he dropped his cigarette butt on the sidewalk, ran over to the police station and yelled in the front door, "There's a riot at the playhouse!" and then headed back to the theater alley. As he ran he pulled a pair of brass knuckles from his pants pocket, put them on his right hand, and hid in the shadows.

Three police cars sped up to the scene and screeched to a halt in front of the theater. Rocks and bottles flew from both sides of the street over the cop cars. Then a baseball bat cartwheeled end over end high above the street and hit the front of the theater's entrance roof. Sparks darted out from the lights underneath and electrical shorts popped and snapped. Two pieces of the roof façade fell to the sidewalk, they were instantly picked up and hurled at the crowd.

The police sprang from their patrol cars and surged into the melee, some blowing whistles while others raised billy clubs trying to keep the onlookers at bay. Police Chief Tom Kelly pulled a megaphone from his black Oldsmobile.

"Everyone clear the area. Now!" He yelled as a few Imperial workers ran from the theater for cover. Others scattered in different directions while more waited and watched from the lobby. When others saw what was going on outside, they went back into the theater. Some tried to escape through the emergency exit while Buck Mullaney and his guards waited and watched from the lobby, holding clubs and ax handles at their sides.

Strikers hid in the shadows of the alley beside the theater, waiting for an Imperial that made the unfortunate mistake of thinking they could escape in its direction or from the side exit.

"Take that, ya damn fink!" one striker yelled as he laid into the scab with a roundhouse bat, knocking the wind out of the guy and putting him on the ground. One quick and clever fellow darted around the next swing, but then got hit in the back by another striker who jumped out from the shadows. The victim cried out, falling to his knees, and a boot kicked him in the nose. He dropped face first to the ground, blood spurting from an open laceration.

Chief Kelly screamed, "People of Everett, I order you to disperse immediately!"

Another man hit the ground in the alley, his face caved in from brass knuckles, red spilled over the gravel as he gasped for breath. More machine bolts were thrown. People were running and shouting as the melee reached a fever pitch. Rocks were tossed, and the bat that hit the entrance roof was thrown back at the strikers, it bounced off the building behind them and landed on the sidewalk.

"Break it up, everybody! Break it up! Everyone is to clear the street immediately!" Chief Kelly yelled into the megaphone. But the crowd would have nothing of it.

"We don't need your help!" one bat-wielding striker yelled.

"Yeah, go back home, Chief!" another hollered.

"I'm ordering you people to clear the area, or I'll arrest all of ya!" the police chief screamed when a bottle hit the ground next to him breaking to pieces.

"If you people don't disperse this instant, I'm going to call in the state police! Now everyone clear the area!" Chief Kelly yelled, his face contorted and red. Boos instantly answered him. Men pumped the air with their fists and started beating the sidewalk again with their clubs.

Two policemen turned their car sirens off and on when the chief, in one last effort to end the riot, pulled his pistol from his holster and fired one shot in the air. The bulk of the crowd turned their focus to the chief as the last dozen Imperial men still waiting inside the theater saw an opening and bolted out the front door, past the crowd, and down Hewitt towards the waterfront.

Someone in the crowd noticed them fleeing and shouted, "Get 'em!" Half of the crowd pursued with their clubs and bats raised. The strikers caught up with them on the other side of Rucker just as two police cars pulled up. The police then escorted MacCullock's men back to the Northern Imperial.

***

An excited David McGivney walked back into the Commercial Club and announced, "There's been a riot at the playhouse."

A hush fell over the room. For the last two hours every member had been whispering about the parade of Northern Imperial workers. All eyes darted around the club and ultimately found Luther MacCullock sitting in a booth with Ralph Edgerton.

"I told you that wasn't a good idea," Edgerton said to him quietly as the club room roared to life.

"What's this? Is this about MacCullock's men?" Lester Blankenship piped.

"MacCullock took his men to the theater, and there was violence in the street!" McGivney said.

"Luther. Why would you march your scabs through the streets like that?" Virgil Postlewait complained.

"There's nothing wrong about MacCullock's men going to the show," Mayor Merrill admonished.

"There is too," Blankenship barked back. "MacCullock's thumbing his nose at all of Everett by pulling a stunt like that. What have you got to say for yourself?" Blankenship glared at Luther MacCullock. The room buzzed with concern.

MacCullock stabbed his porterhouse steak with a fork, sliced off a piece and chewed it with relish. He wiped his mouth with a napkin, grabbed his pipe from the ashtray, stood up from his booth, and strode to the middle of the room as if he were walking on stage, his every step calculated and exact. Luther looked attentively at all the faces, then put a match to his pipe, took a long pull, dropped the match in an ashtray on the table next to him, and blew the smoke out through his nostrils as he gathered his thoughts. He knew his colleagues wanted an explanation about his decision to take his workers to the playhouse, but he had something else in mind.

He cleared his throat and began to speak. "Gentlemen, as some of you might know, forty years ago I was a fresh-faced twenty-two year old captain, probably the proudest young captain in the whole U.S. Army. I'd been assigned to the Fifth Cavalry out in the Black Hills and was put in charge of keeping the supply line open, and safe, from Belle Fourche to Queen City and on south to Deadwood. General Crook had just beaten the Sioux at Slim Buttes, but we were still engaging the enemy in weekly skirmishes." MacCullock stroked his finely trimmed beard as he chose his words and turned his head from man to man while he spoke.

"At Queen City we had about two hundred settlers, farmers and miners, a general store and a hotel, it was a growing village. Besides Belle Fourche, it afforded the best protection from the Indians. There was another settlement on the trail called Iron Creek but it was a smaller outpost, they had a smithy and a stable, a saloon, a few cabins and the hand full of people who lived there called it their home. Iron Creek may not have been much, but it was something, it existed," MacCullock said. The sheriff appeared in the hallway. He pushed his Stetson back on his head and leaned up against the wall to listen.

"I had a company of fine young men who served their country well. What I wouldn't give for a few of them right now in my mill! I'd never seen a better company of men. Well, my scouts had spotted some Indian movement to the south so we went out on patrol and searched for their trail. The next day we were attacked near Iron Creek by a small band of Sioux, maybe a dozen of them, probably just some damn fool young renegades with more anger than sense. They rode up from behind, but we out flanked them and killed every single one, some in hand-to-hand combat with bayonets. The next day we found their camp. I spared the old folks, women and children and ordered them out," MacCullock said to a quiet room.

"I felt those Indian women and children in the camp posed no threat to us or the army, so as captain I gave the order to let them pass. Well gentlemen, I was a young man, and I guess a touch naive. I say that because those Indian women snuck around us and doubled back while we stayed out on patrol. Two nights later they burned everything in Iron Creek to the ground!" MacCullock said with fire in his eyes as he pointed the stem of his churchwarden pipe at the floor and then at Ralph Edgerton and Lester Blankenship like a military baton. "And I promised myself that I would never make another stupid decision like that again in my life."

"Now then — we've already had IWW speakers at the soapbox corner, and today I received a report that they might have set up a union hall here in Everett . . . And the last thing we need is the IWW setting up shop in our back yard."

"What do you mean the IWW is here?" Lester Blankenship asked. Luther fixed an indifferent gaze on him.

"I got word that the Industrial Workers of the World have possibly set up a union hall under the title of Local 248 behind Noah Spanjer's market on Wetmore," MacCullock said as the room buzzed.

"No, that can't be," Virgil Postlewait exclaimed.

"Why would they want to be here?" Blankenship said.

"Gentlemen, please. We *must* deal with the IWW," MacCullock said.

"We're not gonna have some Indian war with the IWW," Ralph Edgerton snapped back.

"You're wrong, Ralph," Mayor Merrill replied. "We *will* have a war on our hands, and Luther's right!"

MacCullock reached into his inside coat pocket, pulled out a slip of paper, unfolded it, and held it up in the air.

"In my hand I have a new city ordinance that replaces the old one and bans all public street meetings," MacCullock proudly stated. "Recently, Mayor Merrill has been working on this new law that will end all these street meetings. It should be far better than the old ordinance, it has been written and recorded," MacCullock proclaimed with bravado.

"What's this now?" Ralph Edgerton said, jumping to his feet.

"What are you talking about Luther?" another member asked.

"Why, this is an outrage!" Lester Blankenship bellowed as he stood up. "You can't just take the right to speak freely away."

"It's better than the other ordinance and it's needed," Mayor Merrill said, clapping his hands. He turned to Edgerton and Blankenship and said, "Sit down. Let Luther speak."

"Members, members," MacCullock continued with a hand raised for quiet, "We have got to give the police and sheriff the tools they need to be able to control these street meetings. Now this brand new ordinance," MacCullock glanced at the page, "number 1746, is what we need to help bring this town under control. The Sheriff and Chief Kelly will use their discretion in how they apply this new law."

"Where were the city commissioners in all of this?" Blankenship said.

"Our fine Mayor and the commissioners have worked together in making this ordinance law," MacCullock replied, "and it is done."

"Nobody's going to follow some silly little ordinance," Virgil Postlewait chided.

"This is an abuse of power! When were the public hearings on this?" David McGivney protested.

Mayor Merrill stood back up and raised his hands, "Gentlemen, the ordinance is law. I can assure you that all three city commissioners voted for this, and I signed it. It is done. Now let Luther finish."

"Gentlemen," MacCullock said with a slight grin, "like our fine mayor just said, this ordinance is on the books. Now, I'm sure all of you read those newspaper accounts a few years back when the IWW was in Spokane and Fresno. In both cases the IWW sent out the word and every bum on the west coast flocked to those towns. There was mayhem in the streets every night of the week in those fine cities because they did not have this kind of ordinance in place. We cannot let that same thing happen here, so this should help deter these parasitic bums," he said as members sitting in chairs and booths with their arms crossed over full stomachs turned to each other and nodded in approval. MacCullock saw the member's positive reaction and continued.

"If we allow the IWW to establish itself here, it will amount to the same thing as those Sioux women. If we give them a pass, they'll burn Everett and all of our plants down, too," MacCullock warned. "These are desperate people we are dealing with and desperate people do desperate things!" He raised his pipe-free hand in the air and persisted, "These members of the IWW are revolutionaries and believe in using violence to overturn everything we hold dear. They will destroy everything we've built, and they import the most degraded barbarisms to accomplish their hellish ends. The Wobblies are agitators who will stop at nothing to blast apart the sound basis of our economy with impossible demands that will sink every mill owner in the state if we let them. They advocate endless wage increases that will destroy our town and ruin our businesses! These freeloaders will use any method they can to overthrow our capitalist system. And one more thing. Let me assure you that my workers having a night at the playhouse was not the cause of any riot. If there was a riot on the streets of Everett it was not because of my men. It was because of the IWW speakers that have already been here to preach their gospel of hate, and they may already have a possible toehold here with a union hall. If not, they will eventually come here, I know it. When they do, they will prolong the strike and inspire our workers with their destructive propaganda that incites nothing but wretched and fowl behavior. We cannot allow these bums and hoboes to take over our town!"

"But we can't fight the IWW. They'll bankrupt the city! And besides, the Wobblies always win," Virgil Postlewait admonished.

"The city can't afford to pay the police to suppress a free-speech fight," McGivney added, "with or without some ordinance. That's why the IWW won in Spokane and Fresno. How are we going to stop them here?"

MacCullock looked down at the banker, scratched the side of his head and thought to himself for a moment while another member had his say.

"David McGivney is right," Virgil Postlewait said. "The city is already spending a fortune repaving Everett Avenue. And I know we're all against raising taxes. Besides, we can't just stop people from coming here."

"If you're concerned about city finances," MacCullock interjected, "then we'll make Everett a fortress using our Commercial Club volunteers. We need to defend this city that we've built. I'm telling you these Wobbly radicals will overtake Everett if we're not careful, Virgil! The IWW will fill our streets with bums that have no interest in Everett except to ruin it! We cannot allow these bushwhackers to steal our town! Never!"

"Luther's right," Mayor Merrill added, "We need to double our efforts. Everyone in favor of doing battle with the IWW if we need to, raise your hand." A cheer went up in the room as nearly every hand was raised.

"We must organize, gentlemen. We need to re-marshal our powers!" MacCullock ordered as if he was a young Captain in the Indian Wars again. "In the morning I want every patriotic citizen banded together in their patrol groups' at all strategic locations. We have to form a barrier around our town. At the depot, in the switching yards, at the Interurban Station, the city pier and on the Pacific Highway coming in from Bothell and Seattle. I want patrols at all of these locations and on our streets around the clock, especially all the way out at the city limits on Forty-First Street, those old skid roads in and out of Lowell, and most importantly, we must protect the gun powder mill out on the Mukilteo Road. I don't want to even begin to imagine the kinds of consequences we'd have if these Wobbly radicals got their hands on all of that explosive material! We must control who comes and goes in Everett. If any of you comes across a Wobbly, offer them deportation first, and if they refuse then take them to the county jail, where the sheriff will charge them with vagrancy."

Chapter 8

MINERAL SPRINGS

In the blue-gray early morning light, Dirty Shirt and Harry waited anxiously in front of the file shop when a dark silhouette emerged from the timber cruiser's cabin. A kerosene lamp began to swing back and forth as it moved towards them and a cool morning breeze blew out of the east from the clear-cut. Like so many times before, Dirty Shirt knew it wouldn't take long to bag a buck.

Since Charlie had gone to the bawdy house down in Sultan on the speeder the night before Shep was the only man in camp with a key to the rifle box. As he got closer they could see his white teeth clenching a corncob pipe, the smoke from his pipe curled around his head, leaving a trail of ghostly wisps behind him.

"Mornin', gents," Shep said with a grin. "Fine day for a hunt if ya ask me."

"Wanna come along?" Dirty Shirt quietly asked.

"Nope, I'm gonna take it easy today," Shep replied as he pulled a key ring from his trousers and unlocked the door. Stepping inside, Shep set the lantern down on one of the saw clamp tables, file tools were strewn about and un-lit kerosene lamps hung from the rafters. On the floor in the corner was the old metal rifle locker, an ancient padlock hung from a rusty hasp. Shep unlocked the long white dust-covered box, it opened with a stubborn creak. A dozen rifles were inside; a Colt Lightning pump, a 94 smokeless, an 1866 Springfield

Trapdoor, and miscellaneous rusted wrecks in a heap, kept around more for appearances and to avoid the trouble of throwing them away. Most were covered with a layer of powdery dirt. Dirty Shirt reached inside for his lever-action Winchester. Harry grabbed the lamp and held it up.

"There's my trusty deer-killer," Dirty Shirt whispered with affection and looked at Harry as he held out his rifle. "Pa handed her down to me, and today we's gonna bag us a fine side-hill salmon," he said with calm anticipation.

Harry smiled at the Winchester and then looked down into the long rifle box on the floor. "What's that new-lookin' one?" He asked as he pointed.

"That's Charlie's Krag. He never uses it," Shep answered.

"Why's that?" Harry asked.

"Oh, who knows why? He had a Springfield breechloader that he traded in when he bought that Krag, and he never used the Springfield, either," Shep said.

"What about those others?" Harry added.

"Oh, a few were owned by men who were killed up here. Nobody ever claimed them," Shep said, "I keep my rifle down at the cabin. The others belong to the rest of the crew. You wanna use one today?"

"Nah," Harry replied, "I'm just goin' along to help Dirty Shirt carry his deer back, as long as he gets one, that is."

It was Sunday, their day off. The paymaster had been up to the camp the evening before and life was good for Harry and Dirty Shirt as they headed out into the clear-cut with a little folding money in their pockets. They hiked along a former skid line where massive old growth trees were once yarded, the woods were beginning to reclaim the gouged out forest floor with a new layer of duff, taking back what was ripped away.

They strode past stumps, rotted tree ends, slash, and decomposed logs as the sky brightened. The golden glow of the sun was coming up to the east behind the Cascades, and the sweet smell of foxglove and fireweed wafted through the air. Two goldfinches appeared in the sky, landed on the limbs of some buck brush and began to follow them, flitting from bush to bush, chirping and singing as they tagged along.

"You do much huntin' down in Oregon?" Dirty Shirt asked.

"No, didn't," Harry replied.

"But huntin's fine sport," Frank offered.

"Just never did is all. Never had the chance," Harry said quietly.

"Whatcha think so far?"

"You mean we're huntin' already?"

"Well, yeah, sorta, I guess. Today we're gonna do what I call a still-hunt. Once we get a little farther out we'll only move about ten 'er twenty feet at a time from stump to stump and stay behind cover. The deer like these clear-cuts. There's lots of new vegetation for 'em to feed on, and the wind's right. We'll just keep movin' into the breeze," Frank said when a brownish-gray rabbit bounded into the middle of the trail, about forty yards ahead of them. The rabbit stopped for a moment, but Frank kept walking.

"Aren't ya gonna shoot him?" Harry whispered.

"Nope," Frank answered.

"I thought we was huntin'."

"No. We ain't huntin' rabbit," Frank said as it jumped out of sight.

"Aw, you didn't shoot it because you knew you would a' missed," Harry said with a grin. Frank stopped.

"I didn't shoot the stupid little thing because I would have scared away all the deer," Dirty Shirt piped.

Farther up the skid road a porcupine waddled into view. Frank held up his hand to stop. "We need to let that critter pass." Once it was out of sight they started out again, and Frank decided to let Harry in on a line of talk he'd been a party to.

"So, uh, I heard a little somethin' last time I was in Sultan."

"Oh yeah, what's that?" Harry asked.

"Well, I heard that there's a strike at the mill and all the other mills down in town," Dirty Shirt confided to Harry in a whisper, "and I guess old man MacCullock's been runnin' scab labor . . . *and then* I heard he marched his scabs to the show-house and there was a riot. I told Reader Bill about it, he seemed pretty concerned."

"What'd he say?" Harry inquired, gaining interest.

"Well, at first he asked me how long the strike's been going on. Then he said that the strikers and their families were probably sufferin' and such and that the mill owners should pay 'em what they want and all," Frank said and then motioned to stop and move behind a stump.

"But there was a riot?" Harry whispered back.

"I guess the whole damn town was waiting for them when they came outta the big theater downtown, and some of the strikers beat the scabs up pretty good," Dirty Shirt said.

"You mean there were fist fights?"

"With fists and bats, I guess. Let's move over to that fir stump."

"Boy, I'd beat up a scab, too, if I had the chance," Harry whispered as he followed Frank, watching every move that he made. Harry observed how he walked softly on the ground, always headed into the wind, and how he worked his way through the forest, going slowly to each area of cover.

Frank finally replied with his nose in the breeze, "Why's that?"

"Because a scab is a low-down rat. That's why."

"Doreen said the strike's been goin' all summer," Dirty Shirt whispered and then put his finger to his lips for Harry to be quiet. Frank knelt down. Harry did the same.

"You hear that twig snap?" Dirty Shirt whispered. Harry nodded. Staying low to the ground, Frank quietly crawled over to another stump and slowly looked over it between some ferns. A five-point buck and two does were working their way through the foliage. Stepping slowly through the brush-choked thicket, their ears straight up, they glanced around between dropping their heads to devour entire fern leaves in one long bite, tails constantly twitching. Frank turned his head around to a hiding Harry.

"Don't move," he whispered and then signaled with three fingers that there were deer. Dirty Shirt slowly rose up to sight in the buck, it was a magnificent black-tail, big and healthy. Dirty Shirt's heart started to pound and his eyes were as big as a full moon. He leveled his Winchester, took a silent breath, held it, and pulled the trigger just as Harry popped up to take a look.

BOOM! The sound of the blast echoed through the woods. The five-point stumbled at first and then bounded off behind the does through the clear-cut and out of sight.

"I think I got him!" Dirty Shirt shouted as he jumped up from behind the stump and started to run. "Come on, Harry. Let's go chase down dinner!"

"I think you hit him in the neck!" Harry yelled after him.

"Ya think so? . . . Cause I aimed . . . at his flank," Frank said as they leaped over decomposed limbs, around vine maple, and up and over a few swales in the ground. They followed the blood trail a good ways through the clear-cut and into the old-growth woods. Dirty Shirt found blood on the mossy forest floor and then some red on a few ferns leading up a short hill. They followed the blood trail down to a creek. A hundred feet on the other side of the stream, the deer was dead on the ground lying in some ferns.

Dirty Shirt leaned his rifle against the closest tree and kneeled next to the massive black-tail. He saw a quarter-sized hole at the base of its neck and the deer's eyes were still wide open.

"Nice shot, Dirty . . . Shirt," Harry said breathing deeply.

"Thanks, but now the real work begins," Frank said. "Ya ever gut a deer?"

"Nope, can't say's I have," Harry replied as Frank pulled a foot-long skinning knife from its sheath hanging from his belt.

"Help me roll this beast over on its back," Dirty Shirt said, "and hold his legs up while I find the sternum."

Frank felt the deer's rib cage, found the spot where the bones came together, and punctured the animal's skin. The foul smell of the deer's insides filled the air. Harry turned away and tried to hold his breath.

"The thing is, ya gotta be careful not to stab the in-tes-tines," Frank said slowly as warm blood spilled on the ground. He shoved his right hand deep inside the animal and searched for the last membrane to cut.

"There it is," Dirty Shirt said with a grin. He reached inside with the knife, severed the last of the membranes, and pulled them free, the huge pile of organs sloshed out onto the ground.

"That'll make a fine meal for some timber wolf," Frank remarked.

"Now let's find us something to carry this beast home with."

Two hard, sweaty hours later, Dirty Shirt and Harry walked into Timber Creek with their prize hanging from its hooves on a fir branch slung between the two of them. Shep saw them from the mess hall door and came outside with his hands on his hips.

"Well, buck me up and push me in the river! That is the finest lookin' deer that's been brought into this camp in a coon's age!" Shep declared with gusto and followed them around to the back of the cook-house.

"We'll have him skinned and quartered in no time," Dirty Shirt said with a grin on his face.

"I'll find Little Stovie an' have him fire up one of the stoves. Tubs went with Charlie last night on the speeder an' gone all day so we won't have to hear him piss and moan about us dirtyin' up his kitchen," Shep said.

"Sounds good to me. We's gonna be fryin' up some back-strap in bacon grease tonight, boys," Dirty Shirt boasted with relish.

***

Harry had been awake for an hour by the time Charlie worked his way down the row of bunkhouses. He'd come to realize that Charlie's morning routine sayings were about the only thing that Charlie Purvis enjoyed.

"Come on, ya bunch of backwoods Romeos!" the head push squawked. "Quit pullin' yer pecker poles in those fart bunks and get up, ya lazy bastards. It's time you ladies start puttin' out some scale. We got logs ta' yard and a raft ta' fill, you sumbitches. Now let's move it!"

Logging gear clanged together in the cool morning air as dozens of loggers tossed their equipment up onto the flatbed railcars. Crosscut saws, axes, stamp and sledge-hammers, bags of wedges, and kerosene bottles hit the car decking as lumberjacks loaded equipment for the morning trip up to Mineral Springs. Jaako tossed a ten-foot saw onto the car and just missed his brother's head.

"Vatch out dar, Jaako, ya yust about gave me a hair-cut with dat dar Swede fiddle," Jorgen said, "an' I don't vant no hair-cut from you."

"Yah, vell, I tot you needed a betta' one for the ladies at the bawdy house," Jaako snickered.

"Shut up, ya stupid Scandis!" Axel Chambers grumbled.

Dirty Shirt snapped his head around to face Axel and bellowed, "Shut yer trap, or I'll part yer hair with my broad ax!"

"You ain't the boss a' me," Axel said when Charlie jumped onto the railcar.

"Yeah, well I'm the boss of all a' ya, and I say ya shut your crummy little faces. We got logs to yard and I want these cars loaded by the end of the day," Charlie ordered. "The raft boom ain't even close to half full yet and the mill needs more timber!"

The engineer blew the whistle three times and the Shay's gear-driven wheels slowly began to turn in reverse. Kerosene lamps hanging from the flatcar load poles swung back and forth as the sky began to brighten. Each car creaked and moaned over the rails as the train lurched backwards through the logged-off land. Past slash, stumps, and uprooted soil, the men sat quietly as another day in the woods cranked into existence.

When the flatcars rolled by the Devil's Staircase, the men knew they were close to the show. After one last horseshoe switch back the train came to a stop at the landing area, where the previous day's logs were stacked next to the heel boom. Men jumped off and headed to their stations with saws, axes, and nose-bags in hand.

Little Stovie ran over to his steam donkey and checked the boiler's water tank. Like every morning, he wanted the water tank less than half full so he could get a good head of steam going fast. Happy to see that the water level was low, he began splitting kindling as the donkey puncher Silas Shotwell joined him, dipping a few freshly cut pieces of cedar into a blue kerosene jug and then tossing them into the firebox. He struck a match and the firebox roared to life.

Harry, Reader Bill, and the other fallers headed into the woods. Dirty Shirt and the rigging crew peeled off to the side they were working on. Axel, his choke-setting partner, and a whistle punk hiked the skid road below the haul-back cable a quarter of a mile away to where their first turn of logs was. The boom operator split kindling for the steam boiler that ran the heel boom loader at the landing next to the train.

Charlie and Shep headed out to timber cruise the next side to be cut and determine the amount of board feet it would yield. Little Stovie checked the boiler's water level again and gave Silas the thumbs up. Silas checked the pressure gauge and opened a condenser valve, hot steam hissed into the cool morning air. Once the pressure gauge rose, Silas opened a piston valve and engaged the main double-drum lever, the donkey chugged to life like a locomotive. He watched both drums turn as one let cable out while the other pulled cable in, and he kept a special eye out for how the cable spun onto the haul-in drum, making sure it wound in smoothly, then he looked at a drum axle.

Little Stovie was watching the haul-back cable as it moved away in the early morning light. He turned back to feed the firebox but then snapped his head around and looked at the cable again. Stovie thought he saw something on top of the cable next to the choker rigging as it moved off, one-hundred feet in the air and then out of sight. *Was that a bird?*

"Stovie!" Silas yelled, "Where are ya?"

"Right here," Little Stovie answered walking towards donkey puncher.

"My haul-back bearings 'er dry," Silas yelled over the noise of the steam engine. "Find me that damn grease gun. Now!"

"Yeah, yeah," Stovie hollered back as the previously silent woods of Mineral Springs now hummed with the sound of work. He ran to the back of the donkey engine where the grease gun hung on a nail and retrieved it.

Every strand of the haul-back cable was made up of a hundred thin steel wires all rat-tail spliced together. Fifty of these strands were then weaved into a one-and-a-half-inch thick cable with the strength to lift and haul a one-hundred-ton log load. The cable operation was a giant loop that circled into the woods with the chokers and back, it was a high-wire ballet of strength and force that pulled timber back to the landing with two freshly cut forty-foot logs on every turn.

The donkey whistle blew once and Silas disengaged the drum lever and closed the piston valve, stopping the cable for where Axel was. Stovie handed Silas the grease gun. He got down on his knees and attached the end of the grease gun to the axle fitting and pumped the gun, but nothing happened.

"Dammit," Silas spat. "The stupid thing's empty. STOVIE! Where are ya?" Silas hollered without looking up.

"What! I'm right next to ya," Little Stovie answered standing beside the donkey engine.

"Here," Silas said handing Stovie the grease gun, "be sure to take it back to camp today. And fill it before ya bring it up tomorrow. That bearing should be OK fer now." Then the donkey whistle blasted three times. Silas stepped back over to his controls for another haul-back.

With every turn at Mineral Springs the logs kept getting bigger. Each log yarded in to the landing had one end suspended in the air from the choker rigging, the other end bounced and bucked along the ground as if it were some crazy Cayuse bronco being broken for saddle. Gouging a path through stumps, brush, debris, windfalls, busted and sawed-off tops, broken limbs, and crushed ferns, the timber fought back like a beast when it was yarded. Its struggle echoed like rolling thunder as it crashed through the forest and up to the landing but there was a problem, the haul-back cable had a fray.

Silas closed the valve, stopped the cable, and looked at his pressure gauge. "I'm losing steam, Stovie," Silas said. "I'm startin' to run a little low. Time to fill the tank."

"OK," Stovie answered as he unhooked the choker cables at the landing. He gave Silas the thumbs up when he was out of the way. Stovie threw another round of wood in the firebox, picked up the bucket, and ran off to the creek. Along the way he slowed down to look at what he thought was a pile of deer scat on the ground, but it was shiny and stringy, *that deer must be sick*, he kept running.

Silas began the process of sending the chokers back out to Axel. He opened the steam valve for the piston rod and then he pulled the drum lever, but it broke off and came free of the linkage where it engaged the drum.

"What in the —" Silas said, holding the heavy lever in his hand. "Fer Christ sakes, what the hell is going on here today? This God-damn thing," Silas cussed and set the lever down. He closed the piston valve and locked the drums in position, stopping the cable, then inspected the drum lever. The machine end that attached to the drum gear linkage looked fine so he got down on his knees to see what the drum gear looked like. Stovie walked up with a bucket of water.

"What's 'a matter?" Stovie asked, filling the boiler tank.

"Don't know yet," Silas replied, not looking up. He felt the drum gears — they were fine and without wear — and then he saw the large washer and a piece of cotter pin on the ground right below the drum.

"Cotter pin broke, and the washer's down there," Silas said standing up. "Crawl under and get it," he said to Stovie.

"All right," Little Stovie answered. He walked out to the front of the donkey's skid logs, got down on his hands and knees between them, and crawled under the donkey engine. He found the washer, and held it up through the machinery for Silas.

"Thank ye," Silas said, grabbing the thick, greasy washer. "And what about the pin? You see it?" Stovie quickly found one piece and handed it up. Silas inspected it.

"Would ya look at that? Damn thing sheered clean off," Silas remarked and scratched his head. "Never seen that before." He walked around to the back of the donkey where tools and parts were stored. Open top wooden boxes sat on a make-shift bench holding various logging gear: rigging hammers, wire axes, a Marlin spike for splicing cable, shackles, an old hindu, short lengths of chain and chain hooks, tree shoes and spikes. Silas found the little metal container with cotter pins in the spike box and then noticed that nearly all of the spikes were gone just as the donkey whistle blasted.

"STOVIE!" Silas yelled. "That's Axel wonderin' what's goin' on. Run on down the skid and yell to 'im we're broke down for a bit and then hurry on back to help."

A half mile away, Reader Bill and Harry Dolson were starting on their first tree of the day, chopping notches for springboards. Harry shoved the metal lip end of the springboard into his notch first and hopped up onto it. He pulled out a can of snoose and put a pinch between lip and gum, then looked over at Reader Bill.

"Dirty Shirt told me about the strike down in town," Harry revealed as he leaned against the tree with his arms crossed. Bill didn't say anything.

"Bill?"

"Yeah, I heard ya," Reader Bill said and then looked at Harry, "So Frank spilled the beans, huh?"

"Sure did, and he told me about the show house riot," Harry answered.

"You tell anybody?" Bill asked.

"Nope, not yet. You think Charlie knows?" Harry asked and then spat a wad of brown goop on the ground.

"Oh, I'd bet you dollars to doughnuts that Charlie knows all about the strike down in Everett."

"Whatcha think we should do about it?" Harry asked, wiping his jaw.

Reader Bill was about to set his springboard in its notch but stopped and looked at Harry. "Well, those strikers and their families are suffering right now for better pay and all . . . and I'm for better pay, no doubt about that. You know, I was a hard-rock miner once and a member of the Western Federation of Miners. But I got sick of going underground mucking ore for Anaconda every day, so I decided to work in the great north woods instead. Been out here for the last six years."

"So you were a union man?"

"Oh yeah, we all were," Reader Bill said as he slammed his springboard into its notch. He leaned the crosscut saw against the tree and swung his ax blade deep into the bark where he could get to it later. Bill climbed up slowly on the skinny platform.

"But they were organized back in Butte. I don't think there's any kind of organization here for loggers, yet," Reader Bill said as he swung the crosscut saw handle over. Harry grabbed the handle in midair. They doused the blade with kerosene and started in on the bottom cut. The blade sliced into the old-growth fir, and they fell into a rhythm. Pulling the saw back and forth, Harry started to sing.

> "Oh Mr. Block, you were born by mistake
> You take the cake, you make me ache
> Tie a rock on your block and then jump in the lake
> Kindly do that for Liberty's sake."

"Hey, I think I heard that one before," Reader Bill commented.

"I learned it in Portland. I got lots of 'em," Harry said as he launched into another with enthusiasm. His young, strong voice boomed out through the forest as they pulled the saw to and fro.

"Long-haired preachers come out every night
Try to tell us what's wrong and what's right
But when asked how 'bout something to eat
They will answer with voices so sweet
You will eat, bye and bye
In that glorious land above the sky
Work and pray, live on hay
You'll get pie in the sky when you die."

"I know that song!" Reader Bill exclaimed, "That's a Joe Hill song, isn't it?"

"You know about Joe Hill?" Harry asked brightly.

"I read all about how the state of Utah killed him last year," Bill said. "Got shot through the heart by a bunch of cowards for a crime he didn't commit."

"So, you've heard about the *Little Red Songbook*?" Harry asked with a touch of apprehension.

"Yep, sure have."

"Then you know about the IWW?" Harry asked with a lowered voice.

"You mean the Wobblies?" Reader Bill asked.

"I mean the Industrial Workers of the World," Harry answered.

"Well, I got nothing against unions, son. But I know for a fact that old man MacCullock and Mr. Charlie would probably just as soon scare you up and shoot you, and that's including every single Wobbly on this here earth," Bill said, and then added, "You hear me, Harry?"

"Yeah. Okay. I get the point. But whatcha think of the IWW?" Harry inquired.

"Don't rightly know. But like I said, I got nothin' against unions."

"But if they was organized, you sayin' you'd join?"

"Whoa there, son. If you start organizing any kind of union 'round these parts Charlie will do exactly what I just told you."

"I'm just askin', Bill. Nothin' wrong with askin' is there?"

"Askin' me is OK, but don't be talking union round here with anyone but me, son."

"I hear ya," Harry Dolson said with a sour look on his face, "and it looks like we're about far enough with the bottom cut."

Reader Bill nodded in agreement and reached over for his ax to start chopping out the undercut. Harry did the same.

***

That Friday Dirty Shirt Frank donated what was left of his deer for a special dinner. Bull cook Tubs Donovan prepared a meal the likes of which the men hadn't seen in years; venison stew with potatoes, vegetables, and a thick hearty broth. Hungry men chowed down as Tubs walked between each table carrying a pot of hot, steaming stew that he ladled into bowls for lumberjacks who rapped the table with their knuckles and grunted at him when they wanted more.

"There ya go," Tubs said quietly as he poured a third helping into Frank's bowl. Jaako and Jorgen were sitting across the table. Jaako whispered, "Dat vas a fine deer you shot, Dirty Shirt. Tank you." Dirty Shirt nodded at Jaako and smiled. Life was worth living for a logger at that particular Timber Creek dinner.

Later in the bunkhouse most of the men were dog tired from the day and relaxing with full bellies while mice scurried along rafters. Men lay in their bunks making and adjusting figures in their pay time notepads as they expurgated stew-gas. Jorgen and Jaako whittled away in the back while Reader Bill sat on the deacon seat that ran along the side of the bunks with his nose in a book.

"What the hell ya readin' now?" Axel Chambers croaked from his bunk.

"*Call of the Wild*," he answered without looking up.

"Any good?"

"Yep."

Axel gazed at the ceiling with a far-off look in his eye and his hands behind his head, then he picked his nose and said, "You know, old Bill, I've always wondered why a guy as smart as you is workin' a stupid man's job out here in the sticks."

But Bill ignored Axel's comment and didn't look up.

"What's sa' matter, you think yer better 'n me?" Axel said with a raised voice. Reader Bill put down his book and stared at Axel across the room as Dirty Shirt jumped down from his bunk.

"I've heard just about enough out a' you, Axel," Dirty Shirt said.

"Why's that? You think yer better 'n me, too, eh?" Axel barked.

"Yer damn right we're better'n you, and older. An' I don't like you or your attitude. Never have."

"Why don't we step outside and settle this matter right now?" Axel shouted, sitting upright in his bunk, his eyes sparking.

"Axel, you are nothing but a barking, whining, low-down dog. And you best be minding your own business," Dirty Shirt shot back when Charlie Purvis walked in the door. He looked around the room and put his hands on his hips.

"What are you bunch a' rotten an' culled timber ants pissin' an' moanin' about now?" the camp push bellowed as the room went silent. "And where the hell is Jaako?"

"I is right here, boss," Jaako answered and stood up in the back of the bunk-house, a lap full of tiny wood chips spilling onto the floor.

"I want you settin' choke with Axel tomorrow and for a while longer. Tubs saw that good fer nothin' short stake I had workin' with him hoofin' it outta camp after dinner, so yer teamin' up with Axel until I get another choke setter, ya got that?"

"Yah, sure," Jaako answered. "But I still be gettin' me riggin' pay, yah?"

"Hell no, I ain't givin' ya yer rigging pay! Settin' choke at this show pays three dollars a day," Purvis piped, staring at Jaako.

"But I been vorking here too long to take a pay cut," Jaako complained.

"I ain't gonna listen to yer bellyachin', Jaako," Charlie snorted and then turned his focus to Axel. "THAT worthless scamp," Purvis said, pointing at the young choke setter, "needs someone out there to keep his sorry ass humpin' logs all day instead of slowin' down the log count."

"Aw, Charlie," Axel moaned, "I don't wanna be workin' with some stupid —"

"AXEL!" Charlie yelled, "You can shut yer chow hole or roll up yer bindle and hit the skids. What's it gonna be?" Axel kept quiet, so Charlie turned to the room.

"Now I want that log count up. You sumbitches been slackin' off all week, and we need to be high ballin' some timber in the morning. So lights out, ladies," Purvis arrogantly said. He turned the wick down on the lamp hanging from the rafters and tromped on out of the bunkhouse.

***

A barefooted, sinewy figure slowly floated along a forest trail like a ghost. Puffy night clouds moved under a crescent moon while tree frogs croaked in the background. With deep, quiet breaths, the silhouette took gentle measured steps, until it was behind a small building. A pocket knife carefully and quietly pried a board loose from the outside of the shack. One board was removed and then another, until there was enough room to wiggle inside. Two hands felt in the black until a pile of crates was located, one already open. Reaching inside, a handful of thin red tubes were snatched and placed in a gunny-sack. The hand reached for more, but hesitated when a night owl hooted, then it grabbed another handful. The figure rolled up the sack, crouched, and wiggled back out through the opening. Once outside, the dark shadow pulled a small rock wrapped in a piece of cloth out of a pocket. It folded over the cloth to muffle the sound and set the first board in place. The body gently tapped the nail with the rock against the cloth, and then did the others until everything was in place. The figure crept soundlessly back along the trail from whence it came.

***

Harry heard the sharp reverberation of clacking cork boots and the sound of that familiar voice working its way down the string of bunkhouses just before daybreak. He'd begun to memorize Charlie's different sayings, each one varied in pitch and whistle.

"Come on!" Charlie hollered, kicking in the bunkhouse door. "Get up, ya bunch of sleepin' beauties. Let's go. It's time you heathens start puttin' out some scale. We got logs ta' yard and a raft ta' fill, you sumbitches. Let's move it!"

Bleary-eyed, worn-out loggers slowly rose out of their bunks, pulled on tin pants and laced up cork boots. Axel Chambers rubbed his eyes and pulled himself out of his bunk, saying, "I swear that damn Purvis is gonna kill us all if'n we don't just kill ourselves out here bustin' our backs."

"Shut up, Axel," Dirty Shirt said. "We's all sick and tired of listenin' to yer bitchin' and belly-achin' every single damn day from hell to breakfast."

"No. Yer the one that can go to hell, Dirty Shirt!" Axel barked. Dirty Shirt snapped his head around with a scowl on his face but then grinned and changed his tone.

"Aw, jeez, Axel, I thought we was already in hell?" Dirty Shirt said as Charlie stormed back into the bunkhouse, hurriedly hitching his suspenders. He held a red pamphlet out in front of him with narrowed eyes and scanned the room.

"Who put this in the outhouse?" Purvis screamed, shaking the pamphlet then holding it higher. "Well, speak up. Who was it that tacked this thing up inside yer outhouse? Behind this fart palace!" The men glanced around the bunkhouse with nervous faces when a voice finally sounded.

"What is it?" Harry calmly asked from the deacon seat, shoving a foot into his cork boot.

"It's God-damned Wobbly crap! Now how the hell did it get up here?"

Reader Bill thought about the conversation he'd had with Harry earlier in the week. He scratched the side of his head and rubbed his chin saying, "There's no IWW up here, Charlie."

Purvis jerked his head around and stared at Bill with his hands on his hips.

"Bill's right," Dirty Shirt blurted out. "There ain't no Wobblies up here."

"Bull-shit," Charlie spat, waving the wrinkled, thin piece of paper, "I got the evidence right here."

"Aw, Charlie," Reader Bill replied. "It could have been anybody. Maybe it was that rigger you fired the other day or the choke setter that quit."

"Yeah," Harry agreed, "I bet it was that choke setter."

"Yep, it was probably that choke setter that high tailed it," Dirty Shirt added.

Charlie ripped the pamphlet in pieces and then opened the wood stove door. He tossed it all inside and turned back to the crew.

"You mean to tell me that thing has been in the outhouse behind this stink shack since then?" Purvis yelled.

"I saw it in there yesterday," Reader Bill said. "Just left it alone."

"Well, then, why didn't ya tell me?"

"Didn't think anything of it," Bill replied. Charlie started to shake his head.

"If I catch anyone up here with crap like that again," Purvis said, pointing an index finger at the stove, "I'll fix the sorry sumbitch fer good. Ya'll got that? Huh? You hear what I'm saying? 'Cause if I hear any kind-a damn union talk, 'er IWW talk up here I'll kill ya. Ya hear me. And that'll be after Luther MacCullock kilt ya. Now let's move it!" Charlie spun on his heel and tromped out of the bunkhouse to the mess hall.

Harry waited for the rest of the crew to leave and then followed Reader Bill towards the door, but the old logger stopped and closed the door halfway.

Bill turned around, tilted his head, and with the tightened jaw of a stern father said, "You better watch yourself, son, and don't be slipping up, ever, because I'm not gonna keep saving your bacon. Understand?"

Harry grinned, blinked, and nodded quickly, then he headed for the mess hall with his eyes looking straight ahead, not turning around.

Chapter 9

CITY OF FOG

O n some days the fog would already be there in the morning, on others it would creep in across the bay like a smoky delusion and filter through the streets, cutting off vision. Sometimes it would be a stagnant, hovering, grey-white ceiling of floating mist with a cushion of damp air underneath that buoyed the great mass of vapor directly overhead, turning the city streets into a series of long tunnels that men and horses trooped through like ghosts.

Then there was the hazy kind of mist that granted a small amount of vision. Or the kind of fog that lulled travelers into a dreamlike state of uncertainty, enveloping in a cloudy wall of white all who would venture out, causing many to lose their way but granting others the ability to hide misguided intentions.

During summer the fog would roll in with the tide overnight and then burn off with the rising sun. Some mornings it burned off quickly, while others it would take until the afternoon. Once the mist began to brighten the clouds would separate and then vaporize, leaving in their wake cool, clean salt air and skies of blue.

Invariably the fog in all of its forms was known to every citizen of western Washington. Moist and damp, grey or white, hovering and choking, hazy, misty, fog.

That morning the fog coming in off the bay was so thick it seemed like it was choking downtown Everett. It slowly worked its way around buildings and up the streets covering everything in its path, clinging to anything vertical and filling in shadows. The hazy vapor was so dense and smothering it was as if it had taken the heart out of the city, acting like a hovering embalming fluid of deception that hushed the city in a veil of nebulous, mummified repose.

Renny Niskanen walked alone through the blanket of smoky, white haze down Hewitt past Myers Photo Studio and the St. Croix Hotel towards the picket line when a low flying flock of seagulls passed over his head cawing and crying. The sound of horse hooves and a buggy whip echoed through the cloudy streets at the same time as a trolley car bell rang out. A curly haired man with a black, walrus-like mustache, swarthy complexion, and a hand-rolled cigarette in his mouth swept the sidewalk in front of Dino's Shoe Repair. Renny nodded to him as he strode by, the man nodded back a hello. Men in overalls were walking the same route as Renny when from around a corner up ahead came a band of Commercial Club deputies with white handkerchiefs around their necks and upper arms, gripping clubs and ax handles in their hands. They were marching right at Renny. His heart began to race as he crossed over to the other side of Hewitt, they did the same, following him. Renny stopped.

"You join the IWW Niskanen?" one vigilante growled as they surrounded him.

"No, I is only a member of the Shingle Weavers Union," he answered.

"You sure about that?" another citizen deputy grumbled.

"Yah. I is sure," Renny replied, staring at the man.

"That's a good boy-o. Cause if we ever catch you with a red card it'll be the worst day in your stinkin' life, and if we find you speakin' on that corner we've got a new ordinance that says you'll be thrown in jail. You got that?" the same watchdog barked. Renny nodded his head in agreement and they let him pass. As Renny continued down Hewitt, he wondered what new ordinance they were talking about.

Down by the railroad tracks he could hear the sheriff's unmistakable voice slice through the thick morning mist before he could see him. It sounded like McRae and his county deputies were in the process of pulling a few hoboes from a boxcar. Renny continued walking until he was close enough to see their silhouettes through the damp, salty haze. He stopped and then stepped behind a railroad storage shed to watch.

"God-dammit! What the hell are you bums doin' comin' to my town? Huh? I know you're not looking fer a job cause there's no work here, unless yer a scab!"

"We're just passin' through, mister. We ain't done nothin' wrong," a muffled voice replied.

"Yeah, yeah. I've heard it all before. Git yer good-fer-nothin' sorry asses out here right now 'er I'm gonna send in ma' troops," the sheriff piped. Three figures jumped down from the boxcar.

"Search 'em, boys," McRae ordered. He took a few steps to the side and watched as his men frisked the bums.

"Sheriff, I got something here," Deputy Irvan said as he held up a red booklet that he'd fished out of one of the hoboe's pockets. McRae walked over to his deputy.

"Good work, Walt. What've we got here? One of those, *Songbooks?*" the sheriff asked as he snatched it out of Irvan's hand and then flipped through the pages in front of the vagrant. He ripped some pages from the book and tossed it all behind him. The hobo said nothing, his head tilted towards the ground.

The sheriff briefly closed his eyes in concentration, put his hand on his blackjack, and then slowly drawled, "Ya'll . . . eye-dubya-dubya?"

"Yep," answered the tramp as he looked up, "we're all members of one big union ya dumb son of a —" Instantly the sheriff clubbed him, knocking the rod-rider off his feet, signaling his deputies into action. Deputy Irvan hit another in the jaw with an upward swing of his shotgun butt while the third drifter was clubbed to the ground by one of the other deputies.

"Cuff these gall damn Wobbly bastards to that switching post, Walt," the sheriff snarled. "We'll come back for 'em after we find some more," McRae ordered and then moved on down the line.

Staying on the bay side of the tracks, the sheriff pushed open another boxcar door and began banging his blackjack against the railcar floor, the hollow sound of the steel car pinging through the salt air. "All right, get outta there, ya worthless bums. Now!" the sheriff hollered.

Vhat is going on in Everett? Renny thought to himself as he watched the sheriff from his hiding place. He'd been beaten up before by the sheriff, but watching it happen to somebody else that he'd never seen before, someone who hadn't done anything wrong, felt worse. A wave of dread rushed through his system, he felt afraid for his town and his union. Then he felt afraid for Petra. *The sheriff might know where I live, he might go after Petra!* He told himself he should start locking the front door of the house every day, watching the violence shocked him, fear bolted through his body like a finger of lightning. Two other strikers walked up to Renny hiding behind the shed. They'd seen the beating.

"What's going on?" one of the men asked.

"I not sure," Renny replied, "but I think those fellows that the sheriff just beat and handcuffed are Vobblies."

"The Wobblies are here?" one of strikers asked.

"Yah. I think so," Renny replied.

"Are they here to walk the pickets?" the same man asked.

"Maybe they'll help us," the other striker said.

"I thought they might help, but I not so sure now. They might make things vorse," Renny said. He headed to the Northern Imperial with rising blood pressure and a reddened face.

At the picket line, Renny took charge. Grabbing a sign that read, "Shingle Weavers Union Strong," he hoisted it as high as he could and chanted.

"Vorkingmen unite!"

"Workingmen unite!"

"Say it again!"

"Workingmen unite!"

"Say it again!"

"Workingmen unite!"

***

Later in the afternoon, Deputy Jefferson Beard got back in his patrol car after another visit to Weiser's Café. He set his fifth cup of coffee on the dashboard, yawned, twisted in his seat to get comfortable, and then took a bite of doughnut.

A trolley car clattered by with its bell clanging as two boys walked past on the sidewalk with fishing poles leaned up against their shoulders.

"You catch anything?" Beard shouted from the cab.

"Couple of bullheads," one of them answered as they strolled along Hewitt.

"What-cha using?"

"Worms," the other said.

"And I had some bread crust," added the first over his shoulder.

"That always worked for me," the deputy replied knowingly.

A woman pushing a crying baby in a carriage came around the corner. She was in a hurry, with a package under her left arm she pushed the carriage with her right hand and shushed her child with every step. A businessman in a suit carrying a briefcase went by the woman, tipped his hat, and asked, "Can I give you a hand?" But the lady paid him no mind and continued on her way. Bored, the deputy took another sip of coffee and wished he was in the railroad yards with the other deputies rather than being stuck on some stake out when a lady in a black-and-green paneled Baker Electric car silently drove by and pulled into the parking lot of American Savings and Loan on the alley corner.

Ten minutes later a Model-T pulled in behind Spanjer's market. Beard hopped out of his car and quickly strolled over to get a look. Two men he didn't recognize got out and began to unload boxes. He watched them make a few trips down the stairs. When they were done, he pinned his badge under his vest, slowly walked down the alley, glanced around, went down the stairs to a wide open door, and stepped inside.

There were single lightbulbs hanging from the ceiling and two massive twelve by sixteen rough-cut old growth fir beams ran the length of the basement supporting the floor system of Spanjer's store above. The customer's muffled footsteps on the creaky wooden floors could be heard overhead. There were brick and timber post walls and two window wells cast a small amount of light into the room, dust hung in the air from a freshly swept rough cement floor.

"Afternoon," a man with a sparse black beard wearing overalls and IWW pins said.

"Howdy," Beard replied.

"How can we, uh, help you?" the same man asked, rubbing the side of his head.

"Oh," Beard said, stroking his mustache, "I saw the sign outside and was wondering if we got a new union in town."

"Are you a workingman?" the other man dressed in trousers and a work shirt asked.

Beard hesitated, and then answered, "Oh yeah, all my life."

"What kind a' work?" the bearded one asked. Deputy Beard thought about the question.

"Oh, farm work mostly . . . drove truck, too," Beard replied.

"Well, you want to be a member of one big union?"

"What union's that?"

"Why, the biggest and best union there is. The Industrial Workers of the World," the other man proudly said, tacking posters up on a support timber. One showed an IWW dagger stabbing a capitalist octopus gripping union men in its tentacles. Beard glanced at it and then stepped over to read a flyer about James Thompson speaking in Everett. It was all he needed to see.

"We welcome all workers in our union," the one in overalls said as he put up another poster and then asked, "How 'bout a copy of our newspaper?"

Beard thought for a moment and said with a grin, "Yeah, sure I would."

"Here ya go," the other man said as he handed Beard an issue of the *Industrial Worker*. "Dues are only a dollar a month. Wanna join up?"

"I'll think about it," the deputy said with a smirk on his face. He turned around, walked out, and headed straight to the county jailhouse.

***

That evening as Renny approached Market Street, a few boys were at the fence in front of Lafayette House.

"I told you not to hang around here," Renny said. "This is no place for kids."

"Aw, we ain't doin' nothin' wrong," one of the curious boys replied.

"Is supper time. Now go," Renny snipped and motioned with an arm, they walked away.

Renny climbed the porch stairs and felt the weight of the world on his shoulders. The strike was going nowhere, the union was running out of picket line pay, and the garden Petra had planted in the spring was depleted. He kicked off his boots on the porch, opened the door, walked back to the kitchen and dropped down on a chair at the table with a thud. Then he noticed the backdoor was wide open. *Vhat is the —?*

"Petra! Vhere are you?" Renny hollered, fearing the worst.

"I is out here," she answered, "in the garden."

Relieved to hear his wife's voice, Renny poured himself a glass of water and went outside. Petra was on her knees with a stick in her hand, plying the ground, searching for the last of the potatoes.

"The landlord came by today," she said, not looking up.

"Vhat did you do?" Renny asked.

"Hid in the closet."

"Good."

"But he vill be back and . . . I don't like hiding from him," Petra said, her voice quavering.

"I know," Renny replied dejectedly.

Petra wiped her brow. She glanced up to her husband and then turned back to her task and asked, "Vhat are ve going to do, Renny?"

"Vhat *can* ve do?" he replied.

"Go to Seattle and find vork."

"No, Petra. Ve already talk about this."

"But ve are starving, ve only have a few turnips left, and I'm not finding any potatoes."

"Everett is our home. Ve are not leaving. Ve have to hold on," Renny said firmly. He took a long drink and exhaled. "Today I saw the sheriff beating up some men that did not do anything vrong. And there are groups of mean men patrolling the streets vith clubs. Things are going on I worried about." Then he softened his voice and added, "But ve just need to vatch out, and be careful and try to stay safe. I think ve need to start locking the front door every day."

"Vaht!" Petra exclaimed. "Now you are going to keep me locked up!"

"I need to know that you are safe," Renny said. Petra turned back to her task. She changed her grip on the stick and held it like a knife, then began stabbing the ground with hard quick thrusts.

After a silent dinner Renny climbed the stairs and fell on the bed. He was asleep in no time. An hour later Petra lay down next to her snoring husband but could not rest. Tears filled her eyes, and a layer of fear covered her trembling body like never before. She thought, *there is no money, no food, and no jobs. Now I am stuck behind a locked door every day. America is not so great.* After tossing and turning for an hour she got up, went downstairs, put on her coat, and slipped out the backdoor.

The night sky still had a touch of the sunset in it and the air was motionless. She quietly walked up the alley, turned west at Twenty-Sixth and crossed Market Street. Petra walked down the next alley until she was at the tall fence. For a split second she thought about how Renny would probably scold her again, but she didn't care anymore, she was starving. Petra pulled on the one board that she remembered always being loose, but it wouldn't budge. She pulled harder and it broke with a crack. Petra stopped and looked around. All was silent save for the pangs of hunger that pitched inside of her. Setting the two pieces down as quietly as possible she got down on her knees and reached into the straw. Searching blindly with her fingers, she dug deeper and farther until she found a straw-covered overlooked egg from earlier in the day. A smile swept over her face when all of a sudden a vise-like grip clamped down on her arm.

"All right, ya little thief! I gots ya!" It was Harvey Keel, the bordello bodyguard.

Petra jerked her hand back as hard as she could. The egg broke between her fingers and she yelled, "Let go!"

"Not a chance, ya damn filch!" Harvey stood her up with a jerk, kicked out two more boards, and pulled her through the opening in the large coop that was built against the fence.

"Let me go!" Petra screamed again and kicked, trying to free herself. Harvey spun her around with a quick flip of his massive arms and bear-hugged her from behind. In a flash he picked her up and headed for the back stairs while she kicked her legs in a frenzy.

"Your chickens vill get out!" she yelled at Harvey.

"No, they won't. They're roostin'," he bellowed with a laugh as he climbed the bawdy house stairs holding her at his side with one arm. Goldie Lafayette and Cora greeted them at the backdoor.

"Well, well, well. I do declare, look at this. What have we got here?" Goldie asked with a hearty southern voice as she opened the door to let them in.

"I do believe we got us an egg robber," Harvey chuckled as he set her down and pointed at a chair. Goldie closed the door and looked at the young woman.

"You got a name, little miss egg robber?" Cora asked coldly.

"Cora, let me handle this," Goldie chirped then added, "Go head hun, sit down. We ain't gonna hurt ya." Petra looked behind herself for the chair and sat down. Goldie crossed her arms and looked at the young, petite lady with long straight blonde hair in her kitchen.

"Well, child. Have ya a got a name?" Goldie asked calmly.

"Petra," she replied quietly.

"Okay. Petra who?" Goldie said.

"Petra Niskanen, that's who."

"Where do you live, Petra?"

"On Summit Street."

"How come you're stealing my eggs?" Goldie asked. But Petra just stared at the floor. Goldie looked Petra over, and thought about what she should do when a wave of womanly benevolence moved through her system.

"You're starving, aren't ya?" Goldie said.

"Yah, ve have no food," Petra replied as she raised her eyes to the madam.

"Your husband out of work?"

"Yah, he is on strike."

"OK, well. Harvey, what should we do with her?" Goldie inquired.

"Can't rightly say, Miss Lafayette."

Goldie put one hand on her chin and thought for a moment then offered, "You want a job?"

"Doing vhat?" Petra asked as she fidgeted with her fingers.

"Well," Goldie said and laughed, "What is it you think we do here?"

"I know vhat you do here," Petra answered curtly. "But I am married."

"Oh, honey, you just told me ya had a man." Goldie smiled and looked at Petra some more. "I don't mean to pry and all. I guess I just can't help myself sometimes, I swear. But darlin', do ya still love him?"

A warm tingle went up Petra's spine. She'd never been asked a question like that before and was surprised that Goldie took an interest in her. She didn't know what to say at first and then replied, "I not sure anymore, yah, I guess."

"Oh, child. I understand. Where ya'll from?" Goldie asked with a warm voice and soft eyes.

"I am from Finland."

"Were ya married when you came here?"

"Yah."

"And now you're not sure if you love yer husband, so much?"

"He thinks he needs to protect me, so he is locking me in the house, making me stay home all day. I have no friends."

"Fer criminy sakes, gal. That's not much of a life. But you came to America with him?" Goldie asked.

Petra looked at Goldie with sad eyes and said the words she had never said before.

"He vas the only vay out. I had to leave, and, I vas in love. Vell, I thought I vas in love."

"Oh, honey. I'm sorry," Goldie replied. "But you're still married," the madam said encouragingly. "Maybe you'll love him again, someday?"

"Yah, maybe, someday," Petra answered quietly. "America not vhat I thought it vould be."

"Yeah, well, honey-child. Ain't that a fact," Goldie said exasperated. "I guess America's about the same for all of us, really. But it's pretty darn good when you got the money!" Goldie said as she threw back her head and laughed. Cora nodded her head yes and Harvey grinned.

"Oh, child, most of my girls were just like you at the start. Married an' unhappy, 'er broke an' starvin'," Goldie said with a southern drawl and continued, "and I just lost a few gals to The Club in Tacoma. They thought they'd go 'n strike it rich in the big city." Goldie looked Petra up and down for a moment.

"Seems you've got a nice little figure, and I know you could use the money from the looks of ya. I'll tell ya what. You can have Dolly's old room if you'd like."

Petra stopped working her hands for a moment and began to take in her surroundings. Goldie stepped over to the counter and leaned against it with her arms crossed. She stared at Petra and waited for an answer. Petra gazed around the room.

Polished hardwood kitchen flooring, fresh flowers on the table, brightly painted fancy cabinetry with stained glass in every door, the biggest icebox she'd ever seen, a cook-stove that didn't have a firebox, colorful wallpaper, and the sweet smell of pine-scented candles. A smile slowly began to form on Petra's face as the pangs of hunger rumbled inside her.

Since they'd been married, Renny and she had been trying to have kids without luck, so she figured the chances of her getting pregnant were nonexistent. Her smile grew.

"How much vould I be paid?" Petra asked.

"The same as all the other girls. Two-fifty a roll. I charge the boys five and keep half for expenses. Whatcha say?"

Petra thought about her financial situation and Renny home asleep. It didn't take long for her to decide, she nervously nodded her head. "Yah, I do it. But I can only vork daytime. I don't vant my husband to know. He can never know."

"Very good then. We have a pretty good-sized lunch crowd. How about if you come by tomorrow 'bout ten in the morning?"

"Yah, but —"

"But what, child?"

"Could I have another egg?"

"Oh, sweetie, sit down and let me fix you a mess a' vittles," Goldie said with a comforting smile, the likes of which Petra hadn't seen in a long time.

Thirty minutes later, Petra opened and closed the backdoor of the house as quietly as possible. She took off her coat and sneaked upstairs. Renny was fast asleep. She slipped under the covers and luckily didn't wake him. The meal Goldie had served her was still warm in her stomach. Petra fell into a deep sleep in no time.

In the morning, Renny leaned over to give his wife a good morning kiss on the forehead, got dressed, and went to the picket line. An hour later Petra got up.

She put on her only dress, a flowered print affair that she'd brought from Finland, did her hair with trembling fingers, and stepped out of the back door wearing the same coat she'd worn the night before. Petra took her usual route up the alley, but this time she moved from fence to fence and barn to barn trying to make sure that no one saw her. She scurried across Market Street at Twenty-Sixth and then down the alley. Halfway there she turned her coat collar up and buried her head in it. Harvey was fixing the fence.

"You can use the gate now," he said and motioned to its location, a brown derby hat was titled on his head and a half smoked unlit cigar in his mouth. Goldie saw her from the kitchen window with her head down, she opened the back door.

"Why, there's my new gal. How are ya today?" Goldie asked with a happy smile from the porch. "Kind of nervous, I bet?"

"Yah," Petra answered into the coat as she climbed the stairs.

"Well, don't you worry 'bout a thing, hun. I'm not gonna put ya on yer back today," Goldie said as Petra looked up and smiled.

A few women sat at the kitchen table. When Petra saw them, she blushed and nodded her head hello.

"Ladies," Goldie said, "this here is Petra, and today is her first day. This is Cora, Lottie, Angel, Pearl, and Roxie. Girls, let's give Petra a warm welcome to our little establishment and make her feel at home."

The girls uttered greetings at the same time and went back to their breakfast. Each one was dressed in a frilly sleeping gown, her hair pulled back.

"Let me show you around," Goldie said. "Today I'm gonna give you a dollar to just answer the door. But how about if we find ya some decent clothes for starters?"

"That vould be fine," Petra said as the madam motioned to follow.

Velvet furniture rested on Persian rugs in the living room. Purple wingback chairs sat in front of an enormous brick fireplace, above which hung a large painting of what looked like a much younger Miss Lafayette. She was naked and reclined sideways on a velvet day-bed, adorned in jewelry, her long auburn hair swept up in a bun. A tiffany lamp was in the center of a large dining room table. A piano with a fiddle on it was in the corner turret room, and a bedroom was off the front entry. Goldie stopped.

"This is Harvey's room," she said as she tapped the door. "He's the house bouncer and bodyguard, and if you ever have any trouble with a john then you just let Harvey know," Goldie said. Petra had a funny look on her face.

"Are all the men name John?" she asked.

Goldie let out a hearty laugh and said, "No, child, *john* is just what we like to refer to the customers as. Now mind you, though, Harvey might look big and mean, and he is all right, don't get me wrong. But he's all soft and cuddly on the inside an' if you ever have a problem, he'll come a running. Let's go upstairs."

A red-carpeted grand staircase climbed to a landing, where the stairs turned. Along the stairway wall hung paintings of New Orleans, stern-wheelers, horses racing on a track with a grandstand in the background, and a picture of Goldie sitting in a chair with a gray-haired man standing in a white suit holding a book against his chest like a preacher. She was sitting cross-legged in a fancy dress with layers of petticoats and high-heeled leather lace-up boots, her hair was done Gibson girl style. The old man wore a black string tie, and his hair was long, he looked distinguished and fatherly.

Down the hall were multiple bed and bathrooms. Petra glanced into every one as they walked by with a child-like look of astonishment on her face. The hallway turned and she saw more rooms. Goldie opened the door to the last one and stepped inside.

"Well, this one's yours hun," Goldie said with a sweeping movement of her arm.

A four poster bed with a frilly white tester was up against one wall. Next to it was a yellow and brown changing screen with clothes and feather boas draped over it. A pedestal sink with a large mirror was across the way next to a roll-top desk, and a walk-in closet held more dresses and clothes than Petra had ever seen.

"Is this my room?" she asked.

"Yes, child. It was Dolly's before, but those are house clothes and free to use here. I'll have one of the girls come up and help you with your hair. Pick out something to wear. I've got to go down and get ready for the day."

As soon as Goldie walked out of the room, Petra went over to the window, pulled back the curtains and looked outside. Not seeing anyone she walked over and sat down on the feather bed, then gazed up at the tester. Petra wondered if she was doing the right thing, when there was a knock.

"Hello in there. Hi, I'm Pearl," the lady said from the door. "Well, really my name's Sarah. Goldie gives us all made-up names to protect us and all. She'll give you a new name, too. Probably today sometime. I bet she's dreamin' one up right now for ya."

"Could I make up a name?" Petra asked.

"Maybe, if she likes what ya come up with. Here, let's pick something out," Pearl said as she grabbed Petra's hand and led her over to the closet. "Miss Goldie asked me to help teach ya a few quick things."

"Like vhat?" Petra asked as she took down a frilly corset and held it up to her body then hung it back up saying quietly, "I already know about sex."

"Well, sure ya do. But this ain't just about sex. Its work, and if you're lookin' fer love, baby doll, then this ain't the place. Now, if'n you want to make money, then that means repeat customers, and if you want lots of business and men askin' fer ya, then, well, you'll just have to act like it's yer first time every time. You understand, child?" Pearl asked with a warm tone. Petra blushed and looked away, then nodded her head up and down.

"I know yer only gonna answer the door today, but, we always try to call the men by their first names, and if they don't tell ya their name then just call 'em john. We never know their last names and some of their first names are probably phony anyway. But ya always wanna get their money first."

"Yah, I vill get the money," Petra said, and then asked, "but vere do I put it?"

"Lock it in the desk drawer. The key is already in it. That long chain the key is on is so ya can hang it around yer neck," Pearl said. Petra pulled down a red and black dress, stood in front of the mirror and held it up to herself.

"I like this one," she said with a smile.

"Looks like it's your size. Try it on."

Petra went behind the changing screen. It fit perfectly. Stepping out, she modeled it for Pearl, holding the skirt out to the side and turning round.

"My, oh, my," Pearl said with a smile. "Don't you just look like a man's dream come true? Now sit here in front of the mirror, and let me do yer hair."

Petra had never been treated with such care in all her life. When Pearl began to brush her hair, Petra felt a tingle go up her spine, and her insides danced with excitement. She felt all warm and fuzzy. She began to think about what she might be called, and the name Dessa drifted into her mind.

***

Down on the waterfront, Renny walked the picket line as he led his dwindling group of strikers in a cycle of chants barely audible over the noise of the Northern Imperial.

"Stand up to the bosses!"

"Say it again!"

"Stand up to the bosses!"

"Say it again!"

"Stand up to the bosses!"

"Direct action beat in-action!"

"Direct action beats inaction!"

"Say it again!"

"Direct action beats inaction."

After marching and chanting all morning, some of the men set down their signs and decided to take a break while black smoke belched from the mill's boilers and scrap-wood incinerators.

"I knew it was stupid to strike. MacCullock's got all the money and his mill is still pumping out lumber and shingles. This is pointless. We're not getting anywhere," a disgruntled, unwashed striker protested.

"MacCullock will just wait us out. He's got nothing to lose," Hank Hillstrom chimed in.

"He's still makin' money while we starve," another striker said.

"Hey, Renny, you ever check on getting us some clinic 'er doctor visits?" Fred McCorkel asked.

"Yah, I ask Jake. But he say not to hold our breath," Renny answered.

"Figures," McCorkel replied.

"We need to take MacCullock's offer of the old wage," one more suggested.

"Maybe we should."

"Yeah. I'll work for the old wage."

"So will I."

"Me too."

"Not me. MacCullock owes us. I wanna raise," one striker argued.

"Whatcha think, Renny?" another asked.

"Yah, vell, I vill ask Jake if ve should do a vote for fifty cents an hour," the shop steward replied.

The Northern Imperial hummed with the sound of saws, steam pistons, fresh logs hitting the saw carriage, and pulley belts running machinery. Outside, the tugboat was pulling another raft of logs from Timber Creek into the salt chuck.

At his shingle bolt station, Tompall Tharp was waging the daily battle with two spinning steel discs of razor-sharp teeth. The automatic steam-driven carriage quickly slid back and forth as the saw blade cut a shingle every second. If he had to cut out a knot or trim it square he'd place it flat on the hinged table in front of him and push down for the trimmer saw to correct the imperfection. Once finished, he'd toss the shingle down the chute to the shingle weaver below, where it was packaged and shipped.

With his eyes and ears wide open, Tompall watched and listened for the time the gleaming teeth told him to reach for the freshly cut shingle or set a new block in the carriage. For hour after hour cedar sawdust spewed from the line of shingle sawyers. Reaching back and forth between whirling saw blades, his arms, fingers, and body in nonstop motion, Tompall engaged in a constant battle with his machine.

He breathed through the water-soaked sponge tied over his mouth until it was covered in sawdust. With a quick swipe across his face, Tompall barely cleared his sponge in between coughs while catching a new shingle every second.

In the middle of a movement pattern, he coughed again. He lost his balance and his right foot slipped on the sawdust covered floor. As he started to fall his left foot came off the clutch pedal but the blade on the old machine kept spinning, his hand hit the exposed spinning razor sharp saw.

Tompall screamed as three fingers from his left hand fell to the floor, covered in sawdust and blood.

"Yeeow!" he yelled, but the sponge over his mouth muffed his voice and the machinery was too loud. Tompall clutched the injury tight as blood spewed from his hand. Dizzy from shock, he rolled over, quickly picked up the severed appendages, and put them in his shirt pocket with his right hand. Then he ripped the sponge from his face and puked on the red-dotted sawdust pile. Tompall pulled himself to his feet with his head reeling, the sawyers on each side of him finally leaped from their stations, they slung Tompall's arms over their shoulders, and staggered down the stairs to the main floor. Butch Barnell was walking his rounds and saw them, he came running up.

"Somebody get the safety kit and stretcher!" Barnell yelled at a few close-by men, "I'll go fire up the truck." Two men ran into the time keeper's office while another had Tompall lie down. A crowd of workers quickly formed around him.

"What happened?" one man asked.

"Sliced off some fingers," another answered as Tompall tried to catch his breath, his mouth and face covered in sawdust and puke.

"Are yer fingers still up there?" another man asked.

"Pocket," Tompall gasped, barely conscious, and shifted his eyes towards his bloody shirt.

"Get out of the way!" the man with the stretcher yelled as he set it down beside Tompall. Another ran up with the kit. He opened it and found a bottle of iodine and some bandages. But the glass container was empty.

"Damn this place," the man with the kit yelled as he threw the bottle at MacCullock's upper-level office.

"Get him on the stretcher," another one ordered just as Tompall passed out.

Outside Renny and his strikers watched as Butch Barnell ran from the mill and jumped into the company truck. He backed it up to the main entrance and hopped out of the cab.

"Buck!" Barnell hollered over his shoulder as he ran back towards the mill, "Open the gate. Got an injury," Mullaney pulled out the keys from his pocket and unlocked the gate as the other guards fanned out.

"Get back, you worthless quitters. We've got a real man hurt!" Buck Mullaney hollered. Renny and the picketers stood off to the side and waited.

"You and you and you," Butch said to three of his workers inside, "help me pick him up and carry him out to the truck." Each man grabbed a handle and lifted Tompall on the stretcher. As they carried him out the other workers in the mill began to yell.

"These saws need to be covered!"

"They need to be replaced!"

"All this machinery is junk!"

"This place is a piece of shit!"

"Shut up! Get back to work," Barnell barked.

"Why? So we can lose our fingers too?"

"Damn it. I said get back to work!" Butch ordered as they carried Tompall out to the truck. As soon as Renny and his strikers saw the worker being loaded they started up with calls of their own.

"What'd ya do? Kill the guy?" one striker yelled.

"We always had to go to the clinic on our own!"

"Yeah! What's with the special scab treatment?"

But the mill manager ignored them as he loaded Tompall on the flatbed and sped away.

***

Luther MacCullock was watching the commotion from his office window across the tracks when he heard a knock on his private door.

"Who is it?" MacCullock asked.

"We're here from St. Paul," said a voice from outside. Luther grinned, unlocked the door, and cracked it open. Two men stood on the landing.

"Are you Luther MacCullock?" one of the men asked. Both were dressed in black overcoats and suits.

"Yes, I'm Luther MacCullock," he replied as he opened the door wider.

"I'm Robert Claymore and this is my associate, Feeney Bradford," Claymore said as he reached out to shake hands. MacCullock shook his hand and then Bradford's.

"Welcome to Everett, gentlemen," Luther MacCullock said with a smile and stepped back from the doorway. "Please come in and have a seat. I hope you didn't mind coming in the back way?" he said, making a gesture to the chairs in front of his desk.

"You were very explicit in your letter about the stairs and private entrance," Claymore replied, sitting down.

"How was the trip?" MacCullock asked from behind his desk.

"Very good," Claymore answered.

"Just fine," Bradford said.

"Should I call you Robert, or Bob?" MacCullock asked.

"Call me Claymore," the first man said bluntly. Luther's eyes narrowed momentarily and his jaw tightened. He stared at Claymore, then he looked at the other man.

"And Mr. Bradford?"

"Feeney's fine," the second said with a slight grin.

Both were middle-aged and of medium height. Claymore had a dark beard and darker eyes. Feeney had a pushed-together face, full of lines and puffy, with a handlebar mustache. Claymore wore a black bowler hat, Feeney a homburg with trim. Claymore appeared to have a scar under his beard, and his face was marked from smallpox.

"Gentlemen," MacCullock began as he lit his pipe, "I've been a responsible and respected businessman here for the last twenty years, and I've done more good in this town than anyone here even knows. I have one of the biggest independent combination mills on the waterfront, and I plan to keep it that way," MacCullock boasted, rocking back and forth in his squeaky chair.

"Now, as I said in my letters and on the phone, I have labor troubles here. I've got a good and fearless sheriff, but he used to be a union officer with the Shingle Weavers and the head shingle inspector for the whole county before he ran for office. So I'm a bit leery of his ability to rein in his old union friends, you see. He's a good man, mind you, a fine sporting man, and I like him. He's taking orders now just fine, but when it really comes down to it, when those Wobbly bastards throw into a fight and bring out the bombs and the union starts their rallies and so on and so forth, I don't know if I can trust him. Sure, he swears up and down that he's with us, and he's as tough as they come, but sometimes I wonder if he'll cave in and lose his nerve," MacCullock said warily. "So I'd like you to keep an eye on him, maybe even keep him out of his own way. In fact, now that I think about it, you should try and make sure he doesn't do himself in, if you know what I mean."

"Yes," Claymore answered, "I think so. You mean he might not recognize the signs of an ambush that we might see coming, or know about, when he doesn't. Is that right?"

"Exactly," MacCullock replied. "He's a good man. I got him elected. But he started drinking when the IWW showed up and now he's drinking far too much. In his current condition he could stumble into anything." Both men nodded their heads as they listened. MacCullock continued.

"The police chief has been instructed for the most part to let the sheriff handle our union difficulties. The goal here, gentlemen, is to break this strike and get the Shingle Weavers Union back to work on my terms, at a reasonable wage, you see. This mess has been going on since May and here it is September already. Not only that, but now I've got hundreds of these Wobbly bums coming to town like ants at a picnic," MacCullock said as he blew a stream of pipe smoke out from the side of his mouth. "And I am going to put a stop to that!"

"I want one of you in Seattle and the other one here. I don't care who's where. I need both of you to do whatever you have to do to get this striker over. I want you both to watch everything, report everything, interfere whenever possible, and try to sabotage their movements from within the Shingle Weavers and the Wobblies. Do you understand?" MacCullock asked, staring at Claymore.

"Yes, sir. We've broken strikes before," Claymore answered.

"We can handle it," Bradford said.

"You see, I don't care about your tactics as long as you keep things quiet. I just want you men to break the back of this strike, and I don't give a damn how you do it. Now I've got you both set up with one room in Seattle at Second and Pike and another at the Everett Hotel over in the Riverside District and, I can arrange the use of a vehicle for the one of you that stays here. "

"I'll stay here," Claymore quickly replied. "But if I determine that transportation is needed, I'll deal with that on my own, thank you though."

"Very well, Mr. Claymore," MacCullock said, then he looked at Bradford.

"Seattle's fine with me, sir," Feeney added.

"OK, good," MacCullock said, handing both men a slip of paper. "Here's my private number. I understand that you're both former Pinkerton's and with your own agency now, but I expect professional work. And, I don't want either of you to receive any outside input. You take your orders from me. Also, I would like to be informed about the things you're doing or might do. Feeney, I'd like you to stake out the IWW hall in Seattle and then report to me daily by phone. That goes for both of you. I mailed your first month's pay a few weeks ago. Did you get the check?" MacCullock asked.

"Yes, we've been paid for now," Claymore answered.

"Very good. You do understand that this will be the only time we meet," MacCullock stated as he stood up to end the meeting. Then the phone rang.

"Excuse me, gentlemen, let me get this before you go," MacCullock said. He sat down, picked up the receiver, and gripped the phone with his left hand then rocked back in his chair.

"Yes?" he said into the receiver.

"Captain, it's the sheriff," the voice answered back.

"Yes?" MacCullock replied.

"Deputy Beard went into that new union hall I told you about."

"So is it IWW?" MacCullock asked.

"Yep, sure is."

"We can't allow them here, never," MacCullock snorted. "If they get a toe-hold here with any kind of a headquarters to operate out of there's no telling what'll happen. Now I want you to go over there and shut that place down. Clear them out!"

"Okay, I'll do it. But don't —"

"But don't what?" MacCullock snapped, his left hand gripping the phone tighter.

"Listen, Luther, I'll do it," the sheriff said. "I'll keep fightin' yer war for ya but don't forget that we still have an agreement."

"Dammit," Luther said firmly, "our agreement stands. You said you'd be able to handle things, not to mention that the whole town is depending on you. So you need to take care of this Wobbly hall. Now!"

"All right. But what about that federal mediator?"

"Hold on a minute," MacCullock said and covered the receiver. He asked his detectives in a lowered voice, "Do you know the status of the federal mediator that's been here?"

Claymore grinned and quietly said, "We just phoned St. Paul on that. He'll be gone in the morning."

MacCullock uncovered the phone and said, "I believe he'll be on the train tomorrow."

"Good," the sheriff grunted. "I'll take care of them after he leaves."

Luther MacCullock hung up, relit his pipe, and turned to his investigators.

"Thank you, gentlemen. That's good work already done. Now, as you just heard, that was Sheriff Donald McRae. Apparently the IWW has established a union hall here and he's agreed to close the place down," Luther said as the two sleuths glanced at each other.

"So like I said earlier, let's keep an eye on him. If he runs into trouble eliminating this Wobbly place then I would guess that we will eventually need you, Mr. Claymore, to assist and quite possibly, intervene," MacCullock said as he pointed the end of his pipe at the detective.

"I'll take care of it, sir," Claymore replied.

"That's the spirit," MacCullock said. He continued after a short pause, "You men look like a couple of straight shooters. But if you have to shoot around some corners to get things done, then that's fine by me."

"I guess it's time to go to work," Bradford said as they stood up.

"Very well then, gentlemen. We'll talk again soon," the mill owner said as he showed the two detectives the door. They headed down the stairs and disappeared into the alleyway shadows.

Chapter 10

LOCAL 248

Dark clouds laden with moisture streamed past smokestacks and around downtown buildings as if they knew where they were going. Soon bullet-like rain pounded every mill and every striker walking the pickets. A spiteful wind picked up and forced rain sideways onto the sidewalks until the gutters of Hewitt overflowed with so much brown water and debris that a respectable citizen could hope that the city's iniquities were being scrubbed clean and swept away.

It was a good old-fashioned gully washer that old-timers loved to embellish. Finally, the rain stopped and the sky began to lighten, but even then the storm clouds seemed to hang around. They shape-shifted into long, flat, low-slung grey sky-shutters that could still darken the outlook of any out-of-work striker. The black smoke that poured out of every lumber mill on the waterfront painted dark stains on the sky's canvas that reminded every man on the picket line that they were losing the battle.

In the jailhouse alley Sheriff McRae opened the back door of his roadster patrol car, Champion Tom hopped in. He slammed the door then unlocked the rear compartment, found the jug of whiskey and got behind the wheel. He turned west on Hewitt, making his daily rounds when Champion yawned from the back seat, belching foul dog breath into the cab.

"Jesus, Tom," McRae said, waving a hand in the air. Two men he'd never seen before were walking towards the waterfront, one was carrying a leather suitcase. He slowed down to look at them, at first with suspicion, but then changed his mind once he saw they were dressed as businessmen. Champion stunk up the cab again.

"For criminy sakes," the sheriff quipped, turning his head to Tom. "I'm gonna have ta' quit feedin' you table scraps."

At the bottom of bayside Hewitt the sheriff turned left on Bond Street and parked in front of the Great Northern train station. Black coal smoke poured out of the city's power plant smokestack directly to the south at the mouth of Forgotten Gulch. He turned around, gave his setter dog a quick scratch behind the ear, and then got out of the patrol car.

He strolled into the large mission-style building with its tall stucco tower and red tile roof. It was the main hub of land-based comings and goings for Everett, and buzzed with activity. People were in line to buy tickets, over-worked baggage handlers pushed rattling carts loaded with travel cases, some of them neat, well-stitched leather valises, but most of them rough and lumpy, bound in brown paper tied with twine. Ticket agents announced arrivals and departures. Travelers sat in pew-like benches as train whistles sounded above it all.

A bulletin board covered with notices and ads was on the far wall. Above it was a massive painting of northwestern Montana mountain peaks and wilderness. McRae wandered over to the board, where he saw two new IWW posters tacked up. One showed a black-and-red cat's face with white lettering that read: "General Strike." The other was a black-and-white drawing of an IWW union member in a work shirt, his muscular arms crossed, and saying: "I Will Win." The sheriff pulled both down, ripped them apart, and threw the pieces in a nearby garbage can when the same two men in suits walked through the entry. The one with the suitcase went over to the ticket line while the other sat down.

The sheriff stepped outside to check on his dog and the patrol car as the trolley rolled up. He recognized the short, overweight, blush-faced federal mediator getting up from a window seat. The man wore a stovepipe hat, a pressed suit with a stiff white collared shirt and ascot tie. He balanced a cane loosely between flabby fingers.

The portly chap steadied himself with his ivory-handled cane and stepped carefully from the trolley. He beckoned to a baggage handler with a free hand and asked, "Could you take these to the east bound gate?" The handler tipped his hat as the smartly dressed mediator dropped a few coins in the opened palm of his hand. The sheriff touched the brim of his Stetson and nodded as the man trundled by, huffing and puffing.

McRae followed the mediator into the building and went over to the bayside window that offered a view of the harbor and rail yard. The sun was beginning to break through the clouds, and a group of men in overalls were walking the tracks with gunny-sacks slung over their shoulders headed towards the Northern Imperial picket line. He placed them in his memory and then turned to watch the mediator, who was chatting with a fellow traveler. The sheriff casually walked over near them to eaves-drop.

"Looks like the weather's gonna let up," the traveler said.

"Yes, indeed, lots of rain this morning," the mediator replied, leaning on his cane.

"Where ya headed?"

"Chicago."

"That's a long ways away. What's the weather like there?"

"Cooling down I suppose. I'm going to miss your mild weather, but not the rain."

"Oh, I guess we're all used to the wet stuff out here."

"How about you? Where you going?" the mediator asked.

"To get a job, I hope," the traveler said with a smile. "Been walkin' the pickets all summer on the 14th Street dock but I'm done. Headed south, Tacoma. Got a job interview with the port."

"Well, I guess you're a lucky man, with the job interview I mean," the mediator replied.

"Oh, hell. Those damn, rich lumbermen. This strike is lost as far as I'm concerned," the former mill worker said.

"Yes, well. I've been here trying to reach a solution and it doesn't seem like either side is about to budge," the labor negotiator said. Then the east-bound train whistle blew. "Oh, that's me. Nice talking with you but I've got a train to catch." The well-dressed mediator touched the brim of his top hat, tipped his head, and ambled away, followed by a baggage handler.

Watching the mediator step aboard the train, the sheriff grinned, turned around, and headed to the patrol car.

Wiping the residue of whiskey from his chin and lips McRae backed out of his parking place and drove up Hewitt. Along the way to the jailhouse he decided to go by Spanjer's basement room to check if any Wobblies were there. Once across Colby he turned into the alley behind the market. The door under the Local 248 sign was closed. He stopped and let the engine idle for a moment, then hopped out of the car, went down the stairs, and checked the knob. It was locked, so he went back up the stairs. Stepping away from the building he put his hands on his hips and looked up at the sign. Two bent-over nails held it in place. McRae walked over to the car and got the tire iron. He pried one corner of the sign loose and it swung down, so he grabbed ahold, levered the sign off, and tossed it in the car's rear compartment.

He slapped his hands together, wiping them off, hopped back in the cab, looked at his dog, and drawled, "Whatcha think, Champ?" then scratched him behind the ear. "How 'bout we stop by a little later an' see if we pissed 'em off? And then give 'em the boot."

McRae pulled up behind the jailhouse and parked. He stepped from the patrol car, pulled out the sign, and tossed it on a pile of garbage. Then he motioned to his dog and said, "Come on, boy."

Champion jumped out of the car, and the sheriff slammed the back door. Tom followed his master as the sheriff tromped into the jailhouse. When he walked past the front desk Deputy Pete Hanigan piped up, "Hey Sheriff, the mayor called. And Jeff said there were some fires last night." McRae stopped and looked at the boyish-faced deputy.

"What'd that mayor want?" McRae asked, turning around.

"He didn't say. Just wanted you to call him," the deputy replied.

"Yeah, well, he can wait. What about those fires?" he snapped.

"One in an alley on Harrison and another on Chestnut," the deputy answered.

"That's fer Chief Taro ta' deal with."

"Just thought it could've been some Wobblies."

"Yeah, well. Maybe it was. Where's Jeff?" McRae asked, heading up the stairs to his office.

"I think he's up in the file room," the deputy replied and then added, "Looks like the sun's comin' out."

In his office the sheriff walked over to the file cabinet and opened the bottom drawer. He pulled out a bottle of Canadian whiskey and a flask, sat down at his desk, and started to fill the small silver container.

"Jeff! Where the heck are ya?" the sheriff yelled at the open door while Champion Tom did his normal spin on the blanket before flopping down.

"Right here," Deputy Beard answered, walking into the room with a clipboard and pencil in his hand.

"Get Hanigan and Walt Irvan and meet me out back in the paddy wagon," the sheriff said, sitting behind his desk.

"What's goin' on?" Beard asked, holding the clipboard at his side.

"Mediator's gone. Saw him get on the train," the sheriff said.

"So where we headed? Wait, lemme guess. That Wobbly hall? Right?" Beard concluded, a grin forming under his bushy black mustache.

"Yep, that's right," McRae said, "We are gonna e-vict them IWW and close down that hall, today! And . . . I saw a few more of 'em down on the tracks, so round up those men and bring the shotguns."

"What's the plan?"

"No plan, we're just gonna go on over to that alley room they call a union hall and shut 'em down," the sheriff replied, standing up. "Kick 'em out!"

"What about Chief Kelly? You gonna let him know?"

"Nope, he knows I'm ahead of him on all a' this Wobbly crap."

"Sounds good to me," Beard said, heading out the door and down the stairs.

Placing the flask in his back pocket, the sheriff started for the door but stopped and looked at his dog. "Sit, Champ. Stay. This won't take long." McRae headed downstairs and walked out the back door into bright sunshine. He got behind the wheel of the paddy wagon and waited for two seconds, then hit the horn.

"We're coming. Hold your horses!" Deputy Beard yelled as he and the two other deputies ran out of the jailhouse and piled into the cab of the large, box-like vehicle.

"Where we headed?" Deputy Hanigan asked.

"Down to the Imperial," McRae crowed, "and then Spanjer's alley."

The sheriff turned west on Pacific and sped through town. Bystanders stopped on the sidewalk and stared as the paddy wagon zoomed by, turning their heads to follow the speeding vehicle. A man in a bowler hat and dark suit did the same and then took a notepad out of a suit pocket and scribbled a few words.

Approaching from the other direction was a black-and-green Baker Electric car. Behind the wheel was the lady with the large hat. McRae glanced at the car, remembered it, *there's that damn lady again*, and then turned and barreled down to the waterfront.

Renny and ten sullen strikers were walking the picket line between the frontage road and the Northern Imperial pier. They were all holding water-warped signs against slumped, wet shoulders and chanting as they slowly walked back and forth. The sheriff wheeled up and came to a stop right next to them. Getting out of the wagon his eyes landed on the gunny-sack-carrying hoboes he'd seen earlier.

"Direct action gets the goods."

"Vhat do ve say?" Renny said, his voice tired.

"Direct action gets the goods."

"Say it again."

"Direct action gets the goods."

Buck Mullaney stood up from his covered perch just inside the mill and motioned for his guards to fan out on their side of the fencing.

"All right! All right!" the sheriff yelled and pointed at the out-of-town men who were now in the picket line. "I want you, and you, *and* you, to step out of that line. Drop yer signs and get over here to the side of this wagon." The pick-eters stopped.

"Why? We ain't done nothing wrong," one of the men said. Another out-of-town man threw down his sign and glared at the sheriff.

"Shut up, ya damn foreigner," McRae grumbled, staring the men down.

"Spitz is right. We ain't done nothing wrong," the second picketer scoffed. "And we ain't no foreigners!"

"I'll decide who's done what and where yer all from," the sheriff barked, stepping toward them. He grabbed one man and jerked him around to face the side of the paddy wagon. "Now spread 'em! All of ya! Walt, search these bums! I can smell a few rats down here today."

The sheriff stepped back from the lined-up hoboes and watched while his men searched them. Renny and the remaining strikers began chanting and walking the picket again. The suspected Wobbly called Spitz made a quick movement with his right arm, and a red card dropped from his hand. Deputy Irvan slammed his blackjack on the side of the paddy wagon and then shoved the Wobbly up against it.

"Watch it," the sheriff spat and jumped at the man with his blackjack, hitting him on the back of his neck. "That's it, he's got a card. Load 'em up, boys! This here trash is being deported."

The deputies pushed the three Wobblies toward the paddy wagon and started to load them in the back. "That's right ya stupid Wobblies!" McRae hollered, "Why yer so stupid and proud ya just got ta' carry them stinkin' red cards with ya everywhere." He pushed the last Wobbly into the wagon and locked the door.

The sheriff hopped behind the wheel and headed up Hewitt, turned right on Colby, and drove out the Pacific-Bothell Highway. Four miles later, where the Interurban train tracks crossed the road, the sheriff stopped, opened the back, and pointed south.

"That's the way to Seattle. Now git!" he yelled as the three deportees ran down the tracks. One of them yelled over his shoulder, "We'll be back!"

McRae jerked his head around and hollered, "We'll be waitin'," and then laughed.

As they watched the three men scurry south and jump over the cattle guard the sheriff announced, "OK boys. Let's go get us some more Wobblies. Jeff, you take the wheel."

Deputy Beard turned the wagon around and headed back to town. The sheriff passed the flask to his deputies. "Local 248?" Beard asked.

"That's right, Jeff! Local 248, say goodnight!" the sheriff joked with a smirk on his face, the gleam of whiskey on his lips. "Yessiree, I'm guessin' that if somebody's there they'll be all worked up 'cause they ain't got no sign anymore. I done ripped the thing clean off the building. Threw it away," McRae said, slapping his knee.

"Ya ripped their sign down?" Hanigan blurted.

"No kiddin'," Beard said from behind the wheel. "Ya didn't tell me that."

"Yeah, well. I'm tellin' ya'll now," McRae said, a grin still on his face.

At Hewitt they turned right and then made a quick left into the alley.

"OK, Jeff," the sheriff said as his deputy feathered the brakes. They could see that the door was open at the bottom of the stairs.

"Go past 'em a little bit," the sheriff said quietly. Beard slowly rolled by, stopped, and turned off the motor.

"Good," McRae said. "I'm guessin' there'll only be one 'er two inside. If there's more, I'll just give 'em the 3-7-77 for now, and we'll leave."

"But if there's only one 'er two then this place is done, today. All right, you boys ready?" McRae looked at his men. They all nodded. "OK, here we go."

The sheriff jumped from the paddy wagon, he lost his balance and stumbled briefly. The deputies got out with shotguns in hand and followed him. He crept towards the stairs and slipped his right hand through the leather thong fastened to his blackjack as he quietly walked down the stairwell. He stopped on the last step, glanced back at his men, and nodded his head. They acknowledged him, he hesitated and then burst in.

He quickly glanced around the dim, musty room. The deputies fanned out beside him, shotguns at the ready. Two men in work clothes sitting behind a table jumped up from their seats.

"What the devil?" one said.

"Who the hell 'er you?" the other snapped.

"I'm the sheriff, and you boys are done," McRae cracked.

At one side of the table stood a yellow and black IWW flag, at the other end was the Stars and Stripes. The sheriff quickly strode over to the table. It was covered with IWW literature, pamphlets, *Little Red Songbooks*, black cat stickers, and fliers about James Thompson speaking in Everett. McRae swept the Thompson fliers off the table with a hand, scattering them in the air and onto the floor.

"That Thompson fella will not be speakin' here!" he yelled and pointed at the posters on the floor.

"James Thompson most certainly will," one Wobbly with a sparse black beard said.

The other one pulled more fliers from a box and set them down on the table. He held them there with his hand and growled, "This is a free country, mister."

"Not anymore, fella," the sheriff bellowed and swung his blackjack down on the back of the man's hand, hitting him squarely. The Wobbly screamed in pain and pulled his hand away.

"Why you — you ain't no lawman," the Wobbly moaned, shaking his hand and then putting it under his armpit. "Yer breakin' the law comin' in here. You got no right," the other Wobbly yelled.

McRae's eyes caught fire, he shouted, "I'm the law dammit! And I'm keepin' law and order. AND . . . I got me a new law that outlaws them street meetings!"

Both Wobblies glared at the sheriff.

"Street law," one said. "Nothin's gonna stop James Thompson or us from speaking freely. Now get out of here."

"Dammit! Don't you be sassin' me 'er tellin' me what to do," McRae hollered. He pulled back his coat lapel to make sure his badge was visible and yelled, "You're out of this town! I'm shuttin' you down. Today!"

"You ain't shuttin' us down. Never. We've heard all about you and yer vigilantes, and we ain't done nothin' wrong. We're here to exercise our right to speak freely," one Wobbly said with a cold look.

"Oh, yeah? Well, you foreigner's got a license to distribute literature?" the sheriff asked, his eyes flashing like a crazy man.

"We're not foreigners, we're from Seattle, and we don't need some license to hand out *free* pamphlets," the Wobbly replied. They both sat down.

"In this town you do," the sheriff spat.

"You got some stupid ordinance against that, too? We got rights," the bearded Wobbly argued.

"Hell, you boys ain't even got yerselves a sign anymore," McRae bellowed.

"It was you, wasn't it? You stole our sign."

"Get yer coats. I've heard enough a yer belly achin'. I am e-victin' an' deportin' you." The sheriff snatched an IWW stencil from the table, tore it to pieces, and cried out hysterically, "Get up. NOW!"

"We're not goin' any-whar," one man mumbled, sitting in his chair.

"Like hell you're not. I'm takin' you boy's outta circulation!" McRae hollered, his eyes blazing.

"We're in the city limits. You don't have any jurisdiction here," the same Wobbly shot back.

"Don't be talkin' words you don't know nothin' about. Yer sayin's ain't worth squat 'round here!" the sheriff roared. "What county is Everett in, huh, ya stupid Wobbly? Tell me that. Tell me. Oh, right, you don't know, do ya? Well, it's in Snohomish County, ya ignorant bastard and I'm the sheriff of Snohomish County. And this is *my* town!"

"We still don't need no license to hand out *free* information," the same man said.

"I told you that you need one in this town. In this county. Now get goin'!" the sheriff ordered.

"Nope," the Wobbly blurted and crossed his arms.

In a flash the sheriff reached across the table, grabbed the man by his shirt and shoved him backwards. The man stood up and took a roundhouse swing, hitting McRae in the neck.

With lightning reflexes Walt Irvan jabbed his shotgun butt into the Wobbly's stomach sending him buckling over and to the floor at the same time that Hanigan and Beard rushed around the other side of the table. They jerked him to his feet, held him off the ground and walked him towards the door. The man struggled as the sheriff hollered at the other one, "I said *now* you little son of a bitch! Get yourself goin' with yer buddy there. Little bastard took a swing at me." The man raised his hands in surrender, stood up, and walked towards the door.

"Jeff, cuff these vagrants and load 'em in the wagon. Then start us a camp-fire in the alley with all their crap. I'm gonna go pay Mr. Spanjer a visit," the sheriff commanded and headed out the door and up the alley. He fumed down Hewitt and around the corner to Wetmore. Moments later he found Noah Spanjer inside his store stocking shelves.

"Spanjer!" the sheriff snarled, "I just kicked that Wobbly mess out of yer alley basement. For good!" Noah stood up from his task and groaned, "What?"

"I said I just kicked that IWW mess out of yer alley room. And I'll do it again if I have to."

"What are you talking about?"

"You damn well know what I'm talkin' about!"

"You've got no right to kick those union men out of that space. They paid rent and can stay, as far as I'm concerned," Spanjer said, facing down the sheriff.

"Are you not understandin' what I'm sayin' to ya? Ya damn Socialist! Those Wobbly bums are criminals. I ought-a run you in fer harboring a pack of felons!"

"Don't you threaten me in my place of business. Now you look here, I'm telling you that you had no legal right to kick those men out. And they're not felons!"

"They got the boot because they ain't got a license to distribute literature here."

"Why, I've never heard of such a thing!" the plump market owner snapped, then quickly said, "What's that, some sort of Commercial Club law?"

"It's the law. Dammit Spanjer!" an out of breath sheriff yelled. "And if you stick any more IWW in that basement I'll shut this whole damn building down."

McRae spun on his boot heel to leave and lost his balance. He bumped into a shelf and knocked some cans and boxes on the floor. He glanced at the mess he'd made, walked past it, and left.

Noah put his hands on his hips and steamed to himself, "Why, that damn, son of a son clutters up my store and —" Then Spanjer went behind the meat counter, ripped a piece of white butcher paper off the reel, and wrote in big, black, bold letters, "WE ARE NOT MEMBERS OF THE COMMERCIAL CLUB," and taped it on his front window facing the sidewalk.

McRae stormed back up Wetmore. When he walked around the corner to Hewitt, smoke was slowly wafting out of the alley and into the street. A small crowd had gathered on the sidewalk, including a reporter from the *Daily Tribune*. The sheriff pushed his way through while a man in a black bowler hat watched from across the street.

A small fire burned in the middle of the alleyway right in front of the former union hall and behind the paddy wagon. The deputies went back and forth from the basement to the fire carrying boxes of fliers, copies of the *Industrial Worker* newspaper, IWW papers, wooden furniture, and anything else that would burn, dumping it all on the fire. The sheriff cracked a grin as he approached, right when a woman poked her head out of an upstairs apartment.

"What's going on down there?" the lady yelled, waving her arm to keep the smoke out. The sheriff took his Stetson off and looked up.

"Official business, ma'am. Just keepin' the peace," McRae remarked, putting his hat back on. She frowned, shook her head, and closed the window.

"Hell, boys, all that Wobbly junk burns good," McRae exclaimed, pretending to warm his hands over the flames. The two Wobblies kicked the metal walls inside the paddy wagon while they watched through the rear window.

"It sure does, boss," Deputy Irvan replied. Pete Hanigan threw the last few pieces of the broken-up table and chairs on the flames and went back inside. Beard motioned to the sheriff. They stepped from the view of the paddy wagon window and the deputy pulled a piece of paper out of his pocket and handed it to the sheriff.

"We found this inside," Beard said quietly. "It says somethin' about Seattle Wobblies comin' up here in a couple a' days."

"Does it now?" the sheriff replied, snatching the handwritten itinerary. He read quietly, "'Tickets have been purchased for train to Mukilteo and boat to Everett.'"

"Yeah, well, we'll see about that," the sheriff cracked.

"Guess they was plannin' a little surprise party," Beard observed.

"Sure does. Looks to me like they're tryin' a new way to get around the blockade. Good job, Jeff. So, where's them flags?" the sheriff asked, putting the piece of paper in a shirt pocket and walking back to the fire.

"Walt!" Beard yelled down the stairs and into the now-cleared-out room, "Get them flags out here!"

"Got 'em right here," Deputy Irvan replied, carrying out the IWW and American flags. "We saved 'em for ya, sheriff," Walt said, coming up the stairwell.

"Good," McRae grunted, grabbing the Wobbly flag. He broke the staff over his knee and tossed both pieces on the fire. The four men stood and watched the IWW flag begin to burn. Black smoke rose from the cloth and floated out into Hewitt, a siren blasted through the air.

Seconds later, the pedestrians on the sidewalk parted and an Everett fire truck turned down the alley. The sheriff grinned when he recognized Sean O'Riley and Duncan McFee sitting in the open air seat of the American LaFrance pumper. As they pulled up and saw what was going on the fireman in the passenger seat quit turning the siren crank.

"Jesus Christ, McRae! What the hell's goin' on here?" O'Riley hollered, stepping down.

"Yeah, yeah, we're just out here doin' the people's business and e-liminatin' these IWWs," the sheriff replied.

McFee hopped off the truck and swaggered over to the fire.

"The people's business? Is that what you call this?" McFee said, greeting the men with a sly grin and a nod of his head.

"I guess this ain't as bad as that lady made it sound," O'Riley offered.

The sheriff nodded his head and rolled his eyes upwards towards the apartment window, and said, "I guess some people just can't leave good enough alone."

"You invite Kelly to this little party?" O'Riley asked.

The sheriff grinned and commented, "Aw, I wouldn't wanna let old Kelly spoil all a' this fun."

"Hell," O'Riley said, "All this carryin' on is like oxygen to you, ain't it? Well, smoky oxygen that is." They all laughed heartily. Two grey-haired men from the crowd on Hewitt came down the alley. One limped and used a cane.

"So, well, well, well. We's been a-watchin' you," the old-timer with the cane brightly piped as they approached, "and we just wanted ta' say damn fine work, Sheriff." The man had a scar on his unshaven, wrinkled face that went from below his ear and across his cheek. A tarnished oval buckle with the letters *U.S.* on it fastened a belt that held worn-out trousers. "I keep hearin' about all the disappearin' justice in this town, and, by God, a line a' talk like that is nothin' but bull-shit on a bed of horse feathers!" he proclaimed and then took a deep breath. "I say justice is right here," the veteran said, nodding his head at the little fire.

"That's a right. Them Wobblies 'er nothin' but a bunch a worthless, intrudin' Jacobites thinkin' they got a right to whatever they want. A menace ta' society, I say," the other offered, his voice like gravel. He, too, had a weather beaten face. The man looked at the fire and spit on it, saying, "They's nothing but trouble."

"Oh yeah, ain't that a fact," McRae replied, rubbing the side of his head. "They sure is."

"Yep, as far as we's concerned, yer doin' good work," the first citizen said, leaning on his cane. "You know, fifty year ago I rode with Slocum in the Twentieth Corps, an' these IWW are nothin' but a bunch a' Johnny Reb's if'n ya ask me. Hell, we took our orders from Sherman himself, an' by gum, we burnt up the whole damn south from Milledgeville ta' Bentonville! Yes sir, I'll tell ya right now, old William Tecumseh would've already burnt down an' eliminated this here entire vermin infested buildin'!" The veteran drawled, pointing his cane at the structure.

"Some people think them Wobblies comin' here's a good thing, but they're nothin' but a bunch a' lazy eye-tinerants, I tell ya," the other validated, nodding at the fire. "Why I was sayin' just the other day that the good Sheriff Donald McRae ain't gonna allow this here trash ta' stay long. And by gum, I was right. Yer doin' good sheriff and don't let nobody say different. Welp . . . I'm thinkin' it's about time ta' shut my mouth. We best be gettin' outta yer way."

The two men turned around. Once they were out at the sidewalk, one proudly announced, "Let's go see if they got any hooch at the Evergreen!"

"That's a damn fine idea," the other replied, "and if they got any whiskey, why I'm gonna ask for a two-finger pour, and then I is gonna spread my fingers wide!" The small crowd cheered and began to follow them down Hewitt.

McRae looked at the firemen. "I guess you boys will be doin' yer job now, eh?"

"Yep, that's right," McFee replied and then chuckled, "We'll get yer, what'd you call it, *people's business*, all cleaned up." They all had a good laugh as the two prisoners began kicking the paddy wagon walls again. McRae looked at the wagon with a grin and then turned to the firemen.

"Thanks boys. But what about those fires we heard about last night down in riverside. You fellas there?"

"Nope, last shift handled 'em," McFee answered, "Guess one was just a wood pile but the other was a shed in the back of Wilber Conway's place. That thing burned right down to the ground."

"Yep," O'Riley added, "night sergeant said it looked like phosphorous. And, they found some black cat stickers on telephone poles and such."

"Oh, did they now?" McRae said, pushing his Stetson up on his brow. "That's a sure sign of Wobbly activity, all right."

"So, Don, we gonna be findin' you around anymore corners and down alleyways kickin' up smoke?" O'Riley asked, starting to pull firehose off the reel on the truck.

"Oh, probably so. But wait. Before you dump yer water, lemme do somethin'," the sheriff said. He turned to Walt, "Gimme them Star's 'n Stripes."

Deputy Irvan handed him the flag, it had a metal stand on the end. McRae grabbed the wooden staff and gazed at the dwindling pile of smoldering ashes for a moment. He pushed a few coals around with the stand to flatten it out and then stabbed the American flag on top of the smoky pile. He stepped back and admired his statement with his hands on his hips.

Black smoke and small white cinders slowly rose up through it, tiny embers hung in the stagnant air and formed a hazy, floating particulate that soon filled the alley. Then a voice from the street sliced through the air.

"Looks like a fine day in America, Sheriff!"

McRae cocked his head slightly towards Hewitt and then turned back to the fire. He stared at it with a scowl. Finally, the corners of his mouth slowly turned into a grin.

"OK, men, let's get to it. Now rip that door off its hinges and toss it back in the room . . . then load up! We still got a couple a' Wobblies to deport!"

***

Two days later, Feeney Bradford lingered at the back of an angry but eager crowd inside the Seattle IWW hall. A fraternity of seasonal laborers stood side by side not only in body but also in their common belief that they could build a new world from the ashes of the old. Anxious, outspoken men with twine-tied blanket rolls strapped over their backs in tattered overalls and worn out boots, all of them workingmen: lumberjacks, grain harvesters, casual railroad section hands, ice-cutters, and seasonal farm hands from all over the western states that heard the call on the jungle telegraph to aid in the Everett struggle had flocked to Seattle by rail and foot.

As they waited for another speaker to step forward a lone voice began to sing, his singular intonation soon joined by a choral brigade dressed in dusty working duds.

"Why don't you work like other folks do?
How the hell can I work when there's no work to do?
Hallelujah, I'm a bum
Hallelujah, bum again
Hallelujah give us a handout
To revive us again
Oh, why don't you save all the money you earn?
If I didn't eat I'd have money to burn
Whenever I get all the money I earn
The boss will be broke, and to work he must turn
Hallelujah, I'm a bum
Hallelujah, bum again."

The singing began to quiet and all eyes focused on a tall, light-haired, broad-shouldered man with a whiskbroom mustache moving through the gathering.

James Thompson slowly worked his way to the front of the hall as a stillness overtook the room. His square jaw was set firmly and his eyes darted from man to man as they patted him on the back and shook his hand. As he got closer to the stage the hall began to fill with sporadic cheers. Once there, he stopped and stood with his hands clasped in front of himself, then he dropped his head down on his chest and mouthed a few words. The cheers in the hall built to a deafening roar. Thompson stepped to the podium and raised a clenched fist, then opened it with the palm of his hand facing the men.

"Fellow workers!" James Thompson called out over the room. "Fellow workers! Greetings. Please, let me start. Please?"

Right when the men stopped cheering a lone voice called out, "Let's give 'em hell Big Jim!" The room boomed with screams once again.

"Thank you! Yes. Thank you. Please?" Thompson said with his hands raised until it was quiet.

"In America," he began, "we are *all* guaranteed certain individual rights. In America we *all* have equal freedoms. In America *we* are all equals and we all have the right to worship and speak freely! But thirty miles north of here there is no America."

"Thirty miles from here there is no freedom. Thirty miles from here there is a town under a crude, illegal form of martial law that is enforced by the end of a club! A town with a self-imposed design to stamp out all freedoms! A town that *burns* all freedoms!"

The crowd immediately responded with thunderous applause. Thompson raised both hands.

"As we all now know, two days ago our Local 248 in Everett was ransacked, and burned by a tool of the Everett lumber trust, Sheriff Donald McRae." Boos instantly filled the air. Every man stomped their feet until Thompson started in again.

"Fellow workers. We have been robbed once again by the industrialists. We have been robbed of our country's constitution! And, we have been robbed of our union hall in Everett!" Thompson hollered out over the room. His face red from the rush of blood.

"Today, my brothers, we have taken up a collection so that some of us can travel by train to Mukilteo and then by boat to Everett in order to take back what is rightfully ours," Thompson hollered to instantaneous cheers. "The lumber trust in Everett cannot burn us out, and they cannot stop us from being American citizens with freedoms and rights of our own. We are going to Everett to demand that we be recognized!" Thompson screamed with his right fist in the air. A deafening roar boomed in the hall. "We are going to engage in our freedom to organize and exercise our right to free speech!"

When Bradford heard of the days plan he had the information he needed and walked out. He looked up and down 2nd Avenue. People milled about waiting for trolleys and reading newspapers while a black and white bulldog wandered in and out of the union's entrance. A passed out down-n-outer was lying on the sidewalk up against the building next door and panhandlers were everywhere asking for change and bumming cigarettes.

Thompson finished his speech and the applause that went up from the crowd was so loud that pedestrians walking by stopped with curiosity and looked into the hall. Bradford moved down the street, and stood in a storefront. The union emptied and the sidewalk filled with IWW members headed south for King Street Station. The detective followed the pack of Wobblies and scanned the group for someone he could approach. A shabbily dressed middle-aged man with an overstuffed ratty pillow-case slung over his shoulder was walking alone. Bradford caught up with him.

"You headed to Everett?" Bradford asked, flashing a friendly smile.

"That's right, takin' the train," the man answered.

"I hear those Everett authorities need to be taught a lesson."

"What's that ya say?" the Wobbly answered and stopped.

The detective pulled a hand out of his trouser pocket and flashed a Smith & Wesson .38, then quickly returned it. "You can have it if you'd like," Bradford offered. The Wobbly stepped back from Bradford and stared at him, his eyes narrowing.

"What are you? Some cop?" he asked.

"Nope, just a fellow looking to help," Bradford replied.

The Wobbly looked Bradford up and down, then said, "If yer a brother how come yer wearin' a suit?"

"Just because I'm wearing a suit doesn't mean I'm not sympathetic to the cause."

"Uh-huh. Yeah, well, no thanks fella. I don't need anything like that," the man said and continued walking.

Bradford saw two more men coming up the street and approached them, raising a hand and forefinger.

"Are you men headed to Everett?" Bradford asked and began to walk with them.

"Who's askin'?" one of the men said, wearing pitch-covered tin pants and cork boots.

"Just a supporter looking to help the cause," Bradford claimed, smiling.

"Izzat right?" the other Wobbly said sarcastically.

"Here, let me give you something," Bradford offered. Holding up his hand to stop the two Wobblies, the detective reached into his pocket and then showed the small revolver. "You might need something to protect yourself up there. I hear those authorities are a rough bunch."

The Wobbly from the woods glanced back and forth from the pistol to Bradford's face, then down the street, and back to the detective with a tight jaw.

"That thing loaded?" the logger asked.

"Yes."

"And you're gonna give it to us?"

"Gentlemen," Bradford said quietly, "I support your cause 100 percent. And I'd like you to have a little bit of . . . a, well, let's call it an insurance policy."

A scowl swept across the second Wobbly's face, and he said, "Nope, forget it. Don't need it fella." They walked away.

The detective ducked into a deli, found a phone booth, and dialed. The phone rang on Luther MacCullock's desk.

"Yes," MacCullock said into the receiver.

"It's Feeney Bradford," the detective answered.

"What is it, Feeney? Are you doing your job?"

"James Thompson just finished speaking at the Seattle hall, he's got the Wobblies organized to move on Everett."

"I swear that man's nothing but an arrogant fool. What is it now?"

"Well, there's a big gang of them that just left the building. They're headed to Mukilteo on the train and then taking a boat to Everett."

"Are they now? How many?"

"I'd say about twenty or so, and some of them are packing weapons."

"Is that so? Packing weapons, you say. What kind are we talking about?"

"Pistols, knives, and brass knuckles. I think they've got violence in mind."

"So these Wobblies are looking to start some serious trouble?"

"Yes, I'd say so sir. Big trouble."

"Well, excellent work, Feeney," MacCullock said and hung up.

He called the sheriff.

"Donald?" MacCullock said into the receiver. The sheriff recognized MacCullock's voice.

"Yes, Captain."

"I just got word that there's a gang of Wobblies headed for Mukilteo on the train. Then coming to Everett on some boat. You need to corral these anarchists."

"Already know about it. Gettin' ready to head out," the sheriff said. "Where'd you hear it?"

"What's that? You already know?" MacCullock replied, "How'd you find out?"

"I'm the sheriff, remember. I'm the one that's supposed to know!"

"OK. Good work. I understand they're on their way and carrying weapons."

"Weapons?" the sheriff said into the receiver. "All right. I'll be ready for them."

The sheriff slapped the receiver onto its hook and yelled out his open office door, "Jeff. Where are ya? Jefferson!"

"Right here, Sheriff," Deputy Beard replied, walking into the room.

"Time to get movin'. Go fire up the paddy wagon and make sure every man is armed."

The sheriff opened the file cabinet, grabbed the jug, filled his flask, and slipped it into his coat. Then he stood up, pulled his Colt from its holster and spun the cylinder, checking for cartridges. Champion got up from his corner blanket and took a few steps.

"Sit Tom . . . stay boy. Daddy's got business to tend to," the sheriff said as his ever mindful setter dog ambled back to his blanket, spun around a few times, and then hit the floor with a thud. He laid his head down on extended paws with a sad look and blew out a big breath of air, jowls flapping.

Stepping into the front of the paddy wagon the sheriff shouted, "First thing, we're headed to the Interurban Station, then the depot, and then the pier to pick up as many volunteers as we can. It's time for a little surprise party of our own."

The sheriff looked at Beard and said, "MacCullock called, he knew all about the Wobblies comin' up today."

"How'd he know that?"

"Wouldn't say. But I'll find out. Anyway, we gotta go find Henry Ramwell about his tug."

After stopping at the Interurban Station to forewarn the blockade vigilantes there, the sheriff and his men drove to the waterfront. Citizen deputies on patrol were marching down Hewitt. Each one had a white handkerchief tied around his upper arm and clubs or ax handles in their hands. The sheriff had Beard stop for the group and told them to get down to the American Tug Boat Company right away. At the Great Northern Depot, McRae jumped out and found more deputies.

"You men hop in back. We've got some work to do," the sheriff ordered. "But a few of ya stay behind. There's a gang of Wobblies headed north on the train from Seattle, but they're getting off at Mukilteo. If any of 'em show up here, arrest them on the spot and bring 'em to *my* jail!" the sheriff commanded.

At the city pier they picked up a dozen white-handkerchief-wearing men, filling the large paddy wagon with twenty vigilantes. When they pulled up to the tug boat pier the lot of them unloaded from the back of the wagon while cars and trucks pulled up with more vigilantes. Close to sixty men milled around with ax handles and long, leather pipes filled with buckshot and ball bearings, stitched at each end. The sheriff went in the office and found Henry behind his desk.

"Well, good afternoon sheriff. What brings ya in the door today?" Ramwell asked and then glanced out the window, his eyes sparked when he saw all the men.

"Aw, we got a boatload of trouble headed this way," the sheriff replied.

"Do ya now? Looks like ya got plenty of help."

"Henry, I need yer boat. There's a mess of Wobblies headed here right this minute and I aim to sink 'em," the sheriff said with a gleam in his eye. Ramwell looked at the sheriff and asked, "How's that?"

"I figure we just jump aboard yer tug and meet 'em out in the bay, give 'em a little welcoming party."

"Yeah, but," Ramwell replied with a questioning look, "what if there's trouble? I'm no pirate on the high seas at the wheel of some gunboat."

"Aw, Henry, you darn well know the captain and his club have declared war against all of these Wobbly bums, don't ya?" the sheriff warned, straight-faced.

"Oh, hell, yes, I do. The whole damn town knows all about Luther MacCullock and his commercial committee. That club of his keeps trying to get me to buy a membership, but what am I gonna do there hob-nobbin' with a bunch of socialites?" Ramwell replied.

The sheriff looked at the tugboat captain and said, "Never mind about that. This is war, and it's us against them. Now I've got plenty of men outside that will make a fine navy. What d'ya say?" the sheriff asked. Then he pulled the flask from his coat and held it out, "How 'bout a little hair of the dog?"

"Criminy, Don, you sure drink a lot these days," the old seaman said as he latched onto the flask, took a short sip, and handed it back. "Yeah, but, who's gonna pay for all my diesel?"

"Aw, fer criminy sakes! Just send the bill ta' Luther, he'll have the Commercial Club pay ya," McRae volunteered.

"Okay then, I guess it's a fine day for a snort and a boat ride. Let's shove off!"

Outside, the sheriff gathered up his men. He shouted, "All a' ya, come on over. Boys, you all know Captain Ramwell, and we are gonna load up on his towboat, so do what he says."

Henry took a moment as he looked at all the men with their clubs and shotguns. Finally, with a stiff jaw and a touch of apprehension in his voice, he said, "OK, men, I want one a' ya on the bowline and one on the stern. Once I get her fired up I'll give the signal and you can cast us off. Now we got ourselves a bit of a tide today and some wind. That means there'll be whitecaps out there, so keep one hand fast to the ship. We don't need any over-boards."

As they pulled away from the dock, the men grouped up on the bow and the stern, some climbed up on the pilothouse roof of the forty-foot tugboat. Out on the bay the wind blew in their faces and the boat plowed through the water south towards Mukilteo.

The sheriff stepped into the wheelhouse and pulled out his flask. He pushed his Stetson up with the spout and then took a drink. He held the little container out for the skipper, saying, "So the captain's been keepin' ya in business?"

Ramwell grabbed the flask and replied, "Oh, more so than the Canyon 'er the Hulbert, even the Eclipse. None of 'em are pulling in rafts like the Northern Imperial." Henry took a swig and passed back the flask. The sheriff looked at the old seaman and nodded his head.

"Well, seein's how the captain's been payin' yer wages lately, and since the good citizens of this town want law and order, I'd be much obliged if ya leave me to my job today," the sheriff requested.

"That's fine, Don. I'll stay out of the way and do what I'm told," Ramwell replied, not looking at the sheriff. Then he confided, "Old Luther's been pretty good to me."

A mile out on the water, Ramwell spotted a craft coming around the point. He picked up his binoculars, leaned against the helm, and said, "There's a mess of men on that little thing up ahead. Why, I'll be damned. It's the *Wanderer.* I'd spot that old floater anywhere."

"Whose boat's that?" the sheriff asked.

"That's Jack Mitten's launch. Haven't seen Jack in a while, heard he was up north chasing sockeye out of Bellingham with his fish boat. Guess he must be back," Henry surmised.

"Lemme see," McRae said, reaching for the binoculars. He looked through them and squinted. "Oh yeah, that's them all right. Head straight at 'em. Mister Mitten is about to get boarded," the sheriff remarked, handing them back. Then he tipped the flask and poured whiskey into his mouth. He sloshed the liquid back and forth between his teeth a few times, and swallowed.

"How d'ya know those passengers on Mitten's boat 'er Wobblies?" Ramwell asked.

"Dammit, Henry. I told ya ta' leave me to my business," the sheriff spat and stepped out on deck.

"Men!" the sheriff hollered. "Let me do the talkin', and keep yer weapons at your side. I'm gonna fire one over her bow to get their attention. Make ready now."

Singing came across the water from the *Wanderer*. Every Wobbly was singing and waving their hats and hands. Dozens were on the fly deck, more on the aft, all of them carrying on like a bunch of young travelers on a holiday.

When the *Edison* was one hundred yards from the *Wanderer* the sheriff raised his single-action Colt, pulled back the hammer, and pulled the trigger, sending a bullet over the top of the Wobbly-filled boat. The singing stopped, but the *Wanderer* kept churning though the water.

The sheriff waved his arms and yelled, "Stop, damn-it!" But the *Wanderer* didn't.

"Damn these Wobbly bum bastards," the sheriff hissed and fired another round, this time at the wheelhouse, hitting it in the sidewall with a crack. Every Wobbly hit the deck, but the boat kept plugging along. He drew a bead on the wheelhouse again and fired. The *Wanderer* slowed its engine, and Jack Mitten, a lanky, grey-haired Swede, stepped out of the pilothouse door and waved his arms.

"You son of a bitch! Come over here!" the sheriff yelled, holstering his revolver.

"What are you shooting at me for?" Mitten screamed.

"I'm the sheriff of this county and I order you to cut yer engines!"

"If you want me, then come over here!" Mitten hollered back and then went inside his pilothouse and pulled back the throttle. Captain Ramwell came about and rafted up alongside. While the deputies lashed the two boats together, the sheriff waited with a scowl on his face and his hands on his hips.

"What are we stopping for?" one Wobbly hollered.

"You've got no reason to fire at us!" another shouted.

"Shut up, all a' ya! Ya hear me? I'm the law of this county and I ain't about to let a' bunch a bums get around my blockade and be a-comin' to my town!" the sheriff bellowed. His scowl worsened and he went aboard, Colt in hand.

"All you bums climb over on my boat, now," he ordered, his legs swaying with the waves as a few deputies climbed aboard to assist. McRae glared at the pilothouse and took a few short, uneasy steps over to it, and kicked in the door. Captain Mitten was standing at the wheel.

"You're gonna get a one piece suit in the nut house for this, Sheriff!" Mitten hissed. The sheriff struck him with the Colt on the base of his neck. The fisherman slumped over in pain and then straightened up. The sheriff struck him again. Mitten fell to the floor of the wheelhouse, bleeding.

"You're a hell of a citizen bringing this bunch here to cause a riot in my town!" McRae snarled, standing over him.

"Aw, you think yer a big man and all, but you wouldn't last two minutes without that gun of yours," Mitten said, pushing himself up to his knees.

"You best be staying down there," the sheriff advised.

"These men are paid passengers, and they're all . . . fine union men," Mitten sputtered.

"You shut yer damn head, or I'll knock it clean off," the sheriff threatened, waving the Colt over him.

McRae went back out on the deck, where one young Wobbly in a knit cap and suspenders was sitting on the rail with his head down.

"Get yer ass on that tug," the sheriff snarled.

"I ain't goin' nowhere," the defiant Wobbly replied, raising his head.

"I said to get your crummy ass on that towboat!" the sheriff yelled, jabbing the Colt in front of the Wobbly's face.

"Nope," the young man said, dropping his head down. The sheriff ripped the Wobbly's knit hat off his head and tossed it overboard just as a rogue wave hit the side of the tug. McRae lost his balance. The young Wobbly seized the moment. He jumped up from the rail and tried to push the sheriff off his feet, but McRae was far too sturdily built for the young fellow.

"Why you little son of a bitch," the sheriff snapped. He grabbed him by the hair, jerked the young man's head around, and struck him in the temple with his Colt, dazing him. Blood gushed down over the Wobbly's face and onto his clothes. The sheriff pulled him back to keep him from falling overboard and let him drop to the deck. Two deputies picked him up and carried the young victim onto the *Edison*.

Stepping aboard the tug the sheriff hollered, "All you bums, group up on the stern, and you men, search 'em all. And keep 'em covered!"

Those deputies with shotguns kept their weapons pointed at the Wobblies as they were being patted down for weapons. Two deputies with rifles climbed up on the wheelhouse fly deck and stood watch. The sheriff stepped over to the pilothouse door.

"All right, Henry, I think we're ready to shove off," the sheriff said.

"Well, I should hope so," Ramwell mumbled under his breath and then yelled out to the deck, "OK, men, cast off."

Just as the *Edison* was pulling away, Jack Mitten stumbled out on his deck, bleeding and shaking his fist. He screamed, "The Coast Guard is gonna hear about this! Go on back to yer damn mill town and rot! Ya bunch a' bastards!"

At Ramwell's dock the Wobblies were loaded in the paddy wagon and taken to jail, twenty prisoners in all.

In the holding tank, a citizen deputy asked the Wobbly called Spitz, "You IWW?"

Spitz answered, "Yes," and he was thrown against the bars.

"What charges are we being held on?" another Wobbly demanded.

"You are being held for vagrancy, inciting to riot, and criminal conspiracy," the sheriff said as he walked around the corner and down the hall.

"We're not vagrants. We paid our boat fare, and we didn't start no riot," one said.

"How can we be criminals? We didn't commit no crime!" another yelled.

"Don't give 'em any blankets, and if you feed 'em, make sure the soup is cold," the sheriff said to Deputy Irvan and went upstairs to his office. Five minutes later a car with two citizen deputies showed up at the county jail. They yanked a man out of the back seat with his hands tied behind his back and hauled him inside. A man wearing a bowler hat stood across the street and watched.

"Where's the sheriff?" Beau Hardee asked as they hauled their captive through the door, "We caught this intruder getting off at the Interurban Station."

"Up in his office," Beard said. He glanced at their captive and recognized him.

"Well, well, well. Would ya look what the cat brought in? The boss is gonna like this. Take him to the backroom, I'll get Don," Deputy Beard said.

"Sheriff!" Beard yelled as he went up the stairs and into McRae's office. "We got Thompson. The boys got James Thompson at the Interurban this morning!"

"What's that? Thompson, ya say?" the sheriff said, snapping awake from under his Stetson and pulling his feet down from the top of his desk.

"Where is he?" the sheriff asked, his once gaunt face now puffy and pale.

"Downstairs, in the backroom. Jeez, sheriff, yer lookin' a bit tuckered out. You OK?"

"I'm fine, dammit. Who got him?"

"Beau Hardee caught him at the Interurban Station," Beard replied.

The sheriff stood up and placed the flask in his vest pocket. Champion Tom followed them out the door. On their way downstairs they could hear the Wobblies making a racket.

"You've got no right to hold us!" Spitz yelled.

"We know our rights," another Wobbly named Skeeter cried.

"We're not vagrants, we're union men," another hollered.

"You're the ones who should be in jail!"

"It's time to build a battleship, boys. Let's tear this place apart brick by brick!" Spitz hollered with glee. "If they can burn out our hall, then we can wreck their jail!"

They commenced ripping the toilet from the floor, then pulled down and cracked a pipe that ran up the wall, hot steam hissed and poured into the cell. While the locked-up Wobblies did their battleship damage they began singing one of their union songs.

"Ta-ra-ra-boom-de-ay!
It made a noise that way
And wheels and bolts and hay
Went flying every way."

Coarse cotton cloth and bed straw flew in the air from the one mattress that was in the holding tank. Straw covered the floor, the mattress had been torn to shreds by the time the sheriff stormed up.

"What in blue blazes is going on here?" he shouted. But the Wobblies didn't let up. One of them had taken a cloth cord from the mattress, made a small hangman's noose, and dangled it in front of the sheriff. The sheriff hauled off and hit him square in the nose through the bars.

"That'll teach ya, you ignorant son of a bitch," the sheriff said and adjusted his Stetson. "You fellas must not go to the same church that I go to."

"The union's our church!" Spitz yelled.

"We don't need yer kind of church!" one Wobbly cried.

"That's right. We don't go to church. We only go to work!" Skeeter barked.

"Bullshit!" the sheriff spat. "You don't work. You only go on strike."

"Going on strike is better than beating up yer fellow man!" a Wobbly added.

"You *ain't* my fellow man," McRae mocked and then added, "And you ain't AFL."

"Yeah, well," an older Wobbly said, "at least we don't work for you or the men that pay your salary."

"Yeah, well, yer union's gonna have to pay for these damages!" McRae hollered.

"That's fine. You can mail us the bill right here," Spitz replied with a laugh.

The sheriff grunted, "Huh?" and then glowered at Spitz with a stony expression. McRae slowly said, "Don't you worry there, fella, you'll get the bill, and yer due in good time."

The casual look on Spitz's face dissolved. He returned the sheriff's glare. His eyes sparked and narrowed, and his back stiffened with fortitude. With a tight jaw, Spitz growled, "Anytime mister lawman. You just go ahead and try bringin' me my due."

"Ha!" McRae scoffed at the Wobbly. "There won't be any tryin' there, fella, 'cause when the iron fist of the law comes down on yer head, yer gonna know it." The sheriff glared at Spitz. He took a malevolent look at the Wobbly and placed Spitz's long, pointed nose and jaw in his memory and then turned on his heel and headed to the backroom as they all started to sing.

> "Fellow workers can't you hear
> There is something in the air
> Everywhere you walk, everybody talks
> 'Bout the IWW
> They have got a one way strike
> That the master doesn't like
> Everybody sticks, that's the only trick
> All are joining now."

Champion Tom bayed and scratched the floor at the base of the cell bars. Hot steam hissed through the cell, and citizens began gathering outside on the street to listen to the pandemonium, including a man wearing a dark pressed suit, wing collared shirt and a black bowler hat.

The sheriff went to the backroom next to the heavily bolted rear door. Beau Hardee stood next to Thompson, who was sitting on a small barrel of gunpowder. Deputy Beard leaned against the wall. Grabbing Thompson by the shirt, the sheriff jerked him to his feet and snarled in his face, "So, you just can't leave well enough alone?"

"Yep, that's right," Thompson answered, staring him down.

"We're gonna fix ya so you won't be coming back here no more. Did you search this speechifyin' bum?"

"Already did," Beau Hardee quickly answered, handing the sheriff a small cardboard box with a wallet, notebook, reading spectacles, and some change in it. Hardee stepped behind Thompson.

"I've done nothing wrong. That's my wallet and —" Thompson said but was kidney-punched by Hardee, sending him doubled-over to the floor. Beard picked him up.

"All right. Let's lock him up in his own cell, boys," the sheriff ordered. "We need to keep him separated from the rest of his kind."

They stumbled out of the back room and walked by the main cell holding the twenty Wobblies.

"Somebody turn off that damn steam valve!" McRae yelled.

"Hang in there, Big Jim!" one Wobbly hollered.

"These swine here in Everett are the devil's children," Spitz exclaimed.

"Satan wouldn't have children this bad," another Wobbly barked.

"Don't worry, you bastards. There's more of us on the way!" Skeeter exclaimed.

Hardee and Beard tossed Thompson in the cell, and the sheriff locked the door.

"Have a nice nap, ya sorry son of a bitch. We'll deal with you after supper," the sheriff said with an exhausted smirk on his face.

"When 'er we gonna let 'em go?" Deputy Beard asked about the other Wobblies. The sheriff scratched the side of his head and then looked at his deputy.

"Well, the way they're wreckin' my jail, sooner than later I'd say."

***

The picketers had heard the shots fired out on the bay and watched the *Edison* go upriver and past the Northern Imperial pier loaded with men. Most of them were too tired, hungry and worn out to wonder what happened.

On Renny's way home, headed east to the Riverside District, he saw a line of strikers, some with young families that were going into the basement of Father Nathan Bywater's church, the Holy Cross of the Virgin Mary. Bywater was out front talking to the men and women waiting and milling around.

"First let the children eat all they want," he was saying, as Renny walked by. Bywater noticed him. The priest smiled and offered, "Please come and have some soup, won't you?" Even though Renny's stomach rumbled with hunger, he didn't want a handout.

"That's OK, Father. I am tired," Renny replied. He continued walking and thought with his head down, *I am not going to take charity.*

He crossed Broadway and wandered through riverside neighborhoods on his way home. At Market Street the usual neighborhood kids weren't peeking through the fence in front of the Lafayette House. He'd forgotten that school had started.

After arriving at his little weather-beaten cottage, he kicked off his worn-out muddy boots on the porch, unlocked the front door, carried his boots inside, and set them down in the entry, then hung the key on a nail. Petra greeted him with the biggest smile he'd ever seen.

"Oh, Renny you are home!" she said brightly. Renny sniffed the air and crinkled his nose.

"Are you cooking meat?" Renny asked.

"Yah! There is a pork roast in the oven!" Petra said with a happy grin.

"A pork roast? How did ve get-a pork roast?"

"Oh, the neighbor lady from across the alley over on Harrison brought me some ironing work today . . . and . . . she pay me vith the pork roast," she stuttered with happiness.

"The neighbor lady? Again?" Renny said.

"Yah . . . She knock on the back door."

"Vell, I guess it vas your lucky day."

"It vas *our* lucky day," Petra said. "Here, sit. I vill get you a glass of vater. How vas the picket line?"

Renny plopped down at the kitchen table and sighed. "Ve hear shots out in the bay and then saw a boat full of men go up the river. I do not know vhat happened, but I did see the sheriff standing on the deck. I guess there vas more trouble. I am tired of this strike. Ve are not getting anyvhere," he said as Petra pulled the pork roast out of the oven. She set it on the stove and stabbed the roast with a fork.

"Maybe ve should leave?" Renny asked.

Not turning around, Petra said, "I vant to stay now. I think you vill vin the strike."

"Now you vant to stay?"

"Yah," she said, facing the stove.

"But you vanted to go."

"I know. But you vorked so hard, and ve vaited so long. It not be right to leave. You said ve have to hold on, remember?" Petra said. She set the fork down and sat on Renny's lap.

"Ve vill be OK," she said.

"Yah. Ok. Let's eat," Renny replied with a tired smile.

***

After dark, Deputy Irvan unlocked and stepped into the cell where James Thompson lay on a cot. Deputy Pete Hanigan stood waiting at the cell door with a hand on his revolver.

"Get up," Irvan said.

"What for?" Thompson said, opening his eyes.

"'Cause we're givin' ya back all yer crap, that's why. Here's yer glasses and notebook, and yer wallet," the deputy said, handing over the articles.

"Where's my money?" Thompson said, looking in his empty billfold.

"We're keeping it to pay fer all the damages," Irvan replied and motioned with a thumb to the cell down the hall.

"What kind of justice is that?" Thompson asked.

"Take it up with yer damn union. Now get up."

Deputy Irvan jerked Thompson to his feet, spun him around, and cuffed him, then led him outside to a waiting patrol car with Deputy Hanigan following. The sheriff was already behind the wheel, Deputy Beard sat next to him. Irvan started to shove him in the back seat.

"We're gonna send you on your way back to Seattle," the sheriff said from the cab, "and Walt, you get in back with him, and Pete, I need you to stay here till we get back."

"Where are you taking me? What's going on?" Thompson asked as the sheriff drove off.

"Well, you came back to Everett. And I told your sorry ass not to come back here. You know, all yer doin' when you come to my town is just a-borrowin' trouble," the sheriff said calmly. "Are you understanding me yet, Thompson? So now yer gonna have to deal with the citizens of this town who do not like your kind, and there is no telling what a bunch of citizens will do."

"What are you talking about? You have no right —"

"I've got the right to keep the peace, ain't I? Sides, you ain't got any rights in my town, you worthless, speechifyin' bum!"

"I'm no bum," Thompson replied, "I'm a union man."

"Union? You mean that IWW thing? That ain't no *real* union," the sheriff barked.

"It most certainly is. Weren't you were a union man once?" Thompson asked. McRae looked at the IWW through the rear-view mirror and then snarled.

"I'm an AFL man, and this is an AFL town. And it's always gonna be an AFL town. That is exactly why we're sendin' yer sorry, damn, eye-dub-ya dub-ya ass on down the road. So shut yer head!"

They headed out the Pacific Highway and stopped where the Interurban train tracks crossed the road. A dozen cars and trucks were parked in the vacant lot on the corner of Scenic Drive and down the street, but no one was in sight. Deputy Irvan jerked Thompson from the backseat and un-cuffed him.

"There's the road to Seattle! So beat it!" the sheriff commanded, pointing down the tracks. He kicked Thompson in the trousers and yelled, "and if'n ya ever make the dumb mistake of comin' back here, there'll be a whole mess a' trouble awaitin' fer ya!"

"Ya got that, Thompson? A whole mess a trouble!"

Thompson started walking. When he was one-hundred feet away, he yelled over his shoulder, "See ya soon, Sheriff!"

McRae turned around, hitched his belt, and yelled, "Ya dumb Wobbly! Ya should-a started runnin' when I let ya go!" He laughed heartily.

A second later Thompson heard a couple of twigs snap. He took three quick steps, and then the sound of coarse trousers moving through the brush filled the damp night air. Fifty men with white handkerchiefs covering their faces rushed from the shadows and surrounded him. One held back and lit a kerosene lantern. The union agitator stopped and slowly turned in a circle. He threw his coat down on the ground and put up his fists.

"You bunch a' cowards. Surround an innocent man with all yer clubs!" Thompson yelled. He stayed in a boxer's stance and slowly turned in a circle, looking at every man.

"The sheriff warned ya," Beau Hardee said from behind his mask. Thompson spun around to face him.

"How about you and me then?" the organizer said, motioning with the fingers of his right hand for the vigilante to come forward. But Hardee didn't move.

"Come on. Let's go one on one. What? You chicken? Fine . . . I'll take all of you on one at a time!" Thompson hollered, moving his fists in tight circles. Still no one moved.

"You're all a bunch of cowards!" Thompson screamed and then lunged in Beau Hardee's direction. At the same time a dark figure rushed from the circle of vigilantes, swung a baseball ball, and hit Thompson behind the knees. Thompson moaned and bent over, feebly trying to keep his fists up. Another blow from an ax handle hit him across the back, and a blanket was tossed over his head. A storm of clubs, boots, and shotgun butts poured onto him until he was lying prone on the ground. Four of the men grabbed Thompson by his arms and legs and dragged him into the woods, laying him belly down across a log, where they tore off his coat and shirt and held him in place.

Beau Hardee tore a limb from a devil's club bush and began to whip his back with the sap yelling, "Take that, you Wobbly son-of-a-bitch!"

Finally, one citizen deputy pushed himself into the group with his lantern raised and yelled, "OK, that's enough! Let him go!"

Beau Hardee hit Thompson one last time and dropped his sap. The citizen deputies walked away leaving Thompson where he lay.

***

Two days later Luther MacCullock's phone rang.

"Yes?" he said into the receiver.

"It's Feeney."

"Yes," MacCullock said.

"There's a picture of James Thompson on the front page of the *Seattle Daily Times*."

"So?" MacCullock grunted.

"It shows his back all whipped and beaten, and there's an article about the brutalities in Everett."

"And what if there is?"

"Well, the IWW hall is full of angry men, and Mayor Gill was just there speaking. He said that he's going to get the governor involved."

"Feeney! I don't give a damn what they do or say in Seattle. This is none of their business."

"I just thought you should know," Bradford explained.

"Yes, yes," MacCullock said and then coughed, "Good work, Feeney."

"OK, sir. Got to get going," Feeney said.

"Hold on, I haven't heard a word from Claymore."

"He's his own boss, Mr. MacCullock."

"And what's that supposed to mean?"

"He's been a detective for a long time, and done a lot of undercover work," Bradford replied. "He knows how to break strikes. He'll be in touch with you."

"Oh, I'm sure he knows how to do his job, but that doesn't mean he can't keep me updated on his progress. If he contacts you then you tell him to call me. I need to know what he's doing and what I'm paying for," MacCullock said, hanging up the phone.

PART THREE

Chapter 11

IN THE BIGHT

Charlie and Shep were the last to jump on the flat car that morning at Timber Creek. A few stars faintly shone in the pale light of another day, glowing kerosene lamps hung from a load pole on each car. Men sat silent beside assorted tools: saws, axes, sledge and stamping hammers, climbing gear, blocks, and rigging rope. The engineer blew the whistle three times and started the backwards climb up to Mineral Springs. Slowly but surely the Shay's gear-driven wheels turned in reverse for the three-mile ride up to the show.

Axel Chambers sat motionless on one flatcar, thinking about how, after twenty years of living on the earth, and spending the last three years of that jumping over logs, setting choke in the woods with a bunch of morons and immigrants, he was stuck way out in the sticks when he should be down in town chasing skirts. His life disgusted him. He stared blankly at the black landscape of logged-off devastation. Axel hated the dark early mornings and didn't like the thought of still having to work with Jaako every day.

At the last horseshoe switchback Axel grabbed his nosebag and stood up, holding fast to a load pole as he waited for the train to stop. As soon as it did he jumped off and darted down the main skid road. The gouged path was filled with large puddles of rain-water and crossed through creeks and swales. After a quarter mile Axel looked over his shoulder, Jaako and whistle punk Ruben Tisdale followed him about fifty yards behind. When Axel got to the work site he sat down on a stump and pulled out his can of snoose. He put a pinch between his cheek and gum then stared at Jaako as he approached.

"Listen here, ya dumb old Scandi, I ain't takin' orders from you anymore. You got that?" Axel growled. "And don't be askin' me anything 'er keep provin' to me how stupid ya are."

Jaako smiled and nodded, "Yah, sure, Axel, I vould not do dat."

Ruben quietly listened to their jawing and headed down to his jerk wire, which hung from a tree at the edge of the clear-cut.

"Good, and just because yer so much older than me don't mean you know it all," Axel grunted. The donkey whistle sounded in the distance, the three loggers turned in its direction. It was the signal that the donkey engine had a head of steam, another day in the woods had cranked into existence.

Axel turned to look at Ruben and raised his right arm in the air, then spun his hand in a tight circle. The whistle punk jerked the wire three quick times and the whistle at the donkey blasted. The haul-back cable began to move overhead. They could hear the chokers clanging louder as the rigging got closer. When the chokers were above the logs to be yarded Axel gave the hand signal again, and the whistle punk jerked the wire once. The cable stopped.

Axel and Jaako ran over to the dangling choker cables, where each of them grabbed hold of one. They pulled the chokers over to separate logs and looped the nub end around the log and then fastened it in the fish hook housing that slid along the cable. They cinched each log tight like a slipknot. Once the two four-foot-diameter logs were choked, Axel and Jaako hopped on top and ran along them. Then they jumped and ran out of the way, each one of them vaulting over a swale in the ground on their way to safety and out of the bight. Axel looked to the whistle punk and spun his hand in the air, the punk jerked the whistle wire three times.

The haul-back cable pulled the choker cables tight, both massive pieces of timber lurched forward through the brush. Each choked end of log then rose in the air, and off they crashed along the skid trail. The overly strained cable stretched taut from the massive load and a new strand fractured at the fray.

When the logs reached the landing Silas disengaged the drum lever and closed the pressure valve. Little Stovie went over and unhooked the chokers. He ran out of the way and gave the thumbs up. Silas opened the valve, pulled the return lever, and the cable zoomed back out into the clear-cut.

Axel saw the cable begin to move and pulled the can of snoose out of his back pocket. He put another pinch between his cheek and gum and then spit. A long, thick strand of brown saliva stuck to his chin and shirt. Jaako watched and snickered to himself.

"Ya got a yiddle on ya dar, fella," Jaako laughed.

"Shut up, you stupid Scandi!" Axel yelled and wiped the spit off his face.

"Yah, sure, ya betcha, sonny."

"And don't be calling me sonny you old worn out son of a bitch," Axel snapped as he spun his hand in the air. The whistle punk jerked his wire once, the chokers clanged to a stop. Jaako ran out ahead of Axel, latched on to a choker cable, and pulled it over to a log that had an end up the air. Jaako quickly choked off his log while Axel had to dig out a gopher hole under his.

"Vat's the matter, Axel? Ya not fast enough?" Jaako teased.

"I'll beat the tar outta you, old man, if'n ya don't shut yer trap!" Axel shouted as he dug a tunnel for the choker cable under the log.

Jaako enjoyed seeing Axel struggle with his task. He spun around on his cork boot heel, ran on his log, and jumped into the slash. He made his way through the buck-brush uphill in the direction of the donkey then jumped on a stump near the two logs. He watched with a grin while Axel cussed and fussed trying to snake the nub-end of the choker under the log. Axel gave up and moved the choker up the tree out of sight in the brush.

Five minutes later Axel was out of the way and spinning his hand in the air. The whistle punk jerked the wire three times. Jaako was still watching with the grin on his face. The chokers tightened. The logs lurched forward through the brush and slash, and the cable strained, then one log started to go sideways. The choked end of the log had hit a boulder hidden in the brush, it pivoted the log, as the other end swung around and lodged against a stump. But the log started to roll upward, it looked like it was going to free itself, then jarred to a stop. Downhill, the tail tree that held the return block bent and two guy wires broke. Jaako snapped his body around at the zinging sound of the breaking guy wires just as Axel signaled the whistle punk. Ruben jerked the whistle wire but he wasn't fast enough.

In an instant the overwhelming tension snapped the haul-back cable at the fray on the donkey side of the cable. It whipped around like a rubber band as Jaako turned back to the logs. The cable's light side sliced through the air like a whip and slammed into Jaako with a force so great it knocked him thirty-feet through the air and into the brush a split second before the heavy butt-rigging side of the cable dropped to the ground.

"Jaako!" Axel yelled, still spinning his hand in the air. "Jaako! Where are ya?" Axel turned to the whistle punk station where Ruben was looking at the shaking tail tree, then at the downed cable, and then at Axel.

"Ruben you worthless bastard! What the hell are ya doing?" Axel yelled as he scrambled over to where he thought Jaako was. Ruben threw his hands up in the air and hollered, "I don't know! I don't know what happened!"

Axel found Jaako lying face up beside a thicket of buck-brush, conscious but barely alive. A gash across his stomach exposed his insides, blood was everywhere.

"Get some help! Get some help, Ruben! Blast that whistle and keep it blasting!" Axel screamed. "Then run and get Charlie! Jaako's hurt bad!" Axel knelt down next to him. The whistle blared until Ruben stopped jerking his wire, he ran up to the landing.

"Oh, Jesus, oh, Jesus in heaven," Axel pleaded. Jaako pushed his elbows down against the ground and tried to get up.

"Don't move. Ruben went to get help," Axel said, holding Jaako's shoulders down.

"Vhere am I? Vhy am I in da bushes?" Jaako asked, his eyes darting around.

"Something went wrong."

"Vhat happen?" Jaako asked. "Vhat happened to me?"

"The haul-back snapped."

"Da haul-back snap?"

"Yeah, the cable whipped back and got ya."

"But ve have to vork now. Ve have to choke da logs!" Jaako said.

"No Jaako, just lie still."

"Vat is da matter?"

"Yer hurt bad."

"Let me up! Vhere is Jorgen? *Jeg vil se min bror*," Jaako begged trying to lift his head up. He tried to grip Axel's arm but his strength was fading.

"Jorgen? He's OK. He'll be here, soon," Axel said, keeping Jaako still.

"Is not so bad. I be OK," Jaako said, rolling his head from side to side. "Let me vork. I vant to vork."

"Hold on, Jaako. We'll get ya taken care of," Axel assured him.

Jaako touched his open stomach, grimaced, and began to shiver. He looked into Axel's eyes and quietly said, "I not feeling anything. It is getting cold."

"It's gonna be alright. Hold on," Axel replied and looked away.

"Yah, vell, I guess I use up my vone mistake today," Jaako said calmly.

"Oh, no. Not so fast. It'll be OK," Axel tried to assure him.

"Are you going to . . . bury me?" Jaako's asked as all the air went out of his body.

"Nah, not yet. Helps on the way. Just be still," Axel said. But Jaako's eyes became lucid, and gained the look of transcendence, his head slowly rolled to the side.

"Oh no, no, no, no," Axel moaned and shook Jaako's shoulders, "Why, why, why?" He got to his feet and the world started to spin, his legs went out from underneath him and he collapsed to the ground on all fours. Losing control he began to convulse, over and over, until his breakfast flew out of his stomach. Axel coughed and wretched a few times and tried to take some deep breaths. Finally, his body relaxed, he went over to a nearby mud puddle and rinsed off his face.

He pulled himself up on a stump and saw Little Stovie coming down the skid path with Silas a good distance behind. He waved his arms until Stovie saw him. Axel cupped his hands to his mouth and yelled, "Tell Silas to go back and get help! Jaako's hurt bad!" He stumbled over to Jaako.

"Help's comin', Jaako. Hold on," Axel said, but Jaako's eyes were empty.

Axel immediately despaired and began talking to himself. He told himself that it wasn't his fault, but he knew he'd be blamed. *How will I duck this if I'm blamed? Should I quit? I can't stand working here. Will Charlie fire me? What am I gonna say? What am I gonna do? Jorgen's gonna blame me for sure. The crew is gonna say I did it on purpose because they knew I hated Jaako!*

***

Charlie and Shep had been two sides ahead of the crew, working their way through the forest flagging lines and scaling board footage all morning. Far away from them the faint sound of the donkey whistle could be heard every ten minutes, followed by the crashing of timber being yarded. White pipe smoke encircled Shep's head as he jotted down figures on a small notepad in between glancing at a map and compass he had on the ground in front of him. Then he heard Charlie cussing through the trees up ahead. Shep put the notepad and compass in his pocket, carefully rolled up the map, and started walking through the virgin forest along a small stream, headed in the direction of Charlie's imprecations.

Fifty yards later he saw Charlie throwing rocks at a short cliff that was flanked by an outcropping of boulders on the side of a small ravine. He swore at the top of his lungs with every throw. Small cedar sprouts that grew between watery cracks in the cliff of boulders had been trimmed back, and the limbs of larger saplings were removed. What looked like a cave opening was in the middle with spring water flowing out of it and down to the forest floor. Some planking was mounted above the cave entrance with black writing that read, "IWW Hotel – All Welcome." Ten feet inside the cave and out of view was a gunny-sack full of dynamite hanging in the shadows.

Two chopped tree limbs formed a make-shift rustic roof above the sign. Another larger cedar tree had the letters IWW carved out of the bark, the yellow cedar wood underneath exposed. A ring of stones was below it all with the charred remains of a campfire, a blackened water pot was next to it along with a hammer and some tree shoe spikes. The decomposed remains of a small homestead log cabin was over against the slope of the hill. Charlie kicked at the fire ring and then picked a rock up from it.

"Whoever the sumbitch is that did this," Charlie yelled and chucked the stone, "is outta my camp? Gone. God-damned Wobbly bastards. They can all go to hell!"

Shep walked up and put his hands on his hips. His eyes darted back and forth as his head snapped around from rock to rock as he read the big black letters that were scrawled in crude writing on every smooth face of light-colored boulder facing downhill: "The IWW is Here" – "One Big Union" – "I Was Robbed" – "Where's My Money" – "Dump the Boss" – "Strike" – "Injury to One" – "Injury to All" – "Beware Black Cat" – "Workers Unite" – "Which Side You On."

"What in the world?" Shep said with a slackened jaw. He took a long pull from his pipe, and, with smoke streaming out of his nostrils, he said, "I'll be go to hell, somebody worked pretty hard on this. Must have roped down from the top, I guess."

"Hard work," Charlie snapped, "This ain't hard work. This is bullshit!"

"Yeah, right. I didn't mean it that way. I just meant it looked like a lot of effort," Shep offered.

"I *knew* there was one of 'em in my camp," Charlie said, staring at the edifice. He kicked at the fire ring stones again.

"What?" Shep said, "You, *knew*? You *knew* what?"

"Aw, I found a Wobbly flyer thing in one of the outhouses a couple a' weeks ago," Purvis said.

"Ya did? What was it?" Shep asked.

"Nothin'," Charlie spat, "just some stupid thing about sabotage and joinin' the IWW."

"What'd ya do about it?" Shep said. The donkey whistle sounded in the distance.

"Just yelled at the crew. Told 'em I was gonna fix whoever did it," Charlie answered. The donkey whistle blasted longer. "The men said there wasn't any Wobblies up here, they said it was probably the choke setter that just quit."

Both men turned their heads at the same time towards the donkey whistle that didn't stop sounding.

"That whistles been blastin' fer too long," Shep said, "Somethin's wrong." Charlie glanced back at the slogans and then tilted his head to listen again. He snapped around and looked at Shep.

"Dammit!" Charlie cussed. They both knew what it meant.

"The accident signal," Shep blurted.

"Let's go," Charlie said as he started to run. Shep was right on his heels. He ran right by a massive old growth cedar but didn't notice that the bark was scarred and torn from climbing spurs.

A quarter mile away, Reader Bill and Harry had heard the whistle in the distance and stopped work on their undercut.

"What's going on?" Harry asked.

"Whatever it is, it isn't good," Reader Bill said. "The last time the whistle blew like that was when Calvin Hartline got killed." Reader Bill hopped off his springboard and began running.

"Come on, Harry. There's been an accident!" Bill yelled.

***

Little Stovie worked his way through the brush-choked clear cut to Axel. Catching his breath, Stovie gasped, "How's he doing?" But when he saw Jaako he turned away.

"Jaako's dead," Axel replied.

Little Stovie's face became ashen. After a long pause he said, "What happened?"

"The haul back got all turned around and hung up, then the cable snapped," Axel said. "It flew back and hit him because Ruben didn't hit the whistle."

"Why didn't he?" Stovie asked trying to breathe.

"Because that gall-derned Ruben is worthless, that's why." Axel said, his nervous voice rising. "And now Jaako's dead. Where the hell is that Ruben?"

Little Stovie turned and looked up and down the skid line. "Don't know. He came up and told us. Didn't see him again."

"That son of a bitch knows he's to blame and probably ran off, I bet," Axel said. He took his shirt off and covered Jaako's head.

"What . . . what do we do now?" Stovie asked with a tremble.

"We'll just sit here and wait," Axel said and then worked his way through the brush over to a stump and sat down. Little Stovie joined him in solemn silence.

The morning air was still, and the woods were quiet. A few goldfinches appeared and settled on a nearby bush. They began to sing, reminding Axel of a church choir. He stood up on the stump and saw two deer in the distance on the edge of the clear cut licking lichen off of a large boulder, apparently unmoved by the events of the morning. Then he noticed Charlie and Shep at the tail tree.

"Up here!" Axel yelled as he waved his arms.

Charlie waved back. Axel and Stovie could see Shep pointing at the broken guy wires while both of them talked for a minute. Then the two foremen walked to where Axel and Stovie were.

"What the hell happened here?" Charlie asked as they got closer.

"Jaako's dead," Axel said, his eyes cast downward.

"What! Where?" Shep barked.

"He's over there," Axel answered and pointed to where Jaako was, his hand trembling.

"For Christ sakes Axel!" Shep yelled. "What happened?"

"The turn went sideways and Ruben didn't jerk the whistle wire. Then the haul-back snapped."

"Why didn't Ruben jerk his wire?" Shep asked.

"Don't know. It all happened so fast. He jerked the wire but it was too late."

"Where's Ruben now?" Charlie asked.

"He ran for help. Ain't come back," Axel said.

Stovie chimed in, "That's right."

"When the cable snapped, it whipped back and hit Jaako. Sent him flying through the air," Axel offered, gesturing with a hand. "Cut his side open and killed him."

"Charlie, where's Jorgen today?" Shep asked somberly, his face drained of color.

"He's a couple sides over below where Reader Bill is," Charlie said, and then started shaking his head, "an' I ain't goin' over there an' tellin' him, nope. I'm stayin' right here. I'll figure out a way to get him to the landing."

Shep knelt down and lifted the shirt off of Jaako's face to look at him. He touched his fingers to his own lips, touched Jaako's pale forehead with his fingers, and mouthed a short prayer. Shep crossed himself and stood up. He went over to inspect the cable and found it on the ground, then followed it to where it had broken. Shep picked up the end and saw that the cable was rusted and rotted out at a fray. A number of strands had separated from the bulk of the cable that were an inch long. He threw the cable down and shook his head, then inspected the logs. One was choked on the end, the other was choked a little farther from its end but still positioned right. He unhooked the chokers, tossed them aside, and walked away to find Jorgen.

"Stovie, run up to the landing, find some rope and bring it back," Charlie ordered.

"What for?"

"'Cause I said so, that's what for, ya dumb kid. Now get ta' runnin'. Axel, find us a couple of strong limbs to build a stretcher with, now!" Charlie snapped as he looked around the landscape.

Shep made his way over to where Jorgen was. As he moved through the brush and slash, the image of the frayed cable reappeared in his mind. His thoughts raced as he walked, he told himself what he knew about the accident. *That cable was old, frayed, rusted, and rotted. All this machinery should be replaced, and if I'd seen or known about that cable, I would have had it replaced. Hell, if I was running this show things would be different, better . . . And this never would have happened.*

Jorgen was high off the ground rigging a spar two sides over and in the process of hammering on the tree shoes for hanging the bull block. He'd already hung the small pass block at the very top to pull up the nine-hundred-pound bull block for the high lead operation and fastened and tightened the guy wires on the spar the day before.

"You yust make sure ya got dat bull strap hooked tight before ya send it up," Jorgen yelled down at a flunky below him as Shep showed up. Jorgen saw him.

"I heard dat vhistle. Vhat's it now?" Jorgen hollered down from a hundred feet in the air.

"You 'bout done up there?" Shep shouted, his hands cupped to his mouth.

"Vee got an early lunch today?" Jorgen asked.

"Yep," Shep said, looking up briefly.

"Yust a minute," Jorgen yelled and then added, "Ve are yust about out of dees nails." He held a spike out for Shep to see and then hammered it, fastening the tree shoe onto the spar, and started climbing down. Shep's heart began to pound in his throat. Jorgen landed on the ground, took one look at Shep's white face, and stopped.

"Vat is it?"

"Jorgen," Shep said with a slight quaver, "there's been . . . an accident."

"Who?"

"Jaako."

Jorgen's shoulders sunk. He bent over, put his hands on his knees and said at the ground, "*Kjaere gud nei, ikke Jaako.*" He shook his head and began to quietly moan. After a minute he stopped.

"Vere is my brudder?" Jorgen said, not looking up.

"They should be carrying him down to the landing by now."

"Vhat happen?" Jorgen asked.

"The haul-back snapped . . . and the cable whipped back and hit him. I don't think he felt a thing. He's in a better place now," Shep said. Jorgen stood up, unhooked his climbing belt, and let it drop on the ground. He slowly took off his climbing spurs and started walking toward the landing with his eyes looking straight ahead.

***

At the landing, men huddled around Jaako's lifeless body. He was covered with a coat, lying flat on a make shift stretcher of rope and fir limbs in the dirt beside the huge pile of decked timbers.

The crowd parted to let Jorgen through as he approached. Not acknowledging anyone, he knelt over his brother and pulled back the coat. He threw himself on top of Jaako's body, then started talking softly in Norwegian while the rest of the men moved away. Shep pulled Axel out of the crowd just as Reader Bill, Harry, Dirty Shirt and the rest of the crew showed up.

"Jaako was a good man, a good worker. I liked him a lot," Shep said.

"Yep," Axel replied.

"He's gonna be missed around here."

"Yeah. I know," Axel said, looking down at the ground.

"How long you and Jaako work together?" Shep asked. Axel's inside's jumped.

"A few weeks 'er so," Axel answered.

"You and him get along?"

"Oh, yeah," Axel lied.

"OK. So, tell me again exactly what happened?" Shep asked calmly.

"Well," Axel began, "we choked our logs and Ruben hit the whistle three times. The haul-back started out OK, but then one of the logs went catawampus."

"How so?"

Axel glanced away, hesitated, and then answered, "It must have hit a stump or a boulder buried in the brush maybe."

"You sure about that?" Shep asked, staring him down.

"Yeah, I think so."

"I noticed one of those logs was choked maybe a bit too far from the end," Shep stated.

"Oh, both a' them logs was choked right," Axel quickly answered. Shep nodded his head, thought for a moment and continued. "Then what?"

"Well, once it got hung up, I turned around to signal at Ruben and I yelled . . . but it all happened so fast," Axel said, fidgeting with his hands. "Then the cable snapped, whipped back, and hit Jaako."

"You ever see anything wrong with that haul-back cable?" Shep asked as he watched every wrinkle in Axel's face.

Axel thought for a moment. "Well, jeez, I don't think so. I woulda said something if'n I did."

"OK, Axel," Shep said.

They walked back over to the crew of men standing around Jaako. They'd seen men killed before, but this was Jaako, a man who always had a smile on his face and a dream in his heart, a dream they all shared: to work in the woods of the great northwest.

Reader Bill began to recite the Lord's Prayer. Every man lowered his head.

"Our Father, who art in heaven, hallowed be thy name. Thy kingdom come, thy will be done, on earth as it is in heaven. Give us our daily bread. And forgive us our trespasses, as we forgive those who trespass against us. And lead us not into temptation, but deliver us from evil, for thine is the kingdom, and the power, and the glory, for ever and ever. Amen."

Reader Bill raised his head, opened his eyes, and said, "Jaako was a friend to us all. I never once heard him utter a bad word. He was blessed with a good heart. Rest in peace Jaako, you will be sorely missed."

A few seconds after Reader Bill's words Shep stepped over to Charlie and pulled him aside.

"That haul-back cable had a fray in it," Shep said as he looked Charlie in the eye.

"What're you talkin' about?" Charlie asked.

"I said that cable had a fray in it."

"No, it didn't," Charlie snapped.

"It had a fray and the cable was rotted out. You did the rig-up when you brought it up here," Shep said louder.

"I checked that cable," Charlie said.

"Yeah, and you hung that cable with that rigger you fired weeks ago!"

"Are you callin' me a liar?" Charlie snarled.

Shep stared Charlie down. The crew standing around Jaako turned toward the two arguing foremen.

"I'm telling you that cable was rusted and frayed where it broke," Shep reiterated.

When Little Stovie heard the word *fray*, he thought back about seeing something on the cable, a shiver went up his spine. Little Stovie turned to look up at Dirty Shirt. He poked him in his side.

"I think I saw the fray," Stovie whispered, white as a ghost.

"You saw a fray?" Dirty Shirt asked Stovie. Little Stovie nodded his head and quietly said, "Yeah I saw it," as the foremen continued to argue. Dirty Shirt's jaw clamped tight, his body stiffened, and he clenched his fists.

"Yeah, well. Even if there was a fray, which there weren't, Ruben should have jerked his wire and stopped the cable," Charlie sizzled.

"This ain't Ruben's fault. Axel says it happened too fast. I'm telling you that cable never should have been brought up here on that donkey!" Shep yelled, spit flying from his mouth.

"That cable was fine!" Charlie yelled back.

"Yer a God-damned liar!" Shep hollered, his face twisting in anger. In a flash Charlie Purvis took a roundhouse swing at Shep and knocked him backwards.

"Why, you cheap-shot son of a bitch," Shep growled and put up his fists.

"Nobody calls me a liar in my camp," Charlie said as he ripped off his leather coat and threw it behind him at the feet of the onlookers.

When the coat hit the dirt, Shep threw himself at Charlie with fists swinging. Charlie took a jab at Shep's head but missed. Shep countered and landed a blow to Charlie's nose.

"That's it, Shep," one man said, encouraging him.

"Get him!" another lumberjack urged as the crowd of workers tightened around the two fighters.

Blood streamed from Charlie's nose, he quickly wiped it with a forearm. Shep saw an opening and hit him again, this time in his stomach. Charlie hunched over, but he righted himself. His fists turned into a brawling machine. Right, left, right, left, Charlie pummeled Shep with a fury until Shep hit the ground. Charlie stood over him for a moment and then stepped back. He turned away from Shep and stumbled around inside the circle of loggers and glared at them.

"God dammit! Ya see? Ya see?" Charlie screamed at his crew and pointed at Shep, "That's what happens when ya talk back to Charlie Purvis. Accidents happen. Ya bunch of brush apes. Now get back to work!" He yelled, trying to catch his breath. Blood streamed down his face as he threw his arms around. "I said get back to work! Now! All of ya scram!"

Nobody moved except Shep. He pulled himself to his feet, put his hands on his knees, and gasped for air. Charlie turned around.

"Can't you bunch of timber bums hear me? I need to fill another raft of logs —" Shep ran and tackled Charlie. They landed in a heap to the sounds of the men cheering Shep on. Shep landed a few blows as they grappled on the ground, but Charlie spun out of Shep's hold, got him in a headlock and stood up, pulling Shep to his feet. Charlie hit him repeatedly with his free right fist. Shep was no match. Charlie finally let go of him.

Shep dropped to the ground breathing heavily.

Dirty Shirt jumped out of the crowd with a murderous look. With his head low and his fists clenched, he rushed a surprised Purvis and hit him square in the jaw, again and again. Charlie took a tired, out of balance round-house swing, but Dirty Shirt ducked and countered with a blow to Charlie's midsection that put him down on the ground. Purvis started to get up, but Dirty Shirt stomped him square in his side with his cork boot, holding him there in the dirt, ending the fight. Joe Frytag and Reader Bill went over and picked Shep up.

"You lying son of a whore," Dirty Shirt spat, standing over Charlie. "You knew all along about that cable and now Jaako's dead! It's your fault!"

"And what about the strike down in Everett?" Harry said, jumping out from the crowd. "You knew about that, too." When Harry said the word strike the ring of men around Charlie began to tighten.

"Go to . . . hell . . . Dolson," Charlie gasped as he lay the ground. "What do you know? . . . You're nothin' but a punk-assed kid."

"What strike? Who says there's a strike in town?" someone in the crowd yelled. "You mean at the mills?"

"All the mills in Everett have been on strike for months!" Harry yelled over the men.

"Charlie here has been workin' us like dogs while everyone in town is starving on the picket lines!" Harry yelled pointing at Charlie. "And he ran that bad cable because he didn't want to lose time 'er spend MacCullock's money fixin' it!"

"And now Jaako's dead because of you!" Dirty Shirt screamed. "You're done, Purvis. Tie him up, boys."

Harry picked up the leather coat and threw it over Charlie's head. The gang of lumberjacks pounced on him. They held him to the ground and tied his hands behind his back with some rigging rope.

"You dumb bastards, what do you think you're doing?" Charlie yelled, his voice muffled under his thick brown jacket as he struggled.

"Looks to me like we're firing yer ass!" Dirty Shirt exclaimed. Harry and Joe Frytag pulled Charlie to his feet while the rest of the crew joined in with whoops and calls.

"We need to ride this low-down piece of shit out of here on a rail," Joe said.

"Stop it! Stop it!" Reader Bill yelled, his voice cutting through the air as he pushed himself into the crowd. "What are you doing? You can't be judge, jury, and executioner here, and you're certainly *not* going to pass judgment on Charlie like this," Bill said, looking larger than life. "Only God can pass judgment on us mortals."

"Aw God dammit, to hell with you," Joe Frytag snapped.

"Take your blasphemy elsewhere, Frytag," Reader Bill commanded. But he was quickly over-ruled.

"We want justice!" one lumberjack proclaimed.

"Yeah, we want justice," another added.

"That's right. He's a killer and a liar!" Frytag yelled.

"Why don't we send him down to Sultan on the flume?" Axel offered as Jorgen began to push himself into the melee.

"Take his coat off!" Jorgen yelled as he made his way through the gang of men.

He glanced around at the men until his eyes landed on Little Stovie. Once their eyes met Jorgen's eyes seemed to spark. Harry ripped the dirty leather jacket off Charlie's head, Jorgen turned and stepped in front of him. Charlie's face was smeared in blood and bruised, his head cast downward.

"*Min bror er dod beause av deg!*" Jorgen hollered as he pointed at Jaako. Jorgen slapped his open palms on Charlie's chest and clutched his bloody shirt, and then he began to pound Charlie's chest like a drum.

"*Du drepte m bror!*" Jorgen screamed as he pounded, his face red and covered in sweat and tears. Jorgen stopped hitting him and glanced at Little Stovie. He turned back to Charlie, grabbed him by the hair, and stared him down. Then Jorgen spit in his face and yelled, ""*Jeg skal drepe deg med bare hendene! Min bror er død på grunn av deg! Du drepte min bror, og nå bli aldri far! Du vil ikke engang bekrefte din egen sønn drittsekk!*" He jerked Charlie's head back violently and then turned his back on him and walked slowly over to his brother's body in the dirt.

Shep and Dirty Shirt got behind Charlie and pushed him forward, stumbling through the crowd towards the spar tree next to the donkey. Dirty Shirt began to tie him off.

"What do you think you're doing? MacCullock will fire every one of your asses!" Charlie growled. "You'll never get away with this."

"Shut up, you worthless dog," Dirty Shirt said with a sneer. He cinched him tight like a choked-off log, and then growled, "Don't move."

They walked back over to the landing where the whole crew was grouped around Jorgen and Jaako.

"Let's get Jaako loaded on the flatcar so we can take him home, Jorgen," Shep said.

"Yah, sure," Jorgen replied quietly as he bent down and grabbed one side of the stretcher. Reader Bill knelt down at the other front handle while Harry and Dirty Shirt grabbed hold of the two handles at the back. They lifted Jaako in unison and walked to the locomotive with the crew following. Halfway there, one of Jaako's bloodied arms slipped out from under the coat and hung at the side of the stretcher. It swung like a pendulum, a grim reminder that the woods of western Washington had no mercy.

Shep walked ahead of the funeral procession. The engineer was standing on the last flatcar.

"What the hell happened?" the engineer asked, his wrinkled face contorted and pale.

"The haul-back snapped, killed Jaako," Shep said as he hopped up on the car.

"Christ, not Jaako!" the engineer said as the pallbearers hoisted Jaako's body up to the flatcar where Shep and the engineer pulled him aboard. Once his body was secured Shep turned to the crew.

"Jaako was a good man, and I will remember him for . . . the rest of my life," Shep said with his voice cracking. Then he coughed and spoke louder, "And since its Saturday, this show might as well be shut down. If some of you left yer gear out in the woods, it'll be fine till Monday. Let's roll up."

Dirty Shirt turned around and pushed his way through the other men. They followed him over to Charlie.

"What're we gonna do?" Harry asked as he caught up with him.

"I don't know what yer gonna do, but I got a damn sight good idea of what I'm gonna do," Dirty Shirt said, the skin on his face as tight as a drum.

Once he was a few paces away from Charlie, Dirty Shirt stepped over to a short piece of rope lying on the ground and picked it up. He looped it around Charlie's head and started to tie it off. Reader Bill grabbed Dirty Shirt from behind.

"What do you think you're doing? You can't treat him like that," Reader Bill said ripping the rope away from Dirty Shirt and taking it off of Charlie.

"Charlie Purvis is a low-down killer!" Harry shouted.

"You don't know that," Reader Bill said.

"He's not worth spit," Dirty Shirt said.

"We need to get the sheriff," Bill urged.

"Shut up!" Dirty Shirt yelled. "This man is a criminal and we are gonna deal with him today!"

"That's right," Harry added.

"Now hold on a minute. I know Charlie's no prince, but," Reader Bill said, "we can't take the law into our own hands."

"Purvis needs to be punished!" Axel yelled.

"For once in your life you're right, Axel," Dirty Shirt agreed.

"He'll be punished, but not by you," Reader Bill said. "Like I said, you cannot be the judge and jury here. We need to get the authorities involved before this gets out of hand."

"And why would we do that?" Harry cracked.

"Yeah, he needs to be dealt with," Joe Frytag added.

"How 'bout if we roll him in sap and stick him to a tree?" one lumberjack said.

"Why don't we just tar and feather him?" another man offered.

"We should tie him up and leave him in the woods for the wolves," a logger suggested.

"Who said we should send him down the flume?" Dirty Shirt asked the crew.

"I did," Axel Chambers replied.

"Well, Axel," Dirty Shirt said with a smirk, "I think I'm beginning to finally like you."

"You can't do that!" Reader Bill yelled. "It'll kill him! Please stop this madness!"

Charlie raised his head. "You can't . . . send me . . . down the flume," he sputtered. "That'll kill me. I'll drown."

"Oh, it won't kill ya, Charlie, not the way I'm thinking about doin' it," Dirty Shirt said as his mouth cracked into a devilish grin.

The Shay's whistle blew, every man turned his head to see the train still waiting. Shep was standing alone on the last flatcar, his pipe in his mouth, white smoke swirling around his head as steam hissed from the locomotive bleeder valve. The engineer stuck his head out of the control house and blew his whistle one more time, signaling that he was ready to go.

Dirty Shirt unlashed Charlie from the spar and, tying some rope to Charlie's belt, Dirty Shirt pulled him stumbling through the uneven dirt of the landing towards the train. Harry and Axel and the crew followed. At the Shay, Shep and the engineer stuck out their hands and helped Dirty Shirt climb up on the flatcar.

"Charlie here needs a one-way ticket to Timber Creek," Dirty Shirt said.

"Why 'er his hands tied?" the engineer asked.

"Tell him why I'm tied up," Charlie snarled through bloody lips.

"This damn bush-wah killed Jaako, that's why. And I told you to shut yer trap!" Dirty Shirt yelled.

"That right?" the engineer asked. Shep nodded his head.

A few men hoisted Charlie up as Shep and Dirty Shirt pulled him on. The rest of the crew loaded up what gear they had. Dirty Shirt tied the end of Charlie's belt rope to a load pole away from everyone and went over to Shep while Purvis fumed.

"You worthless sumbitches. You'll never get away with this. MacCullock will blackball all a' ya. You hear me. You'll never work in these woods again!" The camp foreman bellowed away, but the crew ignored him.

"What's Jorgen gonna do with Jaako's body?" Dirty Shirt asked Shep.

"Not sure yet. They don't have any family here so I guess we'll just take him down to the cemetery in Sultan and bury him with all the other loggers Charlie killed," Shep said, surrounded in pipe smoke. "But I'm wondering what you've got planned for him?"

"Listen, I'd appreciate it if you just stayed out of the way for the rest of the day. I ain't gonna kill Charlie Purvis, just send him on a little trip."

"What kind of trip?" Shep asked, taking the pipe out of his mouth.

"I plan on makin' things right for Jorgen, that's what," Dirty Shirt said. "And I'm gonna send Charlie on a fun little boat ride at the same time."

"OK Frank, I'm with ya as long as there's no more bloodshed," Shep replied, nodding his head. "I didn't care much for Purvis anyway, but there might be some consequences. Work wise, that is."

"Yeah, well," Dirty Shirt said, gathering his thoughts, "I'd rather be alive an' without a payday than dead and buried with all the others."

Shep stared at Dirty Shirt for a moment, took a puff off his pipe, and said, "Yep, well, I guess I can't argue with that."

Dirty Shirt went over to Harry and Axel. They quietly talked.

***

When the Shay pulled into Timber Creek early with very few logs and the crew on empty flatcars, camp cook Tubs Donovan came to the mess hall door. Reader Bill hopped off the flatcar first and walked over to him. Tubs had his hands on his apron-covered hips and a dish towel slung over his shoulder. As Bill got closer, the bull cook's brow began to furrow.

"What's goin' on?" Tubs asked.

"Bad day today," Reader Bill said, shaking his head. "The haul-back snapped and hit Jaako, killed him." Tubs looked over Bills shoulder and saw them unloading the stretcher.

"Jaako? Oh, for the love of Christ," Tubs said as his shoulders sank. "Where's Charlie?"

"He's there," Reader Bill said, nodding his head at the train, "sitting on the flatcar tied up."

"What's this now?" Tubs said, looking at the train. "Why's he tied up?"

"Well, most of the men think it was Charlie's fault," Bill replied.

"Charlie's fault. Why? Wait a second here, are you saying it was Charlie's fault?" Tubs said, his shoulders tightening.

"No. I'm not saying it, they are," Reader Bill said as he pointed quickly over his shoulder at the gang of men surrounding Charlie. "That's nonsense. Why, a man is killed up here every year," Tubs said. He pulled the dish towel off his shoulder and started to shake it at the train as he spoke. "Charlie Purvis never killed anyone. That's just the way things are. This is logging, doggone it!"

"I know that, and you know that, Tubs, but that gang over there claims there was a fray in the haul-back that Charlie knew about, and, I guess, Charlie hasn't been truthful about the mills on strike down in town."

"What?" Donovan blurted. "Oh, for criminy sakes, so what? There's a strike down in Everett all the time. What's the matter with these men? Well, I don't like it one bit, not one bit. But, uh . . . I guess you better bring Jaako inside. I'll tend to him and wash him down. We should keep the men out," Tubs said.

He looked over Reader Bill's shoulder to see Jorgen and a few of the crew carrying Jaako's body on the stretcher toward them. They stepped aside and lowered their heads as the four men carried Jaako into the mess hall and set him down on one of the tables. Reader Bill shut the door behind them and turned back to Tubs.

"OK, so, the crew," Reader Bill said, "they're takin' matters into their own hands. Probably be best to stay out of their way," Reader Bill advised.

"What? Stay out of their way?" Tubs asked and looked at the train with a tightened jaw. "What're they doing?"

Reader Bill looked away and shook his head. "Well," Bill said, looking back at Tubs, "It sounds like they're gonna send Charlie down the flume."

"Oh, for the love of Pete!" Tubs exclaimed. "They can't do that!"

"I know Tubs, but we're outnumbered," Reader Bill replied.

"If they pull a stunt like that Luther MacCullock will fix us all, fer good. Christ I might as well pack my bags right now!" Tubs hollered and turned to go back in the mess hall, throwing the towel on the floor in disgust before he slammed the door.

While Bill and Tubs talked, Dirty Shirt had jumped off the flatcar and walked over to the file shop. He kicked in the door with Harry and Axel right behind. They went straight for the rifle box, Dirty Shirt grabbed an ax from a filing bench and smashed open the box. Inside were the accumulated guns of the settlement, and gleaming above them all was Charlie's barely used Krag. Dirty Shirt snatched his Winchester.

"I'm getting' my rifle while I can," Dirty Shirt announced. "You two might wanna grab one. And take all those bullets." Harry reached into the box.

"Charlie's Krag?" Harry asked.

"Take it," Dirty Shirt said, handing him the expensive gun.

"Well, I want one," Axel said as he latched onto a rifle. Reader Bill suddenly appeared at the file shop door.

"Stop it!" Reader Bill hollered.

"Shut up, Bill," Dirty Shirt said, not turning around. "I'm only getting my rifle. And stay out of the way."

"Don't do this, Frank. You can't pass judgement like this," Reader Bill pleaded.

Dirty Shirt paused, turned, and looked him in the eye. "Listen, Bill, I know you're square with Jesus and God and all that religious stuff, but where was God today when Jaako got killed? Huh? Tell me that — Ya see, the way I figure it, if God don't care enough about us to stop Jaako from gettin' killed, then I don't see much reason for us to care about God."

"But God works in mysterious ways," Reader Bill replied in earnest. "The Lord's ways are not ours. Judgement only belongs to the Creator."

"Well then, the Creator can come on down here and pass judgement on me then. Listen, I ain't gonna kill Charlie Purvis," Dirty Shirt said firmly. "I'm just gettin' him out of this camp as fast as possible and givin' him the ride of his sorry-assed life at the same time, that's all."

The three of them stepped out of the file shop and walked towards the crew. Harry and Axel were behind Dirty Shirt, each with a rifle, their pants pockets bulging with ammunition. Shep and the crew had already unloaded Charlie from the train and were standing next to the flatcar. Dirty Shirt walked up to Purvis and grabbed the rope that was hanging from his belt. When Charlie saw Harry with his Krag strapped over his shoulder his face reddened, and he lunged at him.

"Hold on there," Dirty Shirt said jerking him back with the rope. Shep and Joe Frytag grabbed Charlie's arms from behind.

"Why you little sumbitch! What're you doing with my rifle?" Purvis screamed.

"Ha! You won't be needin' it anymore," Harry said, laughing with his hand on the leather strap.

"God dammit Dolson. I'll kill you!" Charlie barked.

"Shut up, Purvis," Dirty Shirt growled and then turned to the men. "This here son of a bitch has killed his last man. This piece of shit is to blame for Jaako's death, and he's a God-dammed liar!" Dirty Shirt yelled, pointing at Charlie. "So we's 'er gonna send him down the flume."

"We need to get the sheriff up here!" Reader Bill yelled from the back of the crowd surrounding Charlie.

"Get him up here fer what?" Joe Frytag said.

"To investigate the accident," Bill answered.

"Sheriff McRae ain't comin' up here," Dirty Shirt laughed. "From what I hear down in Sultan he's too busy fightin' strikers an' drinkin' whiskey. Besides . . . we ain't doin' any killin'. Old Purvis here has done enough of that today."

"But what happens after we send him down the flume?" Reader Bill asked. Then Shep stepped forward and addressed the crowd.

"Listen up men. We shouldn't be keepin' Northern Imperial stocked with logs so MacCullock can keep getting' rich and pay his scabs squat while every worker in Everett is on strike and their families starve!" Shep yelled out over the crew. Harry stepped forward.

"Those workers on strike have homes and families to support. Most of us don't. They are giving up everything for better pay and better working conditions while we've been up here keeping Northern Imperial stocked with timber to mill. I ain't gonna work for MacCullock any longer," Harry added.

"You dumb bastards!" Charlie Purvis yelled. "If you shut down this camp Luther MacCullock will eat you all alive!"

"Shut up, you little pissant," Dirty Shirt snarled.

"Yeah, pissant," Little Stovie said snickering, "Pissant Purvis!"

"So what's it gonna be, men?" Dirty Shirt asked.

"Hold on just a minute," Reader Bill interrupted. "What exactly are you planning, Dirty Shirt?"

"I say we stick him on a log and send him down the flume," Dirty Shirt answered with a grin. The crowd of men roared back in approval, with the exception of Silas Shotwell and a few other loggers who, seeing the direction of things, took the chance to slink away towards the bunkhouses. The rest of the crew looked at Dirty Shirt with eager faces.

"All right, it's settled," Dirty Shirt announced. "Some of you men find a short cedar log and a piece of lumber about six feet long, longer than the flume is wide. We're gonna build ourselves a canoe."

Some of the men rolled a two-foot-diameter, ten-foot-long cedar log over to the edge of the flume pond perpendicular to the water and placed it on top of two pieces of planking so it was off the ground. Chips flew in the air as Harry chopped out a notch two feet from one end, with each blow he'd snap his wrist, causing the blade to lever out the chunks. He nailed a piece of lumber to the log crossways in the notch and added some hemp lashing to hold it in place.

"With that cross piece, the log won't roll in the flume. We wouldn't want to see poor old Charlie's face scraped off," Harry said with a grin.

"You bunch a' bums are gonna have hell to pay. Especially you, Dolson!" Charlie yelled.

"Shut up, Purvis," Dirty Shirt snapped.

"We're ready," Harry said. Dirty Shirt grabbed hold of the rope still tied to Charlie's belt and pulled him over to the cedar log.

"I ain't gettin' on that thing," Charlie said.

"I just told you to shut up," Dirty Shirt snapped again. "You men pick him up and set his ass on that log."

Four men stepped forward, and each one grabbed hold of an arm or a leg. They picked Charlie up, laid him down on the length of cedar, and lashed his arms to the lumber cross-piece. They looped rope around Charlie's body and legs and the log, fastening him in place.

"This looks like some kind of crucifixion," Reader Bill complained.

"Exactly," Axel boasted.

"He deserves worse," Harry added.

"Pick up the end of that thing and slide him in the water," Dirty Shirt ordered. "Some of you men get pike poles and get out on the dam. Make sure he goes feet first down the flume."

A pack of happy lumberjacks picked up the end of the log where Charlie's head was and pushed him into the flume pond.

"You bastards, you just wait till I get back up here! I'm gonna kill every last one of ya!" Charlie yelled as they dumped him in the water.

Joe Frytag pushed him in the direction of the outlet with a pole. Charlie kicked the heels of his boots against the log and picked his head up and yelled while the men grinned and patted each other on the back.

"You swine!" Charlie hollered. "You're all of bunch of lily-livered, panty-waisted, yellow-bellied, scum-suckin' bastards! If I ever see any of you block-headed sumbitches again I will decapitate you like a spar!" The sight of Charlie Purvis bobbing like a cork in cold pond water was a delight to the crew.

"Good-bye, Charlie," Harry said, waving.

Some of the men began to prance around in a circle like square dancers as they hooted and hollered. A few linked arms and spun around and around while others did do-si-does with their arms crossed, high-stepping.

Charlie slowly floated over to the dam with the current, he rolled his head back and forth on the log and then lifted his head screaming, "MacCullock's got a hundred thugs in town that'll be up here in no time!" At the outlet, a few of the men pushed the log into position with their poles. When Charlie's arms and cross-piece hit the flume gate he stopped, so they picked the cross-piece up and vaulted Charlie over the dam and down the flume.

"God, damn you bastards!" Charlie yelled. His voice echoed and then faded as he headed down the flume. The cross-piece was longer than the flume was wide and acted like an outrigger, keeping him upright, the lumber scraping the sides of the flume as he picked up speed.

"Halleluiah! The son of a bitch is gone!" one of the lumberjacks hollered as the whole crew watched with delight at seeing Charlie Purvis float down the flume towards Sultan and the river splash pond.

"What's gonna happen when he gets to the river?" Little Stovie asked Harry.

"Well, I guess he's gonna go for a swim," Harry replied with a smile.

***

Lum was catching a cat-nap in the flume house while he waited for the logs to start running again. Three river pigs were sitting and talking on the half-full log raft with pike poles at their sides when the bell above the flume rang.

"Lum! Where the hell are ya? God dammit, Lum!" Charlie yelled as he cruised by the flume house soaking wet, his arms straight out to the side. The ends of the lumber his arms were tied to barely missed the framework of the supports of the little building where Lum sat. The river pigs jumped to their feet just in time to see a bloody-chested, beat-up Charlie Purvis arcing into the cold, clear waters of the upper Skykomish River, strapped to an ad hoc lumberjack cross as the flume water cascaded behind him like a crystal waterfall.

Hitting the water like an air-borne torpedo slicing into the depths, Charlie's cross-piece jolted with a crash when it hit the pond, his arms slamming unprotected onto the surface with a cannonball boom and splash.

Lum poked his head out the window and yelled, "What the hell was that?"

With a dropped jaw in the middle of his scruffy face and a grin as big as Puget Sound, river pig Amos Wade yelled, "I do declare! I think I may have just seen the second coming of Charlie Purvis!"

The log bobbed to the surface with Charlie on top. He coughed out a mouthful of water, raised his head off the log and screamed, "You God-damn lazy bastards, get me off of this thing! Now fer Christ-sakes!" The two other river pigs were shocked at what they'd just seen and pushed themselves out to Charlie on a skiff to help him while Amos stayed on the raft.

"Lord Almighty, if this ain't a Charlie Purvis baptism! He's done bathed himself clean in the Holy Waters of the Skykomish Valley!" the dirty old bearded river pig exclaimed.

Holding the pike pole to his side, and with a three-tooth grin on his face, Amos glowed with delight.

"What's next? Ya gonna rise up off that there cross and float on off ta heaven? But what about old Luther MacCullock? Mebbe you should ask for redemption from him first?"

"Damn you to hell, Amos Wade. Hurry up and get me off this thing!" Charlie hollered. The two other river pigs drifted over to him and maneuvered Charlie across the pond over to the raft, where they began to untie and cut him loose.

"You OK, Charlie?" one of the men asked.

"Yeah, you all right? What happened? What's going on up at the camp?" the other asked as Charlie gasped for breath. The stain of red on his work shirt stood out like a target.

Charlie's legs were shaking when they picked him up off the log. He took one faltering step on the raft and collapsed. Sputtering and breathing hard, he finally regained his balance. He kept his head down and stumbled over to Amos, then decked him with a roundhouse right swing, knocking him out before he hit the log raft with a woody thud. Charlie stood over him and glared at the prone river pig for a moment.

"I never did like you ya sumbitch," Charlie spat and then glared at the other two men who'd just saved him.

"Yer all fired!" Charlie yelled and stomped across the raft. Lum had watched and listened to it all in silence from the flume house.

"What's going on up at Timber Creek?" Lum yelled down from the gangway.

"The camp's finished!" Charlie screamed, he turned to walk away. "And yer fired, too!" As he climbed the river bank his steel cork boot spikes sounded out and sparked against the rocks with every step.

***

Harry was in the bunkhouse stuffing his clothes, gear, and ammunition in a gunny-sack.

"What do you think you're doing?" Reader Bill said from the doorway.

"Gettin' out," Dolson said.

"You mean running away?"

"I ain't running away from anything," Harry shot back.

"Looks like it to me."

Harry walked over to Bill, looked at him, and smiled.

"Listen Bill, I appreciate everything you've taught me up here, I hate to go but—"

"But what?" Bill cracked.

"I can't stay here anymore," Harry said looking away.

"Why's that?"

"Because, I'm headed for Seattle."

"What's in Seattle? You got a girl waiting down there?"

"Nope."

"I guess if ya had a girl you would have told me by now."

"I wish I had a girl in Seattle."

"What is it then?" Bill asked, leaning forward. "What's in Seattle?"

"My fellow workers."

"Your what? So I'm not your, *fellow worker?*"

"Bill, I joined the IWW four years ago in Portland. Signed up at Local 93, the same union hall that Joe Hill did back in aught seven. You see, after I ran away from the orphanage I ended up on Burnside Street in Portland, where a few Wobblies fed me and gave a place to stay. I guess I found the IWW as much as it found me. I joined up and been a member since," Harry explained. "The union's my family now."

"The union's your family," Bill said. "Well, I don't have any family."

"Then join us," Harry said, his voice rising. "Become united with our brotherhood! Come with me!" But Reader Bill just stood there staring blankly ahead.

"You see, before I came up here we knew that the Shingle Weavers Union in Everett was gonna go on strike."

"So you knew about the strike this whole time?"

"I only knew they were planning to strike, didn't know when, but I left to get up here before the strike. The Seattle hall was supposed to send another member up here once it happened, but nobody ever showed. I didn't know what to do . . . So, I . . . just kept on working."

"Well, what was gonna happen if one of your members came up here?"

"Bring news and instructions."

"Like what?"

"To organize the camp and go on strike," Harry said. Just then Dirty Shirt and Axel walked in chuckling and slapping each other on the back.

"Boy, oh boy, that was sure somethin' seeing old Charlie Purvis go down that flume!" Dirty Shirt boasted. "Maybe we should ask Shep to break out some moonshine?"

"Yeah, no shit. I could go fer a drop 'er two of 'shine right now," Axel added, "an' boy, oh boy, I woulda loved to see the faces on those river pigs down at the splash pond when that old son of a bitch Purvis hit the water!"

Dirty Shirt noticed Harry's gear.

"What's this?" he asked motioning at Harry's bulging gunny-sack.

"Leavin'," Harry said.

"Just like that? You're leavin'?" Axel said.

"Well, even Shep said he didn't want to work for this outfit anymore," Harry replied.

"Where the hell ya goin'?" Dirty Shirt asked.

"Headed for Seattle," Harry answered.

"There's no more trees in Seattle to cut down," Dirty Shirt said with a laugh. A few other men showed up at the door and began to listen.

"Yeah, I know," Harry said as he slung the leather strap of the Krag over a shoulder and picked up his gunny-sack and bindle.

"Well then, ya got a girl waiting?" Axel asked with a sly grin.

"Nope, just my friends in the union. You should come with me and join!" Harry said, his eyes gleaming. More lumberjacks showed up at the bunkhouse door, so Harry walked outside and stood facing the crew.

"Listen, fellas, I got somethin' to say," Harry began. "None of ya know it but, I'm half Irish, half white, and all IWW. Yep, you heard me. I'm a proud member of the Industrial Workers of the World, and we believe that every workingman in this camp and all the other logging camps shouldn't have to put up with slave drivers like Charlie Purvis. The accident that took Jaako's life today didn't have to happen. Jaako's life was taken from him by the greed for more logs and more lumber and more money over and above the safety of us men," Harry said as a few of the loggers nodded in agreement. "Too many men have lost their lives just to make a few pennies to put bread on the table while the mill owners rake in their profits."

"That's right," Joe Frytag said, "We've been bustin' our asses for too long!"

"But we're all out a' work now. What the hell are we gonna do?" Silas Shotwell said. Harry looked at Silas and his eyes caught fire.

"You'll all work again, there's too many mills that need timber and the mill owners need us. We're the ones with the labor and the production. Don't ya see? We're the ones with the power, not them!"

"Aw, Charlie said he's gonna black-ball all of us! We're doomed!" Silas shouted.

"No! Charlie Purvis don't matter anymore," Harry shot back. "Just because he said that, it don't mean that it's so!"

"Purvis will back up here in no time with a gang a' thugs and we got nowhere to go," another logger said.

"Well, if Charlie does comes back up here, and I doubt that he will, you'll still outnumber him and MacCullock will still need timber to mill. Listen men, the IWW will start organizing all the logging camps once we win the strike in Everett, but that strike ain't won yet, so I'm headed to join 'em down in Seattle first so I can get my orders. And after we win in Everett we're gonna win the hearts and minds of every lumberjack in these woods. And I'll be back because we're gonna bring the strike to the job! We'll wage a war against the timber companies right here in the woods, and soon. You'll see! But, if any of you stick around and keep making Luther MacCullock a rich man, to you I say, slow down on the job. Do eight hours work over a ten hour day and still get the full wages. Start yer own war against these rich industrialists right here, on their own ground. But if anyone wants to come with me and join the Industrial Workers of the World, then pack yer gear and come along," Harry advocated, "because everyone in the IWW is a leader. Join me and be a leader."

"Aw bullshit!" Silas yelled and threw his hands at Harry, "go lead yerself ta' Seattle." Silas walked away, the rest of the men turned and walked with him while Tubs stood watching from the door of the mess hall, his hand on Little Stovie's shoulder. Harry turned around, Reader Bill was glaring at him.

"Well, this is a fine mess you're leaving us with," Bill said with his hands on his hips and shaking his head.

"Bill, I'm sorry. But Charlie Purvis got what he deserved and besides, we still have our lives, Jaako doesn't . . . Anyway, I gotta go . . . Fare thee well, Bill," Harry said, "and you too Dirty Shirt and Axel. Pleasure knowing ya all."

Harry tossed his gunny-sack over one shoulder and hoofed it on out of Timber Creek and down the log train spur. With a new rifle strapped across his back shining against his tattered work clothes, he felt invigorated. The sun was out, Charlie Purvis was gone, and he had some folding money in his right front pocket. Harry grinned a grin so wide it made his face hurt.

In his left pocket was a dirty piece of cloth. When he noticed a good-sized boulder next to the tracks on the tote road he set his gunny-sack down, pulled the cloth out and opened it up. Harry flicked and picked at the chunks of charcoal inside and grabbed one, and then he wrote across the smooth yellowish face of rock in big black letters: "IWW – The Strike Is Here – Fire Yer Boss."

Harry stood back, put his hands on his hips, and admired his statement with a smile. He looked up into the bright sky, and then tossed the rest of the black bits in the air. Harry started to sing as he walked away, his booming voice echoing out over the clear cut devastation.

"Workers of the world awaken
Break your chains, demand your rights
All the wealth you make is taken
By exploiting parasites
Shall you kneel in deep submission?
From your cradles to your graves
Is the height of your ambition?
To be good and willing slaves."

***

Dirty Shirt and Axel went back in the bunkhouse. Reader Bill looked at them with disgust.

"Do you realize what you've done?" Bill scolded. "You know what this means, don't you?"

"It means that Charlie Purvis is finished here," Dirty Shirt said proudly.

"Wake up, would ya," Reader Bill chided. "Charlie Purvis will be back up here in no time with his thugs, and we're the ones who're finished. Don't you understand?"

"Charlie Purvis got what he deserved. Just like Harry said," Dirty Shirt grumbled as he crawled up on his bunk.

"Maybe in Dolson's and your world he received the proper punishment, but all of us are gonna pay for this with our jobs," Reader Bill said as he started packing his gear.

"So yer quittin'?" Dirty Shirt asked.

"Frank," Reader Bill snapped. "We're finished here. You sent Purvis down the flume. Great! But that flume goes to the river, and the river goes to Everett, doesn't it? And who's in Everett? Huh? So Charlie gets down to the mill, and he of course tells MacCullock. Then what do you think happens?"

Dirty Shirt thought for a moment and asked, "MacCullock beats the tar out of Purvis?"

"No," Reader Bill replied, "MacCullock gets that old wolf of a sheriff and as many thugs as they can round up on the train and head for Timber Creek. And then what do you think happens once those thugs and the sheriff get up here? We talk things out?"

"Aw jeez Bill, you know I wasn't thinkin like that when —"

"Of course you weren't! You never think, not when your fists can do all the thinking for you. So the thugs are coming up here, this is for certain, meaning that either we stay here and get the whupping of our lives before losing our jobs, or we walk away now and lose our jobs. Even you can figure out which one of those is better," Reader Bill said with an exasperated look on his face.

Shep walked in the door.

"Been over at the mess hall checkin' on Stovie. What's going on?" Shep asked as he looked at Reader Bill's load.

"Time to get out," Reader Bill replied. "Harry already left for Seattle and the IWW."

"The IWW?! No kiddin'," Shep said, snapping his head around to look at Bill.

"Yep, the Wobblies," Reader Bill answered.

"Well, that's in-er-estin'," Shep drawled. "'Cause Charlie and I found a whole cliff of rock a few sides over with IWW stuff written on it today, just before the accident. Guess it must have been Harry's handiwork."

"What's this now?" Dirty Shirt said.

"Yeah, there's all kinds of black writing on boulders and rocks. Some of 'em says, uh, 'The IWW Is Here,' and 'Strike,' 'One Big Union,' and 'Workers Unite.' The best one I saw was, 'Dump the Boss,'" Shep said. Laughter broke out in the bunkhouse.

"Ah, ha, ha," Dirty Shirt howled, "Dump the boss! Ah, ha, ha, dump the boss! I like that!"

"Eee, hee. Dump the boss," Axel cackled. "That's a good one all right!"

"Boy, oh, boy!" Joe Frytag beamed. "We sure dumped the boss today!"

"And after today, old Harry Dolson by-God, he's gonna be one man that'll be remembered in these woods forever," Shep said knowingly.

"Yeah, yeah, all that's well and good and we're all gonna remember Harry Dolson. But I think it'd be a good idea if we all scatter after what happened here today," Reader Bill said, putting a damper on the festivities. Shep dropped down on the deacon seat with a thud and shook his head.

"Yeah, I guess you're right. I'm sick of working fer MacCullock anyway," Shep said quietly. "Pretty soon the railroad will be hiring men to shovel snow up on the pass. Most of these men will probably head that way. There'll always be more logging jobs in the spring."

Dirty Shirt and Reader Bill looked at each other and nodded in a way that said what they'd just heard was a good plan. Then Shep admitted the obvious.

"MacCullock will have a gang of scissor-bills up here in no time once he gets word . . . Timber Creek is done for now, I guess. But, what the hell," Shep said with a happy change of voice. He slapped his hands on his thighs, looked up at the room of men and brightly said, "How 'bout we gather up the crew an' go on down to the cabin and break out a few jars of 'shine!"

Chapter 12

BEVERLY PARK

The wooden screen door slapped shut behind the sheriff as he stepped into the backyard of his farmhouse, worsening his headache. McRae looked up at the sky, black cumulus clouds hung in the horizon to the west and strings of wild geese were passing overhead, flying south. Walking towards the roadster patrol car he automatically called, "Come on, Champ." But his prized setter dog didn't budge. He just lay in the doorway of his doghouse as the geese honked and flew by.

"Tom. Let's go!" the sheriff called again. But still his dog showed no reaction.

"Champion. Come on!" McRae hollered. Turning around, he could see his dogs tongue hanging out of the side of his mouth. He froze, it looked like Champion Tom wasn't breathing.

"TOM!" the sheriff yelled. He ran over to his longtime companion and leaned over him. A small amount of foam was coating his gums. McRae reached down and placed a thumb on one of Champion's eyes and opened it, it was empty and unfocused. He shook his dog with one hand and stared at his motionless body for a moment. McRae righted himself, ripped off his black Stetson, and slapped his thigh with it. A single cold raindrop landed on the back of his neck, and then another. He looked up at the sky again, it had started raining and the geese had passed.

"Dammit!" he yelled into the air.

The sheriff grabbed his dog's water bowl and threw it against the house. He kicked the doghouse and then began to tromp around in circles in the yard with his fists clenched. Glancing at Champion Tom each time he circled past, the scowl on his face worsened. After a few minutes he went back over to him. He carefully looked around the soft ground next to the doghouse but couldn't see any footprints or anything suspicious.

The sheriff poked his dog with a finger and said to himself, "Tom was healthy and fine. Christ, he was stronger than dirt. He wouldn't have gone down without a fight in the middle of the night."

Standing in the October rain with his head pounding, he didn't know what to do. At first he thought he'd do the easy thing and toss Champ's body in the slough on the way to Everett, then he looked at his longtime companion and thought some more. *Champion Tom was a better friend than anybody I've ever known, he's entitled to a decent burial.* McRae got a shovel from his tool shed and commenced digging a muddy grave next to a willow tree. He wrapped his dog's stiff body in a tarp, rolled him into the hole and covered him up, and then went back inside to change out of his sopping wet clothes.

Five minutes later the sheriff grabbed a jug from the counter and took a healthy pull. Opening the door of a cupboard he grabbed a tumbler and sat down at the kitchen table, where he poured an inch of liquor in it. He dipped a finger in the liquid and tasted it, then ran his index finger along the rim of the glass as he stared blankly out the window at the empty doghouse. He drank the whiskey, set the glass down hard and looked at it, not moving a muscle. Finally he swiped the tumbler off the table and across the room. It bounced and spun along the floor and slammed into the base of the kitchen wall. McRae got up and headed out the backdoor to his patrol car, leaving the glass where it lay.

The sheriff dropped the car into reverse, put his right arm on the bench seat, and looked over his shoulder to back out of the garage. Then he slammed on the brakes, turned the motor off, and jumped out of the car. An IWW black cat sticker was on his rear window. He slammed his fist on the trunk of the car.

"God damn it!" the sheriff yelled into the gunmetal sky. He fumed as he picked at the sticker and peeled it off.

He hopped back into the car and sped down the driveway. *Those stinking Wobbly bastards! Those stinking Wobbly bastards killed Champ last night! How dare they kill my dog! What'd he ever do to them? Those Wobblies are gonna pay*! Forty minutes later he came to a screeching halt in front of the jailhouse and stormed inside.

"Morning sheriff," Deputy Pete Hanigan said.

"Hanigan! What the hell are you doing here? Why aren't you out working the blockade?!" the sheriff thundered.

"Just gettin' off duty. I worked the graveyard shift, there were some arsons last night," he answered.

"What's that?" McRae boomed.

"Some fires were set last night."

"Where?"

"Riverside District again, some trash cans and a tool shed. On Rainer and Baker."

"Figures," the sheriff grumbled.

"Just thought you'd like to know. It could've been some Wobblies," Hanigan asserted.

"Yeah, well, that's Taro and Kelly's problem, and if it was the Wobblies then how the hell did they get past *my* blockade? Huh? You're back on the day shift! NOW! Ya hear me! So go out there and find me some stinkin' Wobblies to lock up!" he hollered, glaring at his deputy with bloodshot eyes.

McRae went upstairs, slammed his office door, and stepped over to the file cabinet. He pulled a jug of whiskey from the bottom drawer and poured more whiskey down his throat, then looked over to his dog's hair-covered blanket in the corner and shook his head. The sheriff sat down, slid his Stetson down over his eyes, rocked back in his chair, and tried to relax. After a few minutes a quiet knock sounded on his door.

"Don?" Deputy Beard said. "You in there?"

"Yeah," the sheriff answered with a tired voice as he sat up and threw his Stetson on the desk. "Come on in Jeff."

Deputy Beard's eyes automatically glanced at Champion Tom's blanket and then at the sheriff.

"Jesus," Beard said, "you're not lookin' too good." But the sheriff just sat at his desk and stared blankly ahead.

"Where's Tom?" Beard asked.

"Dead," the sheriff spat, his eyes still looking straight ahead.

"Dead! What d'ya mean?"

"I found him dead in his doghouse this morning."

"But he was fine yesterday."

"Yeah, well, he's God-damned dead and buried in my backyard today."

"How could that be?"

"I think he was poisoned. Found an IWW sticker on my car window."

"What?" Deputy Beard blurted, "Why in the world would they kill Tom fer criminy sakes?"

The sheriff sat with his eyes now fixed on Champion's blanket. He reached for the jug and took another drink, and then set the bottle on his desk and let his chin drop down on his chest.

McRae looked at his deputy with reddened eyes, his face was pasty white. He said, "Champ didn't deserve to die, he never hurt any of them Wobbly bastards. I have had it with them. Damn their hides. If I see another one of them worthless bums in my town, they'll pay. If any of their kind show up here, why, they'll just be a-borrowin' trouble. Do you hear me? They'll be a-borrowin' trouble, and then there'll be hell to pay. You know why?" the sheriff asked. "Because I am gonna strangle every single stinkin' Wobbly that I can get my hands on!" He took another drink.

***

Scores of laborers filled the Seattle IWW hall. Most of them had been staying there for days, bed rolls were sprawled out over the floor or on cots and washed clothing hung over the backs of chairs and from makeshift clothes lines. A queue of men stood waiting for a bowl of soup while others bided their time in the meeting hall. Anxious members wearing tattered work clothes had flocked to Seattle from all over the western states to join in the struggle against Everett and to fight for the free-speech movement.

Finally their leader emerged from a side room and slowly made his way through the crowd, shaking hands and greeting fellow union men. He moved with a slight limp and had a bandage on his left temple. When he climbed the stairs to the stage his right knee buckled, but it didn't stop him.

Behind the podium he coughed and paused for a moment to gather his thoughts just before he mounted the stand. When he opened his eyes they seemed to be on fire. He looked out over the room, stuck out his chin, and shook his right fist in the air. The crowd instantly roared.

"Greetings fellow workers!" James Thompson shouted from the podium to the boisterous workingmen. "Thank you for such a hearty reception! Thank you!"

"Today I stand beside my loyal brothers. I stand here beside the men who have the moral courage to fight and take back power from these parasites who call themselves patriots thirty miles north of here. I am here with you because you are the men that stand square on your convictions. As I live and breathe, I tell all of you gathered here that I am willing to go to jail for you and go to hell for you. In this urgent hour I am ready to fight every single capitalist in Everett that tries to stop our great and noble cause!" Thompson yelled as every man in the room jumped to his feet cheering.

"Last month a group of us went to Everett in hope of taking back our union hall that was ransacked and burned by what they call lawmen there. We went to Everett to take back what was robbed from us, but we were jailed before we even arrived. The lawmen in Everett may put us in jail, but they'll never put the IWW and every single worker in jail. The prison bars in Everett may separate us from them, but they will never separate our union from us!" Thompson cried out with his right hand over his heart. Men stomped their feet and hollered until Thompson raised his left hand for quiet.

"Hear me, men, when I say now," Thompson shouted, "that the Commercial Club and the industrialists like Luther MacCullock in Everett would have the public believe that the IWW and the Shingle Weavers Union are traitors and thieves. But we are not! They in the lumber trust are the thieves! They are the ones stealing from the working people! They are the ones who should be behind bars. Not us!" Thompson screamed, spittle flying from his mouth. Then he lifted his arm straight up with a stiff index finger.

"Brothers! Sheriff Donald McRae and the members of the Commercial Club have taken control of Everett and its politics. They have forced a crude form of martial law upon the town and initiated a design of violence against any man in overalls walking the street. And, these industrial brutes have now passed another, new city ordinance that completely bans all public speaking, they've shut down any notion of free speech and street meetings," he said pounding the podium. "This so-called ordinance is in direct violation of our country's Constitution, and we must not allow it to stand!"

The hall instantly boomed as though a cannon of screams had been fired. The wooden floor bounced and echoed from stomping boots until Thompson lowered his head and raised both hands for quiet.

"Everett is operating as a closed town. The lumber trust is running Everett as its own private city. The populations of the state can't go there, nobody's welcome . . . all this must end. The strike in Everett has been going on for far too long, and we need to help the Shingle Weavers in Snohomish County. There are daily beatings of any out-of-town workingman walking a picket line, and if they find a red card or any kind of IWW material on a man, he is instantly attacked and left for dead or taken to jail. This violence must end! The industrial will of the lumber baronage in Everett must be broken!"

"We need to fix that town for good!" one man hollered.

"That's the spirit!" one Wobbly shouted.

"Thompson's right! We need to take the fight to Everett!" the union man named Spitz yelled. The rest of the crowd boomed in approval.

"Listen, men," Thompson said raising his hands. "We are going to deal with what is happening in Everett because it is the battleground for the future of every blue-collar workingman in this region and the world. This is a call to arms for the eight-hour workday, the forty-hour work week, better working conditions, and most of all, free speech!"

"Tell us what to do, and we'll do it!" Spitz called out.

"The crisis in Everett needs to be brought to a climax! And we need to go to Everett and openly challenge the lumber trust and Everett's violation of the Constitution," James Thompson said as he reached into his coat pocket, pulled out a piece of paper, and unfolded it. He waited for silence.

"In my hand I have a copy of the First Amendment. Who here will travel with me to Everett and go to the corner of Hewitt and Wetmore and read this sacred document with me there and exercise our right to speak freely?" Thompson screamed to the crowd that was now cheering wildly.

"A ferry is leaving the Coleman Dock later today, I say we take up a collection for tickets to send a group of men north. Who will join me?"

***

Luther MacCullock stared out his office window looking upriver for the tugboat towing his raft boom. All he saw, however, was black smoke filling the sky, pouring from every smokestack and incinerator along the waterfront. He glanced at the last raft of logs in his mill salt chuck, saw that it was nearly depleted, and pondered the orders he had to fill. The phone rang.

"Yes?" he said into the receiver.

"Mr. MacCullock, its Feeney."

"Yes, Feeny?"

"There's a good-sized gang of Wobblies in the Seattle hall, they're headed for Everett today."

"Today?"

"Yep, that fella Thompson has got them all riled up about free speech. He told them it's time to bring the situation in Everett to a climax," Feeney said.

"A climax! Damn this intruding agitator! What are they planning?" MacCullock asked.

"From what I can tell they're collecting money for tickets and then taking the late afternoon ferry from Coleman Dock. It looks like a rough bunch of men."

"Are they now?" MacCullock replied. "Go on."

"There's a good number of harvest workers that just came in on the rails from eastern Washington. They look like a pretty tough gang, and I wouldn't doubt it if some of them have arson on their minds. And they're all armed," Feeney said.

"Arson and with weapons. God almighty, it's Rome and the Visigoths all over again!" the mill owner said into the phone. MacCullock hung up and rocked back in his chair. He crossed his arms, then scratched the side of his head. He picked up the phone.

"Sheriff? It's MacCullock," he said into the receiver.

"What?" the sheriff answered.

"There's a boatload of Wobblies leaving Seattle bound for Everett."

"Who says?"

"I just got word from Seattle."

"From who?"

"I have my sources."

"What's this . . . sources crap?" the sheriff snorted.

"Never mind who I have in Seattle. That's none of your business."

"It God damned very well is my business. I'm still the sheriff of this county, and if you have information then you had damn well better be passin' it on! You hear me?" the sheriff screamed into the phone. But MacCullock didn't answer.

"MacCullock?"

"Yes, Sheriff," the mill owner said. "I'm here."

"Now I've been doin' plenty of dirty work fer you, and you still owe me that job once this is over, remember?"

"Yes, well, I have friends in Seattle that are informing me, and don't worry, the timekeeper's position will be waiting for you," MacCullock reassured him.

"Friends, huh?" McRae grunted. "Well, alright, and by the way . . . those damn Wobblies killed my dog last night."

"They killed your dog? How do you know?"

"Because I know, there was a black cat sticker on my car window, that's why. And those Wobblies are gonna pay!"

"That's a shame Donald," Luther MacCullock replied.

"Yeah, well . . . when's this boatload of trouble coming?" the sheriff asked testily.

"They are taking the late afternoon ferry. It would be best if you organized the Commercial Club deputies," MacCullock said.

"That boat won't be here for hours, but when they land I'll give 'em what they got comin'," the sheriff grumbled and hung up.

***

Stiletto rain poured straight down on the few strikers that walked the picket line at the Northern Imperial. Renny Niskanen marched back and forth as he led his strikers in a desperate chant.

"The boss need you! You do not need him!"

"The boss needs you. You don't need him."

"Say it again!"

"The boss needs you. You don't need him."

"Vhat side are you on?"

"What side are you on?"

"Say it again!"

"What side are you on?"

The sheriff's roadster rolled across the water warped planking and pulled up on the pier. Buck Mullaney stepped out from under cover just inside the mill as the rest of his guards gathered behind him, all of them toting shotguns.

McRae got out of his patrol car, slammed the door, and hitched up the belted revolver and blackjack hanging on his hip as he walked over to the picket line with a determined look on his face. Deputy Beard and Walt Irvan were right behind him, both with furrowed brows and narrowed eyes. Stopping in front of the picket line, the sheriff eyed every striker until he settled on a man he'd never seen before.

"YOU!" McRae hollered, pointing at the man in tattered work clothes. "What's yer name?"

"Who's askin'?" the bum said. The sheriff pulled back the lapel of his coat, exposing his badge. The bum glanced at the badge and then looked over at Renny. The union leader shrugged his shoulders and shook his head sideways. The man turned back to the sheriff.

"Clancy Carmichael," the picketer answered.

"Where ya from?" McRae asked as he placed his hand on the blackjack.

"Riverside. Just moved here."

"Did ya now?" Sheriff McRae said, his eyes narrowing.

"Yep, yesterday."

"You IWW?"

"What business is it of yours?" the man replied.

The sheriff instantly pulled the blackjack from his belt and landed a blow to the side of the man's head, knocking him to the ground.

"Search him," McRae ordered.

Deputy Beard dropped down on the striker, put his knee on his chest, and searched him. He quickly found a red card.

"He's a Wobbly," Beard acknowledged. Sheriff McRae stepped over to the prone man and kicked him in the side. The man screamed in pain while the picketers watched silently, knowing better to intervene.

"Cuff this out-of-town, piece-of-junk, and load him in my rig," the sheriff said, biting off each syllable as he spoke.

The picketers watched as a limp Clancy was pulled to his feet, shoved in the back of the patrol car, and driven away. Renny shook his head in disgust and looked at his few remaining comrades.

"Ve are voting tonight at the Labor Temple," Renny announced to the group.

"It's about time," one of the picketers groaned.

"Ve need our jobs again so ve are going to vote on fifty cents an hour," Renny declared.

"This is useless. It's over, they've already won," Fred McCorkel said.

"We never should have gone on strike," Hank Hillstrom said.

"I'll work for the old wage," another added.

"No, we are not giving in to these bastards. I don't care. We're not quitting," a picketer said defiantly, the rain pelting him in the face.

"Vell, okay. Ve'll keep marching, but ve all need to be at the union hall tonight," Renny said and then raised his sign and began to chant. Hillstrom and McCorkel dropped their signs and walked away. Renny started the chant up again.

"Vhat side are you on?"

"Say it again."

"What side are you on?"

***

Petra walked down the Market Street alley with her face buried under her coat collar, arms crossed, and a black scarf covering her hair tied under her chin. She took measured steps beside fences and behind horse barns, and moved carefully from tree to tree. Right when she opened the gate two boys playing hooky, walked around the corner from Everett Avenue. She ducked inside the fence, sure that they didn't see her, and quickly closed the gate, then waited for them to walk by. Satisfied they were gone, she breathed a sigh of relief and climbed the back porch stairs of Lafayette House. Petra saw the bouncer through the back door window, he was at the kitchen table eating a mess of eggs when she knocked.

"Door's open," Harvey grumbled, not looking up from his plate.

"Good-a morning," Petra said, but Harvey ignored her, and continued shoveling his food. Pearl was at the sink doing dishes. She turned around and smiled.

"Mornin', baby doll."

"Yah, morning," Petra answered.

"I think Goldie's got you booked today. That cute little john with the scruffy black hair you were with the last couple of times came in lookin' for ya last night. I think he loves Dessa," Pearl said with a happy glow. "I guess he's coming back today and wants ya all to himself. Even paid already."

"Well, if it isn't Dessa. You're here bright and early, child," Goldie said as she floated into the kitchen wearing a satin bathrobe. "That handsome young devil you've been keepin' happy was back last night."

"Already told her," Pearl added.

"We best be gettin' you upstairs and all fixed up. Pearl, would you be a dear and maybe teach her a little something special for her man today?" Goldie asked.

"Yes, Miss Goldie," Pearl replied as she dried her hands at the sink and then turned to Dessa. "Come on, baby doll. Let's see what kind of tricks we can teach ya."

Just then Cora walked into the kitchen carrying a suitcase. She dropped it on the floor with a thud.

"Well, I've had enough of this town. I'm headed to the big city," Cora said.

"Are ya now," Goldie replied. "What's the matter? Didn't I pay ya enough 'er somethin'?"

"That's not it. It's not the pay or you, Miss Goldie. I just need more than what this towns has ta' offer, that's all," Cora answered.

"Well, I can understand that. Everett is what one makes of it," Goldie stated.

"You think Harvey could give me a ride to the Interurban?" Cora asked with a smile.

"Sure," Goldie offered, "but I do need to run some errands this mornin'. Tell ya what, I'll use the other one, and Harvey, how about you fire up the old Stanley and give Cora a ride."

"Sure, why not," Harvey said, standing up and reaching for his coat.

***

Singing could be heard from the 112 foot, stacked deck, white propeller steamer *Verona* as it approached the city pier that evening. Longtime Captain Chauncey Wiman stood at the helm in the wheelhouse and barked orders to his crew in the dark over the din of his vocal passengers. Men stood shoulder to shoulder on the covered, upper level passenger deck as they sang in clamorous solidarity.

> "We want all the workers in the world to organize
> Into a great big union grand
> And when we all united stand
> The world for workers we demand
> If the working class could only see and realize
> What mighty power labor has
> Then the exploiting master class
> It would soon fade away."

Across the water were the city lights of Hewitt Avenue going up and over the hill to the east. On the pier was a smattering of glowing flames and bright headlights. As the boat grew closer, those afloat could see that the flames were torches held by men armed with clubs and rifles.

Once the vocalizing Wobblies saw the greeting party on the dock, they stopped singing one by one as each man realized the situation that awaited them. The waterfront became silent.

As the *Verona* eased up to the pier, two deckhands fastened the bow and stern lines, and then one swung the gangplank to the dock. Captain Wiman came out to the freight gangway on the lower deck, and turned to the crowd of citizen deputies and the sheriff.

"What's brought ya out this evening, Sheriff?" the old seaman asked.

"Got a report that some un-dee-sire-ables were blowin' in on the high tide," the sheriff belched as he leaned against a pier bollard.

"Did ya now?" Captain Wiman retorted with a deep confident voice. He motioned to the first passengers that it was OK to go ashore and then turned back to the sheriff. "Looks like you got plenty of help."

"What? These men? Why, they're some of my closest friends, we're here for a little surprise party," the sheriff said, his head and face in shadows, backlit by torches.

The industrial smell of kerosene filled the air as whiskey bottles were passed from hand to hand while yellow-white flames cast an eerie glow. Terrified passengers disembarked to the sight of two hundred armed vigilantes. Each traveler had to pass by the investigative glare of a man with a revolver on his hip and a blackjack in his hand. Two well-dressed male passengers looked familiar as they stepped on the wharf, but the sheriff couldn't place their faces. The two men walked over to the warehouse where they watched, and waited.

Sheriff McRae stood swaying in the inebriated ambition of his design with a horde of Commercial Club and lumber trust brutes behind him, all of them armed, each of them with a white handkerchief tied to his arm, or around his neck. The sheriff eyed each passenger as he or she walked across the gangplank causeway. When the first workingman in overalls and boots stepped on the pier, McRae pulled him aside.

"Over here, fella," the sheriff belched as he grabbed the man's arm.

"What for?" the man said.

"You carryin' a red card?" the sheriff grunted.

"I'm a union man," the man said defiantly.

"Ya'll, eye dubya-dubya?" the sheriff slurred.

"Damn right," the Wobbly replied.

"Well, yer kind ain't welcome here," the sheriff said and shoved him towards his brutes, who had formed a shoulder-to-shoulder circle. Two vigilantes grabbed the Wobbly and shoved him inside the torch-lit corral of deputies, while McRae singled out more Wobblies.

"You and you, over there, you, too," he ordered as his deputies muscled the out-of- towners into the circular pen.

Then Spitz walked across the gangplank. The sheriff recognized his long nose and pointed jaw.

"You! Yer back!" McRae barked. "Get over with the rest of 'em!"

"That's right," Spitz said. "I'm back to ex-er-cise *my* rights."

"You ain't got no rights in my town."

"We'll see about that," Spitz said.

"You just do as yer told 'er else you'll be seein' my jail again."

"Fine by me," Spitz replied. "Hell, I'll remodel it again for ya."

"Take 'em away!" the sheriff ordered. The timber widow Helen Pomeroy and two other women stepped from the ferry carrying brown paper bag packages.

"What's going on here?" Pomeroy snapped at the sheriff.

"This has nothing to do with you, lady. Move along," the sheriff answered, motioning with his arm down the wharf.

"These men have been perfectly civil this whole trip," Helen remarked. "On what basis are you detaining them?"

"I said to move along," the sheriff grunted.

"No, I will not! Not until you tell me what you're going to do with these men," Pomeroy demanded.

"Listen, lady, if you don't step aside I'll arrest you for obstructing justice!" the sheriff yelled, his whiskey breath blasting in her face.

"There's no justice going on here! How dare you treat people like this, and why isn't the chief of police here?" Helen Pomeroy insisted, her voice becoming shriller with each word.

"That's it," the sheriff spat. "Beard, get this old battle ax outta here. Now!"

"How dare you use a name like that? Why, you're nothing but an un-prepossessing drunken fool. This is an outrage!" Pomeroy stormed as Deputy Beard stepped out of the crowd and in between the sheriff and Pomeroy.

"Please, ma'am," Jefferson said and pointed his club down the dock.

Helen Pomeroy harrumphed, looked at her friends, and then glared at the sheriff.

"You will never get away with this. When I get home I'm going to make some phone calls!" Helen shouted as she and her two friends walked down the pier carrying their packages.

Soon enough the sheriff had forty men in his vigilante holding pen when James Thompson appeared. As he walked from the shadows and across the gangplank he held a piece of paper over his head, reciting it from memory:

"There shall be no law respecting an establishment of religion or prohibiting the free exercise thereof, or abridging the freedom of speech, or of the press, or the right of the people to peaceably assemble and to petition the Government for a redress of grievances."

Right when Thompson stepped on the pier the sheriff's blackjack came down on his lower neck and shoulder, bending him over, but he stayed on his feet. At the same time clubs and ax handles were raised over the captive Wobblies, keeping them at bay.

"So you're here again! What are ya, head sick 'er something? I told you to never come back!" the sheriff screamed over his victim. "Get this trash loaded up."

"We are here . . . to exercise our constitutional rights!" Thompson hollered, straightening up and standing to his full height.

"We know our rights, McRae!" one Wobbly yelled.

"Yeah! We're here to have a free speech meeting. The Constitution says so," another one added.

"To hell with the Constitution!" Sheriff McRae hollered. "Yer in Everett now!"

"The Constitution is the law and we are having a civilized, free-speech street meeting tonight," Thompson said over the pier and his rounded up Wobblies. They cheered back at their leader.

Standing off to the side and watching from beside a pier warehouse were the two well-dressed male passengers that had stepped off of the *Verona* earlier, Helen Pomeroy and her friends were standing with them. Deputy Beard recognized one of the men, he pulled on McRae's arm and brought them to his attention.

"Hey, Sheriff," Jeff Beard said quietly, "Judge McAllister is over there."

The sheriff looked at his deputy and said, "Is he now?" He immediately turned to the Wobblies and said, "All right, you can have yer street meeting but not at Hewitt and Wetmore . . . You can use . . . Hewitt and Grand."

McRae glanced at McAllister. The judge and the rest of them began to walk away, but another man nearby in a dark overcoat and bowler hat continued to watch. The sheriff turned back to his task.

"All right, men, let's herd these way-ward, speechifyin, Constitutionals, up the street," the sheriff said with a noticeable slur, "and Jeff," he mumbled quietly, "cuff Thompson right now and . . . stick him in the paddy."

After the Wobblies were searched for weapons the citizen deputies headed them up a deserted Hewitt Avenue on foot while the sheriff in his roadster and a few deputies with cars, trucks, and the paddy wagon followed slowly behind. A procession of forty Wobblies surrounded by kerosene torches made its way up the hill.

Halfway there, one unruly Wobbly said to Deputy Walt Irvan, "What'd you pantywaists do with Thompson? Huh? Well, I think yer all a bunch of chicken-shits. Yer scared of him, aren't ya?" It was all Irvan needed to hear.

"Why, you stinking bum-assed son of a bastard. Nothin' scares me!" Irvan yelled and swung his billy club at the man's head, making a wound that bled profusely down the side of his face. Ax handles and bats were instantly raised in a show of force and determination by the deputies, which kept the rest of the Wobblies at bay, until the sheriff pulled up in his roadster.

"That's it. Stuff 'em in the paddy wagon an' load 'em on that flatbed and then follow me," McRae said to Deputy Irvan from his window opening. In the growing darkness they drove their captive cargo south on Rucker out past the golf course, far from the city limits.

At Scenic Drive the sheriff stuck his arm out of the windowless 490 and motioned the other vehicles to follow him to the left. He parked in the vacant lot on the corner and jumped out of his rig and yelled at the cars as they followed in, "Pull up 'n' get parked. Turn yer lights off. Shut the engines down." The sheriff directed the cars as the citizen deputies all pulled in. Then he motioned them to gather around.

They huddled up in the darkness. "All right, keep them bastards in the paddy and on that truck, we'll wait right here and keep quiet until the Interurban goes by. Once it does we're gonna teach this here pack of vagrants a lesson they won't ever forget. You got me?" the sheriff said, looking around the group.

"We got ya, Sheriff," Jeff Beard replied.

"Good. Now, we are gonna make these worthless IWW walk a gauntlet, so we are gonna form two lines down the sides of those tracks," McRae said, pointing south down the tracks across the highway. A few men turned their heads in the direction. The two steel parallel rails reflected silver from the moon but disappeared into the dark distance. "Once that train spins by I want whoever was drivin' those last two rigs to turn 'em around and point yer lights down them tracks," the sheriff said.

"Ya'll got that?"

He reached into his coat pocket and pulled out a flask. The men that had some hooch did the same. Some lit cigars. Deputy Irvan looked up at the moon, and back at the sheriff.

"What kind a' 3-7-77 are we gonna be applyin' tonight, boss?" the deputy asked. The sheriff grinned, pushed the Stetson up on his brow, and put a hand on his hip. The look on his face cast the control of power he had with his men, and his satisfaction of being in charge.

"Well, let's see. I'd say that these here vagrants have got about, oh, three minutes 'n' seven seconds 'n' seventy-seven breaths left of cool, clean air tonight before they start seeing stars!" The men all had a hearty laugh.

"What's that 3-7-77 about?" one of the citizen deputies in the back of the group asked the man next to him.

"Oh that, it's a warning the sheriff uses when he's kickin' someone outta town. He usually gives 'em three days and seven hours and seventy-seven minutes to git their asses gone. I guess that must a' been a new one," the other deputy replied with a grin. The sound of steel wheels came out of the distance.

"Hear that?" Sheriff McRae said looking up the tracks. "Train's comin'. Let it go by an' stay out of sight. Then we are gonna make these ignorant bastards wish they'd never showed up here!"

As the train got closer it sounded like a rolling party. Hoots and hollers, singing, and then the shrill noise of the whistle filled the air right before the electric train got to the highway crossing. Men were hanging off the side like they were riding a merry-go-round, holding their free arm out in the wind as if they were reaching for the golden ring. The overhead lights in the passenger cars showed couples dancing and carrying on like a circus sideshow, drunk and oblivious. Women threw their heads back and screamed hallelujahs of delight as inebriated boyfriends made them laugh, showing all that Seattle was where alcohol was still readily available. It rolled right by the dark Beverly Park Station without stopping.

"All right men!" McRae yelled. "I figure we got about forty 'er forty five minutes before it comes back by. Light yer torches and turn them two rigs around so we can see. Let's go!"

The two drivers pointed their headlights down the rail lines. Deputy Irvan backed the paddy wagon up so the rear door was facing south down the tracks while the men formed two lines from the wagon and down either side of the rails, ending at a cattle crossing. Then the flatbed truck was backed up and maneuvered into place next to the paddy. Once the vigilantes were in place with ax handles, shotguns, and bats in hand, Walt opened the backdoor of the paddy wagon and took the chains off the rails of the flatbed. The sheriff took a long swig of whiskey from his flask.

"All right you worthless intruders! Get out, and face yer doom!" McRae bellowed and then wiped his mouth with a forearm. He lost his balance briefly, took a quick side step, and regained his footing but stood unsteadily. "You've got no business in my town. Ya don't belong here in AFL country! Ya hear me? Now walk! Walk, ya rotten bastards!" the sheriff screamed. He grabbed the first one by the coat, jerked him down, and then kicked him in the trousers.

"That's right ya dumb bastard! I guess I just eye-dubya-dubbed yer skinny little ass on back ta' Seattle!" McRae yelled. The Wobbly tried to run but was hit in the back with a baseball bat. Another Wobbly jumped out and tried to break through the line but was stopped with a swing of an ax handle. One after another the IWW came out of the wagon covering their heads while more jumped off the flatbed and tried to run. Then Spitz emerged and stood at the paddy wagon door. His face was half hidden in shadow, but the sheriff knew who he was.

"Get going ya bum!" McRae hollered.

"Go to hell!" Spitz hollered back.

"Get that son of a bitch down." the sheriff ordered a nearby citizen deputy as two other Wobblies bolted out from the wagon but were quickly struck. Walt Irvan came out of the shadows and hit Spitz on the shinbone with a billy club. Spitz fell back on the floor, moaning. Irvan and a citizen deputy grabbed him by the feet and pulled him out of the vehicle, the back of Spitz's head bouncing off the bumper.

"There's a wicked sin on yer hands!" Spitz yelled up at the sheriff. The two deputies picked him off the ground, stood him up, and jerked him off to the side.

"Somebody herd the rest of these trespassin' rats out of the wagon and that truck," McRae hollered as he put on a pair of leather gloves and then stepped over to Spitz. The two deputies held him at bay.

"Wicked sin, huh? Boy, I swear you got the mark just as plain as day," the sheriff said. He grabbed Spitz by the throat with his left hand and squeezed, he started coughing. McRae held onto his throat and then hit him in the nose with his gloved right fist, breaking it sideways, and yelled, "And I just knocked that mark right off yer damn face!"

Spitz moaned in pain and gasped for breath. "Yer . . . the marked . . . man. Not me," the Wobbly sputtered, blood streaming down his face. The sheriff pulled on his gloves, tightening his grip, and then hit the malcontent in the mouth, splitting open his lower lip.

"Marks? There ain't no marks on me. Hell, yer the one takin' it on the chin. You got marks all over now!" McRae hollered and laughed a guttural laugh. The sheriff motioned with his hand down the tracks and said, "I don't ever want to see you again. Now git!" The two deputies started to shove Spitz towards the gauntlet.

"I'm gonna get you, McRae! If I ever see you again . . . I swear . . . I'll shoot yer balls off," Spitz said.

"You'll never get the chance, ya dumb son of a bitch!" McRae yelled. He chugged a drink from his flask.

The first vigilante in line coldcocked Spitz with his rifle butt, he dropped onto the rails with a thud. Two others grabbed him by the arms and dragged him along the tracks face down as each citizen deputy kicked and hit the defenseless Wobbly.

"Looks to me like you shoulda stayed in school, sonny boy! Maybe done some extra book learnin' an' taught yerself a craft an' joined a real union instead a' joinin' up with a bunch a' bastards like these here," the sheriff hollered at Spitz with a smirk and swung his hand over his head and down the tracks. He took a pull from his flask, wiped the residue from his chin, and then held it out for a citizen deputy holding a kerosene lantern.

"None for me, sheriff," the deputy said, shaking his head.

"What's that?" the sheriff answered, "None for you, ya say. What kind a' man are ya?" The volunteer looked away for a moment and then turned back to the sheriff, he lifted the lantern higher.

"I'm a man who knows what's right and what's wrong, that's who. And this is not right," the man replied.

"What 'er you talkin' about? These here eye dubya-dubya are nothin' but a bunch of worthless dog killers," the sheriff snarled. "Now I said take a drink!"

"Nope, I've seen enough. You can't treat people like this. You're supposed to be upholding the law. Not abusing it. I'm done with this," the former citizen deputy said.

He set the lantern down, turned around and walked off to his car. The sheriff stared at his silhouette disappearing in darkness. He took another drink, motioned with his flask towards the city limits, and yelled, "Go on then, we don't need yer help!"

The gauntlet was a frantic delirium of vehicle lights, screams, curses and bloodletting. One hundred men on each side of the tracks taunted and hit every Wobbly that passed as they tried to make their way through. The Wobblies were pushed or dragged down the gauntlet and struck with the butt ends of shotguns or kicked by boots.

The flames on the torches flickered, they looked like Roman candles lighting a hellish scene of slaves being thrown to lions. Even those who were fast and elusive runners eventually found the steel supports of the cattle guard, their legs falling through the gaps, pinning and holding them in place for the cruel blows of clubs and the whipping of saps.

One Wobbly was knocked to the steel rails and then kicked repeatedly in the side and face. Men pleaded not to be hit through broken teeth, ruptured lips, and with battered bones. Once past the cattle guard, they stumbled or crawled back to Seattle through the darkness, beaten and bloodied.

A local farmer stepped out of his home to check on his bellowing cows and heard the screams coming through the woods, he walked a quarter of a mile to investigate. From the shadows he watched and winced each time a man was hit or kicked and forced down the gauntlet that ended at his cattle guard.

Finally Deputy Irvan jerked James Thompson from the back of the paddy wagon and pulled him out, stumbling towards the gauntlet gang, he uncuffed him. McRae stepped over to Thompson.

"If I ever see you again I'm gonna be diggin' you a hole that's three feet wide 'n' seven feet long 'n' seventy-seven inches deep! Ya got that, Thompson! Are ya finally listenin' to me now, ya dumb bastard?" the sheriff hollered, standing eye to eye with him.

"I can't hear a word you're saying McRae! You're no lawman! And you'll never —" Thompson said, but a quick blow of a bat across his back sent him to the ground. Vigilantes kicked him in the side. He got to his hands and knees and crawled beneath the flickering torches and curses of community men who knew they were doing the right thing. A willow sap strafed his head and neck repeatedly and an ax handle slammed against the back of his legs, but Thompson kept crawling. Kicked and hit again, over and over, he eventually collapsed on the cattle guard, where he was left next to Spitz.

***

The Labor Temple was packed with strikers. Nervous tension filled the air as Jake Michel strode to the podium. He looked out to all the faces and raised his arms for calm.

"Quiet! Can I have quiet in the hall, please?" Michel asked loudly. Silence slowly came over the room. "It is good to see all of you tonight! It is good to see the faces of the men who have the courage to go on strike for a better living wage. It is good to see those who have been true to themselves and it is even better to see those that have the strength and bravery to speak the truth against the lumber trust. You should all be proud of yourselves and your cause," Michel said to a few feeble cheers.

"We are all here tonight to vote again to end this strike. Weeks ago the Shingle Weavers Union voted to reject the fifty-cents-an-hour wage scale. Tonight we are going to vote again on MacCullock's offer to go back to the same hourly rate that we had when we went on strike."

"We should have never went on strike!" one man yelled.

"I want my job back!" another man shouted.

"MacCullock can go to hell!" a striker yelled.

"No, you can go to hell! I want my job back!"

"People! People!" Jake hollered. "MacCullock offered the fifty cents once before, and if he's a man of his word then he'll keep to it. So tonight we are having an up or down vote on it. If you're against going back to the old wage scale then vote no, but if you're for it vote yes and the strike will be over."

Renny Niskanen got up from his chair and walked to the podium. Michel stepped aside when he approached. Most were silent, but everyone leaned forward to listen to what the shop steward had to say. He stood for a moment as he looked out to the faces in the crowd.

"I know that a lot of you think that it is my fault that ve vent on strike. I am sorry, about all that has happened. But last spring ve all voted to strike after many meetings. Then ve voted again last month, but ve said no. Now ve are going to vote on fifty cents an hour. I vill vote yes. I do not vant to vote yes, and I do not want to go back to work for MacCullock, but I think ve have lost the strike. I vant to go back to vork," Renny said. He bowed his head to a silent room and walked away from the podium. The room stayed quiet as Renny went to the voting table near the entrance.

Jake Michel stepped back to the rostrum.

"OK. The ballots are going to be handed out now, and after you've voted drop them in the boxes at the door."

***

Father Bywater was at the gauntlet location the next morning after receiving a phone call from a parishioner. Pools of blood spotted the ground. Teeth, shoes, clothing, and hats were littered everywhere. Bywater was inspecting the scene when the local farmer who witnessed the attack walked up.

"Mornin'. Name's Lucas Cain. I saw the whole thing," the farmer said as he approached. The priest turned around to address the man.

"Pleased to meet you, Lucas. I'm Father Bywater. What happened here?" the priest asked.

"From what I could tell it was Sheriff McRae and his gang. He must have had two hundred men here last night."

"Yes, a concerned parishioner called me this morning. She saw the sheriff and his committee of men on the city pier last night," the priest said as Jake Michel pulled up in his Hudson and walked over.

"I just heard about this," Michel said as he walked and looked around at the ground. "McRae has got to be stopped. My God, there's even teeth!" he said standing over a pool of blood.

"There are more down by the cattle guard. It's covered with blood, too," Bywater added.

"My union voted yes last night to end the strike," Michel stated.

"Oh, dear Lord. Did they?" the priest remarked.

"That's right," the union boss admonished. "The majority voted yes on the old wage so we should be back to work right away."

"This town could use some good news. But whatever happened here last night was the devil's work," Bywater said as he turned and walked down the tracks shaking his head.

An hour later Jake Michel was at his desk in the Labor Temple. He picked the receiver up off its hook and dialed.

"Yes," Luther MacCullock said into his phone.

"Mr. MacCullock?" Michel asked.

"Yes."

"This is Jake Michel."

"What is it now?"

"I've got good news. The Shingle Weavers voted yes last night to take your fifty cents an hour offer."

"What's this now? . . . They did what?"

"Yes, Mr. MacCullock, they voted on the same wage and approved it. They're ready to go back to work." The phone went silent.

"Hello? Are you still there?" Michel said into the phone.

"I'm here."

"I said the men are ready to go back to —"

"Mr. Michel," Luther MacCullock growled, "I already have men working! Good, solid men, loyal Americans. Why would I want to go back to your lot of quitters? Besides, that offer was only good for forty-eight hours."

"Forty-eight hours? I don't remember anything about forty-eight hours. You mean to tell me that you're not going to honor your offer?" Michel said.

"I told you forty-eight hours the last time we spoke and I honored that offer, it's not my problem if you can't remember things. You're too late. That was a month ago."

Jake tried again, "But the men overwhelmingly voted yes last night to take the old fifty cent wage."

"Goodbye, Mr. Michel," MacCullock grumbled and hung up the phone.

Chapter 13

CITY OF FEAR

Word of the Beverly Park beating spread through town. Neighbors talked to neighbors over backyard fences, people riding trolley cars spoke of what they'd heard, men at business lunches exchanged viewpoints, and every pool hall and café was awash with rumor and speculation. But at the end of the following day no article about it appeared in the *Daily Tribune*.

A swell of confusion swept over the city. Most residents feared that the Wobblies would retaliate. Others felt that the lawless sheriff and the Commercial Club could no longer control their lust for brutality. Since the newspaper printed nothing about the atrocity at Beverly Park, many citizens worried that the brutalities would continue if there wasn't some form of government intervention from Olympia, and soon.

Wednesday afternoon Jake Michel picked up a wooden crate from in front of Noah Spanjer's market and walked to the front of Bachelder & Corneil's Clothing Store on the corner, and set down the soapbox. He stepped up onto it and looked out over the gathering crowd, a sheriff's deputy sat in a patrol car across the way.

"People of Everett," Michel began, "no city ordinance is going to stop me from speaking today! No city ordinance can trump our Constitution, and no city ordinance can stop me from telling the truth about the brutalities that occurred out on the Pacific Highway two nights ago! A boatload of men from

Seattle were accosted at the city pier, loaded up, and taken from the city limits. Once they were far from town they were forced to walk a gauntlet, brutally beaten and then left for dead by Sheriff Donald McRae and his vigilantes from the Commercial Club!"

"McRae has got to go!" yelled one man in the crowd.

"This is all the Northern Imperial's fault," another snarled.

"I know. I know," Michel responded to the onlookers. "On the same night that the Sheriff and his men engaged in the beating at Beverly Park, the Shingle Weavers Union voted to go back to work. But MacCullock has decided to not honor his word to pay the same wage scale that was paid on the day of the strike back in May," Michel said as the crowd groaned.

"MacCullock can go to the devil!" a voice in the crowd called out.

"It's the striker's fault," the little man in the dirty pork-pie hat yelled.

"Shut yer mouth," a bearded man in overalls barked at the little man.

"People, people," Jake Michel said raising his hands, "we must bring fact and reason to our situation here. We are still on strike, but we need to have a public meeting so that our community can discuss and determine what we can do to resolve this strike and deal with the Beverly Park atrocity."

"Like what?" a man loudly asked.

"Yeah, like what?" another shouted.

"Let him speak," Helen Pomeroy chided.

"He's just making things worse for the Shingle Weavers," the man in the pork-pie hat said.

"I said let him speak!" Helen Pomeroy snapped at the little man.

"Citizens, please!" Jake Michel yelled raising both hands again, "Our town's clergy and I think we should have some of the victims from the night of the beating come back to Everett to explain exactly what happened. We need to hear their side of the story."

Helen Pomeroy walked to the soapbox, tugged on Michel's sleeve, and asked to say a few words. Michel steadied her as she stepped up. Once on the soapbox she adjusted her feathered hat, cleared her throat and took a deep breath before starting.

"I was on the ferry the other night coming back from Seattle, and those men were all peaceable and minding their own business. When we got to the city pier I watched Sheriff McRae and his drunken gang round them up and haul them away. And that was after he said they could have a street meeting. Now those men on the boat were all good, decent men, God fearing Sunday worshipers I'm sure, and this so-called ordinance that's opposed to public speaking is against the law!"

The man in the dirty pork-pie hat shouted, "Aw, you're nothin' but some egg-layin' hen rufflin' yer feathers and squawkin' about."

"Let Helen finish!" Jake Michel hollered at the little agitator.

"Yeah, shut up, would ya," a voice in the crowd agreed.

"Oh, I've been called worse than that," Pomeroy said, "and if I may continue. I saw one man clubbed to the ground for reciting the First Amendment! This is America where we are supposed to have the right to speak freely. This kind of treatment and behavior has got to stop," she said to applause and stepped down with her fist raised in the air.

"Thank you, Helen," Jake Michel said remounting the soapbox. "Mrs. Pomeroy is right! We have got to stand up to these lumber trust brutes, along with the city fathers and this ordinance, and end the turmoil that is disrupting our town. So Father Bywater and I are going to ask the IWW to come back here for a public meeting at this corner on Sunday, and demand that Sheriff McRae be present so he can explain himself."

"But if we have the Wobblies come back they're just gonna burn the town down!" yelled a man in the crowd.

"Yeah! You're just fanning the flames for them to come back here and get even," another voice called out.

"McRae and his gang will just have another whiskey brawl!" one more man in the crowd chided.

"I guarantee," Michel promised, "that I will speak to the IWW and make sure that they will come to Everett only to present their side of the story without violence. We must restore our right to public meetings and free speech."

"What about McRae?" Noah Spanjer shouted from the front of his store.

"Well, he's still taking his orders from the lumber trust. Even if I tried to talk sense to him, he wouldn't listen," Michel said.

"That's right," another man said, "and the chief of police has given up his power to McRae, so it's up to us to take back our town!"

"OK then, I'll tell you what," Noah Spanjer hollered, "I'll print and distribute handbills about this Sunday! We need to invite everyone in town so we can maintain our constitutional rights!"

Off to the side of the gathering a man in a dark suit and bowler hat stood listening. For the last few weeks he'd blended into the town without anyone noticing. Detective Robert Claymore was a man who was very good at his job. He felt in control of his secret design to keep each side of the strike warring and end the strike, but now it looked like the IWW was going to be invited back to Everett. He finally felt that he should contact his employer.

Claymore walked to the Interurban Station. He strode into the brick building at the corner of Colby and Pacific and stepped inside a wood-framed glass phone booth. Closing the bifold door, he pulled a small black book from an inside suit pocket, found the number he needed, and dialed.

The phone on Luther MacCullock's desk rang.

"Yes," MacCullock said into the receiver.

"Mr. MacCullock, its Robert Claymore," the detective said.

"Well, Mr. Claymore, it's about time you called. What have you been doing?" MacCullock said testily.

"I've been doing my job."

"Like what?"

"You want me to tell you exactly what I've done?"

"Mr. Claymore, you need to start telling me what I'm paying for," MacCullock snapped.

"I was just at the soapbox corner. Jake Michel is calling for a public meeting this Sunday, and he's going to invite the Seattle IWW."

"What for?"

"He wants the town folk to hear the Wobblies' side of the Beverly Park situation."

"That's madness," MacCullock said. "We can't invite those radicals back after the beating the sheriff gave them the other night."

"So you heard about the confrontation?" Claymore asked.

"Of course I heard, the whole town knows about it. I also heard that the sheriff's dog was killed at the hands of the Wobblies," MacCullock stated. But the detective didn't say anything.

"Claymore? You still there?" MacCullock asked.

"Yes, I'm here," Claymore replied. "The sheriff says the Wobblies killed his dog?"

"Yes," MacCullock answered, "the Wobblies killed his dog and they have prolonged this strike, they've made this situation much worse and I don't give a lick about winning this strike anymore. The only thing I care about now is keeping these Wobbly hellions out of my town! Forever!" MacCullock boomed.

"Mr. MacCullock," Claymore said as he exhaled, "when you hired me you said that you wanted to end this strike. And I would say that it's just about over."

"I'll be the judge of that. But I want more information about this public meeting. Now get back to work, see what you can find out. And I want you to call me every single day from here on out. You got that!"

"Yes, sir, I will," Robert Claymore said and hung up the phone.

***

A freight train slowly rumbled through Lowell and past Sumner Iron Works, the Eclipse Mill, and into the Riverside District. It was coming from eastern Washington pulling boxcar after boxcar of apples, grain, livestock, and hoboes. Most of the rod-riders were from the harvest crews that usually waited out fall on the western side of the Cascades until snow-shoveling jobs on the mountain rail lines opened up. All of them would roam the bars on Hewitt or Seattle's skid row until then, passing time, and sleeping in parks or alleys.

One rider jumped from a boxcar and rolled in the dirt. The man pulled himself to his feet, looked around, and dusted himself off. He staggered along looking like he was about to fall over. Two neighborhood adolescents playing hooky rode up behind him on bikes.

"Hey mister, you lost 'er somethin'?" one asked.

"You one a' them beat up Wobblies?" the other joked.

The man turned around and snarled at them, "Why you little punks. I ain't no Wobbly. I'll kick the tar out a' ya," and stepped towards them, but they bolted up the street, pedaling as fast as they could. The man walked up Everett Avenue to Market Street, where he climbed the front steps of the Lafayette House and banged on the door. Petra went to answer it but stopped and looked through the window first.

"Miss Goldie! Miss Goldie!" Petra yelled, running back to the kitchen, "There is a scary bum at the door. Hurry!"

"Oh, Dessa, where's Harvey?" Goldie asked from the kitchen. Petra shook her head, "I not know."

"Dessa child, we get these all the time. Here let me," Goldie replied. She scurried to the door and looked through the window.

"Oh my lands," Goldie groaned, "Go away. Can't help ya."

"I'm here to see Cora," the man yelled and banged on the door. "I ain't gonna hurt cha."

"What?" a startled Goldie said and then mumbled to herself, "It's too early for this."

"I need to see Cora," the man screamed. "I know she's in there!"

"Nope, there's no Cora here. Get lost fella, or I'll call the cops!"

"The cops! This is a whorehouse, God dammit! Just because yer some kind-a fancy new crib don't mean ya ain't what ya are!" the bum screamed and slammed his fist on the door. "I'm gonna break down this door if you don't let me in!"

Out of nowhere Harvey Keel came running around the corner outside and bounded up the stairs like his legs were spring-loaded. The hobo turned around and got a good look at Harvey just before an enormous fist hit him. Keel belted him with all his weight. The man flew backwards into the door window, shattering it to pieces. Harvey grabbed him with both hands and pulled him out of the opening, held him up with his left fist, and then hit him repeatedly until the hobo fell unconscious in a heap on the porch. Goldie slowly opened the door and carefully stepped outside, Petra stayed in the doorway.

"Boy, oh boy, did you ever show up in time," Goldie said with a grin on her relieved face. She put her hands on her hips.

"You ever . . . see him before?" Harvey asked catching his breath.

"Said he was looking for Cora," Goldie answered.

"That's a right," Petra added.

"Did he now?" Harvey grunted and began to dig through his pockets. "Here's some keys," he said, jingling them in his hand, "and a wallet."

"Any money?" Petra quickly asked.

"There's a bit of money, not much else," Harvey said. "What should we do with him?"

Goldie thought for a moment and then said, "Well, I've never seen him before. He must be some timber bum from up in the woods. Drag him out in the alley and leave him be, but put his wallet and all the money back. We don't need him thinking that we stole his cash. Hopefully he'll just wander away."

From the north end of the alley the same two boys watched as Harvey dragged the man out of the backyard gate and dropped him.

"Looks like that bum," one boy said.

"Yeah, that's him all right," the other agreed.

"That big old bodyguard must a' knocked him out 'er somethin'?"

"Let's go see if he's got any money."

The two boys got on their bikes and slowly coasted down the alley as they looked around to make sure no one was watching. Halfway there one had second thoughts.

"I don't think this is such a good idea."

"Aw, you lily-liver," the bold one said as they got close, "you always chicken out."

Once they were next to him, the bold one quietly hopped off his bike and set it down without a sound while his friend stood, straddling his upright bike.

"Look, he's passed out," he whispered. "I'll do it ya chicken shit." He bent down and carefully slipped a hand in the bum's pockets, he pulled his wallet out with a grin.

"Look, there's some dough!" the boy said, holding up a handful of cash for his friend to see.

"Come on. Let's get outta here before somebody catches us," the diffident one whispered as loud as he could.

"No, wait," the bold one said. He dropped the wallet on the ground and stuffed the bills in his pocket.

"Why? What for? Come on. Somebody's gonna catch us," the timid one urged. The other boy turned his back and began to pee on the bum, he snickered as he sprayed the man's already filthy clothes.

"Tommy, what are ya doin'?"

"What's it look like?" Tommy said. He glanced over his shoulder and looked at his friend with a grin to see his friend's reaction when he peed on the bum's face. It woke him up.

"HEY —" the hobo yelped. He grabbed Tommy's leg and hollered, "You little bastard."

Tommy kicked at the bum with his free leg and screamed, "Billy! Help!" Billy lifted the front wheel of his bike off the ground and slammed it on the bum's wrist as hard as he could.

"Christ! You!" the hobo howled, letting go of Tommy's leg. Tommy jumped back on his bike and they peddled as fast as they could up the alley towards Twenty-Third Street. The bum rolled over blinking, and tried to watch them, but they were out of sight.

Wiping the piss from his face, the man pulled himself to his feet, looked around and found his empty wallet. He rubbed his sore jaw and stared malevolently at the Lafayette House.

"You sumbitch!" the hobo yelled at the bordello and shook his fist, "If I ever see you again, I'll decapitate you like a spar!"

As he walked away, he figured that Everett was a place where he wouldn't stay for too long.

***

Luther MacCullock packed his pipe with fresh tobacco, rocked back in his chair, and wondered where his next raft of logs was. He picked up the phone and called the tugboat company.

"American Tug," a clerk at the company said.

"Who's this?" MacCullock grunted.

"Frank Ramwell. Who's this?" the man replied.

"Northern Imperial here. We're due a raft of logs," MacCullock said into the receiver.

"Oh, yeah, I know. Pa headed upriver with our smaller tug late yesterday on the tide," Frank replied.

"Oh, you're Henry's son?" MacCullock asked.

"Yes."

"Can you radio him? Find out if he's towing my logs yet?"

"Yes, I can."

"Then get him on the horn. I'll wait," MacCullock ordered.

"Hold on," the young Ramwell said. He set down the receiver, pushed down on the radio switch, and spoke into the microphone.

"Tugboat *Goldfinch*, tugboat *Goldfinch*. This is homeport. Come in, *Goldfinch*." But there was no answer. "Tugboat *Goldfinch*, can you hear me?" After a long pause a voice sounded from the radio.

"Go ahead, homeport. This is the *Goldfinch*," Henry Ramwell said over the loudspeaker.

"Pa? Northern Imperial is on the line. They want to know where their raft is."

"You got Luther on the phone?"

"Yep."

"Tell him he's got a problem. There ain't no raft. Lum says there's been some kind of revolt up at Timber Creek and that Charlie Purvis got himself sent down the flume on a log by his crew," Henry explained. "Guess they fired him. Lum says there ain't been a single log hit the splash pond fer days, and the river pigs unlashed the raft. Let every log float off. I guess Charlie hightailed it, too."

"Geez Pa, Luther ain't gonna like this."

"It's no doin' of ours son. Just tell him what I said."

"OK, Pa," Frank replied. "Homeport out."

"Mr. MacCullock?"

"I heard every word on your loudspeaker, son," Luther grumbled and abruptly hung up.

MacCullock slammed both fists down on his desk, jumped to his feet, and went over to the window. He looked across the tracks at his mill with clenched hands on his hips and stared at the picketers.

"Drat!" he hollered. "This damn strike and Charlie Purvis can go straight to hell!" He snatched the pipe off his desk and lit it. Sweet white smoke belched from the bowl, quickly filling the room with a thick haze as he began to pace in front of the window. Each time he turned he glanced at his mill. He finally pulled his pocket watch out of his vest and checked the time. MacCullock went back to his desk and called the sheriff.

"McRae?" MacCullock said into the phone. "This is Luther."

"What's it now?" the sheriff said, his feet up on his desk.

"Meet at the Commercial Club in an hour."

"Why?"

"Don't be asking questions, just be down at the club at lunch time."

"Yeah . . . sure . . . OK," the sheriff yawned.

"Good. Now, I understand you gave the Wobblies a good work over a few nights ago."

"You heard about that, huh?" the sheriff asked.

"Yes. The whole town knows about it, and now I hear the Wobblies are being invited back for a public meeting this Sunday," MacCullock said.

"Yeah, I know. One of my deputies just heard Michel jackin' his jaws at the soapbox."

"And your deputy didn't arrest him?"

"Nope, the crowd was too big, and he was by himself."

"What good is the new ordinance if you're not going to use it?"

"Luther," the sheriff said with a tired voice. "The rest of my men were out on the blockade, and there weren't any Wobblies speaking. So he let it be."

"All right," MacCullock said. "Now if we let these radicals come back here this weekend, they will seek revenge. They would just as soon burn the town down if we let them, and *that* can never happen. Do you understand?" MacCullock barked.

"Yep, I understand," the sheriff replied, rubbing the side of his head.

"Good, I'll see you at the club then. I've got somebody coming today to speak to the members and I want you there," MacCullock said. He hung up.

***

The Commercial Club was packed, alive with conversation. The air smelled of cigar smoke and hamburger beefsteak sandwiches. Ralph Edgerton and Lester Blankenship sat in a booth.

"This whole mess has gotten out of hand," Lester remarked as he picked at his salad with a fork.

"This strike should have been settled months ago," Ralph complained. "Now all we've got is one big out-of-control war, and I have just about had it."

"Did you see this?" Blankenship asked holding up the newspaper.

"You mean the article that finishes with, 'the IWW's entitled to no sympathy,'" Ralph said. "All that damn *Tribune*'s doing is fanning the flames, and that new street meeting ordinance didn't stop anything."

Just then Luther MacCullock walked in with a broad shouldered man wearing a suit. MacCullock took no time commandeering the floor.

"Gentlemen, we have a guest speaker this afternoon," MacCullock announced. After leading the man to the front of the room he turned to the seventy-some members present.

"Gentlemen, members of the Commercial Club, this is Roy Montgomery from the Washington Employers' Organization. Roy is here today to talk to us about the Wobbly scourge that has turned our town upside down. He's come a long way to be here, so let's give him a warm welcome," Luther said, clapping his hands as he stepped aside. The man glanced around the room and cleared his throat. He was tall and clean-shaven, he wore a dark grey suit, white collared shirt, and a black four-in-hand necktie.

"Good afternoon, and thank you Luther and members of the Commercial Club for having me. It's good to be here. I won't take too much of your time," Montgomery began. "As some of you may know I represent many of you here today and over five hundred and fifty employers of this state in both Olympia and Washington D.C. My job is to represent and protect your business interests, advance your success, and make sure that the government does not limit your use of labor, or increase taxes. But today Luther has asked me to talk to you about the Wobbly threat that has descended upon your town, and, I must say, I am pleased to aid you in your fight against this radical union that calls itself the Industrial Workers of the World."

Lester Blankenship stood up from his booth and interrupted.

"We wouldn't have this problem if we didn't have some maniac for sheriff!" Blankenship declared to a few feeble cheers.

"Sit down, Lester, and let Roy talk," MacCullock snapped. "He came all the way from Olympia, so let him speak." Luther nodded to Montgomery and he started again.

"Our sawdust economy owes everything to the men that have the skill, knowledge and wherewithal to build these lumber and shake mills and the other interrelated businesses. The lumber industry feeds everything. It creates jobs, it builds schools, and hospitals, and it has civilized this wilderness. But the Wob believes that their rank and file is improving the workplace by advocating constant general strikes aimed at putting their interests over the company and profit." He pointed a waving finger towards the ceiling.

"But don't be fooled, gentlemen. This union that exhorts one big union for all is nothing more than a front for sabotage, disruption, demonstration, vandalism, and arson. You see, they think of themselves not only as members of a union but as members of a church. Imagine that! They worship the IWW like it's a religion. Here is a group of heathens, bent on the ruination of society, thinking they are on the same level as Christ himself. How dare they think and act like that in this day and age! Wherever they are, these soldiers of discontent that call themselves a union must be crushed, not only here but everywhere," Montgomery advised to an agreeing crowd.

"I understand that you've had a number of conflicts with the IWW and that they have been invited here this coming Sunday, which to me is nothing more than a fool's errand. But I also understand that the invitation has been given and that there is no turning around," Montgomery said.

The sheriff appeared in the back hallway. He pushed his Stetson up on his brow as he leaned against the wall and crossed his arms, his shirttail hanging out. There were bags under his eyes, and the skin on his once rawboned face looked like polished wax.

"This Sunday we must deal with this rabble in the same way that other communities have dealt with the IWW all across our great country. Detroit had to deal with the IWW three years ago at Ford's Highland plant and then the Studebaker plant but in that instance the Wobblies were quickly put down. Then there was the Patterson strike, the Wheatland strike, Spokane and Fresno and well, gentlemen, the list of Wobbly disruptions goes on and on. We absolutely must to do something about this scourge of anarchists," Montgomery explained to cheers and applause. He waited for quiet.

"We cannot be bullied by a gang of un-American renegades and we must fight force with force. I say that Everett needs to show the whole world that this unwashed and ungodly rabble must be stopped, and this is the time and the place to do it!"

"Here, here!" Mayor Merrill cheered, getting to his feet.

"Roy is right!" MacCullock agreed, clapping his hands as he stood behind the speaker.

"Montgomery's a patriot!" another member said when he began again.

"This Sunday is the time for Everett to end the Wobbly threat," Roy said and then he raised his voice, "it is time to take back your town!" The Commercial Club erupted with applause as members looked at each nodding while Ralph Edgerton and Lester Blankenship walked out.

Montgomery was swarmed by Commercial Club members, everyone shook his hand and patted him on the back. MacCullock walked around the group over to the sheriff and motioned for McRae to follow him to the backroom. Luther unlocked the door and they stepped inside, every box of liquor, wine and brandy had been removed and replaced with an arsenal of rifles, shotguns, hand guns, holsters, ammunition, ax handles, and stitched leather tubes filled with ball-bearings.

Pointing out the weaponry, MacCullock boasted, "One of our members is also the commander of the Naval Armory, so I convinced him to relocate most of this here just in case the Wobblies broke into his building and stole it all."

The sheriff glanced around the room and observed, "Would ya look at all this. You've got one heck of a lot-a firepower, here."

MacCullock remarked, "The commander doesn't know it yet, but we will be utilizing this equipment on Sunday at the dock."

"What exactly ya got planned, Captain?" the sheriff asked with a raised eyebrow. MacCullock stepped over to the entry and closed the door.

"The Wobblies will probably arrive by ferryboat. I think we should have every citizen deputy at the city pier armed and ready for them but, we can only use this weaponry as a show of force. You see, my thinking is, if we have two-hundred or more men on the dock brandishing this amount of firepower then those Wobblies will realize right away that we mean business. If they're smart they'll stay on that boat," MacCullock said.

"And if they don't? Then —" the sheriff replied.

"Then you'll have to keep them on it. Under no circumstances can you allow those damn Wobblies to get off that ship! Listen Donald, they'll understand our meaning. When they see all of this weaponry," MacCullock said with a sweeping movement of his arm, "they'll *stay* on that boat."

McRae slowly pushed up his Stetson, looked MacCullock in the eye and said, "And that's all you think I have to do, just show 'em our guns, and keep 'em on the boat?"

"Yes, it's our best option. We just show them down. We'll out man them, and out muscle them. They're no match and they'll figure that out right away."

"Well, all right, but once I take care of this mess on Sunday, I'm gonna be ready for that —"

"Dammit, Donald, listen here," MacCullock barked. "My lumberjacks at Timber Creek found out about the strike and revolted. Plus, they hog tied my foreman to a log and sent him down the flume. So don't start moaning to me about some job down the road, I've got a world of trouble going on right now."

"They sent Charlie down the flume?"

"Sure did, and nobody's seen him since," MacCullock said.

"He'll turn up," the sheriff reassured.

"If he does I want him arrested and brought to me! You got that?" MacCullock snapped.

"What am I gonna to arrest him for?"

"For fouling up my logging camp, that's what."

"But —"

"No buts! Now you listen, if you see Charlie Purvis you cuff him and bring him to me! Do you understand what I'm saying?" Luther MacCullock stormed, his voice full of poison, louder, stronger and more powerful than ever.

"Yeah, OK Captain," the sheriff replied.

Then MacCullock looked McRae coldly in the eye, "And one more thing. There's been plenty of talk about your condition lately, and I think it would be a good idea to leave the whiskey alone come Sunday. I need you sober for once. This is some serious business we're dealing with and this town needs a clear headed sheriff."

McRae glared at MacCullock.

"Don't *you* be givin' me no lecture! If I feel like takin' a drink, then I'll take a drink," the sheriff growled.

"Damn it —" MacCullock spat back. But McRae cut him off. He raised his hand and said, "Nope, I've been takin' all yer orders. But I ain't takin' that one."

The sheriff crossed his arms and stared at the mill owner.

MacCullock inhaled deeply and held his breath for a moment. "OK," he exhaled. "All right. Have it your way. Now, in the meantime we've still got to get ready. Let's go back out and get everyone organized," MacCullock ordered. He opened the door and then locked it behind them.

The main room was filled with the sound of talk. Montgomery was still surrounded by members asking questions while others praised him. MacCullock strode up to Montgomery and shook his hand.

"Can you stick around for lunch, Roy?" MacCullock asked. "This is Sheriff McRae."

"Good to meet you, Sheriff," Montgomery nodded to the sheriff while MacCullock addressed the members.

"Gentlemen. Can I have your attention, again? This coming Sunday the Wobblies will be coming here to wreak havoc on our town. The sheriff has done all he can do to keep them out, but they will not listen or understand that they are not welcome here. We have no choice but to deal with this rabble and we will not, we will never, allow them to set foot in our town."

"We'll show them!" a voice in the room yelled.

"Let's give 'em hell!" another cried. MacCullock raised his hands for calm and then continued.

"Every member that has not been deputized must be so now. We need every man we can to stop these anarchists. There's a very good chance that they will be arriving by boat Sunday at 2:00 p.m., so everyone should meet here well before then. Once you're here we will arm every citizen deputy with a rifle," MacCullock said and then pointed the stem of his pipe at the ceiling, "and we are gonna scare the living daylights out of those arrogant fools because when the Wobblies see our gunnery they'll think twice about stepping off that boat!"

"The plan is to blast the shift whistles from every mill on the waterfront at 10:00 a.m. for a reminder. If they blast earlier or at any other time before then, it means to hustle here right away. But for the time being if anyone hears or sees something suspicious then report it to the sheriff or me."

✳✳✳

Later that day, Luther MacCullock called his mill manager.

"Northern Imperial Mill," Butch Barnell said, answering the phone.

"Butch?" MacCullock said.

"Yes, Captain."

"Timber Creek mutinied," MacCullock explained. "That's why the log raft hasn't showed."

"What?" Barnell said.

"You heard me," MacCullock said.

"Timber Creek mutinied? What's Charlie got to say?"

"Apparently Charlie's crew shipped him out of camp on the flume," MacCullock said.

"They what?"

"I *said*, they sent Charlie down the flume."

"Where is he?"

"Don't know. Hasn't been seen."

"What are we gonna do?"

"Shut down," MacCullock said bluntly.

"Again?"

"Yes. There's no logs coming. So I need you to layoff all those workers at the end of the shift. And then I need you to get on up to Timber Creek and get things straightened out up there. But you can't take Mullaney, I'm gonna need him here. Take a few of his guards with you."

"You're sure about laying off the men?"

"Dammit, Barnell! I said to lay them off, you've done this before. If you have trouble then tell them we'll hire all of them back once we get the logs running again. And then get yourself up to my camp. Today!" MacCullock slammed down the phone.

***

A crowd had been building at the corner of Hewitt and Wetmore all afternoon as one citizen after another mounted the soapbox to speak. By 5:00 p.m. a horde of listeners had gathered from all over town and spilled into the street, blocking traffic. Sheriff McRae and Deputies Jeff Beard and Walt Irvan sat in a patrol car across Hewitt and scanned the mass of citizens. The Salvation Army band played *Onward Christian Soldiers* while Noah Spanjer tried to take care of his customers and watch for shoplifters. Two teenagers with a dog worked their way through the swarm of onlookers as Father Nathan Bywater preached to the crowd.

"Brothers and sisters of Everett, the day will come when salvation greets us all. Our Lord and Savior is watching us now, and we must be vigilant in our deeds and —"

Jake Michel tugged on his elbow and pulled him from the soapbox.

"Everyone! Everyone, listen up," Michel said smiling. "The Northern Imperial just shut down and laid off all of its scabs. The logs have stopped coming, and they have no timber to mill!"

A roar came up from the crowd as a bum with a black-eye and bloody, filthy clothing came up and stood at the back of the multitude. He looked like all of the other bums and suspected Wobblies that came to the mill town, unshaven and unwashed. But he was alone, he looked defeated and forlorn. For some reason he seemed familiar to Sheriff McRae.

"If Northern Imperial is out of logs, then Luther MacCullock will soon be out of money!" Jake Michel screamed at the boisterous, jovial crowd.

When the hobo heard that the Northern Imperial was out of timber to mill, he raised his right fist and pumped it in the air. Then he started walking again.

The sheriff rubbed his eyes as he watched the man move away from the crowd and then snapped his head around to the deputies, pointed from behind the wheel, and spat, "Go grab that bum!"

"Huh? What for?" Deputy Beard asked, sitting up.

"Because that's Charlie Purvis, that's why."

"Jeez, I didn't recognize him," Beard remarked and started to get out of the car.

"Just walk up behind him real slow-like, and ask him to come over here. But once you get him to the car I want you to cuff him," the sheriff instructed from the driver's seat before the two deputies started across Hewitt. "Now just start by tellin' him that I wanna talk to him," McRae added with a lowered voice.

Beard and Irvan nonchalantly walked over to Purvis while Robert Claymore stood in the shadows of a storefront entry and watched, straining his ears. Once they were right behind Purvis, Deputy Beard asked quietly, "Charlie? Is that you?" Purvis spun around and saw the badges on the two deputies' chests.

"How'd you know my name?" Purvis sniffed.

"We know who ya are," Beard said. "Sheriff wants to talk to ya."

"What? He does, where?"

"He's over in the car," Beard said and pointed across Hewitt. Purvis looked over the deputy's shoulder. He thought about it for a second and shrugged his shoulders.

"Sure, I've known McRae for a long time," Purvis said.

The deputies walked behind him while Beard began to quietly pull the handcuffs from his belt. Robert Claymore followed them a short distance behind with his head slightly down.

"Charlie?" Sheriff McRae said from inside the car. "Is that you?"

"Yeah, it's me all right."

"Fer Christ's sake, you look like hell."

"Seen better days, that's fer sure," Purvis said. Then Beard and Irvan pushed Purvis down on the patrol car hood.

"Hey! What's ——" Purvis yelled, struggling, "Why, you sumbitches!" The sheriff leaped from the car and helped hold Purvis down, they started to cuff him.

"I got my orders, Charlie," McRae said and pushed on the back of Charlie's neck, smashing his face against the hood.

"Yer orders. Who's orders?" Purvis sputtered through a squished mouth.

"You'll see soon enough. Get him in the back boys," the sheriff commanded.

"MacCullock, right?" Purvis guessed as the two deputies muscled Charlie into the back seat and closed the door. "MacCullock's tellin' you what to do, isn't he?" But the sheriff didn't answer him. Instead he looked to his deputies.

"Jeff, you stay here and watch the crowd. Walt, hop in, you and me are gonna take Charlie up to the jailhouse."

"You can't arrest me!" Purvis yelled.

"Shut up, Charlie!" the sheriff boomed. "I can arrest anyone I want. Especially a low-down timber bum like you."

Robert Claymore stood off to the side and pulled a small notebook from his coat. He began to jot down a few descriptive words.

On the ride up the street the sheriff reached under the seat, pulled out his jug, and took a long wet pull, making sure that Purvis saw him. "So, Charlie, I heard ya had a little trouble up at the camp."

"Go to hell," Purvis growled.

"Aw, I was just makin' talk. Come on, tell me what happened. How come you smell like, what is that, piss?" the sheriff asked and then took another pull. He looked through his rearview mirror at Charlie's face and snickered. "If'n ya ain't gonna tell me what happened up at Timber Creek, maybe you could tell me what happened to yer face?"

"I said go ta' hell, ya sumbitch. I ain't tellin' you squat."

The sheriff turned down the alley behind the jailhouse and parked at the backdoor. He took another swig, put his right arm on the backrest, and cracked a devilish grin. "Yer just a-borrowin' trouble comin' back here, ya know. Old MacCullock is gonna be mighty darn pleased to hear that I've got the son of a bitch that lost his loggin' camp. Ya see, Charlie, you losing Timber Creek is costing him thousands."

"I didn't lose Timber Creek, some stupid Scandi got himself kilt," Purvis protested as he struggled in the back seat with his hands cuffed behind him.

"You killed another guy up there?"

"I didn't kill anybody, God-dammit. Accidents happen!"

"An accident, huh?" McRae said, he turned and faced the jailhouse.

"Yes, an accident."

"So why'd you come back here anyway?" the sheriff cocked his head to hear Charlie's answer.

"Go to hell, McRae."

"Oh, that's not the answer I was lookin' for. Did ya you come back here to fess up fer yer responsibilities?"

"I said go to hell!"

The sheriff held the jug out for Deputy Irvan. He took a drink and handed it back. Walt wiped his jaw, smirked, and then asked, "Well, what're we gonna do with him?"

McRae glanced at the former logging camp foreman through the rear-view mirror and then looked at his deputy.

"OK, Walt, I guess we're a-gonna be lockin' Mr. Charlie up. How 'bout if you go inside and get a few of the boys to help escort our newest guest to his cell. I'll just sit right here and wait."

"You can't lock me up! I ain't done nothin' wrong!" Charlie hollered.

"Well, that's too damn bad, ya ignorant son of a bitch. Ya should a' never, ever, come back here," the sheriff said, slurring his words.

Charlie mumbled quietly under his breath, "That damn Cora —"

"What?"

"Nothin'."

"You just said a woman's name, didn't you?"

"Nope," Charlie said.

Deputy Irvan came out of the jailhouse with two other men. The sheriff slowly got out of the patrol car and opened the backdoor, nearly losing his balance and unknowingly, dropping the car keys in the dirt.

"All right boys, stick him in the holding tank, and keep an eye on him. I gotta go and make myself a phone call. And keep him cuffed."

Sheriff McRae stumbled into his office and went straight to the file cabinet. He pulled the ever-present jug out, sat down behind his desk, put his feet up, had a sip, and pondered the situation. A grin slowly formed on his face. He grabbed the phone and dialed.

"Yes."

"Captain," the sheriff said into the receiver, "McRae here."

"Yes," MacCullock said.

"I've got someone locked up in my holding cell that I'm thinkin' you just might like to talk to."

"Sheriff, there are more important things on my mind right now," MacCullock snapped.

"Oh, I'm sure that's true. But what if I told you I've got Charlie Purvis?"

"You got Purvis! Where'd you find him?"

"Pulled him out of the crowd, down at the corner."

"Bring him to me!" MacCullock yelled. "Now!"

"Not so fast there, Captain."

"What! Now wait a second, are you drunk?" But the sheriff cut him off.

"Nope, but I've just about had it with you and yer war. I've been toeing the line fer months 'n' doin' yer dirty work, and by gum, I want consideration."

"Consideration? You're drunk, aren't you?"

"I want that timekeeper's job. Right now . . . Today!"

"Sheriff. There's no logs. Purvis lost the camp. My salt chuck is empty, and if there's no logs there's no work, so that means there's no timekeeper's job."

"Dammit, Luther! I've got yer prized chicken down in my tank, and I want consideration. I've had it with this sheriff job you talked me into runnin' for!"

"Consideration, huh? All right then," MacCullock acquiesced. "You can have his old job up at the camp."

"What? That's bull crap, I ain't runnin' no loggin' camp out in the sticks."

"Sheriff McRae! Our agreement is for a job that depends on logs in my mill pond. If there's no logs there's no job. So, either you can run my timber camp, or you can wait until Butch gets up there and gets the logs running again? And then you can have your timekeepers job," MacCullock stormed.

McRae took a pull from his bottle and glanced at his hunting rifle and fishing pole in the corner. Then he began to shake his head as his jaw tightened.

"All summer long I been fightin' yer war for ya when I should've been out snagging trout," McRae said standing up motioning with his arm. "Hell, I should be out hunting this weekend!" the sheriff added, his voice rising and blood beginning to boil. "But instead, I'll be walkin' the line again fer you, Luther, and I want what's due!" McRae hollered into the receiver. He slammed his fist down so hard on his desk the top drawer came unhinged. "This agreement of ours is bein' *renegotiated*! NOW! So, you had better step up to the table 'er else yer gonna be sorry you ever got me elected!"

Luther MacCullock pulled the phone away from his ear, he realized that the sheriff was right. He also realized that the sheriff held a power that was greater than his and that he still needed him. MacCullock put the phone back to his ear, relaxed his grip on the long stem handle and changed his tone of voice.

"Now Donald, you've done a fine job dealing with all of these troubles . . . I'll tell you what. I could deed you over a piece of ground. How'd that be?" MacCullock offered. The sheriff mulled it over for a moment.

"Hmm, a piece of dirt, ya say?" he replied calmly.

"Yes. It'd be a logged-off parcel, but that's all I've got, close to town that is."

"Oh, so yer gonna pawn off one of yer stump farms on me, is that it?" McRae said, raising his voice again.

"That's still good ground, with fine soil. Tell you what, Donald. I'll deed you a twenty-acre parcel on Ebey Island. How'd you like that?"

"Nope, I want timber. No stump farms fer me."

"Sheriff, Charlie Purvis already lost Timber Creek so he's not that valuable to me. However, I do want to talk to him, and I do appreciate the work you've done, I really do. But stump land is all I've got. If you don't take it then I'll have myself a conversation with the governor about you."

"Well, then, maybe I'll have myself a conversation with the governor about you," the sheriff replied, his anger beginning to fade.

"Dammit! All I have is logged-off parcels!" MacCullock hollered.

"All right, I'll take it. Twenty acres, right?" McRae conceded.

"Yes. Good. It's done then. Now bring me Purvis!"

"OK, I'll bring him to ya, be right there."

Luther MacCullock put his hand on the phone and pushed the hook down with a finger, ending the call. He knew what he needed next but his mind raced with what the next move would be after that, and then the next. He nodded his head as the edges of his mouth turned ever so slightly upward. The receiver went back to his ear and he dialed the mill.

The sheriff poured the rest of the jug into his flask, tossed the bottle into the trash with the other empties, and slowly stood up. He walked out of his office door with the flask in his back pocket and reached into his trousers for the patrol car keys.

"What —? Where the hell?" the sheriff asked himself. He turned around and went back to his office, scratching his head. He looked on and under his desk and then around on the floor. "Dammit," he said to himself and went downstairs.

"Walt!" the sheriff yelled as he came around the corner and down the gangway between the cells. "Right here, boss," Deputy Irvan said, stepping out of the back room.

"Go get that extra set of patrol car keys for me. Then get Pete and you two bring Purvis out to the car. But go head and cuff his hands in front of him."

"Yes, sir," Irvan replied. Ten minutes later the two deputies and their prisoner walked out of the jailhouse alley door and shoved Purvis in the back. Irvan handed the sheriff the keys through his open window.

"Pete," the sheriff hollered, "You stay here. Walt, jump in the front seat."

"Where we headed?" Irvan asked as he walked around the front of the car to the passenger door.

"Where the hell 'cr you taking me?" Purvis grumbled from his seat.

The sheriff took a hit off his flask and then looked through the rearview mirror and smirked. He said, "Charlie, I do believe yer about to meet yer maker."

"Why, you sumbitch," Purvis spat, "Yer nothin' but his little errand boy, aren't ya?" The sheriff backed the patrol car up and started to turn around. He looked at Irvan.

"Keep an eye on him," the sheriff ordered. "I don't want Charlie here to be gettin' any ideas."

They turned on Hewitt and headed west. After they crossed Hoyt, the sheriff took his eyes off the road to look at a couple of men in overalls walking towards the waterfront.

"Watch it," Irvan said just as the sheriff crossed the trolley tracks. Turning back to his side of the street, he belched, "Shut up, I'm fine."

When they turned into the alley behind the Northern Imperial head office, Buck Mullaney was there with two lumber trust guards, one holding a shotgun. They saw Charlie in the backseat.

"Walt, you wait here," the sheriff said before he got out of the patrol car. "This won't take long."

The sheriff jerked Charlie from the back seat. Buck Mullaney opened his mouth real wide and said, "Why I'll be washed and starched as stiff as a preacher's collar! If it ain't old Charlie Purvis, the man who lost Timber Creek. Are ya here ta' get what's comin' to ya?" Mullaney started to walk towards the stairs.

"Shut up. I didn't lose Timber Creek, them sumbitchin' lumberjacks done stole it!" Charlie spat out. The sheriff pulled his blackjack from his belt and pointed it at the stairs, signaling Purvis to follow the mill guard.

"Aw, you sorry, dumb bastard. Ya got ta' be either stupid brave 'er just plain stupid, stupid fer coming back to this town," Mullaney said over his shoulder as he climbed the steps ahead of them.

Luther MacCullock sat behind the desk in his walnut-lined office. One window was cracked open, but none of the usual noise from his mill seeped through. He was on the phone talking to a lumber merchant.

"Yes, I realize that you are due a shipment, and I will get it to you as soon as I can. Now good day," MacCullock said, hanging up the receiver. He heard a knock on the door. "Come in," he said loudly.

Buck Mullaney entered the room and walked to the far corner. He crossed his arms as he turned around, and stared at the former logging camp foreman standing at the entry. Charlie hesitated until the sheriff poked him in the back with the end of his blackjack. MacCullock remained seated behind his desk as pipe smoke rose around his head like he was a Northern Imperial smokestack. He looked down his nose through his pince-nez at the foreman.

"Jesus, Charlie, you look like hell," MacCullock grunted. "Go ahead, sit down," he offered, motioning to the chair in front of the desk. "You've got a lot of explaining to do, and I suggest that you tell me just what exactly happened up at my logging camp . . . and I'd like to know why your crew sent you down the flume."

"'Cause he got some lumberjack killed up there," the sheriff quickly said, "that's why."

"McRae!" MacCullock hollered. "I want to hear what Charlie has to say. So?"

Charlie just stood there looking half dead. The blood on his shirt had turned brown and the bruises and lacerations on his face were nearly as swollen as his black eye. He looked behind himself to see the chair and slowly sat down.

"Well," MacCullock boomed and then sniffed the air and wrinkled his nose, "what have you got to say?"

Charlie took a deep breath.

"God dammit, Luther. I'm the one that kept that camp runnin' and pumpin' out logs for months and months after the strike, not you," he said as he twisted in the chair. "I'm the one that pushed those men up there for you, and I was the one that was keepin' yer salt chuck stocked with rafts of timber. Me! Nobody else!"

"And I never kilt anyone up there. Accidents happen, you know that," Purvis added.

MacCullock nodded his head, motioned with his pipe, and said, "Go on. Tell me about the accident."

Charlie inhaled and said, "I didn't see it, so I can't rightly say. I guess he was just in the wrong place at the wrong time. All I know is the haul-back snapped and the cable whipped back and kilt the guy."

"But why'd you get sent down the flume?" MacCullock asked as he stared at his timber foreman. Charlie glanced up to the ceiling, closed his eyes briefly, and turned back to Luther.

"'Cause them stupid loggers thought it was my fault."

"Was it?"

"Nope."

"Then why'd they think it was?" MacCullock prodded, pointing his pipe straight up. Charlie glanced away but this time at the floor.

"They thought the cable was bad," he answered, still looking down.

"Was it?"

"That haul-back line was fine," Purvis said, snapping his head up and glaring at MacCullock.

"So why'd they say different?"

"'Cause they're a bunch of punk-assed timber bums, that's why," Purvis said with a raised voice.

"Hmm."

"Dammit, Luther!" Purvis yelled, and threw his cuffed hands up in the air. "That's it. I'm done."

"You're done? Done with what? I'm not done with you yet."

"Yep, I'm done. I ain't workin' fer you anymore. I quit!"

"What! You'll quit when I say you can, Mr. Purvis. I'm the one that hired your sorry soul, and I'm the one that'll fire it. But I'm not gonna fire you just yet," MacCullock said with a cruel grin.

"Aw, this is bull-shit. What am I, some sort of Northern Imperial inmate now?"

"Oh, I wouldn't put it that way. But I am gonna keep you on ice for a while."

"Why? I ain't done nothing wrong," Purvis snapped back. The upturned smirk disappeared from Luther MacCullock's face.

"You've done nothing wrong? You think you've done nothing wrong!" MacCullock exploded, dropping his pipe, slamming his fists on the desk, and standing up to his full height. "Why, you ungrateful, disrespectful son of a bitch! How dare you say such a thing! My salt chuck is empty! My logging camp is shut down! And my mill is silent! And you think you've done nothing wrong! Damn it, Purvis!" MacCullock roared glaring at the foreman.

"I say we take him back to the jailhouse," the sheriff interjected.

"Shut up. I'm calling the shots here," MacCullock barked. He picked his pipe up off the floor and began to pack it with fresh tobacco. The room stayed silent as Luther struck a match. He put the flame to the bowl and sucked so hard that it went out. "Christ," MacCullock mumbled under his breath and struck another. Once he had his pipe lit he seemed to breathe smoke and fire as he glared at Purvis, his mind slicing through thoughts like a freshly sharpened cross cut saw.

"So," MacCullock began, "the way I see it, Mr. Purvis, your sorry soul is mine, and it stays mine as long as I say so."

"You sumbitch," Charlie muttered.

"You keep quiet," MacCullock said. "Now listen, I've got a mess that is going to be taken care of this Sunday —"

"What mess is that?"

"Well, you see, Charlie, since you've been busy losing my logging camp I've been dealing with this damn strike, as you know . . . And since the first part of August the Wobblies and their union have been here. So I've had my own batch of labor troubles."

"Have ya now," Purvis said.

"Yes, yes I have. And now I'm thinking that I'm going to put you with the citizen deputies this Sunday when the Wobblies are due back."

"What's that?"

"This coming Sunday we are expecting a boatload of Wobbly troublemakers and I'm thinking that you're going to be down on the dock with our little greeting party."

"And do what?"

"And do what you're told, that's what!"

"What are you planning?" Purvis shot back.

"Buck!"

"Yes, sir," Mullaney answered, stepping forward.

"Take Charlie here down to the bunkhouse and keep him under lock and key. Go ahead and feed him, but watch him like a hawk. Leave him be as long as he doesn't stir up any trouble, you understand?"

"Yes, sir, Captain," Mullaney replied with a gleam in his eye.

"And, Buck," MacCullock said, "I want you and your best men to take Charlie here to the wharf on Sunday. But leave some guards at the mill that day just in case the Wobblies try to outflank us and burn the mill down . . . and post two guards here at my office."

"Yes, sir, I'll take care of it," Mullaney agreed.

"Just what the hell is going on here?" Purvis asked, glaring at his former boss.

"You'll see this Sunday, Charlie," MacCullock said with a cold stare. "Now don't give me or Buck here any trouble. Just do what we tell ya, and everything will be fine."

"And what the hell I am supposed to do this Sunday?"

"You just keep your mouth shut and your ears open. I'll take care of the rest," MacCullock said, motioning with a wave of his hand towards the door.

"God damn this place," Charlie Purvis mumbled under his breath and then glared at MacCullock.

"This meeting is over," MacCullock said, gesturing again towards the exit. Charlie stood up as the sheriff opened the door and they began to walk out. Buck Mullaney was the bringing up the rear, but just before he stepped outside MacCullock quickly strode over and grabbed him by the arm, then closed the door halfway.

"Buck," Luther whispered, "be back here in an hour. I'll have my Sunday plan formulated by then."

Mullaney grinned, nodded his head, and walked out.

Chapter 14

BLOODY SUNDAY

It was a clear November day, one of those glorious western Washington mornings that a person never wanted to end. The golden glow of the sun peeked over the Cascades to the east, the moon was still visible to the west, and a slack tide began to pull away from the shores of Puget Sound. The streets of Everett were still and calm.

At 8:35 a.m. the early morning Interurban pulled into the station at the corner of Pacific and Colby with stacks of the *Seattle Post-Intelligencer*. The shipping clerk tossed the banded packages onto the loading dock as bleary-eyed newspaper boys arrived one by one on their bikes. Each one cut the ties that bound their route's papers together and stuffed them into shoulder bags. The article headline reading; "Two-Thousand IWW's Plan to Invade Everett Today – Give Battle to Those Opposing Them."

A city trolley car was parked on the side track, its motorman examining the controls and levers, going over his checklist before rolling out for the first run of the day. Once done with his safety check, he walked over to one of the paperboys.

"Morning, son," the motorman said.

"Mornin'," the boy replied, not looking up from stuffing his shoulder bag.

"You got an extra paper to sell me?"

"Cost ya two cents," the paperboy yawned.

The man dug in his coin purse and pulled out two pennies.

"Here ya go," the man said, dropping the copper coins in the lads open palm. The motorman picked up a paper, read the headline, and looked off in the distance to the west, then he bit his lip as he shook his head. The man turned around and walked back to the trolley where he sat down and began to unfold the paper when the sound of horse's hooves and the snap of a whip filled the air. He jerked his head around and saw a galloping horse pulling a man in a buggy barreling up and over the Pacific Avenue hill. The rider snapped his whip over the snorting, straining grey gelding and whistled at the animal as it pulled its load. They thundered past the station, skidded around the corner and headed out of town, south on Colby. The motorman watched the buggy go out of sight and wondered where in the world the man could be off to. Once the morning was quiet again he ruffled his paper and stared at the front page.

***

Two hours later James Thompson slowly made his way to the front of the Seattle IWW hall with a noticeable limp. Angry union men hollered as the organizer mounted the stage. Thompson wore a threadbare suit coat torn on the sleeve, a white collared shirt buttoned at the top, dirty, dark trousers, and he had thin red scares on the side of his head and back of his neck. When the hall was finally still, he mouthed a few words, raised his head, and stepped to the podium. He looked out to the standing-room-only crowd with steely blue eyes, his square jaw was tightly set, and the lines in his face were many and deep. Feeney Bradford watched and listened from the rear of the room.

"Fellow union brothers," Thompson began, "our purpose here is tenfold! Because this is a day of days!" His deep voice of conviction rang loud and clear over a multitude of men. "Today we shall travel to Everett in the broad daylight. We will no longer allow the lumber trust to use the cover of darkness like they did at Beverly Park. We will travel there because we have been invited to Everett to speak freely to the citizens about the truth of the brutalities committed against us. Handbills have been printed and distributed to thousands of people about our coming there this afternoon. Soon the citizens of that town will know that an injury to one is an injury to all!" The crowd cheered, raised their fists in the air, and stomped their feet, causing the building to rumble like a freight train. Thompson nodded his head up and down while he waited for calm.

"The plan is for every man who was beaten at Beverly Park that can still walk to go to Everett and show the ruling industrialists of that town and its unknowing citizens your injuries and let them hear your story first hand. Because these self-titled patriots, these hypocritical self-serving barons, these thieving mill owners of the lumber trust in Everett, must be stopped before the common family man can no longer work at a decent wage to feed his wife and children!" Thompson shook his fist and added, "We must answer the terrorism of Everett!" The hall boomed with approving cheers while the speaker waited for calm.

"These false leaders must be exposed for what they are. The people of Everett and the world for that matter need to hear about the tactics and ways of the lumber trust and their henchmen in that mill town. They have made their bed of violence and brutality, and we must make them sleep in it. We must expose these red-handed robbers for the brutal and greedy parasites that they are. And. Most importantly! We are not going to stand still while they redefine the American Constitution to fit their self-imposed monarchy of design! The industrial tyranny of the sawdust empire in Everett must end!"

Thompson stood tall at the podium. The lines on his face seemed chiseled as he stood before his peers. The cheers and adulation washed over him like a flood that swept him and everyone in the room away in a flowing tide of great purpose and unity. After minutes of resounding praise and solidarity Thompson raised his hands for silence.

"Since we do not have the funds to purchase gasoline for all the trucks and cars we would need today, we will travel by ferryboat instead. And, every fellow worker going must leave their union card here so we have a head count," Thompson said and then began to motion with his arm. "Sail with me to Everett in the broad daylight, men. Come with me, and I shall stand bedside you and with you. Let us show the people of Everett that the heart of the Industrial Workers of the World never beats a retreat!" Thompson screamed and then raised a clenched fist as the detective in the back of the hall walked out. A deafening roar rose up from the mass of workingmen. Thompson was immediately surrounded by a swarm of Wobblies who rushed the podium and picked him up on their shoulders. They carried him out of the hall and towards the waterfront as the cheering throng followed.

Feeney Bradford hung up after a quick call to MacCullock to confirm the Wobblies arrival by boat and then stepped from the phone booth, he stood scanning the crowd as it marched by carrying Thompson. Hoots and hollers filled the thoroughfare as the mob made its way down Second Avenue. At the corner of Marion a Wobbly stopped, turned around, and yelled, "Hurry up, Spitz! Yer gonna miss the boat!"

"I'm comin', I'm comin'," Spitz yelled back as he ran to catch up with his gang.

Once the bulk of the crowd had passed him, Bradford noticed a tall Wobbly bringing up the rear. The fellow had a confused look on his soot-marked face. His unassuming eyes moved from person to person in between upward glances at tall buildings and then to electric trolleys clanging by. Bradford followed him.

"Hey, fella," Bradford said, catching up. "First time in Seattle?"

"Yep," he answered. "Came in on the rails last night."

"Did ya now? Where from?"

"Well, I was workin' the Palouse harvest, but got stiffed on the last payday. Hitched north and jumped the train in Spokane. Damn thing didn't slow down once, well, till it got here," the Wobbly said, rubbing his face. "Forgot about that tunnel."

"How's that?"

"You know, that railroad tunnel up in the mountains. I didn't have anything to cover my mouth 'er my face. Smoke was bad."

"Oh yeah, right, the tunnel," Feeney said, playing along. "You headed up to Everett?"

"You bet. They gave me a ticket fer free. Just left 'em my card."

"So you know about the strike up there?"

"Hell yeah. Heard all about it, that's why I'm here. The whole territory knows about Everett. An' I heard some of my fellow workers got beat up pretty good there last week. Thought I'd take a run on out an' join the fight."

"Yeah, I hear ya," Bradford said. "Those authorities are a rough bunch. A guy probably needs to protect himself up there."

"I'm ready," the Wobbly said.

"Well, a man needs more than just his fists in that town," Bradford remarked knowingly. He held up a hand to stop and reached into his pocket. He flashed the Smith & Wesson halfway wrapped in a handkerchief for the fellow to see. Once the Wobbly caught a glimpse of the handgun, Bradford returned it, saying, "It's yours if you want." The Wobbly started walking again. Bradford stayed right with him.

"You sayin' I can have that gun?"

"Yep."

"It loaded?"

"Yep."

"Why you tryin' ta' give me a gun?"

"Because I want to help. Too many men have had the snot beat out of them up there, and I believe in your cause. Besides, they all have guns." The Wobbly kept walking and didn't say anything for a half a block. Then he stopped at an alleyway. His stomach rumbled with hunger, and he knew the pistol could be a grubstake.

"So I can have that gun?"

"That's what I've been tellin' ya."

"OK, I'll take it," the fellow said.

Bradford motioned with his head sideways and walked down the alley, the Wobbly followed. The detective stopped up against a brick wall, turned towards it, pulled out the pistol, and held it out on top of the white cloth for him. The Wobbly snatched it and opened the cylinder. He checked that the chambers were loaded and then shoved the weapon in his britches.

"Thanks mister," the Wobbly quickly said and started to turn around.

The detective grabbed him by the arm and asked, "By the way, what's your name?" The Wobbly glanced out to the street and then back to Bradford.

"I go by Dutch," he said and hustled away.

***

At Coleman Dock, Captain Chauncey Wiman stood in the gangway on the lower level of the *Verona*, taking tickets and counting the passengers boarding his steamer. He stopped a young man with a rifle strapped over his shoulder.

"That's a fancy-lookin' gun you've got there, son, but it's not comin' aboard my ship," the captain said. "You'll have to check it at the ticket office and get it when you come back."

"What if I take the bullets out?" the young man asked.

"Nope, that's the deal. No firearms allowed. Next," Captain Wiman said, motioning to the adjacent ticket holder and then he yelled to the rest of the people in line, "All you passengers listen up, there's no weapons allowed on my boat, ya got that! If I find any kind of firearm on anyone during this voyage it's gonna be tossed overboard." A few men glanced around nervously.

The Wobbly with the rifle turned out of line and ran back to the ticket office. Bounding up to the counter, he held the rifle out and said, "The captain says I have to check this with you for the day. Is that all right?"

"We'll put it in the holding room for you. What's the name?" the lady behind the desk asked as she grabbed the gun.

"Harry. Harry Dolson, ma'am. I'm in a hurry. But I'll be back on the last run tonight, thank you," the young man replied cordially.

"OK, I'll put your name on it!" the lady hollered at his back as he sprinted to the ferry. Along the way he got ahead of the walking crowd of men and jumped aboard just before they closed the ramp gate.

Stopping the 251st man, Captain Wiman announced, "That's it, that's the limit. The rest of you'll have to wait for the *Calista* over on Pier Three. It's headed north soon."

The captain stepped aboard his vessel, and the deckhand pulled the ramp back into the gangway. Wiman headed into the lower freight area to make one final check of the cargo and some of his passengers.

He heard them singing a union tune and shook his head. Wiman pulled his watch from a vest pocket to check the time. He mumbled to himself, "Guess we'll see how we do bucking this tide."

Men sat on and in between trunks, bins, and shipping crates on the lower level, most of them singing, smiling, laughing, and carrying on. Dutch saw a man get up from a crate and move away, he hurried over and sat down. There was a group of a dozen Wobblies behind him huddled around each other sitting on two rows of feed sacks on pallets next to a portside window with a crate between them. They seemed to be keeping to themselves, apart from the rest of the exuberant Wobblies.

"Shhh, the captain," Spitz warned, putting a finger up to his swollen lip, now yellow with infection.

Captain Wiman walked by them and Dutch, he glanced their way but paid them no mind. Wiman pulled on the hemp lashing that fastened a wooden shipping box to the side rail cleats to make sure it was secure and nodded to himself. He finished his pre-voyage check and then went up the stairs. Wiman stopped for a moment to look out over his loud and crowded passenger area from the staircase. One Wobbly was playing the old upright piano in the back corner of the salon as others crowded around him singing. The Captain shook his head again then continued up to his pilothouse on the hurricane deck. Wobblies were standing everywhere on the top deck and in between the lifeboats singing and milling around. Once in the wheelhouse he hollered into the brass command tube down to his engineer.

"Make ready, Earnest," Wiman said, he stepped out to the narrow port-side deck, grabbed hold of the railing and yelled down to his crew, "Cast off the bow and stern lines!" He returned to the wheelhouse to instruct the engineer, "OK, give me one-quarter reverse."

From stern to bow the Wobblies covered every inch of deck on every level as the *Verona* set sail and steamed north across the placid, gleaming waters of Elliot Bay and Admiralty Inlet. Spitz and his friends talked amongst themselves at their glassless window opening on the port side. Another Wobbly pushed his way past the standing passengers and sat down on a feed sack next to Spitz.

"Skeeter's all set upstairs, he's under the covered deck right above our heads," the man quietly said to the group.

"That's good," Spitz grunted, "but if that damn buddy of yer's hadn't a' crapped out we'd have this level covered, too. I figured he wouldn't come through."

"Don't worry, Skeeter's a good shot," the man said as he glanced at Spitz's bent and discolored nose. "He'll take care of business."

"But I wanted ta' shoot the balls off a' that son of a bitch. Dammit," Spitz whispered angrily, "Now who knows what's gonna happen?"

"Listen, this ain't my fault, so don't be pinnin' some bugger rap on me," the same Wobbly said, glaring at Spitz.

Dutch had heard every word and couldn't sit still any longer. He turned around and stuck his head into their group.

"If you fellas need what I think you need," he whispered, "then I just might be able to help you out."

Spitz's eyes lit up and he grinned.

"What're ya sayin' there, bub?"

"Mind if I join yer little gang there?" Dutch asked with a smirk. Spitz instantly jerked his head back with an accepting nod. Dutch got up from his crate and traded places with one of them. He sat down across from Spitz and looked at every face closely before he murmured a word.

"Criminy, what happened to yer lip, and yer nose?" Dutch began in a whisper.

"Shut up, and tell us what ya got," Spitz said.

"OK, so, I've got what you need, but yer gonna have to give up a little do-re-mi. It's a .38 piece, loaded."

"What're we talkin' about, money wise?" Spitz said, his eyes sparking with interest.

Dutch looked over his shoulder to make sure no one was listening, and then said, "Not much, just enough so's I can get by fer a few days. How 'bout you take up a quick collection? Get me ten bucks?"

"Ten bucks! How are we gonna get ten bucks?" Spitz said.

"Well . . . I'm thinkin' this boat ride is gonna take a while, *and* I'm thinkin' you got a few friends on board. See what you can come up with. I'll be waitin' right here," Dutch said. He crossed his arms, not moving.

Spitz stared at the man who'd just claimed to have what he direly needed to fulfill his secret plan of revenge on Sheriff McRae.

"Okay, let's see it," Spitz said. Dutch thought about his request.

"I ain't pullin' this pistol out, not here," Dutch quietly replied, "but how 'bout this?" He grabbed the wrist of the guy next to him and placed the back of the other Wobblys hand on the revolver in his pants pocket and pressed. "Ya feel that?" The guy looked over to Spitz, nodded his head yes, and pulled his hand away.

"All right then. We got a deal," Spitz said as he grinned. He looked around his circle of cohorts and quietly said, "How much we got between us?" Hands instantly dug into trousers, and they slapped coins down on the crate between them. Spitz added two crumpled-up dollar bills to the grouping of dimes and nickels and counted it.

"OK, it looks like we got four-twenty," Spitz whispered. "Is that enough?"

Dutch stared at the gang's leader and kept his arms crossed.

"Nope. I said ten bucks. That's the deal," Dutch replied with a straight face.

"Dammit, fella!" Spitz yelled, slamming his fist down on the crate. The men close enough to hear the sound of a fist hitting wood over the din of Wobblies carrying on stopped talking and turned around to see where the commotion came from. Spitz and his boys sat tight.

Once the rest of the passengers resumed conversation, Spitz looked at one of his guys and quietly said, "Freddie, take a walk upstairs an' find Skeeter, he'll help raise some more money for this fella. But take it slow and keep it quiet."

Out on deck hats waved in the calm salt air, and the Wobblies singing floated out across the water like a church choir.

> "Everybody's joining it, joining what? Joining it!
> Everybody's joining it, joining what? Joining it!
> One Big Union, that's the workers' choice
> One Big Union, that's the only choice
> One Big Union, that's the only noise
> One Big Union, shout with all your voice."

The *Verona* was making good time as it churned though the waters of Puget Sound. Harry Dolson stood on the hurricane deck and felt compelled to climb the flagpole on top of the pilothouse. Looking up, it appeared easier to climb than a spar tree that needed to be rigged. He walked over to a close by Wobbly friend for some assistance.

"Hey Hugo, can you help pull me up that pole?" Harry said, nodding and pointing at the flagpole.

"What? No way! I'm climbin' it!" Hugo Gerlot quickly said.

"Nah, what? Wait a second. I wanna," Harry said to his new found union friend.

"But I've been eyeing that pole, too," Hugo said. "I wanna climb it. No . . . I'm gonna climb it!" Hugo said with bright determination. They looked each other in the eye and grinned at the same time.

"You sure?" Harry asked.

"Yep! Sure am," Hugo said. "Come on, lemme."

"Well, OK. If you say so," Harry reluctantly agreed. They clambered up the steel ladder behind the pilothouse while a few other Wobblies watched. Since it wasn't flying a flag Hugo looped the hoist-side rope around his body, then between his legs, and tied himself off.

"I'll help ya," another Wobbly friend named Felix yelled as he came climbing up the ladder. He grabbed hold of the line and pulled with Harry. Hugo was at the top of the pole in seconds. He wrapped his legs around it, to hold himself in place, and then tied himself off to the top of the pole with a series of sloppy half hitches.

"What's it look like up there?" Felix yelled with his hand on his forehead shielding his eyes from the sun.

Spinning around suspended Hugo beamed with delight from his perch fifteen feet above the wheelhouse.

"It's like being on the top of the world! I can see everything!!" Hugo yelled. He pointed his nose into the wind and thought. *This is good. We're gonna go up there and tell these folks what really happened last week and make a fight for free speech and worker's rights. They'll see, they got no choice but to see that we're right.*

***

Shift whistles blew long and loud at the Northern Imperial and all the other mills along the waterfront at 10:00 a.m. Sunday, November 5. Every citizen deputy and new volunteer came in ones and twos, carloads and truckloads to the Commercial Club, where they began to organize. Soon a long line of 40 to 50 men flowed from the door of the back-room armory, through the hall and club, out the door, and onto the sidewalk. Once a volunteer was handed a weapon he was directed out the back door to the alley and down to the wharf.

"Sheriff McRae is already at the pier," MacCullock said, standing next to the line of volunteers, overseeing the process. "Head for the last warehouse. You'll see him and the rest of the other deputies, he'll tell you what to do." Then he spoke loudly over the line of citizen deputies, "And men, keep your weapons at your side. We are only going to show these vagrants our firepower, we are not going to use it. Once they see our might, they will immediately feel a dire need to stay on that ship!"

At the same time Mayor Merrill was tying white armbands on the men for identification. "That's right. Just do what the sheriff says when you're down there and everything will be fine. All we're going to do is not let them land and make them head on back to Seattle," the mayor added. Virgil Postlewait and last minute new volunteer C.O. Curtis were farther back, near the entrance.

"Lots of people," Virgil commented, glancing out to the street.

"Looks like the whole town's headed to the wharf," C.O. replied.

"I'll be glad when this day's over," Virgil said.

"Yep, let's hope MacCullock's right about the Wobblies staying on that boat," Curtis added.

"Yeah, well, I'm gonna try to stay near the warehouse when we're on the dock," Virgil said.

Curtis nodded his head and agreed, "That sounds good. I think I'll try and get a pistol or a Colt. Just in case."

A well-dressed man in a black bowler hat was next in line. MacCullock walked into the room and recognized Robert Claymore immediately, it startled him at first glance, but then he grinned.

"Good to see you today," MacCullock offered, nodding at his detective.

"Yes, sir. Looks like we've got a fine day to deal with this bunch," Claymore said with a quick nod as the mayor finished tying on his armband. He tipped his bowler hat and walked out with a Springfield in his hand.

Citizens, strikers, and laid-off men began to fill lower Bayside Hewitt. Even more civilians crowded the concourse at the Great Northern Depot, where they had a perfect view of the harbor and the city pier. They watched as shotgun and rifle bearing volunteers arrived aboard flatbed trucks and in automobiles who then headed down to the wharf.

When the last volunteer was fitted with a weapon, Luther MacCullock strode out to the front room of the club. People were walking everywhere on the sidewalk and in the street with more residents going by every second. Two volunteers were near the front door, Luther walked over to them.

"You men stand guard outside, and stay there until everything is done," MacCullock ordered. "And keep everyone back from the windows," he said, reaching into his front pocket.

"Yes, sir," one of them replied, walking outside.

MacCullock pulled out his keys and locked the door behind them. He strode down the hallway and locked the door of the empty armory room and then did the same for the door leading to the delivery area as he stepped out. George was waiting in the Pierce-Arrow with the motor running. MacCullock gave him a quick wave, signaling not to bother climbing out to get the back door for him. Luther hopped in and said, "Take me by the head office, I need to make sure my guards are there."

George turned the sedan around and headed to California Street. Once there Luther saw two of his mill guards stationed at his business location, then he watched as people scurried about, all of them headed for the waterfront to greet the arrival of the Wobblies. Kids pedaled bikes and yelled back and forth to each other as they rode by, parents walked with their children, holding hands. George drove the opposite way past them and back to Colby, where he turned and drove through downtown. Once at Pacific he turned towards Rucker Hill and stayed on course until he pulled up to the house on Laurel Drive.

Just as Luther approached the front door, Martha opened it with an expressionless face, she said, "Everything's ready for you up in the sitting room, Mr. MacCullock."

"Good," MacCullock replied, climbing the staircase, not turning around.

***

When the *Verona* sailed into Port Gardner Bay the Wobblies could see the city pier and the crowd of people at the bottom of Hewitt, with more surrounding the Great Northern Depot, the waterfront was covered with people. All of the IWW started to sing, from his flagpole perch Hugo Gerlot waved his hat as he sang along.

> "We meet today in freedom's cause
> And raise our voices high
> We'll join our hands in union strong
> To battle or to die
> Hold the fort for we are coming
> Union men be strong
> Side by side we battle onward
> Victory will come."

"Here he comes," Spitz said, seeing Freddie working his way down the over-crowded stairs. He slowly wedged and pushed his way through the passengers to where the rest of the group had been waiting. Spitz looked at one of his men and gave a little nod to get up and make room.

"Well?" Spitz said. "What took ya so long?"

"You said to take it slow," Freddie replied.

"Get enough?" Spitz asked, his eyes gleaming.

"Yep, more than enough. Five bucks in change," Freddie said, dumping the coins into Spitz's open hand.

"Skeeter says he'd hold off, let you take first shot," Freddie whispered. "Said you had rights." Spitz smiled and winced from the pain in his lip, then showed the money to Dutch.

"Good," Dutch said, pulling the .38 from his trousers. Spitz dumped the money into Dutch's hand, Dutch handed the pistol back and shoved the money in his pants pocket. Still sitting, Spitz kept the gun under his bent knees, opened the cylinder, checked the chambers for bullets, and tried to keep one eye on Dutch until he was satisfied.

"Thanks, bub," Spitz said. Dutch didn't even look at him. He quickly got up from the gang and tried to work his way through the jam-packed boat. More men were coming down the stairs, any kind of movement was nearly impossible, and he wanted to get as far away from Spitz as he could. Dutch pushed and shoved his way slowly towards the stairs.

Thousands of cheering citizens filled Hewitt, from the railroad tracks and the surrounding area up Rucker Hill. People were everywhere showing support for the Wobblies and the free speech movement. Hats and hands were waving in the air, providing a robust welcome for the boatload of singing union men. Behind the crowd, parked in the middle of Hewitt near Norton, was a black-and-green paneled Baker Electric car, its lady driver seated behind the wheel with a straight back. She wore a wide-brimmed feathered hat on top of bobbed hair with a dark tunic suit coat and a pleated calf-length matching skirt. She was dressed in her Sunday best.

Father Nathan Bywater stood behind his ad-hoc pulpit at the base of Hewitt across the railroad tracks from the city pier and tried to speak to the burgeoning crowd.

"The author of all things great and wonderful is watching us right now. Children of Everett, please come under the wing of your Lord and Savior Jesus Christ today. We must not allow ourselves to become victims of evil. Instead we must greet our visitors with open arms. We cannot let the altar of God crumble before our very eyes," the priest said as he watched hundreds of shotgun- and rifle-carrying volunteer deputies roam the immediate area while a few unconcerned hoboes stood next to a burn barrel by the railroad tracks and warmed their hands, not giving a lick about what was going on around them, passing a bottle.

Dozens of citizens ran across the tracks to the pier to greet the *Verona* but were blocked by Commercial Club deputies. At first the deputies formed a human wall across the land's end of the pier, and then they strung a rope across it.

"You can't block us," Helen Pomeroy yelled at the citizen deputies. "This is a public pier!"

"Get back, lady. You ain't going out there!" one deputy yelled.

"I know my rights!" Pomeroy declared.

"Back off, you old goat!" the same deputy shouted, brandishing his rifle. He held it with two hands and swung it across the front of his body, the barrel pointed upward.

"Why you un-prepossessing imbecile," Helen Pomeroy sputtered and swung her purse at the man, hitting him squarely on the side of his shoulder. "You're nothing but a drunken fool!" she said and trundled back across the tracks. The other concerned citizens followed her.

Dutch pushed through the last of the Wobblies on the cargo level and then started to force his way up the crowded stairs. From the starboard side passenger level he saw the massive crowd at the bottom of Hewitt, at the train station, and on lower Rucker Hill. The whole area was covered with people.

What a welcome, Dutch thought and smiled, but there was no one on the pier. He glanced back to the waving, jubilant crowd. *Why aren't they out on the dock? What's going on?*

In the comfort of his second floor sitting room, Luther MacCullock hovered over the wheeled serving table for a moment before he pulled the crystal stopper out of a half-full decanter of scotch and poured himself a drink in his favorite double old fashioned. He walked over to the window, took a sip, and set his glass down next to the sandwich Martha had prepared. Luther stood at the window. The little speck on the water had grown into the white, three-level propeller steamer *Verona*. From his viewpoint it looked to be loaded with passengers. As it slowly floated into the inner harbor, Luther picked up his binoculars, and like the captain he was, he scanned the area below. First the waterfront and the pier, then lower Hewitt, the train depot, and finally, out to the *Verona*. The boat was covered from bow to stern with his enemy.

"Look at them," the old Indian killer grumbled to himself. "Nothing but a bunch of rats on a steamship."

Inside the pier warehouse, stacks of cribbed lumber were lined up ready for shipping. Bins of apples and pears filled one corner, pallets of sacked potatoes were up against the landing dock wall, and empty wooden liquor boxes were scattered across the floor. Citizen deputies lingered in groups holding rifles while others moved sacks of potatoes around the warehouse wall, making room to stand behind but still watch through knotholes and cracks in the siding.

Buck Mullaney stood in the back with three of his guards surrounding Charlie Purvis. They had Charlie's hands tied in front of him. Buck nodded to one of his men and said, "Go ahead, untie him." Buck handed Charlie a Winchester 73.

"Here's yer rifle," Mullaney said. Charlie eyed the lumber guard and grabbed the gun with his left hand. He looked the gun over. Purvis poked his finger in the side loading magazine and tried to look inside, but he couldn't feel or see any cartridges. Then he cocked the lever, a bullet slid out on the chamber carriage. Charlie grinned.

"Just because we're givin' yer ass a loaded gun don't be gettin' any ideas," Mullaney said glaring at Purvis. "'Cause if you do, me and my men will be more than pleased to shoot ya down right on the spot, but, as long as you do what I tell ya to do Mr. MacCullock has instructed me to let you go after we're done."

"Yeah? Well — good," Charlie slowly said, "I'll do what ya say, just as long as yer sure I'm a free man after this."

"Long as everything goes to plan, I'll be lettin' ya go after all this blows over," Buck answered, holding out an open bottle of whiskey. "Go on, have a snort. You might need some extra courage," Mullaney said, and then he spit a greasy blob of tobacco on the warehouse floor.

Charlie looked around at the men in the warehouse. He saw a few of them tipping bottles and turned back to Mullaney.

"What? For this? I don't need any extra courage for a boatload of punk-assed Wobblies. I got all the courage I need for them sumbitches," Charlie boasted, reaching for the bottle. He took a long drink, wiped his mouth, and added, "so, where's that boss a' yer's?"

"Mr. MacCullock? He's up at the club getting the rest of the volunteers all gunned up. He'll be here."

Charlie nodded and took another drink. He licked his lips and handed the bottle back. Buck lifted it to his lips, and then wiped his mouth. He held the jug out, saying, "In a few minutes you'll be a free man."

"I like the sound of that," Charlie said, taking another gulp of rye.

"Sheriff!" a citizen deputy shouted from a side door. "The boat's here!"

McRae snapped his head around, he raised his hand to signal the lookout that he'd heard him, and started barking last minute orders.

"All right, men," the sheriff shouted out over the warehouse. "Today, we are gonna turn back these intruders and not let them land! Now remember, I want everyone to keep yer guns at yer side. You hear me? Make sure that they can see yer weapons, but do not raise them. All we want to do is make a show of force. Everybody clear? Are ya understandin' me?!" McRae hollered as he looked around at all the men with his hands on his hips. The sheriff waited for a moment and then continued, "OK. Deputy Hanigan is gonna lead you out there and form some lines. Deputy Beard and I will come out and stand in front of ya'll. But a bunch of ya stay here in the warehouse and keep watch. All right, here ya go." McRae stepped over to Jefferson Beard to go over a few last second details when a new volunteer stuck an open bottle of whiskey in front of him, saying, "How 'bout a last minute snort, Sheriff?"

McRae glanced at the man and quickly shook his head no, then returned his attention to Deputy Beard, they quietly spoke.

Charlie handed the bottle back to Mullaney. Buck pretended to take another drink, wiped his mouth, and calmly said, "We're gonna walk out with the sheriff." He handed the bottle back to Charlie and then stroked his thick brown mustache mutton chops while he watched Charlie drink, his shotgun held in crossed arms.

As the *Verona* got closer, a backside wind pushed the vessel up to the west end of the fixed height pier where the deep water was. Black mussels, seaweed, and barnacles covered the exposed pier pilings, the tide was out. Seagulls circled overhead and walked about on the mudflat beach that had arisen from the outbound current.

Spitz jumped up and scanned the vessel, he was trapped. It was completely filled with Wobblies wedged shoulder to shoulder thinking that they'd disembark from the lower freight level.

"Crap!" Spitz yelled. "Tide's out. I'm gonna be too low in the water to get a clear shot. Dammit!" He looked up to the dock. It was four feet above his head. "Freddie! What're we gonna do?"

Spitz and Freddie glimpsed a huge group of armed men marching out from the warehouse right in front of them and forming lines as the boat floated up against the pier. Then Spitz couldn't see them anymore, only the mussel-covered pilings that the hull was now scraping against, but he could hear their footsteps. He looked up at the underside of the wharf and saw a few gaps in the planking directly above him.

McRae and Beard materialized from the warehouse and walked to the front of the lined-up citizen deputies with Buck Mullaney, Charlie and the three other mill guards right next to them. It sounded like they were right above Spitz and Freddie. The lawmen stood side by side and waited for the dockhand to fasten the bow line.

Freddie whispered to Spitz, "Skeeter's right in front of them."

"Shut up, I'm listenin'," Spitz said, keeping his eyes focused upward.

Charlie Purvis squinted at the faces on the *Verona*. He thought. *Why am I out here in front? I wouldn't be here at all if that God-damn McRae hadn't a' found me.*

Purvis started scanning the steamer and then saw somebody behind the pilothouse at the rail. Charlie narrowed his eyes, tried to focus in the afternoon sun, and then slightly nodded his head. He was sure who it was, a quickening of hate and revenge surged through his body. Charlie glared at him. *Dolson! So yer a God-damned Wobbly! I knew it . . . And where's my Krag? I bet the bastard sold it! Stinkin' punk-assed kid! You're a dead man.*

A wave of dread moved through Harry's system when he saw a very familiar face with a rifle. *Is that Purvis out there in front? Never thought I'd see him again, and what's he doin' with a rifle in his hands? He's gonna shoot me if he gets a chance. But there won't be any shootin'. We're here about free-speech.*

The sheriff held up his left hand to bring attention to himself, the Wobblies stopped singing, and playing the piano in the passenger area. McRae saw James Thompson staring at him from one of the passenger windows. The sheriff's blood began to race, and then boil as his face reddened.

"I'm the sheriff of this county, and my duty is to uphold the law! Who's your leader?" the sheriff cried out. He noticed Thompson get up and move from the window and towards the gangway. The sheriff's eyes darted around, his Stetson was cocked sideways and the holstered revolver hanging from his waist was to the front of him in clear sight. A hush fell over the wharf, only the sound of stirring, murmuring Wobblies talking amongst themselves could be heard.

Spitz recognized the sheriff's voice. *There's that bastard again.*

"Boys? Who's yer leader?" McRae cried out again.

"We're all leaders!" yelled one Wobbly from the boat.

The sheriff's jaw tightened, and the tendons in his neck became visible. He pulled the Colt from its holster with his right hand and held it high in the air for the Wobblies to see.

Robert Claymore sized up the situation from his knothole post inside the warehouse and listened while slowly taking off his bowler hat, carefully placing it on a nearby crate. James Thompson pushed his way closer to the gangway.

"You can't land here!" the sheriff called out just as the deckhand began to swing out the gangplank. Hugo Gerlot was feverishly untying himself. Glancing back and forth between the wharf and the knots holding him in place Hugo frantically pulled at the snarled and tangled flag line and was just about free. Everyone on the dock, and on land, couldn't help but see the Wobbly at the top of the flag pole.

"That guy," Harry said, pointing at Charlie. "Felix. That guy in the front." Felix quickly scanned the line of men at the edge of the dock. "That guy," Harry repeated still pointing, "He hates me."

With nervous eyes the sheriff scanned the boat for James Thompson and saw him by the gangplank. McRae kept his Colt high in the air and tried to keep one eye on Thompson. When Dutch saw the sheriff raise his revolver from his vantage point he quickly found a corner under the pilothouse stairs and wedged himself between two large upright timbers that supported the ferry's upper structure. Harry and Felix saw the sheriff's action, they moved closer to the pilothouse.

"Hugo. Hurry up. Get down from there," Felix said up to his friend.

"I'm trying to," Hugo replied between glances at the dock, jolts of nervous tension streamed through his body.

"What's taking ya? Come on," Felix answered.

"I said you can't land here!" the sheriff hollered again, still holding the revolver high in the air, he turned his wrist back and forth slowly so the Wobblies from bow to stern could see the Colt. Then the gangplank hit the dock.

From the upper level gangway a deep throated defiant voice hollered back like a cold dark wind, "The hell we can't!" Just as the sheriff began to turn, one muffled gunshot sounded. All heads turned to the stern of the *Verona*. Another shot was fired, a few deputies looked to the bow. Harry saw Charlie raising his rifle. Three more rapid shots went off but no one could tell where they were coming from.

Thundering gunfire erupted from both sides. Wobblies with hidden pistols pulled them out and began firing. Every deputy on the dock did the same. Rifle barrels emerged from knotholes in warehouse walls, and the lines of deputies fired their shotguns and rifles over the shoulders of the men in front of them, a multitude of empty shell casings began to rain down on the dock.

Charlie Purvis tried to focus and aim, he said to himself, "I got you now you punk-assed sumbitch," and pulled the trigger. Harry saw Charlie's barrel aimed right at him, he ducked, and hit the deck as a bullet whizzed right by his head. Harry glanced up and saw Charlie still aiming at him, he covered up. Purvis pulled the trigger again, it clicked. Harry took another quick look.

Purvis dropped down on his knees and cocked the lever, the carriage slid back empty. *Those bastards only gave me one bullet!* He dropped the rifle and began to crawl on his hands and knees under the gunfire towards the cover of the warehouse. Last minute volunteer C.O. Curtis, 35 and a husband with one daughter, hit the dock, a bullet had pierced his heart and instantly killed him. Charlie pulled the revolver from Curtis' holster and continued to the side of the warehouse, he hid behind a stack of fruit bins.

Wobblies took cover and dropped on the fore and aft decks of the *Verona*, blood spilled out over the deck. They quickly crawled to the opposite side of the boat, away from the gangplank and pier, slipping and sliding in vermilion gore. The steamer listed from the weight of them and rocked against the dock. Three men slid on the deck and collapsed a railing on the starboard side and fell into the water as the passenger area piano pivoted, and then rolled over to the starboard side. Bullets slammed into the keys and strings, each jangled note twanged through the air in an out-of-rhythm, nonsensical dirge.

Felix gripped the base of a railing and saw a man with a rifle pointed at the flagpole. He snapped his head around just in time to witness Hugo throw out both arms and fall, the weight of his body broke the flag line. The *Verona* and the warehouse shook from a barrage of lead as every armed man on both sides pulled their triggers as fast as they could.

From his elevated position Luther MacCullock winced behind binoculars and then clamped his teeth tighter on the stem of his pipe.

"Hugo!!" Felix shrieked. Hugo Gerlot was dead before he hit the deck at the top of the stairs in front of the pilothouse. The shooter on the dock quickly spun on his boot heel and ran behind a pile of pallets as a gun barrel slid out of a warehouse knothole above him.

Felix Baran caught a glimpse of the shooter take cover. Baran hid behind the pilothouse, his chest pounding. Harry crawled over next to him and stayed down. Felix turned around and stared in shock at the sight of Hugo's lifeless body sprawled out on the deck bleeding. Hate and revenge moved up into his throat. He pulled a single-action Mauser Zig Zag out of his coat pocket. Felix poked his head around the side of the pilothouse and scanned the dock for the man that had just murdered his friend, he spied him behind the pallets. Harry glanced at the Mauser.

"That guy," Harry sputtered, "just took two shots at me."

"Yeah, well," Felix said, gripping the Mauser, "I'm gonna shoot the bastard that just got Hugo."

"Listen, I'm tellin' ya. I'm gonna need yer gun," Harry yelled and hid his head as bullets slammed into the side of vessel.

A collective gasp came up from the crowd on Hewitt when they saw the man on the flagpole slump over and fall. Cries of horror filled the street. The sound of weapon fire cracked and echoed over the town as gun smoke began to envelop the pier.

Hugo's killer peeked around the pallets. The *Verona* was still listing. He ran out to the edge of the dock and saw a Wobbly hanging out of a lower window holding a pistol. He quickly took aim and fired. The bullet hit the left side of Spitz, his body slumped forward, over the side of the vessel, and into the bay.

The ship lurched, but the bow line held fast, stopping the ferry from capsizing and sinking. The steamer held its tilted position. A bullet-ridden Wobbly rolled off the deck and sunk, other Wobblies jumped ship and began to swim for cover under the wharf.

Below deck, a five-foot-long engine wrench dislodged and pivoted from the listing ship, hitting the firebox door latch and causing it to swing open.

Flames spewed out, and hot coals spilled onto the wooden floor. With the sound of gunfire and bullets hitting the hull, the engineer crawled over, closed the firebox, lifted a floor hatch, and shoved the smoldering coals into the watery bilge.

Bullets smashed into the *Verona* from every direction. The men on the starboard side crawled back into the passenger room for cover. The vessel rocked and then leveled. Right when it did Irish immigrant John Looney was toppled by rifle shot, as he fell another bullet shattered the boats timber frame. A shard of the woodwork impaled his eye, gouging it from his skull, killing him.

Dozens of panic-stricken volunteer deputies fired towards the *Verona* from behind shipping crates, others were shooting pistols around warehouse corners and blindly emptying rifles, firing wildly in any direction, some hitting their own deputies in the back and hips. One volunteer citizen deputy dropped his weapon and ran down the dock past Sheriff McRae screaming, "They've gone mad out there! They're shooting at anything! They shot me in the ear!"

"Get back here ya coward!" the sheriff yelled at the man through a hail of gunfire and quickly turned back to the ship. He saw a man standing next to James Thompson pull a pistol from his coat and aim, but when a bullet hit the man in the leg, the pistol dropped. McRae aimed his revolver at the Wobbly speaker, but Thompson dove and hit the deck. He scrambled on the blood-covered floor, grabbed hold of the dropped pistol, and stayed out of sight.

When Claymore saw the sheriff leveling his Colt at Thompson he knew it was time. With bullets slamming into the side of the warehouse, the calm detective aimed his Springfield, fired, and hit Sheriff McRae in the heel, taking him down and out of the firefight. Charlie Purvis got a glimpse of the sheriff falling, but he sat tight in his hiding place, gripping the pistol. He scanned the top deck for Harry and tried to keep an eye on the sheriff.

"I'm hit! I'm hit! Oh, I'm hit!" the sheriff cried as he fell to the dock planking, firing his revolver wildly at the steamer until he was out of ammunition. McRae unwittingly let go of his empty Colt and began to crawl to the warehouse. Purvis couldn't see Harry but instead saw his chance for the sheriff. He leaped to his feet, raised the revolver, and stuck his tongue in the corner of his mouth. *Time to meet yer maker you sumbitch!*

Harry had been catching glances through the windows of the pilothouse, watching for Purvis. Through the gun smoke he saw Charlie getting to his feet raising a hand gun that Harry thought was intended for himself. In a flash of movement Harry ripped the Mauser from Felix's hand, leaped to the bridge in front of the helm, quickly aimed, and fired. The bullet tore into Charlie Purvis' stomach and lodged up against his spinal cord. Purvis fell behind the fruit bins moaning, he tried to grip his bloody waist, but he couldn't feel or move his arms. Robert Claymore saw Purvis go down, he snatched his bowler hat and took cover next to a stack of lumber in the warehouse.

A bullet shattered the pilothouse window, another hit a spoke on the helm that Captain Wiman was still grasping. As he dropped to the floor he pulled a mattress from the sleeping berth and covered himself against the wheelhouse safe. Harry saw his action, tossed the Mauser back to Felix without looking at him, and dived down against the mattress as well.

Abraham Rabinowitz, a young graduate of NYU traveling the west coast, struggled to stand up from a pile of hiding men on the deck. Just as he righted himself a bullet ripped away the back of his head, brain matter scattered the immediate area and landed on his fellow harvest workers. He died in his best friend's arms.

In the middle of it all, Helen Pomeroy and one of her friends ran back down to the pier and yelled at the deputies, "You're all murderers! You're all a bunch of barbarians! You're all terrible curs!"

"Dammit, lady! I told you already! Now get back, or I'll knock ya up side of the head," the deputy threatened, swinging the stock of his rifle towards her.

"You'll never get away with this! As God is my witness you'll all stand trial for this! You'll rot in jail!" Pomeroy shrieked and then turned to the shoreline, where a group of men were launching two rescue rowboats. The same deputy fired a round into the air.

"Halt! You in the boats!" the deputy screamed. "Nobody's going out on the water! Now get back across the tracks!" The men threw up their arms in surrender and ran back up Hewitt.

Felix Baran hid against the smokestack behind the pilothouse and caught glimpses of the man he wanted to kill. He saw Hugo's killer kneeling down in plain sight, reloading his gun. The killer dropped a cartridge, and reached down to pick the bullet up. Felix saw his chance. He jumped out from behind the pilothouse, aimed, and fired.

At the same time, Buck Mullaney saw Felix's action. Buck aimed his shotgun and pulled the trigger. He shot Felix Baran in the stomach, the wound slowly and painfully killing him. But Felix's bullet missed the mark. Hugo's killer ran back to the warehouse and hid.

Every surface of the steamer's upper structure and pilothouse was covered with bullets holes, the hull was dotted with so many punctures it was a miracle it didn't sink. Between waves of continuing gunfire, one injured Wobbly tried to regain his footing on the gore-covered slippery deck.

"Stand me up, comrades! I want to finish the song!" the bleeding Gus Johnson pleaded. Somehow he found the strength to pull himself upright with the help of the rail to try and deliver the last verse of *Hold the Fort* in a futile effort against industrial tyranny.

"By our union we shall triumph," a bullet hit him in the side, "Over every foe. Fierce and long the battle rages," another piece of lead struck him in the leg. "Fear not," holding to the rail with all his might, "Whene'er it's —," blood spewed from his lips, "Cheer . . . my comrades . . . cheer — " He toppled over with one final shot through his lungs, his singing and dreams, quieted forever, his bullet riddled lifeless body falling backwards, and onto the deck.

James Thompson crawled on his belly across the bloody, slippery floor towards the engine room stairwell with the pistol in his hand. J.F. Billings saw his action and followed him. Sliding head first down the stairs below deck, Thompson and Billings sneaked up behind engineer, Earnest Shellgren, and Thompson jammed the gun in his side.

"Full speed reverse! Now!" Thompson hollered. "Yeah, back this damn hell bucket up, and get us out of here!" Billings yelled. Shellgren raised his arms, turned around, and sputtered, "Only Captain Wiman gives that order."

"I don't care who yer captain is! Give us full speed reverse right now!" Thompson ordered.

"But the captain ain't at the wheel!"

"We don't give a rat's crap! Reverse!" Billings screamed as Thompson shoved the barrel of the gun up against Shellgren's throat. Spinning around to the controls, the engineer yanked the lever into reverse and pulled the throttle to full speed. The *Verona's* propeller churned the bloody waters, and the steamer lurched backwards but was held fast to the dock by the bow line.

"We're still tied off!" Shellgren hollered.

"Keep it cranking! She'll break free!" Thompson yelled over the engine noise and the bullets hitting the hull, determined to save his comrades. The strained bow line broke free with a crack and the *Verona* lurched backwards through a storm of continuing gunfire.

Once the *Verona* was moving, Captain Wiman jumped up and took a quick glance to get his bearings, he turned the wheel just enough to back the boat straight out into Port Gardner Bay. Two hundred yards from the dock, one Wobbly stood up but his legs were quickly shot out from under him by a well-aimed bullet from the pier.

When the *Verona* was finally out of range and the smoke had cleared, two citizen deputies pulled the sheriff up on to his one good foot. Deputy Jefferson Beard, 45 and a father of four, lay dying in the warehouse, a pool of blood oozing from his lungs by a gunshot wound in his back. Charles O. Curtis lay dead in the same building, both had been dragged from the firefight. Well over a dozen Commercial Club volunteers lay wounded, bleeding on the dock or in pier buildings.

"Get these . . . injured men loaded up . . . in the paddy wagon and . . . get 'em to the hospital," the sheriff sputtered as he was carried to the patrol car by Pete Hanigan, forgetting to grab his revolver, his Stetson barely hanging on his head. Injured vigilante deputies were carried and loaded in trucks and cars. Deputy Walt Irvan, injured from a bullet in his leg, was pulled to his feet by two volunteers.

Thousands of citizens had witnessed the bloodshed. A few city police stood around the edges of the crowd while Chief Kelly and the bulk of his police force watched from the south, at the base of Rucker Hill up on Federal Avenue.

Renny Niskanen stood beside Jake Michel, Noah Spanjer, Helen Pomeroy, and Father Nathan Bywater at the front of the massive crowd facing the waterfront. They completely blocked Hewitt. When the sheriff's patrol car, the paddy wagon, and the following caravan of vehicles crossed the tracks, they were stopped by the massive mob of citizens raging to life as bottles and rocks were thrown at the procession.

"You murdering curs!" Helen Pomeroy shouted as she shook her fist at the sheriff.

"Take him to jail!" Renny yelled, pointing at the sheriff.

"They should face a firing squad!" Noah Spanjer screamed over the crowd.

"A firing squad is too good for 'um!" Jake Michel hollered.

"Only God can dole out justice," Father Bywater bemoaned, trying to reason and interject.

"You're all going straight to hell!" a citizen jeered.

"They should have to walk a gauntlet!" another voice proposed.

"Yeah, let's make *them* walk a gauntlet!" someone agreed.

"Gauntlet! Gauntlet!" a striker proclaimed, starting a crowd wide chant.

"Gauntlet! Gauntlet! Gauntlet!" the mob began to shout. They quickly surrounded the patrol car. The sheriff reached for his Colt, but his holster was empty. In an instant his door was opened, and he was ripped from the car. The crowd surged towards the sheriff. Hands reached in trying to hit him while McRae jerked backwards in an attempt to protect himself. People pushed forward, one man crawled over the car hood and kidney-punched the sheriff. The paddy wagon and trucks right behind them were stopped and quickly encircled and besieged. Uninjured deputies threw up their hands in surrender but were torn from the vehicles and had their weapons removed.

"They fired first! The Wobblies fired first!" the sheriff screamed as Renny Niskanen ripped the badge off his chest and threw it on the ground, two strikers grabbed the sheriff. One wrapped the sheriff's right hand behind his back and the other held him by the neck and left arm. They pushed him over the hood of the patrol car. Someone else snatched the Stetson from his head when the sound of a police siren blasted through the air and a voice boomed out of a megaphone.

"Clear the street! All of you! Clear the street!" Police Chief Kelly screamed.

"People of Everett, clear the area right now! Go to your homes and leave the area!"

The police had completely surrounded the crowd from behind on Hewitt and above on Federal and Bond. But the citizens held their ground.

"These murderers need to be dealt with!" Jake Michel yelled at Chief Kelly with his hands cupped to the side of his mouth. Policemen fired pistol shots into the air.

"I will deal with the sheriff! Let him go! NOW!" the chief yelled into his megaphone from the hill above the horde of pressing citizens.

Helen Pomeroy stood at the edge of the immediate crowd surrounding the sheriff. She reached into her purse, pulled out a small glass bottle, and dumped the contents into her right hand. Then she pushed her way towards McRae.

"Out of my way. Let me through!" she hollered as she wedged and pushed her way through the swarm and then pitched red pepper in the sheriff's face, a cloud of scarlet blasting around and past his head.

"There's a dose of medicine, you evil coward!" Helen Pomeroy shouted. "How are we ever going recover from this outrage you've committed today?" The crowd roared in approval while the sheriff moaned in pain and agony, red powder on his face and throat.

"McRae needs to walk his own gauntlet!" a striker called out.

"Yeah, that's the least of it! Gauntlet! Gauntlet! Gauntlet!" the rioting crowd chanted. The police fired into the air again, trying to gain control.

"Haven't we had enough gunfire today?" Nathan Bywater yelled at the sky.

"For the last time! Clear this street! I've already radioed the governor to send a militia! I will deal with the sheriff and take him under my control! You people have ten seconds to begin clearing out!" the chief demanded and then started to count. "Ten . . . nine . . . eight . . ."

The crowd began to disperse, except for the strikers immediately around the sheriff. As soon as Chief Kelly saw the mob's enthusiasm begin to wane, he ordered in his force with billy clubs raised and whistles blowing, they headed straight for McRae. Renny Niskanen saw the police pushing their way into the throng and quickly pulled the strikers off of the sheriff, spun him around, and glared at him.

"Vhere is your boss today? How come MacCullock is not here?!" Renny hollered at the sheriff. But McRae said nothing, his red-peppered face streaked with sweat.

"All Luther MacCullock had to do vas pay us a decent vage, and none of this vould have happened. Vhere is he?" Renny repeated. The sheriff turned to look at Renny and scoffed, "Go to hell, ya filthy little foreigner."

The police grabbed Renny from behind, pulled him back from the sheriff and forcibly pushed him away. They surrounded McRae, grabbed him firmly and led him off to their police cars while the whole town watched, the sheriff's chin down on his chest. A man wearing a black bowler hat came striding up from the city pier. He stood in the back of the crowd, saw the sheriff under custody, and then reached in his pocket for a notepad.

Luther MacCullock flinched when the telephone in his sitting room started to ring. He jerked his head away from the binoculars and stared at the clattering phone. It rang like an alarm, the hanging receiver seemed to rattle off its hook.

MacCullock carefully set down the field glasses on the table next to his uneaten sandwich and walked over to the room's entrance. He turned the doorknob halfway and closed the door. Stepping over to the wheeled serving table, he poured two inches of scotch into his glass and took a drink. The phone kept ringing, he glared at it coldly with an immoveable, tight jaw. Luther walked over to the window, he set his drink down but didn't pick up the binoculars. Instead, he slowly bent over, wrapped the black cloth-wound phone wire carefully around his right hand, and then violently ripped the cord out of the wall. Luther MacCullock picked up his double old fashioned, took a drink, and then sat down in the closest chair.

Shocked and confused, Renny headed slowly up Hewitt. Emotion rushed through his body. He felt pain from the loss of life and for the victims of senseless murder, heartache and sadness for the families of those killed. Shame for being involved in the strike, and fear of what the future would hold for Petra and him. Then he felt anger and disgust for the sheriff and Luther MacCullock. He stopped for a moment and stared at the sidewalk. *How could this have happened?*

The lady seated behind the wheel of her Baker Electric turned around in the middle of Hewitt, and idled east, back to the Riverside District.

Renny started stumbling up Hewitt again and crossed Rucker, his feet felt like they weighed a hundred pounds apiece. *It was never supposed to come to this.* Heartache and pain covered him in a blanket of desperation, but when he looked up, he felt relief at the sight of his wife coming down Hewitt.

"Renny! Renny! Are you OK?" Petra yelled as she ran down the sidewalk to him. She jumped into his arms and hugged him with all her might. She pulled her head back but kept her arms wrapped around him, tears rolled down her face. "I could hear all the shooting, I vas so vorried, I thought you might be killed, I don't vant to live vithout you," Petra said, looking into his eyes. They embraced again. Finally she pulled away and looked him up and down, checking to make sure that he was okay. Satisfied that her husband was safe and sound and away from harm, she smiled affectionately at him, all the way to her bright blue watery eyes and said, "Let's go home."

As she drove by in her silent Baker Electric, Goldie Lafayette slowed down and smiled at the sight of Renny and Petra's embrace. *Oh, my heavenly lands. Thank goodness he's all right . . . I knew it . . . I just knew she'd fall in love with him again.*

Chapter 15

BETTER DAYS

The first thing Reader Bill and Dirty Shirt heard, and then saw, when they hiked into the Smith-Edgerton logging camp east of Granite Falls was a steam donkey with its condenser valve fastened to a fire hose blowing hot steam into one of the bunkhouses. Every window and door was shut tight, white-hot steam still seeped out of every crack.

It looked like it was on fire inside but without flames. A young flunky was feeding the boiler and saw the two strangers. Dirty Shirt was carrying his rifle.

"Howdy," the boy said with a friendly grin and then pitched another round of wood into the firebox.

"Don't look like you need no donkey puncher for what you're doing," Reader Bill said with a smile.

"Sure don't," the flunky replied.

"How come yer blowing steam in that bunkhouse?" Dirty Shirt asked.

"Got lice bad up here. Steam kills 'em."

"Good to know," Bill replied and then leaned towards Dirty Shirt and whispered,

"We never had lice before."

"Yeah, well," Dirty Shirt whispered, "I don't give a hoot. I'm still needin' a payday."

"You know where we could find the push?" Reader Bill asked the boy.

"He's over in the mess hall gettin' grub with everyone else," the boy said as he split another round of wood. He motioned in the direction of the cookhouse.

"OK," Reader Bill said as they walked off. Three steps away he turned to Dirty Shirt with a serious look on his face and cautioned quietly, "You just let me do the talking. Got that?" Dirty Shirt nodded his head with approval as he looked at the ground.

"And make sure that you follow along," Reader Bill instructed.

The mess hall was full of hungry lumberjacks. It smelled of pot roast, wet, rotten wood, corn bread, sour milk, pork and beans and biscuits. The head cook dumped a ladle of beans onto a nailed-down plate as the two new lumberjacks wandered in. Most of the men turned their heads to look at the strangers then silently went back to their meals.

The cook looked at the new men and wearily said, "Grab a seat, I'll bring ya a little somethin'."

The two nodded their thanks and set down their stuffed gunny-sacks and axes next to the door. Dirty Shirt leaned his rifle against a table and they took a seat by themselves. Camp push Rex Holcomb looked over his shoulder at the two fresh short stakes then slowly began to get up from his seat. He waved his right hand over a wooden bowl to shoo away the flies, grabbed a biscuit, took a bite, and strode over to them.

Holcomb was a hulking galoot of a man with shiny, mink-oiled cork boots that stabbed the floor with each step, the tiny wooden bits of shreds trailing behind him. His rough-cut, raw-boned face looked like weather-beaten outhouse siding. He was bald, had a white-and-grey handle bar mustache, and wore a red-and-black flannel shirt and tin pants cut off at the high-water mark.

"Lookin' fer a job?" Holcomb asked with a voice like sandpaper, his mouth full of dough.

"Yep," Reader Bill said.

"Where ya last work?"

"Down in Oregon for Western Pacific."

"You too I suppose?" Holcomb asked Dirty Shirt.

"Yep."

"Whatcha doin' up in this neck of the woods?"

"Dupree's Employment Agency in Everett sent us, said you were hiring ax men," Reader Bill said.

"Jack Dupree sent ya, huh? Old Dupree, he's been sending me timber bums fer years. But mind ya now, I ain't no straw boss. So, yer both a couple of cutters?"

"Yep," Reader Bill answered. "We can fall and buck. Top and rig spar, too."

"Ya got names?"

"I'm William Redbrick, and this here is Frank Cargill," Reader Bill answered.

"OK, well," Holcomb said with a faraway look as he stared at the rafters to think for a moment and then turned back to them, "who's yer closest relative?"

"Haven't any," Reader Bill replied.

"Me neither," Dirty Shirt conceded.

"OK. Are ya right- or left-handed?" Holcomb asked them both.

"Right-handed," Bill said.

"Don't rightly know," Dirty Shirt answered, scratching his head. He lifted up his right hand and pointed at it saying, "This one, but I can swing an ax either side."

"All right then. You know how to stay out of the bight?" Holcomb asked with a solemn look.

"Yep, sure do. Been working in the woods long enough that the good Lord hasn't come for me yet," Reader Bill acknowledged.

"Good. Well, my name's Rex Holcomb, and I'm the head push. I've seen more than my fair share of timber bums come an' go through this camp, and as long as ya keep yer mouth shut and yer ears open we'll treat ya right. Ya got that?" Holcomb said as he looked back and forth between the two.

"Yes, sir," both men replied at the same time.

"Swingin' ax here pays four bucks a day. I'll put ya on the crew, but there's no gamblin', no liquor, no women, no talkin' during meals, no pistols, and that rifle of yours will have to be locked up. If'n ya want to use it fer huntin', that's fine," Holcomb stated as he stared at Dirty Shirt.

"OK," Frank said, nodding his head.

"Ya get Sundays off ta' hunt 'er do laundry and judgin' by the looks and the smell of that shirt ya got on there, Cargill, I'm thinkin' that this Easter Sunday ain't gonna be soon enough."

"Now, if'n ya go to the bawdy house in Granite tonight, or any Saturday night, ya best be back here and ready to get after it come Monday morning. If'n ya ain't back by then, I'll be pleased to fire yer ass. Ya got that?"

"Yep. We're good," Bill answered for both of them.

"Go ahead and fill yer bellies and then take yer bindles over to bunkhouse three and get settled in. I'll get ya all signed up in the morning. Oh, and if'n yer a couple of Bible thumpers, the minister from Verlot is coming up late Sunday afternoon ta' give a benediction."

"Thank you, Rex," Bill said.

"Yeah. Thanks for the job, Mr. Holcomb," Frank added.

Holcomb started to walk away but then turned around and came back. With a serious glower he looked into each man's eyes, and studied their faces for a moment.

"Either one of you carrying a red card?"

Both men knew the question would be asked, they were ready.

"No," they each replied.

"Good," Holcomb snorted. "And what about that new thing they're talkin' about startin', the Four L? You boys part a' that?"

Reader Bill and Frank looked at each other. Bill shrugged his shoulders and said, "Don't think we've heard about that one. What is it?"

Holcomb stared Bill down and then said, "It's some kind-a legion of loggers and somethin' 'er other. The government is supposed to be startin' it."

"Well, we's ain't a part a' no union," Dirty Shirt replied.

"Good. Keep it that way," Holcomb snorted. He turned to go back to his meal and then said over his shoulder with typical camp-push arrogance, "Welcome to Wiley Creek, ladies."

***

The next morning organ music filled the cathedral of the Holy Cross of the Virgin Mary. The brass pipes boomed out over the choir and the parishioners singing

Amazing Grace, the church seemed to shake with the power of the Almighty. Once the hymn was finished Father Bywater stood before his congregation with a Bible against his chest and a smile of grace and brotherly love on his face. He placed the holy book on the podium and looked out into his overflowing sanctuary.

"As I gaze into all of your wonderful faces on this Easter Sunday, I can't help but feel overjoyed to be here with you," Father Bywater said warmly. Then the tone of his voice changed, "I understand that some would like to forget about the tragic circumstances that occurred in our town last fall, but we cannot. We must remember it and we must learn from it. *And*, we must carry forward what we've learned for the sake of our children, so that we leave a better world for them. This we must do. Let us all move together, forward, everyone, equal in God's great light. For I pray that we never see those dark days again. It's time for us to walk into that glorious light of our Lord and Savior and bathe in the glow of eternal life, on this greatest day of the year."

"Our Easter sermon today comes from the words of Saint John Chrysostom, who lived in the fourth century. I've chosen the words of Saint John because he was known for his denunciation of the abuse of authority. His words that I am about to repeat hold great meaning to this very day. Let me begin."

"'Are there any weary with fasting? Let them now receive their wages. If any have toiled from the first hour, let them receive their due reward, if any have come after the third hour, let him with gratitude join the feast. And he that arrived after the sixth hour, let him not doubt, for he too shall sustain no loss. And if any delayed until the ninth hour, let him not hesitate, but let him come too. And he who arrived only at the eleventh hour, let him not be afraid by reason of his delay.'"

"'For the Lord is gracious and receives the last even as the first. He gives rest to him that comes at the eleventh hour, as well as to him that toiled from the first. To this one He gives, and upon another He bestows. He accepts the works as He greets the endeavor. The deed He honors and the intention He commends. Let us all enter into the joy of the Lord! First and last alike receive your reward, rich and poor, rejoice together. Sober and slothful, celebrate the day. Christ is risen, and the demons are cast down. Christ is risen, and life is set free. Christ is risen, and the tomb is emptied of the dead. For Christ, having risen from the dead, is become the first-fruits for those who sleep. He be glory and power forever and ever! Alleluia! Alleluia!'" Father Bywater said and then gazed upon his flock with a warm and gracious smile.

"These words of Saint John are as relevant today as they were fifteen hundred years ago. As I look out to your faces and into your hearts today I also look out beyond all of you here and to all of the members of this community to begin anew," Father Bywater said.

"Let us pray," Father Bywater said as every parishioner stood and joined in with eyes closed. "Our Father, who art in heaven, hallowed be thy name. Thy kingdom come. Thy will be done, on earth as it is in heaven. Give us this day our daily bread, and forgive us our trespasses, as we forgive those who trespass against us, and lead us not into temptation, but deliver us from evil. For thine is the kingdom, and the power, and the glory, for ever and ever. Amen."

The timber widow Helen Pomeroy looked up from her prayer and beamed with joyous hope from the front row pew, her two children at her side.

***

The sun rose over the Cascade peaks in the east like a glorious, illuminating, warm gift. Its glow and fervent benevolence was another reminder of spring. Renny Niskanen had that same optimistic light on his back as he turned on Wetmore from Everett Avenue. Once he was closer to Spanjer's he could see all the unused wooden crates beneath the sidewalk fruit racks. Nobody had touched them all winter.

Renny unlocked the front door to Spanjer's Dry Goods & Grocery and flipped over the open sign. He pulled a rolled-up white apron from his back pocket, threw the top strap over his head, wrapped the strings around his waist, and tied them off with a slip knot. Noah walked in.

"Good morning," Spanjer said, greeting his new assistant. "Looks like it's gonna be a fine day."

"Yah. Good-a morning," Renny replied with a smile.

"Did you have a good Easter?" Noah asked.

"Oh, yah, and you?" Renny said.

"The wife and family had a wonderful Easter," Noah said.

"That ham you gave us vas very good. Thank you again for that," Renny said.

"Well, you're welcome, glad you liked it. I see that nearly all of the flowers sold on Saturday," Noah remarked happily, looking around the store.

"Yah, maybe the rest vill sell today" Renny said as a horn sounded out on the street and a bundle of newspapers landed on the sidewalk. Renny went outside, picked up the papers, and carried the load inside. A front page article of the *Daily Tribune* read: "Defense in IWW Trial Makes Good Beginning - Much Testimony to Come"

That afternoon Renny was behind the counter of the market when Petra came in. Her pregnancy was showing.

"Petra!" he exclaimed. "That vas a long valk. Are you all right?"

"Oh, yah. I fine. The valking is good."

"Here," the proud father to be said, "take my chair. Sit vith me."

Renny ran around the counter, took his pregnant wife by the hand, and led her to the chair. Noah poked his head out of the storeroom, looked at the couple with favor, and went back to his task. Renny plucked a yellow lily from one of the arrangements and held it out for Petra. She gazed into her husband's eyes and smiled.

Time stood still with his simple, loving gesture. Everything in their world was right and just. Everything they'd been through was in the past. The future was right there in that moment. All of their hopes and dreams came together, all the reasons for coming to America were fulfilled. Their lives arched into the heavens and back in a rainbow moment of life affirming transcendence, pure and clean. The miracle of wonder touched them in a sparkling flow of emotions.

And the child that Petra carried would be their one and only child.

An American child.

"*Mina rakastan sinua,*" Renny said to his wife softly.

"I love you too," Petra replied with the glowing, affectionate smile of a new beginning. She took the flower and held it to her heart. Renny placed his hand on his pregnant wife's tummy and felt their child move. Their dreams were carried forward and everything was as it should be.

The End

POSTSCRIPT

O fficial figures state that five IWW members and two deputies were killed at the Everett City Pier on November 5, 1916 although six union cards were never retrieved from the IWW Hall in Seattle upon the Verona's return. Eyewitness accounts claim to support that possibly seven more Wobblies perished that day either on the *Verona* or drowned in the bay. A combined number of fifty men were reported wounded.

Sheriff McRae nor any members of the Commercial Club were arrested or stood trial; seventy-one IWW from the *Verona* were jailed and charged with murder but were all eventually acquitted.

Donald McRae didn't run for re-election and drifted into a life of obscurity. He moved to Ebey Island for a handful of years and then left for southern Puget Sound where he lived out the rest of his life quietly as a groundskeeper at the state capitol.

Charlie Purvis spent the rest of his days at Currier Private Hospital as a bedridden quadriplegic.

Luther MacCullock continued to run his mill until he suffered a massive stroke and died alone in his office, face down on his desk, broken pince-nez on his nose, Churchwarden pipe gripped tightly in his hand.

James P. Thompson was sentenced to 10 years in federal prison in violation of the Espionage Act in 1918 for speaking out against World War 1.

Harry Dolson worked in the logging industry for the rest of his life and rose through the ranks becoming a hook tender, foreman, timber cruiser, and log scaler. He got married, had ten children and lived to be the proud and doting grandfather of thirty-six grandchildren.

The *Verona* was fully repaired and plied the waters of Puget Sound for 20 more years. In January of 1936 it suffered an extensive fire after returning from Bainbridge Island and was shortly thereafter dismantled. Its nameplate, as of this writing, is on display at the Poulsbo Maritime Museum.

ACKNOWLEDGMENTS

Words can barely express my gratitude and heartfelt thanks to the people that helped and inspired me to fully realize this project. Without their encouragement, insight, and aid, I could have never brought this work to fruition. I would like to acknowledge all of the following for the help, and support they've shown and provided. Thank you: Susan Harrell, Miles Auckland, Tom Davies, Cynthia Neely, Royce Ferguson, and Cassidy Cuthill.

I would like to convey a very special thanks to: Miles Auckland for assistance with logging terminology, and to Everett historians David Dilgard and Larry O'Donnell for their willingness to share their knowledge and expertise of early day Everett.

I'm exceedingly grateful to my editors; Allison Hitz and Skyler Cuthill. They worked long, hard, and tedious hours. I couldn't have had a better literary team at my side.

From the beginning I have felt that this would not be my book, but Everett's book. Much has been written and said about the Everett Massacre. Told and retold, the story has been covered for a hundred years by journalists, historians, residents, theorists, and even a few novelists. This author has attempted to bring a new view to a well-known story and possibly show what life might have been like for those living on Port Gardner Bay during 1916.

ABOUT THE AUTHOR

J.D. Howard is a native of Everett, Washington. Over the last 45 years he has been an avid student of history and literature, a foundry moulder, welder, door maker, glazier, wood cutter, carpenter, land broker, proud father of two wonderful children, fisherman, and handyman. Sawdust Empire is his second novel.

Made in the USA
Monee, IL
24 March 2022